THE PANAMA LAUGH

T0105419

THE PANAMA LAUGH

THOMAS S. ROCHE

Night Shade Books
San Francisco

Cover art by Lucas Graciano
Cover design by Claudia Noble
Interior layout and design by Amy Popovich

Edited by Ross E. Lockhart

First Edition

Printed in Canada

ISBN: 978-1-59780-290-1
eISBN: 978-1-59780-354-0

Night Shade Books
Please visit us on the web at
http://www.nightshadebooks.com

To Bridgitte,
for the living,
and to all my dead.

Perhaps I know best why it is man alone who laughs; he alone suffers so deeply that he had to invent laughter.
—Friedrich Nietzsche

War is fought by human beings.
—Carl von Clausewitz, *On War*

PART 1:
CARIBBEAN ICE

When I showed up on Isla Pescado in sunny Kuna Yala to find Van Fish tending his Holy Ghost orchids on the terrace, he reacted pretty much like you'd expect.

He said, "*Buenos dias*, douchebag," and punched me in the face.

Van Fish throws a right hook like the 5:15 to Chiriquí. Nobody gets punched by him if they can help it. At the time it surprised the hell out of me; it shouldn't have, but I was in a one-sided love-fest with Van at the very moment that the son of a bitch decided to beat me bloody. Five minutes before *that*, I'd been dead-set on punching *him*. I didn't know where I'd been or what I'd been doing for five years, but I knew I wanted to give Van Fish a knuckle sandwich. In fact, it was the whole reason I'd hitched a thousand-dollar ride out of Golfo del Urabá with a Colombian "fisherman" to visit Isla Pescado at eight in the morning.

But once I arrived, everything changed.

I hiked up the path carved into the island from the makeshift dock where he'd moored the *When She Was Bad* and the *Speedy Gonzales* and the *Jerry Bear* and the two half-disassembled mahogany Chris-Crafts with strings of bullet holes where jackass Van had left the safety off an AK-47. I saw his half-deflated Zodiac and two jet skis with open panels and that piece of shit Cessna of his, the *Bush Soaker*, with the goofy Maggie Billman illustration of a devil girl, and the jackass floats scavenged from God knows where half-secured with baling wire. I saw the big pile of camping supplies near the *When She Was Bad*—a big red cooler and cases of Balboa and bottled water and MREs and canned beans and fishing gear and tents and tarps and cases of ammunition—it just all seemed so lovely and familiar. That shit broke my heart.

I couldn't do it. I couldn't hit him. I couldn't beat Van to a pulp any more than I could have bitchslapped my own brother.

I suddenly knew Van hadn't sold me out to Virgil Amaro. I knew he hadn't betrayed me—and, far more importantly, I knew he hadn't betrayed *her*. I realized in an avalanche of brotherly love that I'd been barking up the wrong tree ever since I woke up in the jungle with a gun in my hand and mud on my schvantz. I knew Van loved me—and, damn it, I loved him, in that special way that only guys who occasionally beat the shit out of each other can love each other.

As I threaded my way up the path from the beach to the house, my anger just... *vanished*.

I saw the massive hirsute Van rising from a crouch by the orchids—the national flowers, the pale white souls of Panama. The hairy prick looked like a Sasquatch that'd had let itself go. He coulda been mistaken for a silverback gorilla, only no sane ape would have dressed like that. His cargo shorts hung down his thighs almost to his knees. He wore cheap Tijuana-style *huaraches*. His beard was grey, as was his moppy hair. They'd always been shot through with silver; now they were almost entirely that way, like the rest of the carpet store that was Van Fish's body.

But in his essence, in his holy and sacred essence, he was exactly the same. He was Van Fish, the only lunatic dumb enough to befriend me, and the one I had trusted with the soul of my beloved.

In this big and brutal world, reader, allow me, for argument, there may be no such thing as God.

But there's Van Fish, and that'll do.

It was all so *gorgeous*: the light and the jungle and the sea and the sand and the heavy-light air of Kuna Yala, the sea breeze and the sky and the glorious wisps of white clouds pirouetting overhead.

I huffed Holy Ghost orchids.

Van came for me, grinning.

I put out my hand for a shake and said,

"*Como esta usted, amigo?*"

...Which is pretty much when he punched me.

Did I mention Van hits like the 10:10 to Reno?

Express.

☠

I went down. I landed six or eight feet from where I'd started. I landed on my gym bag with a soft suffusive *whump*. The thing was stuffed with cash, so it provided a pretty soft landing except for the matching automatics, which hurt like hell jabbing my kidneys.

I got up and went back to Van, grinning.

I said brightly, "I'm glad you got that out of your system. ¿*Que tal, compadre?*"

Which is pretty much when he punched me again.

This time, I took it—but I didn't like it.

I stood my ground.

I said, "You wanna knock that off, Bubba?"

He didn't. He drew back and swung again—first and second mistake.

His fist came at me fast but I saw it coming, caught it, stopped it with my open right hand.

I snarled savagely:

"What? No *buenas dias* this time?"

—and let him have it, right in the kisser. He went back with a yowl; he came back and I ducked a haymaker and gave him a right of my own, which he ducked, and a left, which he didn't.

Oldest trick in the book.

He reeled back and looked pissed, and stood there growling and frowning and nodding as I stood my ground.

I said, "I'm glad we got that out of our system."

He nodded, said, "Me, too!"

And then he kicked me in the balls.

I doubled. He gave it to me, fist-to-face; I gave it to him. We clinched; we rolled; he howled: "You broke her heart you piece of shit," and punched me in the face, and I caught him with a haymaker coming up from a crouch. "Don't you think I know that? It wasn't my fault," I growled as he smacked me again, and he said, "Save it!" just before he smacked me. We struggled to our feet and clinched Greco-Roman style, his bigger bulk dragging me around in circles with my pointy-toed black leather boots ripping Holy Ghost orchids out by the stems. I heard orchid bulbs going *Crunch!* underneath me.

I saw his crazed grimace. He had murder in his peepers—the kind where every smile is poison.

We clinched, panting.

I said, "Let me explain, *compadre*."

"Don't *compadre* me," he snarled.

Then I smelled *her*, lingering, ripe on his clothes, under the scents that struggled to dominate. I smelled *her* on *him*; that smacked me hard in a way Van's fists could never have done.

I went apeshit.

I tore free and hit him *hard*. He hit me back. We rolled around, slaughtering orchids. He said some nasty words.

He pinned me and smacked me; I pinned him and smacked him; it went downhill from there.

Van Fish is six-foot-three and would wear a size fifty-four jacket if you could get him to wear a suit. I'm six-two, maybe six-two-and-a-quarter, depending. We are not matched in size or stamina; I am usually the bigger badass, but I felt wasted and empty after everything that'd gone down. Therefore, it was a good sign that I could still hold my own against Van, who may have had years on me but had spent most of them smacking the shit out of much tougher assholes than me in half the hellholes liquor and oversized *huevos* could build on five continents. I was pleased with my performance.

But getting the shit kicked out of me was not a lot of fun.

I had a matched pair of Belgian pistols in my gym bag, in ballistic-fabric holsters. Rather than getting slappy with Van, it would have been far less effort to get away and make for the handguns. I didn't, because it was evident from the first that Van did not intend to kill me. If he had, one of us probably would have been dead already because, like a jerk, I'd forgotten to jack a Taser. That's pretty much what it takes to reason with Van when he gets like this.

She showed up after we were both good and bloody, panting, tears running down Van's face, blood down mine.

Her scent blew through the Holy Ghost orchids like the wafting stink of pungent ecclesiastical incense. I got drunk and stupid huffing it for about a second and a half—which was roughly the time it took her to shove a shotgun so far up my ass I was wearing it as navel jewelry.

It was a pistol-grip Ithaca pump. A credible weapon, in case you were wondering.

"Get off the Wookiee," she told me. "Back away slowly." I did.

I dripped blood on Van's lost *huarache* as I rose.

I put my hands up, backed away. She took quick short steps backwards away from me, Ithaca trained on my head.

Van was panting too hard to say a word, either; or maybe the rat bastard just wanted to see her shoot me. He mostly just glared.

"Now turn around," she said. "Slowly."

I did. It took her a minute. She hadn't recognized me from behind; it had been that long.

Her eyes went wide. Her mouth dropped open.

God almighty, she looked like Heaven. Dynamite packed into a frame far too small to contain it. She wore sun-bleached cargo shorts and an Ani DiFranco T-shirt. A tiny Venus of Willendorf danced from a choker at her throat. Her long hair blazed like threads of bare, coiled copper wires; her eyes glittered emerald from beneath it and from above her sunny freckles. She had wrinkles but not a hint of grey. She was the most beautiful woman I've ever laid eyes on, and I've laid eyes on 'em all over the world. I was riveted. I couldn't have moved if I'd wanted to.

She said, "Frosty Bogart."

She let the pistol-grip Ithaca dangle at her side.

I said grimly: "Don't call me that."

She shook her head. She grinned and said, "Have you lost weight?"

Then she punched me in the face.

If Van hits like a train doing sixty, Trix hits like a DIY-nitrous-jacked dirt bike doing one-eighty-five.

It was not the first time *she*'d hit me, either.

Lest you think me and my friends go around doing practically nothing but punching each other... well, look. I don't have an ending to that sentence. Guilty as charged.

Rubbing my jaw, I said, "I'm not really sure. Haven't got a chance to hop on the scale lately. Good to see you, too, Trixie."

—which is when she gave me a left, having passed the Ithaca pump to her right hand. Trixie's, as they say, ambidextrous.

"That's for Pinogana," she told me.

I rubbed my jaw.

"What was the first one for?"

"Being an *asshole*."

Trixie's from the Peace Corps. She's here to help you.

She's also a doctor. Open up and say *Aaaah*.

☠

At least she got it out of her system fast. One smack per paw and that was it.

Then she was hugging me, putting her arms around my shoulders, all stinking-hippie scent of morning glories and sandalwood. She buried her face in my neck before I could even back away screaming for fear she'd smack me again. She still held the Ithaca as she hugged me and kissed me; its heat shield rattled against my bruised skull. I would have liked to mention it, sort of a friendly "point your shotgun elsewhere, *amiga*," but I didn't think it'd be prudent. The smell of her took me back to times when peace was a real possibility. I got *drunk* on it. I felt light-headed. I wanted to let it all out. I wanted to tell them *everything*.

For several long minutes, she held me; I could feel Van's glare boring into the back of my head; if he coulda nudged the shotgun down and pulled that hair-trigger, he woulda. But *fuck* him.

"If anyone needs me," he growled, "I'll be sharpening my machete." He stalked past us and into the house.

Trixie ignored him. She said: "You're too busy to write?"

I said, "Yeah, kinda."

She looked at my T-shirt in horror.

She asked, "What's 'The Rimbaud Fiasco?'"

I told her, "I have no idea."

She said, "Which one of us was right—Van or me?"

I said, "Which one of *who* is *what?*"

"Van claims the videos were real. I say they were faked."

"Excuse me?"

"Which means," said Trixie, "that he thinks they were faked, and I think they were real. Some of them, at least—I mean, not the crap about Bigfoot and Mothman, obviously."

"Obviously," I said.

"I mean the stuff about the laughers, and the viruses, and Virgil Amaro. I figured that part was real. Van said no, but now he's not so sure. Is it corporate misinformation or private inspiration? I mean... until the chuckleheads came around, everyone figured you were just fucking around."

I looked at her blankly.

She looked back at me blankly.

I looked at her blankly some more.

I racked my brains. I honestly hadn't the faintest idea what she was talking about. I remembered a sunrise on the Corredor Sur; I remembered heading toward me with murder in her peepers, saying "C'mere, Dante, C'mere!"

...then I remembered *squat* until I woke up as an understudy in the role of Mowgli.

So I said, "Huh?"

She punched me on the arm.

She said, "Same old sense of humor, Dante. What are they, parody or exposé?"

I said, "A little of both, like most things. What are we talking about, again?"

She said, "The *videos*, dipshit."

I said, "Okay, wait a second. Are these the ones Van shot in Rio? 'Cause I had no idea it was that kind of strip club." I rubbed my jaw. "By the way, did they ever let you back in the Peace Corps?"

She scowled. "No. I lost my contract. Thanks for that, by the way."

I said, "You're welcome. You got Scotch?"

Trixie said, "Dante, it's 8 a.m."

I said, "Vodka, then."

"There's still dew on the flowers!"

"Come on—from the looks of that boulder on your finger, I'm entitled to a toast. And I'll give you twenty-to-one Van doesn't stock any Dom Pérignon."

She waved the back of her hand at me. "You noticed."

"Oh, come on," I said. "I practically arranged it. Ex-soldier living off the grid in a Caribbean paradise, convinced aliens live in his muesli? Peace Corps doctor who carried the collected Whitley Strieber to every third-world hellhole where children had rickets she could cure? You two were made for each other. Can I see the diamond?"

She held it up and said, "It's not a diamond."

I whistled. "Bullshit. That's some Caribbean ice, lady. Like the kind you're gonna give me for my Scotch."

She said, "Uh-uh," she said. "It's cubic zirconium."

I rolled my eyes.

"You prick—it's not because he's a cheapskate."

"He *is* a cheapskate."

"Of course," said Trixie. "But he *tried* to buy me a real one. I made him take it back to the dealer in Panama City. You think I'd wear a blood diamond?"

I rubbed my jaw, impressed.

"Aren't there cruelty-free diamonds?"

"Uh-uh," She said. "The whole industry is corrupt."

"*Claro*," I said. "There's a lot of that going around. Did someone mention Scotch?"

We went inside.

☠

"Claro" means sure, that's so, of course it is, I know. The expression is used throughout the Spanish-speaking world, but in my experience its use is particularly endemic to Panama and Colombia. It was the first Spanish word I learned that didn't come with a side of guacamole, so I have some abiding affection for it.

That's because "Claro" says some things that can't be said with any word in the English language. It's not so much that we don't have a word for it; it's that we have a thousand of them, and none of quite mean "*Claro.*"

☠

Van Fish had cooled down, but he declined the offer of a drink. He told me, "Dante... it's 8:10 a.m.!"

"Why does everybody keep telling me that? And if you're worried about it being so early, maybe you shouldn't go punching people."

"You asked for it."

"Asked for it? All I said was '*Como esta usted!*'"

Van glared at me. Steamed, he went back into the bedroom and changed his shirt. I'd done a number on the tattered 4-XL iron-on Lou Reed bootleg he'd been wearing when we fought. The one he changed into had cut-off arms and airbrushed wolves howling at the moon. He looked like a random sexual deviant in a Quentin Tarantino movie.

The Scotch was a sickly-sweet MacTavish, which, the last time I checked, was the cheapest single-malt Scotch in the world—competitive with some brands of lighter fluid. Van was a man who appreciated the finer things, as long as he could get them cheaper than dirt.

Needless to say that since it was a single-malt, I hijacked Trixie's handful of ice away from my tumbler and planted it on my bruised noggin. I poured the MacTavish out neat, two fingers, three, four—then well past the point of digital measurements. As I drank, Trixie dabbed half-assedly with a wet towel at the blood on Van's face. Chunks of potting soil clung tenaciously to the injury. As she cleaned him up, they both looked at me like I was completely crazy.

Trixie asked, "Why do *you* look so happy?"

I said, "I'm not."

She said, "You're smiling."

"I'm not."

Van said, "Dante, I gotta go with Trix on this one. You're grinning your ass off. It's a little creepy."

I shrugged. "I guess I'm just really happy to be alive," I said.

Van and Trix looked at each other.

"Then it's *really* creepy," said Van. "What have you done with Dante, pod person?"

I growled, "Can't an asshole be happy around here without getting Gitmo'ed?"

Van growled back, "Not you, goth boy. By the way, Bubba, you gonna tell us where you've been for five years?"

I scowled.

I said, "I'd love to."

Van said, "Okay."

There was a big long empty. I sweated.

Trixie and Van both looked at me, irritated.

"Waiting with bated breath," said Van. "This worm tastes like shit."

I said, "I don't remember."

Van said, "Huh?"

I stared.

I took a deep breath.

I drank. I poured Scotch. I drank.

I said: "Look. Here's what I know. Like eighteen hours ago, I woke up in the jungle—"

☠

—naked, filthy, and clutching an automatic.

I sprawled shivering in my birthday suit on a bed of matted rotting mangrove leaves. Acetylene streams filtered down through the canopy far, far overhead.

I took a huff of jungle stink and gunsmoke. I hauled myself to my knees, then my feet, then came down hard, head swirling. While the dizziness passed I sat there with rotting leaves sticky-sweet on my ass, and looked blankly at the weapon in my hand.

The slide locked open, the thing was empty. It stank of cordite. I dropped the empty mag. I looked at it, slammed it back in; it settled in with a happy polymer *click*. It was an FN Five-seveN—get it? The capital N at the end reminds you who made it, in case you give a damn while you're being shot at. It is a credible sidearm nonetheless, which is why it had supplanted the haphazard smattering of Glock 19s and Beretta Model 92s that had marked the early days of Bellona Industries. The five-sev is a breeze for daily carry, because it's relatively light and doesn't have the kidney-caressing sharp edges of, say, a Model 1911 or most revolvers. You can also pack twenty rounds into a flush-fit magazine, or thirty into an extended. More importantly, its small but high-powered round provides considerably less recoil than a nine-millimeter, creating a very accurate handgun that will defeat many types of body armor.

This one, however, was worth fuck-all under the circumstances. The weapon was empty.

It had been fired very recently; it was warm.

So was I.

But I was cold, too, alternately, in great screaming waves that wracked my body from chill to fever to chill again. It wasn't awesome. Every muscle in my body ached. I took stock of the short suppurating incisions on the backs of my wrists and half a dozen fresh hypodermic insertions on the soft fleshy insides of my elbows. I had more on my thighs. My feet were newly cut and bleeding with far less precision—slashed by rocks and branches, the cuts caked with jungle humus. I also had plenty of cuts on my knees, like I'd crawled, and on the palms of my hands.

I felt my head: *no hair.* I'd been shaved. My face, too—smooth. Much of the rest of me was shaved, haphazardly where I'd apparently been stuck with needles.

I looked around me.

I'd left big gushy footprints in the wet groundcover. I didn't see anyone else's prints, or any empty shells in my immediate vicinity. This wasn't where the gunfight happened.

About ten meters away, I spotted something glinting in a stream of sunlight slanting through the canopy. It was a shell casing. I tracked back and picked it up. It was a five-sev—it had to be one of mine.

I spotted another, three meters past.

Then another—two meters. More beyond that.

I followed the trail of 5.7-millimeter breadcrumbs. This must have been the path I'd followed, shooting.

I heard a distant scream—a New World monkey. Yes, I know the difference. All right, then—this wasn't Africa or Asia. That was a start.

Naked, I followed the trail of expended cartridges, cursing and grunting as my feet sank into groundcover writhing with bugs. My bare flesh itched all over.

Through breaks in the rainforest canopy, I saw a looming mountain overhead. Unfamiliar. White waterfalls poured down the sides in several places.

I heard chittering; I looked up. A small flight of bats pirouetted, outlined against the pale grey clouds.

I followed my brass-breadcrumb trail to an empty magazine. I retrieved it and picked up my trail again. The distance between footsteps told the story: I'd been running as I fired.

I started running now.

Running and firing a pistol is not a thing that anyone who knows their shit would do. As difficult as it was to believe I had done it, I felt something tickling my insides that told me I had. It was something like terror: the lingering scream of absolute panic that bubbled up from memory where no memory existed. I knew who I was. I knew what I did for a living. And I knew I didn't panic. Scared? Sure. No one serves under fire and doesn't get scared. But panic?

I'd dropped panic as an option.

Not knowing what time of year it was, I wild-guessed it was probably three in the afternoon. There were dark clouds overhead, and I could hear faint thunder.

If that rain came—and it almost certainly would—the trail would go cold.

I ran faster, picking up cartridges on the way.

Ten minutes later, I found the first body.

The guy wore body armor and a load-bearing vest with fragmentation grenades and flash-bangs. He'd been shot in the face at an upward angle with a large-caliber round, almost certainly a hollow point—not the Five-seveN, which fires a small-caliber bullet without a hollow point. The wound as made by something like a .44 or .45. I hadn't shot him—at least not with the weapon I was holding.

The back of his skull mingled with his brains in the mangrove tangle.

I kicked him over with my filthy bare foot. Most of the expansion had occurred after the bullet had entered his skull at the upper lip, scattering most of his teeth somewhere deep into brain tissue. He had been shot from a low angle, likely while he stood by someone on their knees or belly or back. His face was not in what I would call good shape, but I could tell he was Latino. He wore plain black fatigues and had worn a beret until it became part of the jungle mulch.

He wore no insignia.

I racked my brains. I heard more monkeys; I knew this was the New World, and the middle swath of it. Colombia, Panama, possibly Ecuador or Venezuela. Neither of the latter have governments likely to join the Dante Bogart fan club any time soon. It was far more likely that I was in Colombia. In that event, the guy I just kicked over could have been FARC—Fuerzas Armadas Revolucionarias de Colombia, Ejército del Pueblo—or EPL—Ejército de Liberación Nacional—or the Cartel de la Costa Atlántica—the North Coast cartel. For that matter, he could have been Los Zetas or the Gulf Coast cartel, both from Mexico, both of which had made inroads into taking over Colombian drug operations, and with some frequency showed up in the jungle, either defending transshipment points or whacking competitors.

But I knew homie wasn't a gangster. I didn't know much—but I knew that.

This prick was Bellona.

I found his ID in the front right pocket of his bush vest:

Hans Gonzalez, country of origin Paraguay.

The logo and corporate name on the ID was for some outfit called "In Country Security Consultants." But I recognized the typeface and the configuration of the magnetic strip on the back—slightly narrower than a credit card.

I got the kind of shiver you'd get unexpectedly encountering your ex-wife at a strip club. If she turned out to be there with your *Dad*.

I'd seen these ID cards a million times over the years; I'd *carried* one a million times over the years, for companies named things like Western Executive Protection, Malraux Security Consultants, Shur-Shield Embassy Contracting. Such outfits, and dozens more, were all Bellona Industries. Named after a Roman goddess of war, the group was owned by Virgil Amaro—if he was still alive—and his annoying sons Mark, and Luke, and John.

The three brothers had formed a Trinity of pain-in-my-ass for fourteen years now. Mark was the kind of prick who starts wars in African nations to drive up the price of diamonds. Mark's younger brother Luke was a failed USC-educated filmmaker who got into private security mostly because Daddy paid him plenty of greenbacks to do it. The youngest son, Johnny Boy Amaro, on the other hand, was just a garden-variety Canadian psycho. Encountering John Amaro in-country, I could expect either to be lectured on the benefits of methamphetamine to mental health, or challenged to a game of Irish Standdown. John was a hemmorhoid on the ass of the world of military contractors, and that's a world with a very big ass.

Virgil also had an annoying fifteen-year-old grandson named Augustine—Luke's boy—who, in the old days, had occasionally been handed off to me for "executive protection," aka babysitting.

I strained to remember the last time I'd seen any of them.

As for Hans Gonzalez, neither his pistol nor his rifle had been fired. The rifle looked as if it had been forgotten, dangling from its strap. The strap now crossed his trachea, tangled in the gore of what had once been Hans G's face. There wasn't much left—he'd been killed with a very hot load, fired close.

He'd been surprised. His pistol's security strap hadn't even been unsnapped.

I unsnapped it now, and took the handgun—another five-sev. I checked the action; it was cocked and loaded, the safety on. He had two spare mags for it. I wasn't really interested in carrying the rifle. Getting un-naked seemed like a higher priority for me. It's not that I care if New World monkeys eyeball my junk. It's just that I was getting itchy, with sweat dribbling places it was not meant to dribble. Especially not while one was handling firearms.

Unfortunately, Hans's clothes were soaked with gore.

I checked the safety of the fresh five-sev, blew the most egregious chunks of dirt out of the other and slapped a new magazine into it. Now I had one muddy pistol and one that was basically clean. I carried one in each hand, ready to party. Look at me, fuckers. I'm The Shadow.

My own trail of footprints continued on well past Hans's; he had obviously been tracking or chasing me. But if I'd been shooting at him, why was his rifle dangling, and why wasn't his pistol out—or at least unsecured in its holster?

His boots were caked with mud and blood—blood that couldn't have been his. But whose was it?

I started running again.

I spotted more empty 5.7-millimeter cartridges—whether mine or someone else's, I didn't know; I only knew they didn't belong to Hans, since he hadn't fired his weapon. I followed. I ran.

It took me ten minutes to follow Hans's trail of running-footsteps, a couple dozen spent cartridges and three empty magazines more than a kilometer back to the place that, as near I could tell, I—or *someone*—had started firing.

The trail of footprints, blood and shells T-boned at a scene that wasn't pretty.

I entered a clearing. One black Toyota four-wheel-drive SUV had face-planted into a mangrove tree, taking a black-fatigued Bellona merc with it. The guy slumped across the Toyota's hood, crushed at the pelvis, a pistol in his hand; he'd blown his brains out.

For his part, the SUV's driver had been impaled on the steering column and hadn't lived long. Its doors were open. A second identical model SUV sat intact with its hood nudged against a mangrove, its door-open warning buzzer sounding weak and reedy. This one had Colombian government plates but no other markings. I got close enough to see the police- or military-style Mobile Display Terminal on the dash had gone dark.

I stood there, naked and barefoot, feet caked with mud, holding both pistols and trying to remember.

It was all murky.

I remembered... I remembered...

... I had to fight for it.

I shut my eyes tight and massaged 'em with my palms. This is not the world's best idea when holding two handguns, but I didn't have a waistband to stick those damn things in. I took deep breaths and the pain of remembering lasered from backbrain to nutsac; something was ugly, here, and I didn't wanna remember it.

Something exploded in the vicinity of my thyroid—that is to say, midway between brain and heart.

I caught fragments like shrapnel:

I remembered Trixie and me, the *Corredor Sur*. Rainforest. Trixie playing guitar. I dropped her on the beach in Kuna Yala. I had business.

I recalled driving up the coast to borrow Señor Mike's phone on the *Bubba Love*.

I remembered arguing with Van over a crackly, warbly satphone connection. I heard him say: *Who killed Kennedy? The Bilderbergs? The Greys? The Illuminati? The Space Sisters?*

I knew I'd told him, *Don't sleep with Trixie.* I knew he'd said, *No promises, Frosty—she's at the mercy of the Fish Family mojo. You know damned well I've got no impulse control, and Trixie's a good-looking woman, if a bit annoying...*

Brain pain. Gut pain. Nut pain. Heart pain.

I stopped trying to remember. My path seemed clear: Get dressed, get moving, get Fish. Smack some respect into that Sasquatch, and sort the *Family Circus* out later.

I started for the nearest Toyota. All four of doors were open wide; the key was in the ignition. The car had stalled out—it hadn't been turned off or destroyed in a wreck.

Four men in body armor, bush vests and boots sprawled in a trail from the SUV to the edge of the clearing. Long guns lay discarded near them: Two more AR platform rifles and a Benelli shotgun. A fifth body could be seen distantly; it had died running and appeared to have been shot in the back, a rifle still in its hand.

The men had all been opened up in various ways. Many had chest wounds, too, but every last one had a headshot. The cure for what ails you. Or what ails the guy who shot you.

I turned them over one by one. All five were Anglo. Two had large-caliber entry wounds in the face, the backs of their heads destroyed. Two appeared to have smaller entry wounds of about a quarter-inch, but tangled oblong exits. These had also been fired at a very short range. The bullet from a 5.7x28-millimeter round, like that from its larger cousin the 5.56x45 mm NATO round, is known for "tumbling" upon entry to flesh, providing a buzz-saw effect. With exits like that, I voted for the 5.7s. But someone had shot Hans Gonzalez and two of his closest friends in the face with a higher-caliber hollow-point round. Who was shooting .45s in the jungle?

All four John Does had other abrasions—or so I thought at first glance. As I bent down, something went *click*. The scrapes were all wrong. They weren't scrapes. They were—

I kicked over one who still had a face.

I almost screamed like a little bitch. He had a face, all right—it was peeled back and frozen in a sick-weird happy face—like he'd died in the throes of the funniest joke any son of a bitch on Earth had ever heard.

He'd died *laughing*.

He had blood and goo and strings of flesh between his teeth.

He'd died *chewing*.

His eyes weren't soul-empty like those of a corpse; they were alive, frozen in a final instant of hilarity.

"*Blow my brains out?*" his frozen mouth seemed to say. "*That's a good one! And this steak tartare is hilarious!*"

It was more than a little bit creepy.

I went over to the other two bodies with the smaller entry wounds.

I bent down and looked at their "abrasions."

They were *bites*.

My heart poured on the juice.

I decided it was time to get the fuck out of here.

I reached in the Toyota and removed the key.

The keychain had a blank brass medallion with no insignia and serial number. I know those brass fobs well—they come from the Bellona Industries motor pool.

I got a weird, cold feeling in my gut.

I found the second guy who appeared to have an intact face.

I kicked him over. He was the same: he'd died laughing and eating.

I stood there blinking, trying to piece it all together. My brain was running a million miles a second; I couldn't get it to stop. Goddammit, what was the last thing I remembered?

It hit me like a sledgehammer: Memories, like the corners of my mind, misty water-colored memories of me strapped to a table, a black-haired beauty swimming around me in the sterile air, crying, screaming, "put a mask on him!" and scalding me with sobs while titters echoed every-where—and sticking me with needles. Big ones. Stark naked and shivering in the 80-degree heat, I stalked over to the last corpse—the one with a face—the distant guy who'd died fleeing. He was maybe forty meters away, running for the river, when he got taken out. He'd been shot in the back, not the head, but apparently not by a large caliber round. The shot was distant enough that it if had been fired by a handgun, it came from someone who was a hell of a shot—or maybe just lucky.

The dead man had a gym bag slung over his back and a big rolling aluminum suitcase tipped over next to him—about a 26-inch airporter with an elaborate locking mechanism that looked high-tech. The latter hadn't much liked getting dragged along behind him; it was battered. Inexplicably, in the hot jungle it had gained a distinctive sheen of condensation, as if the contents were refrigerated. There was even the faint imprint of one big snowflake on it, a crystal structure disintegrating under the jungle heat. The suitcase was cold to the touch. It had shoulder straps as well as wheels and a handle. If the running man had hoisted it onto his shoulders, it might have stopped the bullet. He might still be running.

The guy had a pearl-handled .45 automatic in his hand.

The slide was open—the pistol was empty.

I disengaged the gym bag and kicked the body over.

Holy *crap*.

It was an Amaro, all right—I saw it right off. He had that Amaro nose, the Amaro forehead, the Amaro cheekbones—they're all unmistakable. But something was seriously wrong.

It looked like Augustine—"Little Augie." Luke Amaro's son. But it wasn't him—it couldn't be. This guy wore eyeliner—who wears eyeliner on a military operation in the jungle? Then again, who wears a crucifix dangling from one ear, a robot-spider choker and a *Mörbid Örchid* T-shirt?

The guy's porkpie hat dangled pristine from a jagged shard of mangrove about two meters from where he'd fallen. I remembered that: Augie always had a thing for hats.

It couldn't be Augie. But the resemblance was too eerie to be a coincidence. Last time I'd seen the little prick he'd been… what, fourteen? He'd been five-four and round with baby fat.

This kid was nineteen or twenty—six-two and skinny.

That was bad.

If this was Augie, I'd lost more of my life than I thought I had.

That was *very* bad.

I unzipped the gym bag. In it, I found a bunch of clothes—thrift-store pinstripe suit pants pegged in as tight as such things can go, a spare pair of pointy deathrock boots, T-shirts from asshat bands called "Isambard Kingdom Brunel" and "Felonious Monk" and "Hölles Eierstock," boxer shorts with ironic sayings about Colombia and cocaine. There was a grey thrift-store vest in case poor Augie, you know, got, like, blood or something on the one he was wearing. There was a charger for the cell phone, some boxes of .45 pistol ammo and $100,000 cash—a 10K bundle of Franklins, and the rest in what looked to be well-laundered twenties.

To a longtime mercenary, the sight of that much lettuce is arresting enough that it made me forget that there were some missing years between the Little Augie I knew and the Little Augie who apparently cruised the jungle dressed like a fruitcake.

I tried to open the aluminum suitcase. The lock system had three thumb-print panels covered with black plastic sheaths. Three separate people—or, at least, three separate thumbs, which meant at least two people—would be needed to open it, unless you were the bomb squad.

Needless to say, I didn't try to open it.

Those asshats you see on the television who need to open a lock so they point their gun at it and just start firing, and the thing goes *snap*? When a guy tries that in real life, he only loses one toe, kneecap, earlobe or testicle before he says, "Right. We'll try something else next time."

I reached in Augie's thrift-store vest and felt around for his Bellona ID. First I found his cell phone: One of those hot-shit pieces of crap that not only sings and dances for you, but gives you all the latest beats and tells you what international socialite has been playing footsie with Justin Timberlake. I knew it must have international service—that was easy enough to get if you have the cash. But the battery was dead, and all I got when I tried to turn it on was a satisfying chime, a flash of light and then a quick blacking-out of the screen.

I finally found Augie's ID in the pocket of his vest.

It was Augie, all right.

I racked my brains. Could I be mixing him up with one of the younger Amaros? One of Mark Amaro's rugrats, or a long-lost child of one of Virgil's paramours in... I dunno, *Fruitystan*?

I panicked.

I got in the driver's seat of the Toyota; I set the five-sev on the passenger's seat and turned the key in the ignition.

The motor complained and whined. The battery was half-drained from however long it had sat with the door-open buzzer going.

It was an automatic; I couldn't have push-started it if I wanted to. I pumped the gas and tried again; the groaning starter went *whirrrr-choke-whirrrr!* and the engine caught.

The tank was about half-full.

I started booting the dash display. It was the same Mobile Display Terminal Bellona vehicles used when on deployment. Unlike the more elaborate displays used by certain law enforcement and military vehicles, it does not provide video or voice uplink to other Bellona locations worldwide; it's a text-only gig. The big advantage is that there's no way hostiles can track its signal in combat. It is generally batched with a secure GPS display, which this one appeared to be.

As the MDT booted, happy logos blinked at me, showing dancing globes and corporate names and slogans like *Bringing You the World* and *We Get You There!* While I waited, I got Augie's cell phone charger shoved into the dashboard adapter and started it juicing.

When GPS came online, I watched a spasm of static go through the screen. Somehow, the GPS unit had been damaged. The screen was cracked and swirls of color filtered across a mottled image of southern Panama. I couldn't see the date.

But I could still read my future on the map.

I was in the Darién Gap. That's southern Panama, a narrow strip of rainforest just north of the Colombia border. Just past the northern terminus of the southern branch of the Pan-American highway, it's basically the middle of nowhere. Because of the rugged terrain, the highway had never been built to cross this swath of jungle. If you wanted to reach Pinogana, the southernmost terminus of the northern half of the Highway, you'd need a four-wheel drive vehicle, and preferably a padded codpiece, too.

I knew where I was going: to the only place in Panama where I could start a serious argument about whether or not the Council on Foreign Relations had yet succeeded in assassinating the Everglades' last Skunk Ape—and then end said argument with a well-deserved sucker-punch, followed by beer and bonghits to the soothing strains of Jethro Tull.

I flipped open Augie's cell phone and saw the *date*.

My blood ran cold.

Five years.

It had been five years.

The MDT beeped.

The message said: **ATS LOGIN?**

ATS: "Above Top Secret."

That had to be Luke Amaro playing Army; there is no "Above Top Secret."

I paged through the address book on Little Augie's cell phone and found… *voila*. Right under "A": *ATSway Oginlay*. Nice going, Augie; highly secure. The entry had a 20-character password; I punched it into the MDT.

The MDT blinked and purred like it didn't want to take it; I waited on eggshells. I heard copters: distant, but getting less so every second.

I almost panicked; I didn't want to wait around to get nailed by the cops, by Bellona, by angry townspeople with pitchforks.

The thing purred and whirred some more; then it coughed up.

The message said: **GOD'S MERCY DEPARTING VALPARAISO NOON GMT FALSE-FLAGGED UNDER LIBERIAN REGIS-TRATION AS THE VS LEONARDO. VIPS COPPOLA AND HIPPOCRATES ON BOARD. VIP BRUNEL HAS PACKAGE SALVATION. VIP BRUNEL TO BOARD AT CASCO VIEJO, BAHÍA DE PANAMÁ. ENTRY CLEARED FOR QUEUING AT MIRAFLORES. GOD'S MERCY TO RENDEZVOUS WITH GOD'S GRACE AT COLÓN FOR ARMED ESCORT TO MALTA. VIP PALEHORSE REMAINS IN COMMAND OF PALE BIRD SQUADRON DARIÉN CLEANUP TASK FORCE. GOD BE WITH YOU.**

I said, "God be with *you*, shitbag."

These cats had come up with a code any idiot could break with two fingers and thirty seconds in Wikipedia. The first two were obvious. **VIP COP-**

POLA: Luke Amaro, the wannabe filmmaker. **VIP BRUNEL**: Augustine "Little Augie" Amaro—I'm figuring, from his favorite band name—based on the T-shirt. The other two Amaros took a cursory reading of either the Book of Revelation, or 1990s comic books. **VIP WHITEHORSE**: Mark Amaro, the military brother, raised by Virgil Amaro's South African second wife; he was the only one among them who I would have trusted to field-strip a salad spinner. His moniker, clearly, came from the White Horse of the apocalypse—Conquest.

And **VIP PALEHORSE**? That had to be Johnny Boy Amaro—Mark's bigger, meaner half-brother, who became an Army Cayuse pilot, then almost got court-martialed for heroin—*almost*. Obviously, he had too many connections for his Uncle Sam to do him that way without a reacharound. John Amaro got administrative discharge, a civilian license and an operational job with his pops, not to mention a bazillion-figure salary.

Johnny Boy's horse was pale, which made him bad news for bald ex-mackerel-snapper mopes standing naked in the jungle wondering why their pubes were shaved.

But… "Salvation"? What the hell was that? Was "Salvation" me, or Augie's steamy little suitcase, or… what? And who was **VIP HIPPOCRATES**?

My heart pounded: was there any chance Virgil or Luke had gotten Trixie?

The message was timestamped two hours ago.

Another message, similarly secured, had followed it—five ago.

DARIÉN FACILITY COMPROMISED. CONFIRM VIP BRUNEL HAS BEEN EXTRACTED WITH SALVATION.

—and another, five minutes ago:

CONFIRM EXTRACT OF SALVATION WITH VIP BRUNEL

—and another, moments before the Mobile Display Terminal finished booting.

CONFIRM EXTRACT OF AUGUSTINE AMARO AND PACKAGE SALVATION CONFIRM URGENT

RESPOND AND CONFIRM RESPOND AND CONFIRM.

I looked over at Augie's body; I frowned.

His cell phone played "I Melt With You."

I flipped it open.

There was a text message received, from "Dad."

Jesus Christ. Not only did this ass clown let the VIPs pick their own dumbass monikers; now he was using his son's cell phone in what I could only assume was a war zone.

The text said:

Augie secure voice is down u.s. justice dept has compromised use text only do you have the package are you out of the Darién facility????? ur uncle John is goin 2 blow it

They were going to blow it, all right.

I frowned at the phone.

It seemed a bad idea to tip Luke Amaro off to the fact that I wasn't his son. I racked my brains for how one sought to sound like Augie. I remembered I got stuck playing babysitter to the little bastard one week in Riohacha, back when he was about thirteen and I was *career-minded*. He spent the whole week sexting with some older girl, bragging to me about how chicks always got hot and bothered by his expert use of online slang and sent him topless pictures of themselves.

I'd watched Little Augie's sexting hijinks like a hawk, not because I wanted to see the pic of his sophisticated paramour but because if he shared it, I planned to cockblock him with a right hook and a boot to the *huevos*. Some *chica bonita* innocently sends you a naked picture of herself and you share it with the grizzled prick your father assigned to make sure the Gulf Cartel doesn't whack your sissy ass? Amaro spawn or no, that would have earned him a well-deserved lesson in manners.

Lucky for my career, Augie's *muchacha caliente* never posted her *tetas*, but I got a crash course in how Augstine Amaro's mind worked, or more often *didn't*.

So, channeling poor, dead Gen-Z asswipe Augie Amaro, I typed back:

LOL

I waited on pins and needles until a message came back about twenty seconds later:

god b praised bogart eliminated per orders???

I got goosebumps.

I typed back:

confirmed... dante is dead lol

The message bleeped back:

confirm u have salvation???? utmost importance

I typed:

totally ROFL i have salvation LOL

The response came with a speed that blistered my thumbs just to think about it.

ur uncle john in command pale bird squadron
but NOAA predicts lightning storm darien

heavy winds john sez copter extract impos

ur ride intact?

I typed back:

i m fine dad will c u @ rendezveuz panama city w00t!!

W00t? Pretending to be a nineteen-year-old pinhead was even easier than I thought it'd be.

Luke responded:

god b praised

confirm u r clear 1 mile?

fire in teh hole :-)

My *goosebumps* got goosebumps.

My hands shaking, I typed back:

LOL

The copters were louder, now.

I gauged the distance from the sound and saw the shadow; the copters were coming in out of the sun. They were Bellona's Little Birds—McDonnell-Douglas 530Fs, the same craft as the U.S. Army's AH-6s—descendents of the Vietnam-era Cayuse. These were armed to the teeth with folding-fin rockets, and unmarked except for white sans-serif numbers across the belly.

I rummaged like a maniac around in the SUV and found a pair of field glasses. I climbed on the SUV's hood; I was still naked and mud-slippery. I braced myself against the bumper and peered at the mountain.

My jaw dropped.

There it was: the gaping mouth of the facility in the side of the mountain. It had been camouflaged by rock and underbrush, carefully-positioned jungle vines hiding a secured entry that looked like the south-facing entrance to Fort Knox.

Now, the jungle was scarred by blasts, the face of the mountain blackened. The entrance gaped wide.

People spilled out and lumbered down the mountain. A hundred, two hundred of them. People in shirtsleeves, people in lab coats, people in hospital gowns. People stark naked and bloody, sprouting tubes. People with huge gaping chest wounds, hours old; people with fresh gunshot wounds still spouting. People in Bellona-issue body armor and black fatigues.

Or, rather, things that *had been* people.

Hundreds of them.

I could see their chests working, mouths open.

They puked out wet sodden streams of death and hunger and anti-mirth, yukking it up to a joke only they found funny. They were much too far away for me to hear them, but I could hear them anyway. I heard them in my nightmares—the kind of nightmares you have while awake. Awake, and naked in the jungle.

They were laughing the Panama Laugh.

LOL.

I wanted to puke. I felt dizzy. I almost went down, but I stayed steady. I kept watching.

They lumbered down the mountain toward the lowlands—toward me. They were still perhaps two klicks distant. My heart pounded.

Were those things actually *coming after me?*

Could they smell me *two kilometers away?*

I remembered laughers further north in Darién: menacing Colombian orphans; menacing Trixie. I remembered driving to Colón in the middle of the night. I remembered going feverish...

The Little Birds came in for the kill, trailing wisps of low-lying cloud from their skids. They cast shadows out of the sunset. There was thunder above them.

Rockets flared: Hydra-70s, high-explosive warheads.

The rockets hurtled over the heads of the laughers, who glanced up only briefly before continuing their down-the-hill lumber toward—presumably—me.

The missiles hissed into the gaping vault.

I put the glasses down and shielded my eyes.

The blast came: distant thunder as, far overhead, the clouds roared.

I uncovered my eyes. Hot jets of flame poured out of the vault. Vents on the side of the mountain spewed smoke and dust. There were more blasts, deep inside. One, two, three, four—

—the mountain came down.

The Little Birds peeled off and vanished into the clouds as thunder rumbled; the second flight came in low, laterally over the heads of the lumbering escapees as the dust settled over them.

The thunder cracked hard overhead.

There was a flash of lightning.

The creatures looked up, cackling.

Behind them came an airplane—a black Super Tucano. A turboprop aircraft of Brazilian manufacture, it was a counter-insurgency, border-security and smuggling-interdiction aircraft designed for close-in ground support, low-level strafing, and the precision bombing of targets in rough terrain.

This one bore a single package, loaded centerline.

The creatures looked up.

Thunder erupted from the clouds; there were flashes of lightning.

I saw the weapon exit the Super Tucano's underside rack.

The plane climbed fast and disappeared into the clouds as the bomb fell.

I got down on my belly on the far side of the SUV and said, "Hail Mary, full of grace—"

The fuel-air bomb ignited at altitude.

☠

This was not the first time I had seen the laughers.

My memories were fuzzy; they came back to me in waves, but each wave had a laugh track.

I'd killed these things before, or things like them—things that laughed, things that cried, things that just wanted to eat me. Things that lay and twitched and said nothing. I knew I'd killed them in Congo; I knew I'd killed them in southern Libya; I knew I'd killed them in the Philippines. I'd seen them packed into rail containers in terrorist camps, writhing and laughing.

Worse, I knew I'd uttered that laugh myself.

I knew I'd howled with sickly-dead bliss.

I knew when I laughed it… I got *hungry*. I knew I'd craved the flesh of my fellows.

Staring up at the hillside full of chuckleheads, I reached through the fog of memory.

I remembered saying, "More kisses *now*, loverboy.…"

…and feeding. Then blissed-out catatonia till the hunger returned. Chuckles as it grew. Hunger taking over…

…Till I was laughing the Panama Laugh.

☠

I shoved my palms against my eyes again; it felt like someone set my brain on fire. I remembered a deathrock angel swimming through my brainpan.

She said: "My contact at Scripps asserts it's just an involuntary violent contraction of the lungs, caused by the same cascade that causes the hunger. But a neuropathologist I know at Walter Reed thinks it's semi-voluntary."

Virgil Amaro: "But in his Mauritania debrief after the Libya operation, Dante said it *felt* like laughter. Sort of, you know, sort of—" his hand made dismissive gestures in the air— "*Emotionally.*"

The deathrock angel wore a lab coat. She hovered before me.

Virgil sat behind her, in a wheelchair.

The croaker said: "I know. Your visiting USAMRIID neurologist claims it's cachinnation."

And Virgil, coughing, his lungs cancer-wet:

"Cachinnation?"

"Laughter without apparent cause. Like in schizophrenics."

"Does it accompany an emotional response?"

"Well, in certain cases of traumatic brain injury—"

"Forget I asked," interrupted Virgil. "I have to Skype with Defense in ten minutes and I don't have my makeup on yet. Here's what I need to know. Do these the victims have emotions?"

"I'd need more information. More brain scans."

"Fine, I'll tell Luke to sign off. Now give me your gut feeling."

She said: "It depends on the strain."

"Then with some strains, they're alive. They can think."

"Well," she said. "They can *feel*. For a while. With the primary strain, all cognition has ceased and won't come back—we know that. But yes, my gut tells me they think it's funny, at first. Or *feel* it. But then they die laughing. They keep laughing. So, no, at that point it's just laughing. It's not even cacchination. It's just—" her voice caught. "But with Bogart's strain, I'm not sure."

"About which part?"

The black-haired sawbones with the cranberry lips bent down down and shined a penlight in my eyes. I fought against the straitjacket, trying to get a bite of her tender Iberian nose. I fought with my straitjacket, howling.

She told Virgil, "What I'm not sure of… is if he still thinks it's funny."

☠

I was two klicks distant when the bomb went off.

Even so, I fancied I could smell them, like I felt the blast of heat, burning my shoulders. Like I smelled the sickly scent of the smoke. Like I felt the steam, the hammering pour of a sweet Panama rain all vaporized in the scouring blast of thermobaric Armageddon.

When I looked up, there was a mushroom cloud. The flames swirled up and merged with the low-lying cloud cover.

There might still be bones there, but I doubted it.

The bomb blast opened up the rainclouds.

They burst.

Rain hammered down.

I held my arms out wide like Christ on the cross, looked up into the Panama shower and let it wash me as the fuel-air sent a mushroom up to Heaven.

Things got *steamy*.

☠

I drove through the jungle, steaming, stewing.

Van Fish had sold me out: I knew it, or thought I knew. Maybe one of the Amaros had come to see him and Van had finally gotten that new fifty-foot Catalina he'd always wanted. Or a decent Cessna float plane, or more likely a two-week soiree in Rio, pickling himself in rum-and-lime denial.

Or maybe Virgil tracked down Trixie. Maybe Van *had* to sell me out to keep her breathing. Maybe he'd done what he needed to do, or what he *felt* he needed to do.

I still owed the prick a knuckle sandwich.

I made good time through the jungle; GPS helped.

There were no more messages on the Bellona MDT. No more texts from Luke Amaro to his dead son Augustine.

I was tempted to try, but I'd left enough spoor as it was.

I broke the rainforest near Arquia and found a swamp I'd used before. The GPS was dead by then; I jacked the MDT out with a tire iron.

I packed Augie's gym bag with two pistols, ammo and magazines, plus the cheesy boxer shorts and T-shirts that said weird-ass things. The rest, I left in the jungle.

I found an empty case for the MDT and strapped it to the suitcase.

I sank the Toyota into the black muck of the swamp.

I rolled the suitcase behind me, its little wheels sinking into the mud.

I found a dirt road with a sign that said,

Santa María del Cordero
10 km

I shouldered the gym bag. With the suitcase rumbling behind me, I started the walk to the sea.

☠

Trixie was stunned, like she couldn't decide what to believe. Christ, the eyes on that woman. The wind blew in from the terrace, carrying the scent of the orchids. I took a deep breath of it and went back to talking.

I said, "I made it to the town, found a fisherman—drug runner, actually, but he *said* he was a fisherman. He gave me a lift."

At the mention of the case, Van had dragged it over and started peering at it. The man knew a thing or two about locks. On this one, he had already passed judgment.

He said, "You're not getting this open. Not without the fingerprints."

I said, "It's important. That frost you're seeing means it's refrigerated. I think it might be the cure to the laughing sickness."

"Well you're not getting it open."

I said, "Have you got a hacksaw?"

Van said, "You're not getting this open. Not without the fingerprints."

I said, "How about an acetylene torch? Is Señor Mike still around? The *Bubba Love* has metal pontoons—"

Van said, "You're not getting this open. Not without the fingerprints."

I said, "I've still got connections in Buenos Aires and Montevideo. I can get thermite."

Van said, "Frosty—"

I said, "Some kind of acid?"

Van growled, "Frosty, did I stutter?"

I said, "There's gotta be some way."

"D-man, you're not getting this thing open unless you have the fingerprints. This is the kind of thing they ship really dangerous samples in—Ebola, Marburg, smallpox. Governments, big companies that deal with serious biological stuff. It's got integrated electronics. If you try to crowbar it open or use a cutter or thermite or shaped nitroglycerine or do anything other than use the thumb pads, it ignites and destroys the samples."

I said, "Why do *you* know?"

He said, "Trust me."

I looked at Trixie.

"Does this make sense what he's saying? About the medical samples?"

She said, "Sorry, dude. This isn't my area of clinical specialty. Talk to me if you find any kids with cleft palates."

I said, "So what are our options?"

Van said, "Well, let's see. Get the fingerprints, get the fingerprints, or get the fingerprints. Or you could always get the fingerprints."

I said, "I don't know whose they are."

He growled, "Probably one of your erstwhile employers."

I shrugged, "Sure, but which one?"

Trixie said, "Anyone but Virgil. He died years ago."

It hit me like a slap. I didn't remember much, but I remembered that I wanted a long, dark night of the soul with Virgil and some power tools. Looked like it wasn't to be.

I said, "When?"

She told me, "Not long after you went... uh... wherever you went. It was lung cancer."

I rubbed my jaw. I said, "I shoulda hacksawed Augie's hand off."

Trixie said, "Couldn't you just bring a bottle of wine, like normal people?"

I said, "No, I mean... it coulda been him. I wasn't thinking straight. If we can't get our hands on any Amaros, then do we have *any* options? Someone who might know more about this than you?"

He and Trixie exchanged a look.

"The San Francisco people might know."

I did a spit-take with my Scotch.

"San Francisco?"

Trixie said, "You got a problem with San Francisco?"

I said, "A problem? Yeah, I'm from Oakland, so, yeah. I've got a problem with San Francisco."

Van said, "Who doesn't? But these are the guys to ask. They know all sorts of stuff about computer security—stuff I'd never know. Conspiracy people."

I said, "Oh, man. Oh, hell. Oh hell, no. Shit, no. Hell, no. Shit, no! Hell no, no. Just... no."

"You got something to say, Frosty?"

I said, "Don't call me that! Are these the shitheads who freeze people and make porn?"

Van snarled, "Hey, fuck you, asshole! They're not shitheads and they don't just make porn! They're called the Inferno now, and they're also hacktivists."

I reeled back as if Van had smacked me in the face.

"Did you just say 'hacktivists'?"

"Why, did I stutter?"

Like its owner, Van's kitchen table is kinda on the big side; he was too far away to punch. So poured myself another tall Scotch and slammed it. It didn't help.

I said in horror, "'Hacktivists.'"

He said, "They're dedicated to getting the truth out. Some of them have pretty weird ideas, but basically if you give 'em a chance you realize they're talking sense."

I said, "Sounds like a cult."

Van said, "It's not a cult. It's more like a commune."

I said, "What's the difference?"

"Oh, man," he said. "That's just asking for it. Get with the program, Frosty. You've been away a long time. Information is power—you taught them that."

I said, "Huh?"

Van said, "They were just garden-variety conspiracy nuts before you and your videos came along."

I said, "Huh?"

Van and Trixie looked at each other.

Trixie said, "Dante, just how far back do you remember?"

My head throbbed. I massaged my eyeballs; I remembered a gorgeous view of sunrise over Bahía Limón, and—

Big vague memories thundered over me. Then it hit me. Tears rolled from my eyes. I buried my face in my hands and began to weep softly.

I heard a sound across the table. No guy like me doesn't recognize that sound. It's often not good news when it's coming from across a table with Scotch on it, even at 8:20 in the morning.

Van looked guilty.

Sheepishly, he held up his silver .45 automatic and said, "Okay. See, I'm sorry. I'm sorry. There, I said it. I thought you were laughing."

My blood went cold.

I said, "You know about the laughers."

Van said, "Duh, Frosty."

Trixie said, "Didn't you notice all that nodding while you were telling your story?"

I felt like I'd been smacked with a two-by-four. I felt my head spinning. I had to fight not to pass out.

That's when an airhorn sounded outside.

It was the kind of horn that comes from a can of compressed air—the kind you take to a baseball game. Panamanians love their baseball. The sound grated on my nerves.

Van and Trix exchanged another look.

Van got up from the table. He said, "Sorry, Frosty, but when those Kuna boys start blowing the airhorn, there's no time to fuck around. Can you still shoot straight?"

I had broken away from my tears and the shakes.

I growled, "Depends on who's paying."

Van glared at me for a minute and said, "Can you make a five-hundred yard shot into a boat in this weather?"

I sneered, "With what, Old Smokey?"

He said. "My uncle's .308."

"Which uncle?"

"Uncle Joe's. Uncle Stan's is a thirty-ought, remember?"

"Oh," I said, remembering vaguely. "Right. Is the boat moving?"

"You could say that."

"Oncoming or lateral?"

"Coming straight at you."

"Scope?"

"Zeiss."

I shrugged. "As long as I'm not shooting at Kennedy."

"Nah," said Van. "I already shot him once. Trix, baby, will you get the rifle?"

She ran to the bedroom.

Van said, "Do you have a sidearm, too?"

I said, "Sure."

He said, "How much ammo?"

"Enough."

"I wouldn't be sure," he said. "Bring it. I'll meet you on the terrace."

Van ran out the door and left it open.

A calm, sweet Panama breeze blew in after him.

I heard Van shouting in Spanish to someone down by the dock.

More air horns blew outside.

Trixie reappeared in the door from the bedroom. She carried a AK-47 over her shoulder and the promised .308 Winchester with a scope—both loaded. She'd also shoved a .45 Smith & Wesson in the waistband of her khaki shorts. Her pockets bulged, distended in box shapes.

She handed me the Winchester.

I took it and said, "What the hell's this about?"

Trixie hoisted a case of .308 shells—20 boxes of 20—from under her arm and slammed them on the kitchen table, right next to the Scotch.

She said, "Pirates."

I looked at the ammo.

I said, "That's a lot of pirates."

Trixie said, "You're telling me."

☠

That word, "Pirates," didn't sound as exotic to me as it might to most other mopes. As a contractor with McTucker Associates, a Bellona affiliate nominally of Cyprus and wholly owned by Virgil Amaro, I had spent two years doing pirate interdiction on the *God's Blessing* out of Dubai all up and down the Somali coast and the Gulf of Aden.

But Trixie? Last time I saw her, she couldn't even hear me say the word with a straight face, let alone say it herself. To her, pirates were something you dressed up as for Halloween.

I retrieved both my five-sevs from the gym bag and clipped their holsters to the belt I'd jacked from poor, dead Augie Amaro.

I shoved extra mags in my pockets.

☠

The air horns had been sounded by a small group of Kuna youths in dugout *cayucos* who had, apparently, befriended Van and Trixie.

The Kuna are a dark, small-statured people. They speak a language called Dulegaya among themselves, but most speak Spanish—especially the young ones.

The kids wore an amalgam of jean shorts and native wraps, T-shirts and reverse- appliqué Kuna *molas*, traditional sandals and cheap plastic made-in-Taiwan *huaraches*. One kid wore a Rey Mysterio T-shirt; I figured that one for a gift from Van, who had once told me that Lucha Libre was his favorite sport, but only because there were serious moral issues with bullfighting.

The kids had moored their dugouts to Van's private dock, the same place the Colombian fisherman had moored his drug-running boat when he'd dropped me off an hour ago. I counted three rowboats and six Kuna youth. Three had AK-47s. Two had hunting rifles. One, the youngest, had a spear. They held them cautiously at port arms—like they'd been thoroughly trained on them.

The San Blas archipelago is the maritime component of Panama's Kuna Yala province. Technically an autonomous region or *comarca*, it is governed by the Kuna, and they don't sell their real estate to outsiders. And yet here Van Fish was, on a private island called Isla Pescado, which was either within the San Blas Islands or just outside them, depending on how you reckoned such things. Here, Van Fish had carved himself a relatively cozy piece of Heaven with a reverse-osmosis water filter, a state-of-the-art septic tank, a hydroponic garden and solar panels mail-ordered from the back of *Popular Mechanics*. What exactly Van Fish had done to secure himself a parcel of paradise from a people who don't sell it was a matter of rampant speculation among the very small number of fishers, beach loungers and pot smugglers who had the fortune and/or misfortune to have known our Mr. Fish.

What I knew about Van Fish could fill a 55-gallon oil drum of fermenting nightsoil, but I still didn't know much. He alternately claimed to be a Georgia Jew, Florida white trash, and third-generation Hollywood royalty from el-lay—West Pico and South La Cienega in specific. But more significantly, and with great colorful flourish, he claimed to have served in the U.S. military—which branch changed with the number of cocktails consumed—and to thereafter have been a mercenary all across Africa in the tumultuous years of the oil-and-diamond wars.

The world of military contractors is not a small one; it is infinitesimal. And yet, I had encountered almost no one who knew him, which should have made me suspicious. When we had first met he had struck me as one of those weirdos who tells stories about the horrors of Nam, vague on the details, and then you find out he just got mugged there once while on vacation. Van didn't claim to have served in the Vietnam War, but he did have some pretty weird stories about caves in Cambodia—and he even had a '60s-era bloop tube he'd fire if you asked him real nice (or got him drunk enough).

And when it came to more recent service in the armed forces of the world, he certainly dropped the right names and knew all the right places from Niger to Dubai to Samarkand, and he could not have been full of shit all the time. He had served, all right.

But just who had he *actually* served with? I've never been able to find them.

What really mattered, though, was that I knew Van Fish was possibly the best man in the world to have on your side in a bar fight in Barranquilla or Panama City or wherever the hell else you felt like getting in a bar fight, which was nowhere as far as I was concerned... and yet, I kept seeming to get into them, especially when Van was around.

Trixie was another story. I sometimes thought I knew her better than I knew myself. And none of it added up, even remotely, to being the kind of girl who shouldered an AK. They don't really cover that in medical school—let alone the Peace Corps.

But Trixie was more than just a two-term Peace Corps veteran. After her post-college tour with the Corps, she had received from some venerable institution a combined MD and Masters of Public Health and, with the chance to stay Stateside and earn six figures, instead signed up with the Physicians' Emergency Fund for an extended tour of meeting the bright-eyed children of the world, stitching up their shrapnel wounds and telling them not to practice their tap dancing in the minefields. At the end of that tour, she elected to go back the fuck to Panama to have relationships with losers like me. With three fellow doctors, she formed a health-education nonprofit and contracted with that selfsame Corps to provide medical services to certain of their Latin American volunteers, making just enough money that she could moonlight delivering lectures on health to Colombian orphans, accompanying herself on guitar while singing songs about heat rash.

And speaking of music—that violin music you hear? That's being played at your funeral if you're ever stupid enough to ask Trixie why a wholesome hippie like her dates so many criminals, vagabonds and soldiers. Her dad was an Army man—thereafter a cop. He did some not-so-nice things. She's got issues. Don't ask if you don't wanna know.

And if you wanna know? Have your head examined, or she'll do it for you—with a claw hammer, or whatever's handy.

If you can manage to not piss Trixie off, you'll have taken an important step toward not existing in a world of hurt.

And you'll be doing better than I do, half the time.

☠

I joined Van and Trixie at the flagstone-paved place where the three paths split for different sides of the beach.

I said, "You wanna fill me in?"

Van said, "Pirates."

I said, "I got that."

He said, "Dead pirates. Catch my drift?"

I said, "Not really."

He gave me a look of enormous pity.

Trixie did the same, stopping mid-sentence in her conversation in pidgin Spanish/Dulegaya to glare at me while the youngest Kuna trembled.

He said, "You remember Colón, don't you, Frosty?"

I said, "Now *you're* gonna start?"

Van said, "Look. Trixie's pretty good, but she's a beginner. You know I can't shoot worth a damn with anything except my bloop tube. Once they're within fifty meters, I'll let 'em have it. But I've only got two grenades left, so they've got to count. Until then, you're our only qualified marksman."

I said, "Van. I don't get it."

Van frowned and said, "Cuba's in chaos. Pirates flooding south. They like the look of my boats and my plane and my house."

I said, "I'm glad someone does."

"Keep it up, laughing boy. Also, word on the waves is I got like a hundred grand in cash stashed here."

I said, "Do you?"

Van said, "Yeah, Frosty, you just brought it."

He gave me a walkie-talkie and field glasses, and pointed to the water tower.

He said, "Topside. Watch for catapults."

I said, "*Catapults?*"

He said, "Uh-huh."

I said, "Seriously. Catapults?"

Van said, "Did I stutter?"

☠

Casa Fish had been augmented since my departure. What I thought was a water tower was in fact a *sniper* tower.

I mounted the tower with the Winchester slung over my back, the five-sevs jabbing me in the guts, and the boxes of ammo tucked under my arm.

I still felt woozy.

The walkie crackled.

Van said, "You loaded, Frosty?"

I punched the walkie and said, "Don't call me that."

He said, "Frosty?"

And I said, "Don't fucking call me that!"

So he said, "Please, douchebag. There are children present. Watch your fucking language."

"You wanna tell me what I'm shooting at, Chewbacca?"

Van was unflappable. He told me, "The things that *move*."

"Lots of things move."

"Yeah? Well these things *shouldn't*."

I suddenly had one big fat goosebump where my throat used to be.

Then I heard the airhorn blare outside, from the close ocean side of the island, down on the beach below the rock face.

The airhorn blared: Short. Short-long. Short-short-short. Long.

The walkie crackled. Van said, "East. That's your cue, Frosty."

On that side of the tower interior, the top half of the wall had been marked, rather helpfully, with a crudely-painted sunrise to indicate East. The bottom half was open, giving me a straight shot to the ocean.

I got on my belly behind and peered, first through glasses, then through the scope.

The scope was all katywonkus. I punched the walkie.

Crackle: "A screwdriver woulda been nice, Van."

Crackle: "Radio silence, Frosty. Those *piratas* can hear us."

Crackle: I said, "If you're not going to maintain your toys—"

Crackle: "Shut the fuck up, Frosty."

"Don't fucking call me that!"

Since I didn't have a screwdriver, I reached in my pocket for a Colombian 20-peso coin I'd gotten as part of the change for a Jackson at the seaside tavern in Santa María del Cordero last night. I used it to work on the screw of the scope and got it to where I could stand it; I went back and forth between them: field glasses, scope, field glasses, scope—not seeing *shit*.

Then I saw them.

I saw them, out there in a big wide-open aluminum skiff, running hot on an outboard opened up full. Then another. Then another. Then another. Then another.

Packed in close.

Raving, drooling, howling—

—laughing.

I got a good look through the glasses, then through the scope. I couldn't hear them, but I could see them, and just seeing that spasmodic jerking of the chest and the grim wicked twist of the face gave me shitstains in all the underwear I'd ever worn in my worst fucking nightmares—like, retroactively.

My blood ran cold. There were twenty or thirty—eight, ten to a boat. Their skin, where it was intact, was drained white and pasty; in various spots, it was lumpy with blue-black distensions. Where skin *wasn't* intact, it had long since gone gloppy with congealed rust-colored matter. Bones had been broken; limbs hung, rubbery, still jerking with movements as the creatures' open mouths emitted peals of tittering laughter. Extremities swelled with pooled blood.

My goosebumps got goosebumps.

I shit a fucking brick.

Crackle: "Van! Van! Van! Motherfucker!"

Van, nice and easy: Crackle. "Yes, Frosty?

Crackle. I said, my voice shaking: "These are *things*."

Pause, crackle, pause, crackle, pause.

"You don't say."

"They're, they're… *kids*."

Pause, crackle, pause, crackle, pause.

Crackle: "Sorry, Frosty."

I said, "And girls. Women—*young* women."

He said, "I *know*, Frosty. They're not alive."

I said, "I know! But—"

Screech! We stepped on and squelched each other.

A moment of silence.

Van said, "You gotta do this, Frosty. Someone does. You're Annie Oakley around here."

Trembling, I looked back through the scope.

I said, with a walkie-crackle:

"*Claro*."

I looked: There were two, maybe three dozen of them. Packed into three decayed, dented bent-up fishing boats, outboards lashed in place by inexpertly-knotted line. They were aimed at the shore, hurling in at twenty, twenty-two knots. More than a half-mile distant, now—closing. Soon they'd be in range, if I could shoot like I used to.

Crackle. Van said, "You know about the head shots, right?"

Crackle. I said, "I know about the head shots, asshole."

Another airhorn sounded.

Crackle: "West, Got it?"

Crackle: "Got it." Trixie's voice.

Crackle: Van. "How we doin', Bogey boy? Are they laughing?"

My voice trembled as I said, "They're laughing. They're *kids*."

Crackle, crackle. Van, growling: "Kill 'em."

Crackle, crackle. "*Kids*," I said, weakly, shaking.

There was a squelch and a howl as Trixie hopped on the line while Van tried to speak.

There was a moment of silence.

Crackle: "Kill 'em, Frosty."

It was Trixie.

I took a deep breath.

Took a bead on one.

He was too distant, of course, for me to hear that awful sound—but I could see jerking spasmodically all over, howling soundless like this was the funniest thing on the planet.

I probably couldn't have heard him even if I was close, because his chest had been opened by some sort of ordnance. His lungs hung in strips out his shattered ribcage.

But still his mouth opened, closed, opened, closed, a terrible grimace turning his face into an obscenity.

Trixie: "Frosty?"

I said, by way of exhalation: "Don't call me that,"

—and fired.

☠

That first one was twelve or thirteen years old. Nothing much seemed funny to him once the back of his head exploded from my .308 round.

He fell dead in the water, his foot hooked. He trailed behind for a while, leaving blood on the wake.

I worked the bolt, aimed, fired. A hysterically grinning little girl went down—eight, nine, drooling, howling, spewing putrescent goo in great steaming gouts through her screaming laughter.

I aimed, fired. Aimed, fired. Aimed, fired.

A ten-year-old dark-skinned Cubano boy, twelve, chest already opened by a shotgun and suppurating, oozing grey puss through his white *guava-jara*. He jiggled and huffed with the Laugh. His eyes were wild, smiling, dancing with the cracked-up broken-faced grin of an empty guffaw.

I blew his brains out.

I got two more; some tumbled over the edge of the boat and into the water. Others just dropped and went dark as their blood and their brains blew behind them on the wind. Others splattered and twitched in traumatic convulsions when my glancing shots weren't bulls-eyes. It tore at my guts to see them writhing like they were in pain, but that was stupid. Laughers couldn't cry. Right?

The first batch got close. I sighted the outboard.

It took me three tries to put a bullet in the motor.

The thing sputtered, died; the boat hit a rock and swerved; it tipped. The dead things went keeling over and half-hung into the water over the edge. The little boat capsized.

They writhed and squirmed, broken-boned and rubbery, for the few seconds before they disappeared before the waves.

That's when I saw the black boats.

I focused the scope.

The black boats: twin power cruisers, forty, forty-five feet, cruising back and forth in big wide serpentine patterns, packed with guys in shades, hoisting rifles. One with two belt-fed thirties, amidships and bow-mounted. The other —

—catapult.

They'd strapped a young gyrating laugher to a big makeshift medieval number that looked like a science project from the sixth-grade class at St. Anastasia of the Siege of Byzantium.

I howled, "They've got a catapult!"

Van said, "Didn't I mention that, Frosty? Don't stress. I bet they can't hit a damn thing with that piece of crap. Those laughers on the west are getting pretty close!"

"No shit. I could use some help."

I heard a crack from down below—from where, I didn't have a clue; when I looked through the scope an adolescent dead thing was lolling back, throat ripped open, head half-severed but spinal column still, apparently, intact: his mouth worked viciously even as the laugh spewed from his half-opened throat.

Van was a crappy shot; what's more, I was pretty sure that crack hadn't come from a thirty-thirty. More like an AK. That was Trixie, shooting with iron sights. Pretty damn smooth. She finished off the one she had opened up with the first round. The laugh stopped short and blood geysered out the back of the thing's head.

The boats were approaching almost parallel; they were fast and getting closer.

I tried the trick with the outboards again, but the dead things were crowded in too tight and they were coming at me almost dead-on; I couldn't get a shot on either of the boats. It had only been through methodically thinning the dead that I had gotten a chance at the first outboard. The angle was all wrong by the time I started in on the second and third boats; they closed too fast on the shore.

Both boats ran aground at full speed close together on the rocky beach about a hundred meters from Van's dock. Boats tore across rocks and sand, scattering dead things, breaking into pieces, breaking *them* into pieces. Bits of what had been human hit the rocks, got mowed over, ground into pulp. I heard the wet sounds of bones breaking, sickly-sweet cackles wrapped around each *crack*.

What was left upright started lurching for me: those boats had been *packed*. They were eight, ten, twelve, maybe fifteen years old. Girls, boys, missing arms and noses and ears and throats and shoulders. Swollen guts distended with rot. Teeth bashed out. Wrists scarred and bloody from manacles: that must have been how they were kept in line until forced onto the boats.

Crackle: "Meet you on the beach, Frosty!"

Crackle: "I'll bring the sunscreen."

I scrambled down the tower's makeshift ladder.

I jumped the last ten feet.

My boots hit the soft, sodden ground at the base of the tower and headed for the beach. Maybe ten feet from the tower, the rich, wet soil blended to gravel, then to Caribbean sand that made a crunchy sound under my feet.

I started running.

☠

The Winchester 70 is a bolt-action rifle, excellent for long-range work but not much fun for a hoedown. It's a damn good weapon, but I'd left it in the sniper tower because it holds five rounds and its integral magazine has to be reloaded manually.

I ran for the beach, the first five-sev in my hand. Laughers were rising, half-broken, from the sand.

Out on the water, the catapult *ka-thunked*. A ten-year-old laugher pirouetted through the air, screaming right for me delivering the best medicine right to my doorstep.

I blew his brains out at distance—not a bad snapshot with a pistol. He went down wet and bloody in pieces. The black speedboats closed in; I saw them reloading the catapult; I saw Van Fish coming down the slope between the house and the dock, puffing, carrying *Old Smokey*, working the lever action, firing wildly. I was a hell of a lot closer to the beach than he was, and the fucker couldn't hit shit to begin with; in fact, I was in fact mildly concerned he'd hit me, which seemed far more likely than him hitting a laugher.

But he meant well, which is really the most important thing in military engagements, right?

Big sand-scoured lumps of bleeding dead things were lifting themselves on half-broken arms and legs, having scented human flesh. They moved up the beach toward me, driven by ravenous hunger, bleating. *Ha ha. Ha ha. Ha ha ha.*

Howling out the Panama Laugh.

They were eight, ten, twelve, thirteen, fourteen years old when they died. They picked up speed as they closed on their meal. I was thirty meters distant. The ones that could run did exactly that; others lurched on broken legs and limbs with muscles ripped from flesh.

I aimed the five-sev and blew out brains. The range was too far for perfect shots from a sidearm with the sand and the wind in my eyes, with my heart pounding like that and adrenaline raging. I wasted some ammo.

The hot slide of the polymer handgun locked open, pouring smoke.

I watched them come for me, gape-mouthed—both of us. Me in horror—them, *laughing.*

They were so *little.*

More of them came for me.

Van screamed, "Hey!" at one of the laughers. He hefted his thirty-thirty and fired again. A rotted youth jerked, hit in the shoulder.

Van was a hundred meters distant; from the configuration of the beach, the children moved toward him in jerky, shambling runs, then scented me—closer—and came at me.

I was cut off.

Thanks for the help, asshole.

I lifted the field glasses: out on the breakers more pirates were waiting; there were a half-dozen black speedboats in reserve. The two boats approaching Isla Pescado weaved serpentine, the crew firing AKs in the air and at the water, sending up plumes of smoke and spray. One vessel had a loudspeaker, blasting perky *guaracha.*

Van's eyes and mine met across a hundred meters of rock and sand. I flipped him off.

He ran for the house.

I slammed another mag in the five-sev, racked the slide and started shooting.

The kid Van had winged went down, forehead holed and back of his head blasted out in a spray of rotten dark gristle. I dropped to my knees on the sand, big rocks biting into bare knees, pebbles stuck in my pointy-toed boots. I worked the action, sighted, fired. What had been a young girl met the same fate.

They closed.

I took another. They lurched. I took another. They closed on me. They were close, now: close enough to smell. The smell hit my guts before it hit my brains. My intestines froze as the stank hit me: cheap perfumed kiddie-soap and rot, mixed with gas from swollen guts and the contents of death-voided bowels. It all poured hot and wet all over me and my throat closed up, my vision swimming. They came to five meters, lurching.

I dropped one final laugher, and I was out.

They closed on me. I pulled a New York reload, took a Weaver stance and fired at the closest.

A girl at four meters. Three more behind her, bam-bam-bam, the meaty-musk stink of brains rolling over me with the bright scent of blood. I took them down, striking one in the chest first, wasting ammo, too freaked and panicked to shoot like I oughta. Three meters. Two behind them, now at point blank but my adrenaline working against me, recoil foiling me. Head-throat-head, *blam-blam-blam*, more misses, the hot slide of the pistol locked open, now, pouring smoke.

I tried to pull another New York reload; I fumbled the mag. I went down. Before I could get it, they were upon me.

I ran.

I missed them by inches; they almost surrounded me.

I dodged a pair of them, then a trio; they lurched ever closer, close enough to trip themselves, to foul each other. I ran, like a man fleeing a gang; if I steadied a second to reload and fire on them, I'd be screwed.

I went running for the thinnest strip in the dead—two across, and a break in the crowd: open beach. I got another magazine out and rammed it in the five-seven; I racked the side, aimed and fired.

My aim went to shit as I ran across wet, rocky sand. I dodged groping flesh-scoured fingers, skeletal fingertips poking through pulpy pin-red goo: three dead, three for seven. Then I got caught by the closest, a boy of ten, maybe twelve, his arms around me, teeth working as he belched out the Panama Laugh; I punched him hard in the face; he went down and I slithered free, hitting hard on one knee and scrambling back to my feet.

He lurched up and caught me as I ran. He got my leg. I went down and kicked. His teeth had almost closed on my calf when I shot him.

He went limp as the bullet transited his brain. Green things poured out of his bare, brown chest and over my foot. I was already firing, straight up, both hands on my weapon, seeing brown children's faces looming over me, aim-fire-aim-fire-aim-fire no matter how many teeth I saw, coming close.

The slide of the pistol locked open. Grey smoke poured, sooty, whirling on the ocean breeze.

Nothing moved around me but the smoke.

I popped out the mag without thinking. I slammed the next mag into its new happy home in the five-sev.

I lurched up into a sitting position, hopped to my feet, took a crouch, pulled a slow, wide-eyed circle.

High above me, I heard a laughing scream and the hiss-whistle of incoming ordnance: a preadolescent projectile coming down fast, cackling, trailing streamers of goo and a long trail of ropelike intestine. It was not going to hit me but I fired and fired and fired until the slide locked open and poured smoke. It pulped on the rocks and did nothing but squirm; all its bones were thoroughly broken.

I thought, *Good going, soldier. You just wasted a magazine.*

I got another mag out of my back pocket, jammed it into the warm five-sev. Then I got out the cold one, slammed my last mag home. I jacked the action.

I held both guns and trembled all over.

Dead things littered the beach in pieces—really dead this time, as in, actually dead. No longer moving. No longer crawling and shambling toward me. Pieces of brain and skull and face sprayed over the pristine rocks of Isla Pescado. Bones broken. Fluids leaching into the sand, gooey, wet, draining, gurgling. Pale gorgeous aquamarine waves lapped over broken skulls with their brains leaking out. Except one.

I'd put them all down—except one.

Far away, down the beach, a hundred meters, a small girl—eight, nine years old, had sat her ass down in wet sand and started weeping.

She sobbed. She screamed. She howled.

My blood ran cold. She was covered in gore. She was living. I'd blasted some laugher's brains all over the little girls' face. Maybe her brother. Maybe her sister. Maybe her friend.

She sobbed and screamed at the top of her lungs, weeping openly, screaming, howling, rocking back and forth as she sat in the sand.

I trembled. Guilt washed all over me; I'd blown her friends away. I'd killed; I'd killed dead things; I'd killed *many* dead things, but even dead things had once been living. In no small way I'd made them dead, before I'd ever pulled the trigger. The young girl howled. I felt a sudden longing to stop that infernal crying, to go down and help her—do something—stop her, stop her stop her. The crying was worse than the Panama Laugh. I hated how it made me feel; I wanted to help.

But I wasn't alone.

Something moved on the water—no longer serpentine. No longer approaching, but having *arrived*.

Two big black flat-bottomed boats loomed over me, deck guns trained on me.

The pirates had anchored.

Music blared.

Six grinning skinny brown boys in bare feet waded toward me, aiming bayonet-fixed AKs at my head.

Music blared: "*¡Viva Cuba!*"

Music stopped: "*¡Dejó la pistolas, gabacho!*" Drop the pistols.

It was a woman's voice. It crackled over the loudspeaker.

I put up my hands with the pistols held loosely, pointing skyward; I lowered myself slowly into a crouch and laid both guns on the beach. I put my hands up.

The loudspeaker crackled: "*¡Muchas gracias, cabrón!*"

From high above, on the rocks, there was a thump.

I'd know that sound anywhere.

There was a whistle in the air—coming down fast —

—and there was *light*.

☠

The sound of incoming ordnance caught the attention of the boys with the AKs, who were covering me close. That's why I didn't catch an AK slug in my belly.

The pirates heard the thump and saw the grey-smoke blast of Van's bloop tube from the low cliffs overlooking the water; they immediately freaked out. Whether they knew what it was or didn't, I don't know.

The Vietnam-era M79 grenade launcher makes a strange, distinctive *whump* when it goes off at the operator end, hence it's nickname, the "bloop tube."

The ordnance travels slowly enough that its arc, described by wisps of smoke like morning fog, can clearly be seen in the sky; at the range Van was firing, you've got maybe a second, two seconds to work. Move fast enough, you've even got a small chance of shooting it down. Except you don't—because chances are slim, unless you're firing a shotgun and you're a hell of a shot with it.

But you *think* you do.

They were dead the second Van Fish pulled the trigger.

When an explosion is imminent at sea, a moving boat can be abandoned and maybe—maybe—you can survive. But jump off a boat close-in, like these two, and you get pulped by shrapnel in the water; this is not pretty.

But none of that shit was probably known to these guys; they just knew a big projectile was hurtling toward them. I knew how they felt. To a man, they panicked.

It's therefore not that surprising that maybe three of the six pirates on the beach covering me with AKs started shooting wildly at the rocks from which Van had yelled. A string of plumes blasted up—dusty, smoky.

The other three started shooting wildly at what looked like a faint contrail on the Panama morning.

The fact that I, an experienced bad motherfucker, had two pistols close at hand, never even entered their fucking minds.

I dropped to one knee, grabbing both pistols fast and aiming up.

On each boat they'd mounted a .30-caliber machine gun; the operators were kids—older than fifteen, say, but far less than twenty. One of them was not experienced. He spun and fired like a whirling dervish, freaking out; he tried to shoot at the grenade in the air like the three on the beach had, but his thirty was not mounted for anti-aircraft work and in any event, like I said, the chances were shit.

The second machine-gunner started firing at me.

He cut down his friends and came damned close to cutting down me. The ones he didn't kill I had downed in the seconds before the blast. The M79 is also fairly quick to reload; a second grenade was on its way before the second machine-gunner got a clue and stopped shooting at me; the side of the cliff lit up with plumes of AK fire; had he done that right away, he maybe could have saved them.

Van scored a hit.

One pirate boat went hot like the sun, splintered pieces of it spiraling out everywhere. The blast from the first boat hit the second—tipping it well to its side and nearly capsizing it.

I hit the wet sand and covered my head. One of the thirties on the first boat blasted open as its operator caught fire; bullets raking the decks of the other. Something behind it exploded—jerry-cans, probably—and the thirty went dead. Streams of burning liquid misted.

The second boat tipped, thirty-cal blazing; it righted itself, but there was a huge hole in its side where a piece of the first boat opened it up.

Then Van's second round rattled off the broken wood deck of the first boat and bounced to the second.

The second blast ripped all of it to shreds. Chunks of boat went *gurgle* and lodged in the mud. Guys in board shorts did the same. Ruined bodies with AKs squirmed in wet sand.

Pistol at the ready, I found bodies and kicked rifles out of their hands. AKs: new from the factory. Chinese. Both boats burned twenty meters offshore. Screamers writhed in the water, afire from gasoline.

Black smoke hovered on the waves.

Distant, down the beach, the sobbing of the eight-year-old girl intensified.

I looked up at the cliff; Van came out of the trees, M79 on one shoulder, thirty-thirty on the other.

We flipped each other off.

I approached what was left of the six pirates in the shallows.

One of the kids groped after his rifle, his face burned, his body nearly bisected by the thirty-caliber machine gun.

His fingers weren't working. They were broken, only he didn't realize it. He was in shock.

I looked into his eyes.

I aimed one of my pistols.

I said, "Don't go for it."

His fingers twitched, limp on the rifle stock. He was out of his mind.

I aimed the pistol and said, "Hands up, vato."

He looked at me.

His head exploded with the crack of the bullet hitting.

He went down wet.

The AK-47 fires a supersonic bullet—so I'd seen the Cubano kid go down before I'd heard the pop of Trixie's weapon behind me.

Looked like she'd gotten to be a pretty mean shot.

She approached, rifle ready, scanning the water, where pirates writhed.

I frowned at her bitterly.

"He woulda surrendered," I said.

She sighed.

She shook her head.

She didn't even look at me.

She never took her eyes off the water and the bodies and the pieces of broken, ravished boat.

She said, "Dante, I'm starting to think you really *don't* know what's happening."

She spotted a shattered Cubano in a life jacket, desperately dog-paddling for shore.

She aimed and fired. The kid's head exploded.

I lunged at her, grabbed the rifle and tried to yank it out of her grasp. She clung to it, pulled away; I got ugly. I used a hold I knew and took the gun away from her.

She squealed, her wrist smarting. She glared at me.

I looked into her eyes and saw murder.

"Trixie, what the fuck?"

She looked at me, shook her head again.

She said, "We've got a hell of a lot of talking to do."

I frowned and said, "Goody."

☠

Generally speaking, I have never been a man of visible temperament.

When people are shooting at me, I don't scream; I don't frown.

When people argue with me, I look at them blankly.

If I beat the living shit out of them or god forbid blow their fucking brains out, I do it without malice and, generally speaking, without evident emotion ninety-nine times out of a hundred. Or I *did*. I used to.

It's not—or it *wasn't*—because I'm not scared; it's because I don't show it.

It got me a nickname: Frosty.

I despised that nickname the way a man can despise only things that grow from himself and take on a life all their own, like murders and novels and excreta, when you piss too close to your campground. The nickname "Frosty" was like the stink of piss blowing into my tent in the middle of the night and the middle of winter when it was too big of a pain in the ass to move, and the night yawned ahead long and very, very cold.

That hated nickname had followed me from Fallujah to Mosul to the Gulf of Aden to the Philippines to Nigeria to Somalia to Tanzania to Angola to the Caucasus to Singapore and three times back around the world again.

How it got to me, I'll never know.

Without ever cracking a grimace, I bitched, I complained. I pointed guns at people and told them not to call me that.

Guys called me Frosty Bogart, Frosty B, The Frost Man.

For the twenty-something gimme-cap tough-guy "consultants" I worked with, it was different. There, a nickname is—or *was*—your badge of honor. Guy without one? He's not *real*. Guy with *one* nickname? Barely real.

A guy with a hundred nicknames is as real as they get.

There's a lot of time to kill in war zones; fucking with your coworkers is about the only truly engaging entertainment that doesn't run the risk of getting you indicted at a United Nations tribunal. Making up nicknames is a pastime. I'd heard Frosty Bubba, Frosty Ba-da-Bing which became Frosty Bing, Frostante Bogarte which became Michael Frostante for this L.A. douchebag I knew who liked the Red Hot Chili Peppers, Icy, Bog-ice, Frosty the Snowman—that one's a gimme. This wannabe Rat Packer I knew in the Philippines called me "Buh-buh-buh-Bogart, Like, Frosty, Man!" which was fucking annoying but essentially innocuous. Frosty Bogardo became Frosty Bog-*Tardo*, which got someone punched just before it became Frosty *Ricardo* by Texas guys faking a Cuban accent and chanting "Loo-ceee, I'm hoooo-oooome" while blasting .223 rounds into the side of rusting Somali derelicts.

I hated that name because I hated what it meant: That I *endured*, despite the heat of battle; I froze, and did things a man with emotions could not.

To quote a Bellona Industries corporate motto, I was *Glacium belli*. I was frost on the flames of war.

Until I saw Trixie on the beach, there, rabid with murderous heat.

And that's when Frosty Buh-Buh-Buh-Bogart boiled over and blew.

☠

Even with the gunsmoke pouring out and the dead things raining down upon the beach—and more than a few still-living ones—I'd begun to piece a few memories together. So when I looked in Trixie's eyes, I saw things I hadn't remembered, or hadn't known I'd remembered—or maybe things that never happened at all. It's hard to sort that shit out sometimes nowadays.

I saw: Trixie, tie dye, arguing viciously with me over a plate of vegan hash at Feliz de Huevo, Via España, Panama City. Face going pinker as I got her Irish up. I wasn't even trying. It's just… Mention you squooshed a spider in her shower? Congratulations! Your reward is an hourlong lecture about shepherding souls through the first Bardo and oh, by the way, what about all the feral cats in New Orleans, chased by mad dogs through the vales of the city? Should *they* be squooshed, you sexist asshole?

That's why, there on the beach on *Isla Pescado*, San Blas Islands, Kuna Yala province, Panama: I looked deep in Trixie's eyes, Trixie Ferguson, Trixie *Fish* and I *saw* her. The new Trixie. The Trixie I'd left, but changed.

Become something I'd dreamed she could never become.

A killer.

And not *just*; we're all killers, *vato*, given a gun in our hand and a shadow in the window at 3 a.m. when we wake from a bad dream. I'll admit that a man like me has a very strong ulterior motives to hold this belief, but we're all budding murderers. We're all killers, given the bad men in jeeps who want to come take our children. We're *all* killers, with Osama or Hitler or Stalin or Ted Bundy or a grim faceless predator or the man who killed your wife or the beast that raped your daughter, one of them—whichever one's on your freebie list—blindfolded and hogtied face-down in a locked room, somewhere, nowhere, a gun in your hand, clean ballistics, no serial number, no one knows you're here, no eyes to look into, six guys with mops outside and the incinerator going ready to whisk your sins away, you don't have to clean, no one will ever know and this beast will walk *free* if you don't pull the trigger.

Would you or wouldn't you?

You may say you're not a killer; I say you are.

And if you're not, then I don't even want to know you.

But this wasn't that; this wasn't *anything* like that. Not anything close. Not anything even reminiscent. She hadn't just killed Ted Bundy; she'd just killed a prisoner, pulped and bleeding, scared out of his mind. She'd shot him in the head.

I'd just watched her *murder*. I'd watched her murder in cold blood, like she had done it a million times and would a million-million more. That kid was down. His hand was just *twitching*.

Pirate or no, someone puts a kid down in circumstances like that, she's damn well *looking for an excuse*.

Which, last I'd heard, I knew Trixie'd never do.

And I'd done far worse. I'd done far, far, far, far worse—a hundred times. A thousand. Not just a minute ago—years ago. Starting young. Starting very, very young.

I had more blood on my hands than Trixie could ever have, if she clipped live people, dead things, children, babies, squirrels and fuzzy-wuzzy mockingbirds from now till the day she shuffled off this mortal coil. I was a *monster*.

So, then, why was I crying?

☠

Trixie glared at me.

Her face went red.

She made a disgusted noise and said, "Grow a pair, Frosty."

Trixie stalked down the beach to the lone young survivor.

My voice caught in my throat when I tried to say, "Don't call me that."

So it came out a strangled squeal.

I stood there weeping like a bitch and staring after her, thinking.

That's it, then. The world is over. Trixie kills children, and Frosty B cries.

I watched Trix walk down to the sobbing little girl. I stared at the rifle in the sand, the broken-open head of the young *Cubano* pirate.

I heard the Panama Laugh from the waters.

It hit me.

I said aloud, "Oh shit."

I screamed at the top of my lungs.

I started running.

☠

It happened on the last day I remembered clearly, before I woke up in the jungle.

Pinogana, at the edge of the Darién Gap, about fifty klicks from the Colombia border:

Gringos in chinos and sport shirts, aviator shades, bulges at their belts, followed Trix to the orphanage in Pinogana, the southern terminus of the northern half of the Pan-American highway, at the edge of the Darién Gap.

I followed them.

The shirts were long enough to conceal the eagle-and-anchor tattoo on one's upper arm, the beret and knife and DE OPPRESSO LIBER on the other's. Long enough to conceal them, until they got hot and rolled their sleeves up, not knowing I was watching from the jungle.

The smiling brown schoolchildren didn't know they were eyeballed by killers I mighta done tequila shots with at a expat bar in Dubai.

They were The Good Guys. Except for the killer part.

But then, there was a lot of that going around.

The smiling brown schoolchildren were orphans, some displaced from the drug war or rescued from trafficking; Colombians, Nicaraguans,

Salvadorans, Hondurans, four to fourteen.

Trixie and I had been fighting. I suspected we were not far from mutually surrendering—not to each other, but to the gap between us. I had followed her from Panama City not because I was stalking her, but because I had just touched down at Tocumen, and something in Virgil Amaro's text message had rubbed me the wrong way. "Suggest not talking to Justice. Suggest STRONGLY REPEAT STRONGLY. Consequences."

I'd been on one side of that "consequences" equation enough to know what that might have meant. I'd left my ditty bag to the mercies of Copa Airlines and sprinted for the Peugeot in long-term parking, carrying only my laptop case.

Trixie the laughing gringa treehugger led the children in "Kumbaya" on a maple-flame Takamine, open chords only and a capo, lyrics altered to be about clean drinking water and what to do if you find a landmine.

I found them.

In the jungle near the school crouched predators: guys with guns ready to pounce. They coulda been there singing "Kumbaya" right along with kids—at an orphanage in Lebanon or Nairobi or Haiti—taking the weekend off from dropping landmines themselves from AH-64 Apaches or Kamov Black Sharks.

Me and them: Today's protectors of Democracy.

Let's put it to a vote, then.

How say yea, Gentlemen?

Guys get lazy. Killers, more than most. "Consulting" is often just that. Some douchebag asks your opinion, and you say "I'd go with the 7.65-millimeter hollow-point round, Governor," and pop another beer. Your gun grants you the authority to watch and nod and cash a paycheck; usually, nobody shoots.

You walk around like God's gift to the third world, and the local cops call you *compañero* or *compadre* or Captain or Boss and they pat you on the back and introduce you to their sisters. And you walk around and get the kind of respect reserved in your crappy hometown for the mayor, the owner of Cal's Chrysler-Plymouth, the captain of the football team and the guy who can always get weed.

With a bulge at your belt you never have to use.

You get lazy. Complacent.

Then the shit goes down, and you hate yourself for getting fat.

These pricks would be hating themselves for a while.

This is what I dreamt of: I had them down before they knew what was coming. I had blue latex gloves and a crowbar. I broke a nose, a jaw, a kneecap. One lost his eye; it hung out, wet and dangling, while he writhed. Both hands had reached for nine-millimeters. Both hands had broken fingers when I took those guns away.

It's easier to search guys once you break a few things. I only had to smack Army Airborne twice on the back of the head with the crowbar. I emptied their pockets: cell phones, IDs, wallets, pocketknives. I cuffed them with their own cuffs. Smith & Wesson: nice. Airborne had a Taser; I pocketed it.

Passports: Canada. James T. Briggs. Michael L. Martin.

Jesus H. Christ.

I looked at their pistols.

If they had been Glocks, HKs, $600 or $1,200 or $1,500 guns, that woulda been one thing. I would've called it a day with some broken bones and a traumatic facial injury or two.

If they had been the guns of cops or soldiers with honor, I woulda chilled. They weren't. I didn't.

These were a Bersa and a Makarov; both ancient, chipped, decaying, with an extra magazine each. They were the kind of guns you bought from the trunk of a car. Cloth tape covered the grips and triggers, plus a strip on each side of the slides. I didn't have to look to know the serial numbers were filed.

They were guns for a killing—not a snatch job.

USMC also had a .38 at his ankle—this one wasn't a disposable. Smith & Wesson, Five-round short-barrel wheelgun; bad luck for leathernecks.

I dumped four rounds and spun the cylinder.

One foot on his throat, the other on his knee, I aimed the gun at his balls. I cocked the hammer.

I told him, "Are you from the government? I'm here to help you."

Click! The hammer hit an empty chamber.

His eyes went wild. He screamed: "Stop! Don't!"

"Are you fucks after Trixie?"

I spun; I cocked; I pulled.

"Stop! Stop! Stop! Who?"

The hammer clicked on empty.

I said, "The redhead! The redheaded doctor! Are you here to kill her, grab her, or damage her?"

"What are you talking about?"

I said, "From the looks of your hardware, *kill*. That's bad news for soldiers, prick."

"I don't know what you're—"

I spun and thumbed and pulled and spun; hard sharp clicks like the half-remembered fragment of a Buddy Rich drum roll.

"Yes! The Teacher! But we're only—we're only spot—watching! Who are you? What are you doing?"

I spun the cylinder again and aimed it at his nuts again.

"My name is Dante Bogart," I told him. "I used to be a military contractor."

A wave of sheer terror went over his face.

He said, "Crap."

I said, "Call off the dogs."

He shook his head. "Frosty, don't make me. They'll kill me."

Spin. Click. Spin. Click. Spin. Click. USMC screamed. Army moaned. I punched him hard on the back of the head and he stayed down. Bulldog tried to get up. I kicked him so hard in the balls I wasn't sure he'd spill the beans.

Three more spins and clicks got him spilling, but no beans came out. Just a scream.

I said, "Time's a wastin'."

I heard the *chop-chop-wuh-wuh-huh* of the copters—distant, low like a tease, like a dream, in the depths of my hearing.

I shoved his walkie to his face, stuck the wheelgun to his head, and said, "Dogs? Off? Call? Or brains? Squoosh? Go?"

He nodded fervently.

I punched the walkie.

He said, "*El objetivo no está aquí. Abortar. Abortar.*"

The radio said, "*Claro. Adios, muchachos.*"

I threw the walkie into the jungle.

I said, "You pricks were gonna snatch and grab my girlfriend?"

"Way I heard it, she's your ex."

I kicked him, hard.

"Dude! Stay frosty!"

I kicked him harder.

"Why do you want her?"

"Not to hurt her!"

"For Virgil?"

"Come on, man! What do you want me to say? They'll kill me!"

I said, "*I'll* kill you."

"Don't, man. I'm your kind. I'm your people. We just ended up on opposite sides for a minute. It'll be different tomorrow, man. Cut me a break."

Click. Spin. Click. Spin. Click.

The guy howled. "Come on, man! Virgil didn't want to hurt her! He just wants you to come in from the cold!"

I growled, "Seems plenty warm in Panama." I jacked his huevos with my steel-toed Dickie. He didn't like that much. Who would?

Fueled by his pain, Bulldog got nasty.

"What do you want me to say, Dante?"

I said, "I want you to say you'll help send Virgil to prison."

"That'll never happen. You know he's too connected, Frosty. Besides, why do you care? What, are you on *their* side?" He jerked his head toward the kids a few hundred meters off in the jungle.

I said, "Whose?"

He said, "The terrorists."

I said, "Those are *orphans*, dipshit."

He snarled: "That's not what I mean! I mean the drug gangs, Al Qaeda, the Marxists. I was in the Marines, Frosty, just like you. I know your reputation—you fought for your country like a real man. You gonna be a sob sister now? Virgil Amaro is the best chance this country has of bringing down the mercy on those evil motherfuckers."

I said, "Which country and which evil motherfuckers? It's a fuckin' smorgasbord out there on both counts."

He screamed, "The *terrorists*! The bastards who want to hand over America to—"

Spin. Click. Spin.

He screamed: "Stop that!"

"Just cooperating with law enforcement," I said. "Wanna read me my rights?"

He glared.

"Frosty, I could be you. I know your rep. You work for the highest bidder, just like me. You play it cool."

I said, "That was the old Dante. I think maybe I was a little outta touch with my *feelings*."

"Come on, you're cool, man, you're a legend. You're Frosty the Snowman, buddy—Frosty Buh-buh-buh-Bogart, right? Stay frosty, Frosty."

I stared.

Marine said: "Come on, man. We're Bellona, right? We're the gods of war, man! We don't worry about this mortal shit! *Glacium belli*, buddy! We ice the fires of war, right?" He looked at me desperate. "Come on, man.

You're not just like me, Frosty. You *are* me. *Glacium belli*, buddy?"

"*Semper fi*," I said, and blew his balls off.

☠

Trix heard the gunshot.

I caught her just before she saw the bodies.

I caught her stalking toward us through the jungle, holding a machete. Looking scared.

When she saw me, she didn't look scared anymore.

She looked *pissed*. Enough to separate my head from my body with a machete.

I had the pistols in my belt behind my back.

"What the fuck, Dante?"

"Keep them back!" I said. "Keep the kids back!"

"No shit! They're under their desks. Jesus Christ, Dante, what the hell—"

"They got someone to watch them?"

"Of course."

"Hear those copters?"

"Hell yeah, I hear those copters. They're here all the time—drug interdiction patrols. It's one of the reasons these kids have PTSD. Maybe you and your Army friends could—"

"Get in the car."

"What the fuck, Dante? I've got a *job*. I can't just leave. This is the Peace Corps. What does it say if I just leave?"

"Get in the car. You hear those copters?"

"Dante, stop—"

"Those are bad guys, Trix."

She said, "No shit, asshole. We've been having this conversation for nine months! You're the one who's always defending them—drug war this, cocaine trafficking this, heroin ghosts on the streets of Los Angeles that, blah blah blah like I'm supposed to start playing a violin for drug addicts when right here in the jungle the drug war is—Dante, why are you wearing gloves?"

I got her in a hold, but she was sweaty. She gets that way when she plays guitar, and it was over ninety in the jungle.

She slipped from my grasp. She was gone.

But she didn't run.

She gave me a right so hard she sent me reeling back against a mangrove tree.

She still didn't run.

She came at me grinning, rolling up her goofy crepe-cotton sleeve, with lots and lots of Crazy in her eyes.

She snarled, "What's that, Dante? You got something to say to me?"

Don't hurt me seemed like about the only option, so I didn't say shit.

I just Tasered her.

☠

The truth is, I had attacked Trixie with good intentions. I didn't want to hurt her; I just wanted to tie her up and shove her in the trunk of my car. It sounds somewhat less magnanimous than it seemed at the time—but believe me, in humanitarian terms it was an improvement over what I'd *been* doing the last few weeks.

I didn't have the heart to put her in the trunk, so I tied her up and stuffed her in the back seat. By the time I got back to the site of my spirited conversation with my new friend the jarhead, he and Army Airborne were nowhere—but nowhere—to be seen.

I pulled the Makarov and said, "Here, kitty-kitty."

They'd parked their Toyota off the side of the little access road that led to the school. I'd bitch-slapped them off toward the edge of a thicket, leaving them cuffed and bleeding, one of them gunshot, on the wet ground of the forest. I had their car keys.

Meaty ribbons of flesh lay stripped on the ground, tangled up with their wallet, watch, spectacles, testicles, four live rounds of .38 Special. Bloodstains. Switchblade. A rusty machete; a roll of Colo Pesos. An ancient MP3 player. One fucker's shoe.

I'd picked the Makarov 'cause I knew it. I'd used one for a job in Uttar Pradesh. It was one of the most available sidearms in the world following the collapse of the Soviet empire. Chambered in nine-millimeter Russian, it held eight in the mag and none in the chamber, which I didn't have to check to know. Like I said: lazy. *Pezzonovante* fuckers.

I jacked a round in and did a spin-take, looking. Looking, looking, looking. Looking. Looking.

There was a flash.

I breathed the Darién steam. The clouds hung pregnant.

Silence churned under the dwindling *whup-whup* of copters. This was bad. The rainforest *never* shuts up.

Thunder cracked.

I looked; I spun. I backed toward the car.

There was a flash.

There was a howl.

Airborne came at me, roaring like Ed McMahon.

He came at me out of the mangroves, trailing oleander blossoms. He came at me out of the tournefortia, dangling strips of his flesh from one wrist, where he'd wrenched it to bone, trailing handcuffs from wrist two, where he'd broken it yanking free. It hung limp and boneless, half-crushed but too swollen for the cuff to come off; he trailed clearwater cryptantha branches and the hanging distended glob of what had been his own eye, which I'd smacked out of its socket when I hit him with the crowbar.

Army Airborne came at me out of the hot pulsing screaming gouts of pouring rain, never slowing when it hit him full in the face, never blinded, never slowing, never seeing anything but me, because I was the closest living flesh.

He came at me, hard, fast, emitting that sickly wet *huffing* that sound from a mouth spewing fluids: *huh-huh-huh-huh-huh.*

The sound of weeping. The sound of laughing.

Coulda been either: *you* figure it out.

He came at me, howling out laughter, face crowbar-ruined, hands mangled.

I screamed like a bitch.

I raised the Mak.

I fired.

He hit me full-on.

Mouth spewing LOLZ—or something like 'em.

☠

It is inviolable dogma of non-sniper combat engagements that if you have to shoot, shoot more than once. There's a good reason Lyndon Johnson never sent Barney Fife to Nam. Shoot to wound, you've got a pissed-off asshole with your bloody violent death on his to-do list. And either he's pointing a gun at you, or you shouldn't have been shooting him in the first place.

Empty the magazine, though? That's just Chow Yun Fat shit. Tempting as it is with modern hair-trigger designs, if God had meant us to pull a *Miami Vice,* he'd have made it even remotely possible to actually hit something firing full-auto. Ditto if your finger gets twitchy and you empty the mag in one go, even with a semi-auto, even with one with as famously rough a trigger pull as the Makarov.

It took him only a few seconds to cross the space between the jungle and me.

I gave him six rounds fast because I wasn't thinking. I didn't miss. I hit him six times in the chest, mostly up and to the left, a spread of six inches maybe, to judge by the spray.

He was all over.

Then I got my brain back, thought like a man for the space it took me to tap off two rounds—maybe a second. I achieved two head shots; bully for me, motherfuckers.

But I didn't get any *brains*.

He was shorter than me; most guys are. I didn't *think*. I aimed for his face, not his grey matter. I hit him at a down-angle, once through the roof of the mouth, leaving his teeth intact but his palate bisected off-center about half an inch—and once through his cheek, at an angle, the 9mm round peeling it halfway off him like opening a book with pink illustrations inside.

Then he hit me.

He landed spread-armed atop me, hands dangling, eye twirling on his optic nerve, chunks of his throat hanging on strings of meat and blood dripping onto me. I went down wide-eyed, still pulling the trigger. The pistol clicked raw and empty under his laughter as hot Panama rain washed the swirling cordite smoke out of wet air and down into the wide-open slide of the Mak.

I went down.

Laughing, he set on me, mouth working violently. I don't know what happened to the Mak. I got my hands around his throat and squeezed and jerked and twisted.

He slapped and flailed. His rubbery cuff-ruined hands hit my face. We grappled under hot Darién rain. It hit us like fists.

I thought, *God damn you, die*, but he'd already obliged me and it really didn't work out the way I wished it would.

His clacking teeth got closer, chopping. He'd broken some thrashing on the ground, ripping his hands free.

I struggled.

He clacked. He dripped goo and pieces of face on me. Parts of his hands were stripped of flesh. One finger jutted out, bony and fleshless, from a ruined mass of gooey paw.

The thing huffed out laughter and each time he did he sprayed blood over me to mix fine and misty with the cloudburst.

His teeth got closer and closer.

He almost had my nose when the whole world exploded.

There was a thunderous *sproing*! Kind of like an open-A, but a little flat.

Pieces of Takamine rained down wet and laminated around me.

Rain poured.

Army Airborne turned and *huff-yowled*, laughing, or belching something *like* a laugh, only ten times as weird.

I wrenched Airborne over, got my knee in his ass and got him on his belly. I forced my arm around his open, bloody throat until the wet mass of flesh felt like carne asada against the inside of my elbow. He *huff-laugh-guffawed*.

I broke Airborne's neck.

A gawky Colombian girl about fourteen stood over me being rained on, the ruined pieces of Trixie's Takamine hanging on bright steel strings from her hand. Her face was scarred; at some point her left side had been scored by shrapnel. Her eye was milky.

I said, "Thanks, kid."

She said, "I'm not a kid."

I looked at her scar-dappled cheeks and said, "*Claro*."

☠

Trixie had just reached the young sobbing girl when I started screaming.

I didn't scream loud enough.

I didn't move fast enough.

Trix was far down the beach; my feet were blistered; I ran slow. I hadn't slept; I was wiped. I was adrenaline-cooked. I was burnt and hoarse and broken from sobbing. I ran. I screamed:

"Don't touch her!"

I watched it like a nightmare:

Trixie crouched down and said something like, "It's okay, sweetheart."

And the young girl erupted in the Panama Laugh.

I couldn't hear it; we couldn't hear each other. My scream was hoarse; it didn't carry. I saw it slo-mo, screaming, sobbing.

But the Panama Laugh carries far on the wind.

The girl sank her teeth into Trixie Fish's arm.

Trixie stumbled back; she fumbled at her pocket.

The girl was on her—clawing her, pinning her, preternaturally strong.

Trixie got her pistol out about the instant I lined up the little girl's head with the iron sights of the AK. The girl lunged violently and her mouth closed on Trixie's face.

I blew the girl's brains out.

The thing went flat, arms wrapped around Trixie's throat, teeth wide around Trixie's nose.

Trixie screamed, shoved; the thing didn't want to go. It had gone rigor-mortis atop her.

Trixie lay wailing, her hand outstretched, a pistol dull and dead in a hand slack with pain.

Close enough now to be sure of the shot, I shot the kid in the head again; the face distended and crumbled; Trixie kicked the ruined thing off of her, screaming.

All that was left of the head was the face and some stuff, strings and bits of it streaming out wide across the sand behind the grinning mask of the girl like an octopus in flight.

Trixie sat up. She was covered with gore. She started panicking. She went white. She clutched herself, trembling.

I reached her, gaping, and dropped the rifle.

Tears steamed their way from cheekbone to jaw. I felt the Panama wind on them; they vaporized, leaving a trail of salty and tight on my eighteen-hours' growth. The Panama wind blew clean; then it changed and I smelled burning diesel, flesh.

Trix clutched her arm, face screwed up, first in pain, then disbelief.

She said, "The bitch got me."

And then she was down, body tight with convulsions.

Van ran up, dropping his thirty-thirty and his bullhorn and the M79 and a bandolier of projectiles in a string from the base of the cliffs to the beach, panicking, screaming "*Trixie, Trixie, Trixie!*"

I said, "I'm sorry."

I said, "I wasn't thinking."

I said, "I shoulda told her."

I said, "It's my fault, it's my fault,"

… and burst into tears.

Van looked at me like I was a motherfucking lunatic.

I sobbed, "Don't shoot her! Whatever you do, don't shoot her."

Van said, "Are you fucking insane? She got bit, Dante—fuck, man, it's *over.*" His voice caught hard, tight on over, like he couldn't even say it.

Van dropped down to his knees; his eyes went wide and he started sobbing, hyperventilating.

He loomed big and hairy, high over Trixie Fish as she started in with the convulsions.

High above the beach on the rocks, I saw the Kuna kids watching with rifles, gesturing to each other frenetically. They looked scared.

I tried to speak, but I was crying to hard.

I finally sobbed, "Don't kill her."

And Van sobbed, "What?"

I sobbed, "Don't fucking kill her."

And that was all I could get out. My chest was convulsing; I was crazy with sobs. I exploded. I heard the Panama Laugh from the shallows.

Things were rising.

No convulsions, *vato*.

Things wet with gore and seawater and sweet-burning diesel were hauling ass out of the water, coming for us.

I started madly for the waves.

☠

I found him several hundred meters through the jungle. I thought he was laughing.

He wasn't.

USMC sat there in a lump, his chinos blown into shreds at the crotch, his balls hanging free. He would have bled to death if something hadn't killed him.

But something else got him first.

Marine Corps sat there and chirped and shuddered and hugged his hands to himself; he wept.

He sobbed, inconsolable, crazed and uncontrollable. His sobs mounted quickly; he buried his face in his hands.

I'd seen far worse.

I'd *done* far worse—so much worse, I don't even want to tell you. Maybe I'll have to, sooner or later, but for now let's just say: you won't like me. You shouldn't.

I've killed sobbing men so many times you'd think I was bullshitting if I told you.

I've done so much worse it would curdle your blood.

I've seen weirder, too, before or since—weirder, when men get into battle; blow their balls off and they do things you'd never expect. Sitting there crying's the least of the weirdness—but he should have been comatose.

Maybe in shock. Not sitting up, rocking back and forth—having clearly run a few hundred meters with pieces of him dangling dark and bloody bouncing on strings of meat. He shouldn't have run. He couldn't have run.

But that wasn't the Panama Laugh.

I came at him slowly, Bersa at the ready, trained on his head. I'd learned my lesson with Airborne: double-tap headshots; I'd learned it and learned it good.

But curiosity does things horrible to the brain.

I came in close.

He sobbed.

He retched; he choked he buried his face.

I aimed the Bersa at his head and gritted my teeth.

He drew back his hands and showed me his pain.

Then he moved—so fast he dodged the bullet.

☠

Technically speaking, Marine Corps didn't dodge a bullet; he dodged my wide, crappy aim. As he came at me, the bullet went wide; it screamed through his cheeks and ripped one inward-off and one outward-off. Molars and tongue scattered everywhere, and then the thing without a face was on me. His ruined upper jaw still had its front teeth; incisors dug through the latex gloves, deep into my trigger finger and bit so hard I lost my grip. He slammed me into a mangrove tree and kept his teeth down tight on my hand while I grabbed the Mak and pistol-whipped him.

I broke what was left of his nose. I broke what was left of his jawbone. I broke his face. I cracked his skull. I pounded the Mak through his eye socket; it made a sick wet splitting noise. I broke every bone in his face, and still the thing sobbed.

I got my knee in his chest and pinned him down; I finally pried the Bersa free and rammed it up into his open, empty eye socket. I aimed down.

I felt the blast and the wet on my hand as I killed him, and finally his teeth pulled free.

Clutching the gore-wet Bersa, I started running. I fell, got up again, fell, got up again, fell. My eyes rolled back.

I started screaming.

I didn't go out; I was awake the whole time. I lay face-down and convulsed; I screamed. I felt it all—every muscle in my body pulsing hot with pain and jerking, violent—

—and out of my mouth came the Panama Sob.

I heard myself crying; this was not a familiar experience. Coming up quick from the round of convulsions, I crawled for the car; I froze and went down; I convulsed some more.

I finally got to my feet and took deep heavy breaths.

I started walking, my muscles going stiff.

My hand hurt like hell; I gritted my teeth against the pain.

The fourteen-year-old Panamanian girl stood amid the chunks of Trixie's guitar and wept.

My eyes wide, I aimed the Bersa at her.

She watched me approach, her face a mask of terror.

She said, "*¡Monstruo! ¡Riendo Monstruo!*"

She pointed at what had been Airborne.

His neck broken, the thing still squirmed. His head twisted and jerked on the top of a rubbery neck; his body lay deflated and empty.

I put the Bersa down and pointed furiously at the schoolroom. I told her to run. She did, sobbing.

I looked down at Airborne, my right hand alive with pain I can't even describe. Something burned through my veins.

Airborne's mouth opened up in a wet, wide, empty, silent laugh. His chest contracted violently.

But there was no link between the two.

He didn't make a sound, beyond gushy slurpy wet noises.

I'd crushed his windpipe when I broke his neck.

The tears came—rolling hot down my cheeks as I watched Airborne writhe. My chest contracted; I fought to keep the fear down. I struggled till I stood, cool and even, over the bleeding mass of pulp as it spasmed.

I watched Airborne try to laugh for a little while.

Then I blew his brains out.

☠

The Peugeot was a manual. It had a lawnmower engine and front-wheel drive. I had never intended to stay in Panama long; loading up on a big diesel pickup or a black SUV like every other Bellona contractor in Panama City never seemed like a good idea.

It seemed like a *great* idea now.

There are few things I've done more difficult than driving a four-cylinder manual-transmission city car over the dirt roads, gravel, rock, sand vines and jungle of Darién Province with the raging infection from hell pulsing hot up my arm.

But I made it; I tore off the dirt roads and hit the highway. I kept it at the speed limit, twitching all over, fighting to maintain control of the car.

As I turned off the *Corredor Sur* to head for the coast, I heard a voice.

"You wanna tell me what this is all about?" Trixie asked, her voice a tightly-controlled package of high explosives with a fuse about a micrometer long.

I said, "Do you have your cell phone?"

She said, "Not on me."

I said, "Do you have anything that gets a cell phone or internet signal? GPS, satphone—"

"Oh, yeah, Dante, sure. I'm glad you reminded me. I always keep a satellite phone tucked away in my lady parts. I'm surprised you haven't noticed it. You wanna tell me what this shit is about? Why do you have blood on your clothes?"

I said, "It's a funny story."

She said, "I'm not laughing." Her voice got tight. She said with grave fury: "Dante, did you hurt my children?"

I said, "Fuck no."

She said, "You promise? You swear? You fucking *promise*?"

I said furiously, "Trix, I *promise*, I *swear, and* I *fucking promise*, I didn't hurt those children. They'll all grow big and strong and live long to get bored off their asses by a hundred more lectures from do-good *gabacho Norteños*."

She sneered, "That's redundant."

And I said, "No shit. Lectures and bored off their asses. I didn't hurt your children."

"Whose blood is it?"

"The Bad Guys'," I said. "And some of mine."

"You're hurt?"

I said, "Not bad."

"Let me look at it."

"Sorry, Trix. No dice. I know you must think this looks pretty bad."

"Dante, you're covered in blood. I don't know *what* to think."

I said, "Yeah." I said, "I don't know either."

She said bitterly, "When you figure it out, why don't you tell me?"

I said, "Trix, I had to kill some guys to help you."

"Why did you need to kill them?"

"Because they were after you."

"Because they were after *me*, or because they were after *your girlfriend*?"

I said, "I'm sorry."

She said, "Did you have a *very* good reason?"

"I had a reason," I said.

She said, "What is that supposed to mean?"

"They were going to hurt you."

She said, "Am I supposed to thank you?"

I said, "Thank yourself. By letting me take you someplace safe."

She asked, "Did you bring my guitar, at least?"

I gulped and said, "It's in good hands."

"It better be. It was my father's. Who is it that's after me, Dante?"

"They're after *me*," I said. "You were just in the way. They're my former employers."

She said, "Like a drug thing?"

I said, "Huh?"

She said, "I always figured you were a drug smuggler. You know. The Colombia trips."

I said, "Trixie, I do security consulting and piracy interdiction."

She said, "Right. 'Cause anyone really does that."

"Trixie, don't you watch the fucking news?"

She said, "I watch the news. But I wanted to see how you'd react if I said that. Dante, I don't think you do pirate interdiction."

I thought about it for a while.

I said, "Sometimes I do."

"And other times?"

I was getting a fever.

I said, "I've done a lot of bad things."

She said, "I figured."

I said, "I've done some *really* bad things."

She said, "I know."

I said, "I've done a couple really, really, *really* bad things."

There were tears in her eyes. Her lips got tight.

She said, "Just a couple?"

I said, "Things you wouldn't forgive me for. For money."

"Oh," she said, voice shaking. "Not just for fun?"

I said, "I don't think my career history really gibes with your global politics."

"Dante, I figured that out on our second date."

I said, "I'm not good for you. You know, interpersonally."

There was a big long empty, till she said, "I figured that out a long time ago, too."

I said, "I wish I was good for you."

Trixie lost it. I'd told her things she either took seriously or didn't take seriously—to tell you the truth, I don't know if she believed me, then. She might have thought I was talking about securities fraud. I doubt it, but anything's possible.

But Trixie's a crusader. She believes—or believed—that every social and political ill can be corrected if a pissed-off hippie is willing to yell loud enough.

"Thanks, Bogey! Thanks a lot! I'm glad you want to have a healthy relationship with me!"

"Trixie, don't get started—"

She hit her stride: "Don't get started? Don't get started what, telling you thanks but no thanks with the whole working your inner child thing? I'm so glad to hear you want to be good for me, Dante! That's going to work out just fine! You've got the not murdering people at my workplace part down fine—oh, wait. You fucked that one up. But at least you didn't kidnap me—oh, wait. You fucked that one up, too. Um, maybe your next step can be not to tie me up and stuff me in the trunk of a car?"

"Back seat!" I snapped. I'd just been *thinking* trunk.

She'd gotten going; now she couldn't stop: "You think human beings can just be racked up on an abacus. Healthy relationships aren't about getting what you want out of someone. They're about supporting them when they face all the fucked-up crap that people have to deal with, we all have to deal with, Dante, in this shit world that people like you and my father and Bob Geldof and Richard Branson helped build. You know what the trouble with guys like you is Dante? The problem with guys like you—"

Sadistic pleasure suffused her voice, but my eyes had glazed over at "Thanks, Bogey." Why listen when I knew what she was going to say? The problem with guys like me was blah blah blah; the military-industrial complex was yada yada yada; what her father and I had in common was ba-da-bing, ba-da-bang, ba-da-snore. She coulda saved it, 'cause I knew it all by heart.

But this was different. I didn't have long. I felt the ache through my shoulders. I felt sick. The Peugeot wobbled slightly.

I tried to talk over her, shouting: "Trix, listen, I know I fucked up bad this time, but I've got to save us, I've got to save you, I've got to save—"

My voice caught. As she ignored me and rambled on, I took a deep breath…

… and started crying.

She stopped hard, in mid-word; it mighta been "codepend—" or maybe "family of origin ish—" One of those, maybe; they all kind of always blurred together with Trix.

She gasped in shock.

I sobbed, disconsolate. I howled. I wept. I went to punch the dash, but there was nothing behind my punch. There was only sadness.

I saw her eyes in the rearview mirror. She stared. She gaped. She looked stunned, scared, confused; she kept staring as I glanced at her, red-eyed, seeing the sun sink low over the deep green canopy while she watched me get ahold of myself, after long, long minutes of sobbing.

She said, "I've never seen you cry."

I said, "No one has."

She said, "I wasn't sure you could."

I said, "No one is."

She said, "I'm not sure what to think."

I said, "Don't think anything."

She said, "This sounds like a breakup talk. You just kidnapped me. Bad form."

"I'm sorry I Tasered you."

"Yeah, I'm pretty pissed about that. You're kind of an asshole."

I said, "Thanks for the news flash."

She asked, "Can you please untie me?"

I said, "Later. I can't stop right now. You're in danger. I'm taking you someplace safe."

She said, "Where?"

I opened my mouth to make something up—but I had nothing. My sobbing had taken it out of me—every clever thought I'd ever had. I felt spent.

So I told her the truth: "I've got this friend."

She said, "No no no."

I said, "He's a little weird, but—"

She said, "No no no no no no no no no, not that off-the-grid solar panel weird hippie freak crackpot alien abduction pothead—"

"Hey," I said. "Let's not get ugly—"

"—dope-running fish taco single-bullet-theory—"

I said, "He only *advocated* the single-bullet theory as being *physically possible* in a combat situation—"

"—Bigfoot-hunting Loch Ness Monster boat captain South American high-colonic chromium picolinate popping coke-snorting wannabe gangster Greatful Dead chasing—"

It went on like that for a while.

My fever climbed *fast*.

I felt inside me the emptiness that comes from a really good cry. I'd seen it in Trixie's eyes.

It was a big, rich, beautiful kind of empty—gorgeous as the morning, and twice as cold.

I heard Trixie drone on and thought, *This might be the last time I'll hear her go on like this.*

Trixie finally ran out of rant and let it go—her words just sort of trailed off, her voice a hoarse and raspy choke, like my sobs had done.

And I said, "Yeah, Trixie. Him."

She said, "Whatever."

☠

Trixie stretched out on the back seat.

The sun sank gorgeous and bloody and bright, darkening into the rainforest.

Life was good; the day was over.

I was alive, for now, and going down fast; I had nothing to lose but Trixie, and I'd already lost her.

So that's when you kiss her goodbye and say, "Fuck it."

Life was good. Life was *gorgeous*.

I could feel it coming on fast. I was sick, but soon I'd be well.

I was about to take a loading dose.

… Of the very best medicine.

While Trixie snored, I leaned on the gas; the Peugeot leapt ahead, farting miserably.

☠

I wound down a dirt road to this glorious cove I knew near Vuelo Puente, about ten minutes from a town—if you can call it that—known as San Juan del Risa. I knew of a tour office there. A guy named Señor Mike lived upstairs. He drank heavily. He'd be home. He had a phone. He was

Jersey trash like the best of us: *Americano. Gringo. Gabacho. Expatriado. Pescadero. Guía turístico.*

There was a full moon.

The beach below was gorgeous.

That shit could move me to tears.

I got out of the car.

I had the Bersa nine-millimeter in my hand—like I was going to do anything with it?

I left the driver's side door open and tipped the front seat forward. I backed away.

"A little help?" said Trixie.

I shook my head "Uh-uh."

She struggled out of the car, wobbling on legs unsteady from hours spent at improbable angles. She stood steaming.

She said, "Mind if I pee, you son of a bitch?"

I said, "In a minute. Turn around. Face *that* way."

I pointed away from the car.

She sighed and obeyed.

While she stood there, I popped the trunk and rummaged. I always kept a gym bag back there with a change of clothes and some Kleen Wipes (*Fresh Scent!*) I unzipped the gym bag and took out an old Dickies jacket. Trixie was looking pretty dirty, but I needed the wipes; I pulled out five of them. They smelled like gardenias. I got out an old blanket, a flashlight, a case of Power Bars (New Chocolate-Cranberry-Acai!), and a year-old copy of *Guns & Ammo* (*Mini-14 Stress Test!*) The only other reading material back there was a yellow-edged paperback, its back cover stickered: Señor Shakespeare's Used Books, Maracaibo—Inglés y Español. Guess whose? I looked at the cover:

The Intimate Core
Let the Wisdom of Agartha and Atlantis
Improve Your Love Life

Someone had drawn a pencil mustache and pointy goatee on cover's the bikini-clad Nordic Atlantean priestess.

I tossed the paperback on top of the Power Bars, blanket, the jacket, the magazine the flashlight and the big wad of Wet Wipes. I left it all in a pile behind the car.

I approached Trixie cautiously the way one approaches a hemorrhoid-plagued Siberian tiger.

"Stretch your arms back behind you," I told her.

She did.

I took her wrists and gently marched her.

Trixie said, "Ow. You're really a prick, you know that?"

"I think it's finally dawning on me."

I took her about fifty meters away from the car, down the road by the cove. I got my knife from my pocket, flipped it one-handed. I grabbed her wrists.

I said, "Wait right there by the cove. He's not far off the coast, but it'll probably take him an hour or so."

"And what if I get kidnapped in the meantime?"

I said, "You mean *again*?"

"Very funny."

"I left you some reading material and a blanket and a jacket. And some Power Bars."

"Oh," she said bitterly. "Great. High-fructose corn syrup."

I cut the ropes and started running.

She started after me.

"Dante, come here," she snarled, murder on her face, her fists working violently—*killkillkillkill*, they said.

I was sick and hot with fever—but she'd lost a shoe in the struggle. I had Israeli tac boots. The asphalt was baked and sharp with stones; she stopped about twenty meters into the chase and hopped back and forth, saying "Ow!" and panting under the bright Panama moon.

I'd left the car running.

I jumped in as if pursued by the Devil—which I was.

"C'mere!" she howled.

"Just chill! He'll be here to get you!"

Silver in the moonlight, she limped toward the car and screamed: "I'll get *you*!"

About five meters away, now, she suddenly looked freaked. She said:

"Dante, you don't look so good."

I popped the clutch. I smelled it burning as I tore up the gravel.

In the rearview I saw Trixie staring after me, wide-eyed.

Gorgeous like the moon, and just as distant.

☠

A mile from where I left Trixie, I pulled to the side of the road, got out and stripped off my clothes. My bloody jeans and shirt were crusty with gore but too wet with my sweat to catch fire. I tossed 'em in the rainforest. I used up all the Wet Wipes and threw those in the rainforest, too, with the bloody latex gloves. Leave only footprints, Bubba.

I didn't even try to clean up my hand. It was swollen and ugly; it looked hilarious. I fought down the pain. I fought down the laugh at how dumb my hand looked.

I put on the fresh set of clothes; they felt stiff from months in the Peugeot; they stank like trunk. I got back in the car and hit the road, driving north.

I had a fever. That seemed suddenly hilarious.

I laughed till I cried.

I careened across the road, guffawing.

I pounded my fist on the dash until it was bloody.

I fought it down to a chuckle. The laughter was gone.

Five miles away I found the *La Dolce Vita Tours* office, which was in fact a houseboat staple-gunned together out of US Army cargo pontoons and what looked like a 1950s-era Airstream trailer that someone at some point had christened the *Bubba Love*. Fixed to one side of a ramshackle dock, the office faced a forty-eight-foot flat-bottom named the *East Jersey Lady*, from which I heard the soothing strains of *vallenato* and cheering, laughing voices.

Señor Mike and his poker buddies had a hell of a drunk on. I rapped on his window.

I said, "Can I use your phone?"

He called back, "Who is it?"

I said, "It's the boogey man, *vato*. Open up."

He peered through the screen into the darkness, shaded his eyes against the bug light.

"Dante?"

"Boo," I said.

"D'you bring weed?"

I said, "Open *up*."

☠

Three shattered pirates crawled up the beach, laughing: *Buh-Bang*. Burned, broken limpers shambled in panic, the laughter starting while they were alive enough to know what was happening. *Rat-a-tat-tat*. Ruined bodies steamed and smoked, draped with the charred remains of shredded board shorts and pastel *guavajaras*. The laughter went wet with hissing cracks as bullets hit bones.

I blasted their brains out into the clear blue Caribbean, each in numerous pieces, trailing like jellyfish back toward Cuba.

I found a wriggler tossed on the shore, torso bisected by a cheap, pitted plane of maritime windshield. Her sidearm, an old Tokarev, had been driven up into her body cavity by the blast; it now lay glinting in what had been her ribcage.

Her almond-colored *chiquita* face was pretty as hell, rimmed with inky black hair that would have shined maybe just a few days ago. I mighta felt like a dirty old man eyeballing her in El Cangrejo.

I looked into her red-rimmed eyes as she howled at me, spewing wet cackles—hungry, starving, *ravenous*. Wanting me.

I blew the girl's brains out.

I took a brief circuit, slow and smooth, round in a half-circle. Out in the clear warm water things were moving still, bubbles breaking the surface. I couldn't get shots. They'd be on land soon enough, I knew.

I started back toward my friends.

The three Kuna toughs watched from the cliffside, rifles clutched to their chests: watching, waiting, watching to find out if they had to put us all down. They were scared. Their eyes were big, like the ones you see in the airbrushed Christian inspirational art—but scared out of their minds.

Trixie was sick. I'd started crying again; my voice caught in my chest as I tried to say Van's name.

Trixie'd sat up; her teeth were chattering. Van held her. He clutched his short-barreled .44 in his hand, fingers curved around the fat five-round cylinder. He held her and rocked back and forth with her, trying to summon up the *huevos* to put the .44 to her head.

She said, "I don't feel so good."

Van said, "I know, babe, I know I know I *know*."

She said, "Just do it."

Van said, "I know."

I said, "Don't do it!"

She said, "Shut up, Frosty, I'm sorry, I'm sorry—I love you—I love both you assholes."

That got us both going. All three of us, actually, but Trixie was so sick you couldn't tell the crying from the shakes.

On his knees in the sand, Van laid Trixie down and edged back, raising the .44.

I said, "Don't do it."

He said, "I've have to."

I said, "No."

I put my gun to his head.

He looked at me sadly. "Dante, she'll turn."

I got my hand around his .44 and held the barrel of my five-sev at the base of his skull.

I said, "I know."

Shaking all over as he looked in his dying wife's eyes Van looked more betrayed than I'd ever seen him look.

He said softly, "What the fuck are you doing?"

I said, "Let *go*. I'm going to count to three—"

He sneered, "Don't pull that, Dante. I *invented* that shit."

"I just perfected it. Give me the six-shooter."

Van said weakly, "It's got five." He let go.

I took the .44 away from him. Trixie clawed for it, her eyes rolling back. She said my name, delirious.

She looked sick already—this shit was *fast*. Five years was a long time.

She said, "Dante, for fuck's sake, I don't want to be like them—"

I stuck the .44 in my belt.

I said, "I don't have time to explain." I gestured at Van. "Back away," I told him. He did.

Trix clawed for her own pistol, which she'd dropped in the sand alongside her; she couldn't really see, since her eyes were running so bad. I kicked it away with the toe of one sodden *huarache*.

She was starting to jerk. She looked horrified.

Trix squealed: "Kill me!"

She bleated a death rattle, soft:

"*Ha ha. Ha ha ha.*"

Her eyes went wide; she looked more scared to hear it coming from her own lips than she'd ever been to hear it from another's.

Then she was gone.

She writhed, laughing softly in her sleep. It chilled my blood. Van said "You hear that shit?"

I said, "Pick her up."

He said, "She's turning!"

"I know! Pick her up. I can't explain."

He did.

"Up the beach, *vato*."

"You wanna explain?"

"*Up the beach!*"

In his arms, Trixie spasmed and moaned and rocked back and forth. She chuckled, her eyes wide and roving when they were opened, pouring tears when they were closed. Her hand had swollen. It oozed pus.

Trixie's eyes rolled back and poured tears. She choked out guffaws—three sickly peals of nightmare, fast and grating.

I gestured with the pistol. He walked. We passed the end of the dock where the *Jerry Bear* was moored, and I told him to stop and wait for a second. He did, looking madder every second.

I opened the dock box and took out three lengths of nylon line, tied off neatly into fifty-foot segments. Trixie's work: Van couldn't tie knots for shit.

He glared at me. Rope in one hand, pistol in the other, I jerked my head toward the house. He started walking again.

Van said as he walked, in measured tones, "Dante, you dipshit, I can't get that case open. We can't cure her!"

I said, "Take your wife home to bed, *vato*. Then tie her up."

He said, "Tie her up?"

I said, "Did I stutter?"

☠

The fever had passed for now; I no longer laughed.

Under the clouds of marijuana smoke drifting in from the deck, I sat on Señor Mike's stinky orange couch and got Van on his satphone. It was the only way to reach him short of the internet; they don't build a lot of offshore cell phone towers in Kuna Yala.

I said, "You sober, *compañero?*"

And he said, "What time is it?"

I said, "Just after one."

He said, "Then what do *you* think?"

I said, "Can you pilot your skiff?"

He said, "Could Jimi play 'Little Wing' on acid?"

"Stop answering questions with questions, you fucking Yiddish grandmother."

He said, "Define 'skiff.' I just got the *Jerry Bear* running again."

I said, "How about the Speedy?"

"I'd have to siphon if you want me to go more than a hundred—"

"Uh-uh," I said. "Just a snatch-and-grab. Vuelo Puente. Remember that cove you showed me?"

"Like the back of my hand. But you know I don't run drugs."

"It's not *that* kind of snatch-and-grab," I said. "I really need you. I'm in a hell of a lot of trouble."

Van said, "What have I been telling you, Dante? Scour the globe busting skulls and breaking kneecaps for Coca-Cola and Texaco, now you come crying to Daddy 'cause your—" water gurgled "—crypto-Nazi Jerry Falwell Union Carbide baby-killing prison-privatizing three-strikes sex-in-toilets Republican Proposition 13 black-helicopter UFO-flying child-molester bosses decide to hammer you down since you're the squeaky nail. Why is that *my* problem?"

I started talking and he said, "I mean, you run an empire based on prohibition and next thing you know the religious right is conspiring with Russian oligarchs and the Iranians to jack up the price of oil and steal our hard-earned—before you know it we'll all be a mash-up of Shiite and Southern Baptist and caffeine will be outlawed, pal—what, you think you can beat karma?"

I said, "Finished?"

He said, "Not really. I got a week's worth of it."

"Yeah, well, you're about to have an appreciative audience."

I heard a gurgle.

It hit him. He coughed.

"No," he said. "No, no. Not her. No, no. No, no, no—"

I said, "Just for a few days!"

"No!" Van howled. "Not that pompous vegetarian Berkeley hippie doctor Peace Corps all-organic Majarishi-following crystal-healing born-again Buddhist war protestor—"

"Yeah," I said. "*Her.*"

"She's a *monster*," he said.

I rubbed my jaw. "She's from Portland, not Berkeley, and come on, she's a pussycat."

"More like Tatiana the Tiger, asshole. She's *Colombian*."

My teeth chattered; spasms ran through me. I said weakly, "Just a few days. It's a big island. Stick her in a tent on the cliffs. She'll be happier that way. Give her a Richard Bach book and a lunchbox packed with tofu salad sandwiches on whole grain bread with quinoa blossoms—she'll be *fine*. And she's *not* Colombian."

He said, "I know. I'm just fucking with you. That girl is *nuts*."

"Van, I'm begging. I wouldn't ask if I didn't really need it."

He sighed and said, "Just few days?"

I said, "Yes."

He said, "You're sure you really need this?"

I said, "I need *you*."

He said, "Why me, Dante?"

I said, "You're the only guy within driving distance with more guns than brains."

He cackled.

"Guilty as charged," he said. "You're really going to owe me on this one, Bogart. You know she has serious Daddy issues, right?"

I said, "Discuss it with her. She loves spirited debate."

He got solemn. He said, "You're really in deep shit, *compañero?*"

I said, "Hard to imagine it could get any deeper."

"Get out of the business, Dante. Before it turns *you* into a monster."

I shivered all over and said, "*Claro*, buddy. Listen, Van—"

I heard gurgling on the other end.

He said, "What? I'm listening."

I said, "Van, there's one thing I need you to promise me—two things. Really important. One soldier to another."

He said, "I haven't been a soldier in ten years, buddy."

And I said sadly, "Neither have I. Just… the bro code, then."

"Dante, that brand of douchebaggery doesn't become you. Just tell me what you want."

I said, "First: She doesn't want to go. But you've got to get her to Isla Pescado, and you've got to keep her there—at least for a few days. She won't want to be there. This girl is going to try to leave, maybe using force. She'll try to get a ride to Colón or something; she'll want to go back home. She *can't*. She can't even contact anybody for a while. Not her foundation, not the Peace Corps, not the consulate, not her family, not her friends. She can't leave the island."

He said, "Yeah, I think I used to watch that TV show. Do I get, special numbers to read her every forty-five seconds? I've already got a bitchin' smoke monster." Gurgle.

I said, "I'm serious. You have to promise to keep her on ice?"

"It's ninety degrees here at midnight, Dante. Nothing's on ice but the beer and the acid. But trust me, once she skinny dips in those sapphire waves and kicks it on these diamond-strewn beaches, she'll be tryna buy real estate. I bet I have to *evict* her."

I said dubiously, "Uh-huh. And once she cops a squat in that high-class septic tank of yours, she'll—"

"Hey, fucko! That's *ecological*. Green."

"Yeah," I said. "So's my face whenever I need to unload there. Promise you'll keep her there?"

"Is this gonna take, like, *violence*?" he asked.

I said, "Probably on her part."

He said, "Remind me why I love you again?"

"You don't, remember? This is life and death. Promise."

"Sounds like it'll probably be my death we're talking about."

I said, "Yeah, well, I wouldn't suggest being around her unarmed for the first few days."

He made a disgusted noise.

"I want some serious favors for this, Bogart. We're talking weed, cocaine, hotel suites full of amber-skinned—"

"Put it on my tab," I interrupted. "Second favor."

Gurgle. "I'm listening."

"Don't sleep with her."

Van cackled and said, "No promises there, Frosty—she's at the mercy of the Fish Family mojo. Have I ever mentioned that the San Francisco Lesbian Alliance pays me a stipend to remain south of Campeche?"

I said, "Right."

"Besides, she's gonna be busy punching my lights out. How exactly does her beating the shit out of a guy end with her falling into bed with him?"

I sighed. Through the haze of mounting fever, I thought about it.

I said, "You know, I've been asking myself the same thing for almost eighteen months."

He cackled.

"I'll research the question."

"There's one more thing, Van."

Gurgle. "Christ," he said. "*Three* favors?"

I said, "Yeah. You still got internet on *Isla Pescado*?"

He said defensively, "Intermittently."

"I need the name of that conspiracy forum you like so much. The off-the-grid one. The one with the paramilitary weirdos."

"Dante, which one?"

I said, "There's more than one?"

He said, "Hell yeah. There's twenty or thirty I watch."

I said, "There are really that many assholes out there wearing tinfoil hats?"

And he said, "Hell yeah, Dante. There's a lot of mind-control rays."

I said, "I need the *big* one. The really, really big one."

Van said, "There are a lot of big ones."

"The biggest."

He said, "Well, are you talking uniques, total readership, actual page loads? Now you shouldn't use the term 'hits,' because that's outdated at least in the sense that every time a web page loads—"

"I mean what's the biggest in terms of, like, cultural impact. If something *really* needed to get out, you know—something big. I mean a *real* conspiracy. Not some bullshit fantasy. I need to get a theory out. Where do I do it?"

He said, "Okay, sure. Purgatorio."

I said, "Huh?"

He said, "Purgatorio. In San Francisco."

I said, "The porn company?"

He said, "Oh, you know it, pervert?"

I said, "Long story."

He cackled. "Yeah, I bet! Dude, they're *way* more than a porn company. They're a social activist *army*. They're rebuilding the way America sees both reality *and* sexuality. They're the ones behind that viral video, *Who Killed Kennedy—Sasquatch—The Greys—Subterraneans—The Space Sisters?*

"That sounds like a long video," I said.

"It is," he said. "Four minutes."

I said, "Those idiots are actually important now?"

He said, "Don't call them idiots, man. They live in a castle. Used to be some kind of weird-ass Spiritualist commune. Burning Man, that sort of thing. But the second dot-bomb was a game-changer. So was Wikileaks. Now it's this huge collective hacker house."

"That makes porn."

"Okay, they make a little porn. What's the crime? What are you, turning sex-negative in your old age?"

"Anyone can upload?"

"Hell, no. You need an admin account; then you can set up usernames."

"You got one?"

He said, "That depends, Dante. Are you gonna troll?"

"Just give it to me."

He did. I wrote on the back of my hand. He gave me a URL with lots of tildes and backslashes and whatever, and his username and password:

"Sasquatch Israel."

I told Van, "Watch it. Watch your little freakshow. Say, about sunup tomorrow. Make sure Trixie's watching, too."

He said, "Dante, this conspiracy shit isn't like you. Just how crazy is your theory?"

I said, "*Crazy.*"

"Important?"

Chills wracked my body.

"No," I said. "Just crazy."

☠

Among American expats in Panama, great amusement is shared at the widespread Latin American view that Colombian women are both sexy and, well, *feisty*. Trixie was both; that didn't take a rocket surgeon. But Van actually *calling* her Colombian told me everything I needed to know.

The very stoned Van Fish had just disclosed more about his interest in Trixie than he'd meant to—but then, that was the point.

I knew that if Trixie was presented to him as a sexual challenge—nay, a partnering *possibility*—he would not only be a perfect gentleman for a change, but he would follow her around like a puppy dog.

He would die for her. More importantly, he would kill for her.

It's like this: For all his crude assertions about women, his periodically sexist appraisals of their reasoning capabilities, and his frequent and mildly defensive holding-forth on the sexual insatiability of certain Brazilian latecomers to the feminine gender, Van was a little boy inside, like too many of us. Without women, we're monsters—and we know it, but *they* don't. We live our lives in fear that they'll find out.

The corpulent prick wished no one—*no one*—to know it, but under that reeking jiggly assemblage of hair and fat and ill-advised tattoos and curiously-colored board shorts and obscenely-distended Zeppelin t-shirts, the little fuckbag was the dorkiest schoolboy around showing up for his date with the prom queen wearing a bad tux, a half-wilted bouquet and a four-foot skull bong.

I knew what a pussy he was. Despite having cruised the coast of South America footloose for the better part of ten years and made many acquaintances, Van didn't have many friends. He didn't have *any* friends other than me who had been around to see the short and tragic tale of his relationship with Consuela—equal parts war booty and mail-order bride.

No one had seen the hairy, hostile, heavily-armed obscenity-spouting freak staring sob-wracked into his wife's fading eyes and weeping to his wife:

"Baby, don't die. I can't live without you."

The prick would be in love with Trixie before he knew it. He'd be braiding her hair by tomorrow evening.

And if anyone fucked with her? If Virgil Amaro came after Trixie?

Then God have mercy on Virgil's soul…

… because Van Fish sure as hell wouldn't.

☠

Van walked across the garden, crushing Holy Ghost orchids under his feet.

He growled, "Where do you want her, asshole?"

I said, "Does she still treat sick kids at home? Just like old times?"

"Nah, she cooks children into sausage now, fucker. She's Trixie. What the hell do you think?"

"Then she's got a sickroom?"

He said, "*Si.*"

I said, "*Está bien.* Will those Kuna kids sneak up on me blow my brains out?"

He said, "Probably. But I taught 'em to shoot, so…"

"Oh, no problem then. Keep moving, Bigfoot."

Van carried the shivering Trixie back through Casa Fish, threading through an obstacle course built out of cases of thirty-thirty ammo, sacks of brown rice marked in Portuguese, cases of penicillin, stacks of decaying *National Geographics.*

Dolphins and starving kids grimaced from the covers.

The sickroom had a hospital bed that looked like it had been scavenged from a commercial about in-home care. In Ukraine.

Van asked, "Dante, you know what you're doing?"

I said, "Not a clue. Put her down."

☠

From the *Bubba Love* I hauled ass through San Juan del Risa on the Kuna Yala coast, threading down dirt roads and onto what passed for a *Carretera* in these parts. I found my way to the Pan-American highway. It was black. I had a fever. As I drove, I felt sleep fighting hard to take me over. I tried not to think. I floored it. It was a starry night, with no moon.

Darién nights are bright above, but on the ground they're dark as nightmares.

I had a few of those, there on the highway, coming out of the night at me fast. I saw Jesus, Buddha, Indrid Cold. UFOs over Chilibre. Bigfoot mooning me in the jungles of the Parque Nacional Rio Chagres. I wept at the skies.

I kept control of the Peugeot with staggering effort and fought away the need to sleep and the craving to succumb to the fever. I got hotter and more feverish. The pains in my body came, went, and returned, and each returning was more painful than the last. I sweated all over. I thought about Trixie and wept. Tearing through Nuevo San Juan, I cried "… Holy Mary, mother of God pray for us sinners now and at the hour of our death…" while dragons and dancers pirouetted in the skies over Lajo Alajuela.

It was a long drive to see the sun rise over Lemon Bay.

This may seem irrelevant to you; it may seem I ought to have bigger fish to fry. But men like me are children inside. At moments of consequence, we become mired in sentiment; the smallest detail of our experience becomes critical.

It's the curse of my people: proud men who built Rome.

We also talk with our hands.

☠

I made Colón before daybreak.

I left the Peugeot in a basement garage in Old Cristóbal.

I walked through the empty streets to the Beaumont Colón, a mammoth luxury resort structure overlooking the expanse of Bahía Limón—Lemon Bay—and the cerulean paradise beyond.

I had to see the sunrise.

I fought the shakes and the laughs.

I saw the skies turn from black-with-stars to deep-purple-aquamarine, and in the backscatter I saw Trixie's face.

I thought bitterly, *You're welcome.*

Passing a fisherman I smelled an early-morning haul.

I got an image, suddenly, of black-faced boys on Somalian speedboats, waving AKs. Frozen in time with .308 holes in their foreheads, brains spread behind them like Superman's cape.

I chuckled: *What a riot.*

I entered the Beaumont. I hit the front desk.

I made my face American-dopey, my tone the friendly expat.

I said, "Hi, I don't have a reservation—do you have a room?"

The clerk was a perky Panameño, twenty, twenty-five, teeth at rakish angles, cranberry lips, one nostril bigger than the other—hair the hue of kávé in Budapest, flesh like mousse on the Champs Élysées. She would for ten, twenty, thirty, forty minutes occupy a place in my rogue's gallery: the most beautiful woman I had ever seen. Because she was to be the very last.

She said, "I'll have to charge you for the night."

I said, "*Está bien.*"

She said, "Cash or credit card?"

I pulled the Bellona card out of my wallet and said, "Let's do American Express."

Would Virgil's people be watching for charges to my company AmEx?

Could Jimi play "Little Wing" on acid?

The charge went through; I signed.

They gave me a key card and a pass to the breakfast buffet and two complimentary tickets to the ferry and a brochure for Panamá Tránsito Tours and the Colón Museum of the Panama Canal.

And a code to access wireless internet.

She said, "Breakfast is six until nine…"

… and I trembled all over and said, "*Claro. Gracias.*"

She said, "The gym is on the fourth floor…"

… and I shuddered and said, "*Claro. Gracias.*"

She said, "Any baggage, Mr. Bogart?"

I had lots of baggage, but I patted my laptop bag and said, "Just this."

She said, "Will anyone be joining you?"

"*Si,*" I said. "My whole fucking family."

☠

I trained the sev on Van's big face and told him, "Back."

He backed.

Trixie was tied to the hospital bed, with tangled segments of rope. Van tied the shittiest knots of any sailboat owner north of the South Sandwich Islands. But they'd have to do for now.

He said, "How far?"

"All the way."

He got against the wall on the far side of the sickroom. Trixie shuddered on the bed. She was starting to laugh. There were tears in his eyes. His heart was breaking. He trembled.

He growled, "If you let her suffer…"

I said, "Everybody suffers. Listen up: I should send you out of the room for what I'm about to do."

"If you hurt her—"

"You were gonna *kill* her."

That did it. He broke. He started sobbing. Tears ran down his fat, hairy face.

That started me off. I wept.

Trixie started laughing.

She did it quietly—her eyes wide, roving in terror. Trixie fought it. She was still there, locked in her mind, feeling it go, feeling the horror begin inside her. I said, "Just sit tight. Don't stop me. I'm not just fucking around."

Trixie's chuckle became a titter, then a tortured giggle titter. Her eyes went crazy, wide and terrified.

Van gaped at us.

Suddenly, Trixie howled.

She blasted out a peal of that shit. It drove into my brain like shards of glass.

Then she stopped, staring up blankly. Her mouth hung open, her lips slack.

I only had a few seconds.

I barked at Van: "Stay!"

I lunged forward and kissed Trixie hard on the lips.

"What the *fuck*?" sobbed Van, his jaw dropping.

Things got ugly.

☠

In the elevator, alone, I thought about shrapnel-dappled orphans in Niamey and Congo, and legless Calcuttans on skateboards in front of the Hôtel Argenté.

My fever mounted. I howled. Legless fuckers: *Hilarious.*

I laughed my ass off.

☠

Back to my usual serious self by the twenty-first floor, I exited the hallway with the dull dead weight of the Bersa in my laptop bag.

I thought: *Fuck this. Just pull the trigger.*

I thought: *That'd be a laugh riot.*

I parked my ass in Room 2135, on the Canal side; I faced a big picture window and a glorious sunrise over Bahía Limón with Colón trailing pieces of cloud, bloody and brilliant in the flesh of blue sky. Behind me a wall-sized color photo of the Gatun Locks—*glorious.* Before me was the sun coming up over Lemon Bay—*glorious.* Beyond the window were sprawling purpose-built vistas packed with early-morning Sanfords and Bertrams and Reginalds playing golf while their Leonas and Hillarys and Elizabeths sat doing the *New York Times* crossword puzzle on terraces far below, sipping $28 carafes of premium Rwandan coffee and eating croissants.

I plugged my laptop in and while it booted I washed my face and my hands. I thought *Food* and thought *Puke*, but I couldn't do either.

I took the Bersa out of the bag and set it on the table.

I sat my ass in front of the laptop.

I found the internet signal. I logged in. I turned on the webcam.

The screen showed me an off-color webcam image of my white, sallow face, my eyes bloodshot and dying.

I took a very deep breath.

I started recording.

I said: "My name is Dante Bogart. I used to be a military contractor. For the last fifteen years I have been employed by the private military company Bellona Industries and its various shell corporations, all owned by the Amaro family. I have provided military and law enforcement training consultation, piracy and smuggling interdiction, black ops services and hard method interrogation services to government and private clients in many parts of the world."

I said: "For the last five years, I have been employed privately by the Amaro family on a private project to acquire exotic viral and bacterial agents and advanced biological warfare materials from third-world sites, foreign research facilities and terrorist paragovernmental black sites facilities with the intention of developing viral-based radical life extension technology for both offensive and defensive military application—"

Like that. My fever mounted as I spoke; my shakes got worse but I fought them down. My voice cracked sometimes when I talked about blowing people open, even in the vaguest of terms; I never quite lost it, but I was damn close, at times.

My hand rested sometimes on the Bersa, sometimes on my guts, sometimes on my throat, sometimes on my forehead, which popped out fifty-cal sweatballs with an ever-increasing rate of fire. I never wept. I never broke. I spoke with even tones. Clinical language, facts only—like that, Bubba. Never raised my voice.

Every now and then I had to stop the cam so I could start sway and cough and sneezed and tremble.

Sometimes I'd laugh. Did I really think this shit would work? *Hilarious.* I got through it.

Half an hour after I started, I quit the webcam, hit the browser, opened my email—

—a dozen messages from Virgil. "Please check in." "Consult needed." "Urgent: Contact Me." "Dept. of Justice Involved." "WHO conducting inquiry into," "Libya operation compromised," "URGENT URGENT URGENT!"

I sent Trixie a last message: "I know why Man laughs, Doc—Love, Frosty."

I burned my email account. I purged. I logged out. I started scouring.

I had planned for this moment, in some way—in my biz, you have to. Not that I thought I'd run afoul of the Amaros, at first; really, you never know who's gonna flip. Until very, very shortly before the incidents at the Beaumont Lemon Bay, I thought it'd probably be the FBI coming for me. It wasn't.

I stared at the screen; I barely breathed until the blue screen flashed: it was empty. Not even an operating system.

No ghosts of my past could lead Virgil to Trixie.

I said to myself, "Hail Mary, full of grace—"

—and then the laughing started.

Spasms wracked my body. I groaned. I twitched. I guffawed. I giggled. My muscles tightened. The pain screamed through me. I chuckled. I picked up the Bersa. I checked the clip a hundred times. I thought about stretching out on the bed. I thought if I did I'd probably never get up. Especially if I took the Bersa with me; I wanted to put it in my mouth. Which suddenly seemed hilarious.

There at the end, I was never quite sure what was happening.

I sat down in the hotel chair with the Bersa in my lap. I went all fuzzy. I tittered. I howled.

Then suddenly, the laughing was done and the misery hit me like a piledriver; it was like having my soul slammed into a vat of liquid nitrogen. I heard myself sobbing. Everything about me shivered and shattered, and as I wept uncontrollably, the *only* thing I knew was that somewhere in the world, maybe several or many somewhere, I'd done some really fucked-up shit.

How fucked-up?

Not half as fucked-up as what I was *about* to do.

That got me laughing again.

I faced the door with grin on my face. I felt my lips tear back in a rictus. I felt my breath coming out hot.

Ha ha ha. Ha ha ha. Ha ha—

My fever was spiking. I could feel myself going. Flames danced in the corners of my vision.

The windows shattered. CS canisters burst and hissed out howling. I laughed till I cried. I heard boosteps in the hallway.

In the moments before the no-knock ingress, I started laughing.

I said: "Stop me if you've heard this one."

I said: "Guy walks into a hotel."

I said: "And no one walks out."

I howled. I busted a gut.

I got to my feet and opened up *wide*.

☠

A 12-gauge breach round blew the lock. I hovered there shrouded in tear gas and nightmares; I stood there grinning with a smile that could melt flesh from bone. They'd sent *dozens*, trotting up the stairs on laced-up Bates Tacticals. Strapped into Kevlar, toting railed-up M-4s, looking confident.

They came for me, locked and loaded, through the choking clouds of tear gas.

But then I came for them… and I'd had all the tears I could stand.

☠

They heard before they saw, but they didn't get the joke.

Even if they had, they wouldn't have had much time to laugh; quick as a shit they were silenced, slurping CS, bone fragments, blood.

They went down wet… which if I may say so was a fucking laugh riot.

They'd brought my cure, or so they thought: Quarter-inch entries, with tangled, oblong exits.

But I had the best medicine.

So I gave 'em an *overdose*.

PART 2:

THE FATE OF *GOD'S MERCY*

Yearse ago: Me, fresh from security gigs on Nigerien uranium mines, with detours to kidnapping cases of PRC nationals from oil facilities near Owerri and excursions into southern Chad. Me, fresh from the field, cracking wise to pretty Panamanian faces and scrawling my name at the Bellona contract office in the Miraflores Tower, El Cangrejo, Panama City. One of Virgil Amaro's half-dozen assistants was a smoking twentynothing in a straight blue wool skirt, plain jacket and granny blouse. She helped me fill out forms to get my bonus and smiled with eyes of Panama Brown.

I was jotting down account numbers from memory, having checked the box for "Euros" under the currency of the receiving institution.

Panama Hot got a buzz on. It went off near her slender hand, from an intercom rig marked *Claro*!

"Blanca, is Mr. Bogart still down there?"

"Yes, Mister Virgil."

I got goosebumps.

"Send him into my office as soon as he's done."

Blanca smiled at me, sharp eyebrows high.

"Looks like you're moving up in the world, Mister Dante."

I said, "*Claro*."

☠

I went upstairs. I met the Boss. He asked me questions and told me he was impressed with my record. He asked me if I knew that with my breadth of command experience, I'd become something of a legend to the younger consultants under the Amaro family umbrella.

I told him, "*Muchas gracias*."

Then he bored me senseless for an hour, droning on without passion about geopolitics, China's Indian Ocean empire, military privatization and, finally, the application of modern technology to the problems of life extension, and by the way, did I know about how researchers at MIT were mapping the human connectome? I was bored off my ass.

At one point he said, "You *are* still a Catholic, Dante—am I correct?"

I fingered my dangling crucifix and said, "Yes, Sir. I went to St. Magdalena's."

He said, "In Oakland, California."

I'd walked into it.

"After your father died—rest in peace—"

I looked at him like he was crazy.

I said, "Yeah. I moved back to Oakland to live with my grandfather."

He said, "Rest in peace."

I shrugged. "If you like. Gramps preferred a party."

Virgil said, "Men without women, Dante: we're dangerous. We become monsters."

I said, "*Claro*, Mr. Amaro."

He said, "That was your father's father? The one who gave you the name?"

I said, "Well, he gave himself the name. He made it legal before my father was born. But it started out as a stage name."

My future dangled from a thread. His lip curled. "Hollywood?"

"Vaudeville."

Virgil looked relieved.

"What year was this?"

I said, "My father and grandfather were both on the older side when they had kids. It was before his service in World War II."

"Your grandfather served honorably?"

I said, "Oh, yeah. He slipped on many a banana."

Virgil squinted at me.

He said, "How well do you know the Port of Oakland?"

I'd stolen things from there, but I wasn't going to tell him that, so I just said, "Pretty well."

He said, "Want to take a vacation from the third world?"

I guffawed. "And go to *Oakland*?"

He didn't think that was very funny—but then, neither did I.

☠

A week later the *God's Glory* was moored in the Port of Oakland, and I was being driven across the Bay Bridge in a two-tone burgundy-and-black hearse by a little pissed-off-looking Latina in a black men's suit with a skinny tie. Her hot pink dreads were stuffed up inside her chauffeur's cap.

She said, "So you're the famous mercenary Frosty Bogart, eh?"

For a man of my stature, this is like someone asking a Mafia hit man if he is a made man or just an associate, while toying lackadaisically with the skull of the last man he whacked.

I said, "Hopefully not famous, since my name's Robert Denard."

"Huh!" she said. "Right."

"And that's an awfully rude question. And don't call me Frosty. And what gave you that impression?"

She said, "You work for the Amaros."

I laughed my ass off.

I said, "What was your name again?"

She said defiantly, "Guadalupe Grope."

I said, "Um… okay. Is that 'Miss Grope—'"

She barked, "Ms.!"

"—or can I call you Guadalupe?"

She shrugged. "My friends just call me Lupe."

I said, "Oh, so am I your friend all of a sudden?"

She glared at me, looked me up and down lasciviously, sneered, tossed her head and flared her nostrils.

She said, "I doubt you could handle it."

I said, "Guadalupe, I work for Kochevar Maritime Security in Cyprus. I'm a maritime escort."

She guffawed. She laughed so hard she almost puked. "OhmiGod, I'm a maritime escort, too! I see this client with a 40-foot sailboat—"

I snarled, "I'm fully bonded and insured. I'm licensed by the European Union to provide antipiracy services for—"

She guffawed. "See, he likes me to dress up with an eye patch and stick his face in the bilge, and—he likes to be bonded, too!"

I growled: "—companies registered in member states. Look, lady. You mind telling me why you're laughing?"

She fought down her guffaws and said, "You work for the Amaros and everyone knows it."

I said, "Who's everyone?"

She said, "Well, the FBI for one, and Immigration and Customs Enforcement, and the Coast Guard, and the—I mean, not that I like those fuckers any more than you do, but—*Pick a lane, fascist!*"—she swerved around an SUV and flipped the guy off, hanging both hands out the window and driving with her knees. She screamed, "Margaret Thatcher fart-sniffing Kuwaiti butt-licker! No blood for oil! Pick a lane!"

I said, "Looked to me like he'd already picked several of them."

She put one hand back on the wheel and lit up a joint. She said: "All I'm saying, Dante, is that… look, this driving for Paradise is just my day job. I'm also a blogger."

I said, "What's that?"

She looked like I'd punched her in the face. I knew what a blogger was, of course. You ever killed time at a uranium mine in Niger? That satellite internet shit is your *lifeline*. But those were the days when enough people *didn't* know that she could still look wilted when someone said so.

She said haughtily, "And a poet. Do guys like you know about poetry slams?"

"Those are the things you fry up with peanut butter and marshmallow, right? I thought you said you're a bugger."

She frowned. "Blogger!" Then she guffawed. "Though I do bug people sometimes, sure."

"You're bugging me," I said. "You're really good at it, in fact."

"Look, Dante, I'm a real journalist, but I work without the sanction of a private para-governmental corporate power structure."

"Wow, that sounds serious."

"It *is* serious, asshole. We're the only ones who really know what's going on."

"I'm glad someone does."

Her tone went from vicious to compassionate in an instant.

She said, "All I'm saying, Dante, is that you might want to consider whether you're lying down with dogs."

I said, "My girlfriend prefers cats."

She burbled: "The hired killer has a girlfriend!"

I growled, "She's Colombian. And my name's not Dante. It's Bob Denard."

She rolled her eyes. "I've got public-domain pictures of you in Mosul."

I said, "I've never been to Mosul."

She gave me a sarcastically innocent look and said mildly, "If you had, do you think you would have killed many babies?"

I said, "That depends, do they blog?"

"You've got a hell of a sense of humor about infanticide."

I said, "You should see me do impressions. How about you? You're my chauffeur. If you think I'm a murderer, doesn't that make you my wheelman? An accomplice?"

She said, "I work for Ellis personally. He's completely obsessed with me."

"Is that why he has you driving cabs?"

"That's Malign. Ellis is crazy and he knows it—he's so fucking obsessive in relationships. So he and Malign have this weird thing; Malign locks down the business side, and when Ellis has some new dominatrix he gets obsessed with, then Malign finds her a job. Ellis would marry me if he could, but I'm like, no, stupid fucker, marriage is a tool of patriarchal capitalism, so, like, bite me!"

I said, "Who's Ellis?"

She made a disgusted noise.

"Ellis Osborne IV, asshole."

"Wow," I said. "There are four of him? Is that, like, a cloning thing? Are there more of *you*, too?"

She said, "Paradise Life Extension just went bankrupt. Lloyd Strong—that's the founder—went to jail in Thailand. Ellis knew Lloyd and Malign from Burning Man. He bought the assets of Paradise Life Extension, including the building. It isn't Paradise anymore."

I said, "There's a lot of that going around."

"Dude, EO4 is *huge*."

"Did you just call him EO4?"

"That's what we call him."

"Hey, I think I know this guy. Is he like, three feet tall and shaped like a trash can? Makes bleeping noises? Used to have his own ride at Disneyland?"

"You'd like EO. You and he could bond. He was in the Army. He was a helicopter pilot. He saw combat in Iraq. He saw first-hand what you scumbags do to helpless babies with Napalm."

"Hey, I *never* let my babies play with Napalm."

"But then EO met Deepak Chopra and became an Ayurvedic pacifist adventurer and dot-com entrepreneur."

"I don't know which part of that sentence disturbs me more," I said.

"Hel-lo! He took an autogiro across Siberia. Ring a bell? No? Jeez, don't you read the papers?"

I said, "I try not to. It hurts my bank account."

"Well, this is EO4's new adventure: Purgatorio Multimedia Entertainment."

I said, "And what's the adventure?"

She gave a wicked chortle; she looked over and her dark eyes did a suggestive up-down, saying *I've got a secret...*

She told me: "Let's just say they're still doing things to bodies."

"OhmiGod!" I said. "Me too!"

She hissed, "That's creepy."

I said, "You have no idea."

☠

The remains of the Paradise Life Extension Foundation—now Purgatorio—occupied the giant Moorish Castle called the Armory that you pretty much can't miss if you're driving down Mission or 14th Street. I knew the history of this monstrosity from when I was a kid, but I'd lost track of it when I'd moved away from the area. Erected in the teens to serve as a rallying point in case of Union riot—which actually occurred in the 1934 Waterfront Strike—it once upon a time dominated the entire neighborhood with its imposing form. It had turrets and kill slots and '60s-era metal rollup doors and a huge set of marble stairs that were bitchin' to skate across.

The facility had been decommissioned in the '70s and sat around rotting for years. Several years before, Guadalupe Grope informed me, an outfit called the Paradise Life Extension Foundation had purchased the building and used it to set up shop doing experiments and providing Life Extension Services, whatever that is supposed to mean. The founder, being an old computer genius from the sixties turned dot-com zillionaire and, apparently, being a bit of an acidhead, had sought to hire people from the "trusted fringes" of San Francisco's underground as far back as the late 1980s.

From the back roll-up door, a deep ramp led down into the basement, where the stables had once been. Lupe explained this brightly as we descended at an improbable angle. Her personality had hugely improved once she got finished calling me a baby-killer, and she discussed the use of military steeds at the Armory during the teens with some excitement. I guess she dug horses.

She parked the hearse and turned me over to a muscled, tastefully-unshaven jeans-and-wifebeater type with long black hair and a stick-and-ball tattoo of Substance P. He introduced himself as Malign and offered me a cigarette.

I accepted, and he led me through a decaying marble-lined lobby that was probably opulent about eighty years before.

He said, "You know what you're picking up, Bob?"

I said, "Twenty oblong crates."

He said, "You know what's in 'em?"

I said, "Not a clue."

He said, "Good man!" and gave me another cigarette.

He led me down a long hallway lined with metal bars; it looked like an Old West jail, which I thought was pretty freaky—but hey, don't ask, don't tell. The guy seemed to be checking his cell phone.

I asked him, "That works in the basement?"

He said, "Oh, yeah—we've got a repeater. Wanna know the best part?"

When people ask that, you can usually figure what they're about to tell you isn't the best part at all, and in fact is probably boring as hell.

So I shrugged.

He said, "It'll even work if the towers are down. It's wired in to our backup satellite internet, and through that into this sort of back door version of the MEECN."

"Sorry?"

"Minimum Essential Emergency Communications Network. Ellis is big into emergency preparedness. He might be a little bit paranoid, but if there's an earthquake, or a tsunami, or a terrorist attack, or even a *nuclear war*? We're gonna be the ones still updating Live Journal. Pretty neat, huh?"

"No shit. What do you do here now that you need that kind of setup?"

I almost got bowled over by two mostly blondes chasing each other down the hallway. Both wore dog collars and ball gags. One wore high heels, with the result that the other was gaining on her. But those marble floors were slippery, and the one with the lead was upping the ante by waving twin bottles of intimate lubricant behind her, unloading serpentine strings of it as she ran.

The result was that the chase continued until both girls vanished around the nearest corner.

A guy in Converse Hi Tops, wraparound shades and nothing else came puffing after them, hoisting a camera on his shoulder.

As I stared, dumbfounded, he went down hard on his ass with an "Oof!"—holding the camera aloft to keep it from falling. With difficulty, he hauled himself to his feet, cupped one hand and howled behind him:

"Lupe, we need a cleanup here! Lupe! Lupe!"

Down the hallway, Lupe showed up with a mop, a pissed-off look on her face. Her chauffeur's cap was gone, and her hot pink dreads spilled everywhere in a frenzied curtain past her shoulders. Her black suit was half-off; she wore tight black bicycling shorts and the white shirt mostly unbuttoned, but with the black tie still knotted.

She stalked furiously down the marble hallway, mopping.

As she passed me, she purred mockingly, "Is my friend Malign treating you right, Mr. Denard?"

"He keeps giving me cigarettes," I said. "So we're cool."

Malign watched Lupe strip off her chauffeur's uniform, eyes wide behind his John Lennons and his tongue hanging out. Lupe and her mop vanished down the hall.

I said, "You were telling me what your new business is."

Malign looked at me.

He said, "I'll give you a hint. We still do things to bodies."

"That's what Lupe said. I told her, 'Me, too.'"

"But our bodies enjoy it more. Are you familiar with the Life Extension Movement, Bob?"

I said, "Nah. It's not really my skill set."

He said, "Mine, either. I only agreed to sign on as CEO because Lloyd and I are old friends. But it's like I told him. The planet's too taxed for resources. If more people live, more people die."

"Hard to argue with logic like that," I said.

"Lloyd believed all people should live forever. But EO is smarter about it. The trick is to increase the *quality* of life. People don't necessarily need to live longer... they just need to *enjoy* it more. That's the idea behind Purgatorio."

From down the hallway, there was the sound of a whip cracking, and a feminine scream.

Malign saw my eyebrows go up. He laughed nervously.

"Hey," he said. "Pleasure is subjective, right?"

I said, "Don't I know it!"

☠

Ten minutes later, an ancient bread truck had been backed down the ramp into the basement. The side of the truck had been recently whitewashed; it now said "Purgatorio Multimedia Entertainment" over the image of a winking devil-girl.

The back of the bread truck was open. Blue-mohawked guys in sunglasses and Bauhaus T-shirts hefted oblong crates into the back.

This Malign cat was explaining to me: "... and Ellis did pretty well in the first round of ISP buyouts back in the day, so when Lloyd got arrested, Ellis was like, okay, bitch, fork over the building and nobody gets hurt! But it wasn't technically a repossession."

"Well," I said, blowing smoke. "That's a relief."

"Anyway, Ellis and I figured, let's keep the business going and just change course, right? So he kept me in charge. I mean, if you run one kind of thing, you can run any kind of thing, right?"

I said, "I had that thought about an Abrams once. Turns out it didn't drive quite the same as my Kawasaki."

"Anyway, so I asked Ellis, what's your *dream*? And he said, 'To balloon around the world, smoking weed and getting poontang.' So here we are."

I said, "Uh... he wanted to balloon around the world smoking weed and... uh... so here we are making porn on an Army base?"

Malign said, "This wasn't Army—it was National Guard."

I thought, *Army, Navy, Air Force, Marines—it's all pink inside after the seventh margarita, buddy.*

Malign said, "And that's not really what I mean. The porn is just a means to an end."

"What end, the weed or the poontang?"

"Ellis was being facetious. He's like that. You'll see that when you meet him."

"I'm going back to Panama tonight," I said. "I doubt I'll meet him."

"Oh," said Malign. "I'm sure you'll be back. You have an open invitation. Come back and party with us any time, Bob! Seriously. Any time. Any time at all."

I said, "Thanks. It's a very tempting offer. 'Cause what maritime security contractor doesn't love weed, ballooning and poontang?"

"It's not just about weed and poontang."

"Right, I got that. Ballooning."

"It's about adventure!" he cried, waving his arms. "That should just about do it, Bob. You got help unloading on the Oakland end?"

I said, "Malaysians."

He said, "Huh?"

I said, "The international shipping industry has a lot of Malaysian sailors this year. It has to do with exchange rates. Last year it was guys from the Philippines; before that, PRC Nationals. Russians and Ukrainians before that."

He said, "It's different every year?"

I said, "It seems to be, just like your business."

"Tell me about it! It's been *Hungarians* lately."

I said, "Fucked-up language those people speak. How many g's and z's and k's does any one word need?"

"No shit! We took Ellis's blimp over to Hungary to shoot a strap-on thriller with this one girl he's completely obsessed with. Wanna know what the name of her town is? Székesfehérvár. You believe that shit? *Székesfehérvár*! Jesus, save some letters for the rest of us!"

I said, "I'm sorry, did you say—"

"Strap-on thriller. *Buggery on the Orient Express*. It's all about fetishes nowadays, Bob."

"I didn't know you could fly a blimp to Europe."

"Sure you can! As long as you've got charging stations!"

"Charging stations?"

He looked apologetic. "Yeah, they haven't perfected the photovoltaics yet, so the *Ocelot* is only partially solar."

I said, "It's an electric blimp?"

"Well," he said. "We had to be towed part of the way by the Portugese Coast Guard, but… sure, it *will* be electric!"

I said, "I have this hippie pilot friend in Panama—well, he *thinks* he's a pilot—who tried to talk me into a balloon trip to the Galapagos."

Malign turned slightly green. He said, "Well, bring your Dramamine."

"Yeah… I keep telling him, Van, you fuckin' cheapskate, just buy a fuckin' seaplane."

"Good call." Malign said. "Get a Cessna 172 or something. No motion sickness, no birds crawling up your nacelles, no problem. Just convert 'er to ethanol, get yourself a nightsoil fermenter, set up your still and you're good to go."

He slapped me on the shoulder and shook my hand vigorously.

"Thanks for coming, Bob. Remember what's in these crates?"

I said, "What crates?"

He gave me a cigarette.

When I climbed into the passenger's seat of the bread truck, I said tartly, "Crrrrrrrap."

Guadalupe Grope glared at me. She had changed into engineer boots and blue coveralls; she'd left the zipper of the latter most of the way down and apparently had gone commando underneath, which she remedied with an accusatory glare by zipping up. She adjusted the knit wool watch cap that housed her hot pink dreads and said, "It got hot waiting for you, Frosty."

I said, "How do you even know to call me that? And, *don't*."

She rolled up the windows and blasted the air conditioning. She took out a clove cigarette and lit it. Malign had required so many protestations of ignorance that I had ended up with a shirt-pocket full of cigarettes. I jammed one into my mouth and gestured at the lighter.

She looked at me, put the lighter away deep in her coveralls, and blew clove spoke in my face.

"Can I have a light?"

"No," she said.

"Are you a professional bitch?"

"As a matter of fact…"

"Answer my question. How do you know to call me that?"

She chuckled, glanced around and said, "Shhhhh, Frosty. The dildos have ears."

"That's what my girlfriend tells me."

She thought that was hilarious, which was strange, 'cause I had no idea what it meant, and I'd said it. She put the bread truck in gear and edged us up the ramp into the alley.

Once we were clear and making the turn onto 14th Street, she said, "They don't know I'm a blogger."

I said, "Clearly, or they'd put you in charge. What's a blog slammer again?"

She scowled at me and punched the gas; skateboarders went scattering, screaming obscenities. She careened around the corner and headed for the nearby onramp to Interstate 80, swerving around little cars with rainbow stickers and massive SUVs.

She glared at me. She said, "You're good at this."

"I'm good at most things. What am I good at this time?"

She hit the onramp doing forty, swerving around cars. She said, "Psychological warfare, Frosty."

"Don't call me that, and… thanks?"

"If you ever decide to work for the forces of good, you'd make a hell of a blogger."

Now I *really* almost punched her in the face.

She said, "Maybe even a video blogger."

I said, "Over my dead body."

"You could make an impact if you tell what you know."

I said, "You know what I know? The world's a fucked-up place."

She said, "You helped make it that way."

"That'd be an awful lot of responsibility for one guy."

"In dreams *begin* responsibilities," she said chidingly.

"You know," I said. "If I really am a baby-killer, you might not want to antagonize me."

She blew clove smoke at me.

"I have to, Frosty. You're into bad shit. I want you to know how deep it gets."

I looked her up and down and said,, "Pretty deep, apparently."

She said, "Do you know what's in the back of this truck? You think it's—what? Guns, drugs, gold? Stinger missiles?"

I said, "No, and I don't want to know."

She said, "Bodies. Frozen bodies."

I leaned in close and whispered conspiratorially, "Porn stars who got caught blog slamming?"

She went seven shades of red. She blew clove smoke at me furiously.

She said, "Your bosses don't want to die."

I said, "Who does?"

She said, "*Ever.*"

I said, "Who does?"

She said, "Virgil Amaro and his cronies want to bring about the End Times."

I said, "Look, they're a little hot on the Christian Zionism, sure. But their hearts are in the right place. As are their wire transfers."

She said, "I don't think you get my meaning, Frosty. They want to *cause* the End Times. And profit from them."

I said, "Huh?"

"They want to bring about the end of the world." Lupe was getting swiftly worked up. She foamed at the mouth, blowing clove smoke and spattering drool. She said, "They're not happy waiting for the End Times to happen. They want to make them happen, ensure that they're protected so they can survive the Trials, and profit from them." She was as pink as her dreads. "Oh, don't get me wrong, Frosty. I'm all for it. The human race *must* depopulate, if the planet is to survive. But these assholes want to depopulate everyone *else*, and live forever themselves. They're willing to break the laws of biology to ensure their own eternal life! That's fucking crazy, Dante, that's crazy!"

I told her, "Say it, don't spray it."

She took great heaving breaths and said, "They don't care who they have to hurt."

I squared my shoulders and growled, "Are you on the list? 'Cause I'll sign up for that."

She gave me a sour look. "Yes, or I will be. If you tell them I talked to you. You wanna get rid of me? Go ahead. There'll be a thousand more of me tomorrow."

I said, "I doubt that. But don't worry, I won't narc on your buggery. That's not my style. I'm hired on a per-contract basis. I don't owe these douchebags shit."

She gave a disgusted laugh, "That's the spirit, Frosty. God Bless America. Maybe someday I can find the cash to have you fight on *my* side? What would it cost me to buy your soul—a hundred thousand?"

"That depends," I said. "Would I have to blog?" I traced the wisps of her clove smoke, huffing it but trying not to *look* like I was huffing it. I said, "If you're so outraged about what they're selling my asshole bosses, why don't you alert the Coast Guard?"

She said, "They already know. They've been paid off."

I said, "The Coast Guard?" Now I knew she was seriously off the deep end. I've met those cats. They recycle their tinfoil.

She shook her head. "Not the Coast Guard. Higher than them. Much higher. This conspiracy goes to the highest levels of government, Frosty. And not just the U.S. government—the world government."

I whispered, "Bilderbergs?"

She chortled.

"Sure, you could call them that, but only if you don't know that the Bilderberg organization is a sock of the Illuminati."

I said, "*Claro*," I said. "And I bet it stinks."

She said, "I'm serious! It's all the same bullshit patriarchal, privileged white male feudal colonialist first-world thinking, Frosty. Everything's about acquiring more resources and spending them to prove your dick's bigger. It's like this Lloyd Strong fucker who started Paradise. I mean… increase the human lifespan? You believe that shit?"

I said, "I know! Doesn't he know us smart guys are trying to shorten it?"

She brightened, "Yeah, I know, right? I mean, people in the first world can't just live forever. It's exactly that kind of bullshit that's gonna sink this planet. We live longer and longer and longer, and keep having babies, and the whole planet's just gonna disintegrate. I mean, huh, 'Paradise Life Extension'? Bullshit. How about 'Inferno Life Abbreviation'?"

"Hell," I said. "I'd invest in that shit. It's my skill set."

"That's what I'm saying! Like *Logan's Run*!"

"Aw, come on," I said. "Floating in the air? That's fruity. Much easier ways to accomplish the same end."

She said, "It's not crazy. Everyone lives to a predetermined age, then—come on, don't look at me like that. Everyone's gotta go sometime. May as well be voluntary!"

I said, "See, there's where you lose me, Lupe. Take the West Grand Exit."

As she exited, she pleaded with me: "Don't think I'm some weirdo. Listen to me, Frosty. The only thing that can bring down the Amaros is if men and women of conscience come forward and bring it down. Men like you, Frosty. Heroes. People who have fought for democracy—"

I said, "I fight for a paycheck."

"—and against terrorists, Frosty—it's time to fight the real terrorists. Join me! Blog with me!"

I said, "You had me at 'fight the real terrorists,' but you lost me at 'Blog with me.' You San Francisco people gotta work on your revolutionary rhetoric or everyone is just going to point at you and laugh. And I fight whoever's unlucky enough not to have a healthy bank account, you punk freak."

She howled angrily: "I'm not punk! I'm Candy Commando!"

I said, "Is that your name?"

"It's a movement!"

I sighed. I said, "Back up to the gate here at Yard 23, will you?"

She did. She sulked in silence, smoking at me. Her slow-burning cig was almost gone; she'd seriously bogarted that shit.

I got out.

The Malaysian hands of the *God's Glory* had been hired from an Argentinean maritime personnel service. Travelling without papers, they had been instructed not to leave the port. Now they flooded around us, smoking American cigarettes and wearing Bruce Springsteen T-shirts. I opened the back of the bread truck and helped them guide the crates onto carts for transfer to the cargo elevator.

Some of those crates were pretty cold on the outside.

When everything was loaded, I found Lupe leaning up against the driver's side of the truck, looking green against her dreads, her booted feet crossed jauntily, spent clove coffin nails scattered around them.

I looked at her. She glared at me.

"Thanks for the ride," I told her.

"Don't play Han Solo with me, asshole. I know your rep."

I said, "That makes one of us."

"I know about Fallujah."

That got my attention.

I told her, "That makes one of us."

"I know about Karen Klein and the Wolf Women's Academy," she said.

I told her, with a dull and savage menace: "That makes one of us."

"You're a real warrior, Dante Bogart. What I can't figure is why you're fighting on the wrong side."

"'Cause the other side's got haphazard fashion sense, *Ms.* Guadalupe Grope."

She crushed out her last clove cigarette and stalked up to me and got in my face.

"I know guys like you. I slap 'em around all the time."

"When you're not mopping up lube?"

She said, "You *want* to be a hero, Dante. I can tell. You *want* to fight for the right side. When you do, I'll be waiting to help you."

She rammed her finger into my chest.

If a guy had done that, I would have been duty-bound to break it.

But I didn't do that.

She told me, "And when you do come around, you'll be my hero."

I said, "Goody."

She backed to the driver's door, opened it, stood at attention and saluted me. "Awaiting orders, asshole. Your move."

Then she flipped me off with both hands, and disappeared back into the truck.

I shook my head.

I asked a Malaysian sailor: "Does everyone from San Francisco talk in riddles?"

He asked me, "*Que?*"

☠

Van said: "Hey, asshole! You're kissing my wife!"

Trixie's eyes roved as I pressed my lips to hers.

Her eyes went wide and crazy, swirling, spinning, gyrating. Her lips trembled.

I felt the air escaping as her lungs contracted violently.

He started forward. I waved the pistol, vaguely, and he stopped. I kept kissing her as the expulsions of air got stronger, more aggressive, until with a violent spasm of her body, she surged upward and bit.

I'd pulled away at the very last instant; Trixie was reaching for me, her body going rigid.

She tried to lunge up and bite me, but her muscles were weak. The knots held, but barely.

I looked at Van with distrust.

I said, "You still can't tie knots worth shit, probably, huh?"

He looked wounded. He said, "What the hell are you talking about? I tie knots just fine! I'm a friggin' boy scout!"

She lunged up with greater force and snapped her teeth together. The laughing had started in earnest. She chortled. She brayed.

I got her ankles tied; she was pulling so hard she made the bed shake.

Van said, "Holy Christ."

Trixie surged up against the ropes.

The whole room shook as she thrashed on the bed.

She screamed at the top of her lungs.

She howled.

I said, "It's better if we leave her now. She'll quiet down if there's no one in her immediate vicinity."

He looked at me, furious, ready to kill.

Van said sadly, disbelieving: "What did you do, Dante?"

I said, "Maybe nothing. Let's go have a drink."

☠

I made Van get out glasses and Scotch. I made him pour.

In the sickroom, Trixie howled.

I poured. I hoisted my glass. I nudged his at him across the table.

"Let's drink to Trixie."

"To her life or her death?" His voice caught.

I said, "Always drink to someone's life. But if she does die, it was a brave death. She was trying to help that kid."

Van glanced at the sickroom, his face red with anger. "The way I see it, that wasn't brave, it was *stupid*."

I raised my glass high.

"Then let's drink to that. That's the way I see it, too. That's why without her, you and I are monsters."

"Come again?"

I said, "Just something a very dumb man told me once."

He drank to that.

Trixie howled. Van winced. I made him pour again. He said, "Dante, I'll never understand how a douchebag like you got hooked up with a number like that."

I said, "Neither do I."

We clinked our tumblers and slammed our Scotch.

This time he made the bad-Scotch sound—which is kind of a glottal explosion midway between the Panama Laugh, a scream of ripe agony and a profoundly furtive howl of forbidden carnal pleasure.

He looked at the gun.

"You plan to explain yourself, Bubba?"

I put it down on the table. I said, "It's a little complicated."

"Not unlike our mutual paramour," he said, jerking his head toward the sickroom. "And this ray gun of yours."

He picked it up and peered at it disapprovingly.

"Would you have shot me?"

I said, "Probably not. I couldn't even punch your lights out."

"That's right," he chortled. "You couldn't."

That wasn't what I meant, but it seemed like splitting hairs at this point.

Van said, "Where I come from, if a gun fits in one hand it's made out of metal and wood. It's either got a cylinder, or it's a .45. Or else it's fruity European shit. This crap you idiots carry nowadays—it's space-age. It's weird, Dante. It's not natural. How the hell does anyone keep track of all these moving parts?"

"I ask myself that a lot lately."

He looked at me with sympathy.

"So explain a few of 'em," he said. "You say it's complicated. Does it have something to do with that kiss?"

"What else would it have anything to do with?"

"I don't know, that coulda been, just like, what Trixie calls a 'behavioral tic.' You do kinda have *sexual issues*, Dante. The kiss coulda just been you being *fixated* or something."

"It wasn't."

"Is it going to cure her?"

I shook my head sadly. "I'm not sure."

Trixie laughed in the bedroom, the sound growing slowly while Van and I listened, both too horrified to plug our ears or walk away or talk over it.

When she quieted down a little, Van grinned weakly across the table.

He said, "You ever try that shit with me, *compañero*, I want plenty of tongue. And do you mind tweaking my nipples a little? I'm really into that."

I said, "That's not funny."

"The tongue or the nipples?"

I said, "The nipples were kind of funny. But I've had plenty of tongue for now."

He said, "Aw, come on, *vato*. I thought the new Frosty Bogart was comfortable being vulnerable in front of his friends."

Trixie laughed at the top of her lungs, violent uncontrolled guffaws mingling with sobs shaking Casa Fish to its foundation. She wept savagely, then laughed again.

I said, "Yeah, I'll get to that. Things are coming back to me. But you talk first. I remember Colón now."

"The rest of the world remembers it, too. But no one's quite sure what happened."

"Catch me up on what happened to you," I said. "The night I gave you Trixie."

He said, "Gave me Trixie?"

I said, "Sorry. Slip of the tongue. I didn't mean it like that."

He frowned at me. "Well. Don't let her hear you make that slip."

I growled, "*Claro*. Now *spill*."

He remembered out loud.

☠

There were things I hadn't told Van and Trix over MacTavish because I didn't remember them. I was only getting my memory back in bits and pieces as I watched people and things die around me.

The memories poured into my brain, all mixed up with the death and the fever dreams. I couldn't always be sure what was real and what wasn't. I didn't always know whether it really happened to me or if I just saw it on YouTube.

The days and hours leading up to my incarceration and relocation to the Darién Gap had started as fuzzy streams of nothing, awful things happening beyond a curtain of night. The curtains were parting, but there were too many missing pieces.

Van filled in a few of them.

☠

Van had found Trixie wrapped up in my ancient blanket reading *Guns &*

Ammo and crying on the sand. He said ¡Hola!; she called him an asshole and demanded an immediate ride to Colón. They argued for a while on the beach. He told her he'd take her to Colón. Trixie hoisted her batiked hippie skirt and waded onto the *Speedy Gonzales.*

He took her instead to Isla Pescado, which kinda pissed her off.

She told him she'd have him arrested for kidnapping.

He said, "This is Kuna Yala. The Panamanian cops aren't even sure how to get here. The Kuna elders have jurisdiction, and I'm their *pal*. I'm a hero to the Kuna nation. They call me *Hombre Mantequilla Borracho* —it means 'Great Hero With Plane.'"

It doesn't mean "Great Hero With Plane," but Trixie apparently didn't tell him that. She told him, instead, that I was clearly unhinged and needed psychiatric help. I was violent.

He told her, "Dante's crazy and violent? Are you sure? He's also not that smart, or haven't you noticed? Also very lazy, and he almost never pays attention when you lecture him. Oh, and does that asshole *ever* wash a dish?"

She decided she liked him.

Van had plenty of beer, and his island did indeed have a smoke monster. Trixie chilled; they got blasted; she played him "Tangled Up in Blue" on Van's beat-up Washburn, clucking and tsking over its condition. She explained the complicated provenance of her name—Trixie as a nickname for Beatrice being only part of the story. They argued politics a little, said Van, but got along pretty well on the political front since unlike me, Van said, he's always been basically left of center, a Libertarian opposing monolithic corporate and governmental control but not exactly advocating Trixie's exact brand of socialism from a government model but more in the form of, say, cooperative weed farms and worker-owned sex toy collectives.

He and Trixie had not slept and were still slightly baked about an hour before dawn when Van remembered that I'd made some vague cryptic remark about how he should check his freaky conspiracy forums at daybreak or something.

Trixie told him he was nuts for believing that stuff, until he laid down some crap that blew totally blew her mind. Trixie had never realized the Illuminati were so involved in Saudi politics.

They figured they should check to see what lunacy had led me to kidnap her and start spewing conspiracy crap to Van; Trixie got upset when she remembered that I'd had blood on my clothes. Maybe I'd really killed someone.

"He said they were bad guys," she said. "You think?"

"Unless it was animal blood," Van told her.

Trixie sobbed, "Sure! Just a little voodoo! No big deal!"

He held her while she cried, the prick. She cheered up. They jawed for a while about what an idiot I was, and then decided to watch the sun rise.

Eventually, they both decided they were tired, but Van said, "No, man, don't crash now, you'll get a highover," so Trixie made coffee and bitched about his French press, while Van fired up his laptop and tweaked the satellite internet connection he'd jerry-rigged. It wasn't always stable. He couldn't always get a decent signal.

He got one this time.

Panama occupies a single time zone, the same one as the east coast of the United States. That means as the sun came up at Casa Fish, it was something like 2 a.m. in San Francisco, where the Purgatorio servers were located, along with most of their followers and hangers-on. The Fogtown wingnuts were just getting back from their long nights out spanking each other at metasexual orgies with LEDs glued to their private parts. It was prime time for looney-tunes and conspiracy nuts.

Isla Pescado is in the same time zone as Colón. But Colón is on the central stretch of the North coast of Panama, whereas Isla Pescado is far to the East off the coast near the Colombian border. The sun rises there roughly twenty minutes earlier than in Colón.

Which meant they watched that shit virtually as it happened.

They might even have been among the first to see the video upload from user **NotBobDenard** that started: "My name is Dante Bogart. I used to be a military contractor…"

And they were among the first and *only* to see the news stories linked from the forums:

American Security Firm Assaults the Beaumont Colón.

They saw the posts, Van remembered; from guys named **NotFoxMulder** and **NotLorenColeman**—"Is it related to *this* video?"—and someone had matched the wall-sized print of the Gatun locks visible behind me in the video to a photo on Flickr of someone's vacation pictures taken at the Beaumont Lemon Bay—"Panamanian television reports terrorist attack in Colón,"—and footage from a boat of the Beaumont on fire—"Canal locked down"—and the windows blown out on the top floor—"American-Owned Panamanian firm involved in Colón slaughter"—and screenshot of the Bellona Industries site—"Gatun locks under military control"—and a high-res US Army photo of me in desert camo with my hand in front of my face—"Lago Gatun patrolled by black copters"—"Death in Colón—American contractor involved?"—screenshots of a rape investigation in Fallujah—screenshots of my face visible in the back window of an Apache over a Philippine Air Force base—"Security footage from the Beaumont Colón," promised as "Hacked from the NSA computer"—and ten-second clips of guys being thrown down stairs—some with their faces ripped off, others *broken in half*—"Satellite footage"—the Beaumont burning—"Counterinsurgency?"—shots of a copter landing on the helipad on atop the Beaumont—"Images from Google Earth," a fleet of copters chopping through black smoke pouring out of the top floor—and then the bullshit started—mashups, remixes, my face saying "My name is Dante Bogart" over and over again as I sang out the Hamster Dance and conspiracy theories came everywhere—

And then the Purgatorio servers crashed.

Van told me the operators would later claim that they had been subjected to what looked like a simple Denial of Service attack of Russian origin—Vladivostok—but that was a total red herring. They would discover, later, that their servers had been targeted by a series of Trojan-infected zombies scattered throughout—wait for it—Panama City.

My video was gone.

The footage of the Beaumont was gone.

The satellite shots of the place on fire were gone.

So was most of the thirteenth floor.

None of it was ever seen again, except the thirteenth floor which was rebuilt with a plaque in the room where a Yemeni national with Chechen connections named Abdel Mahari had blown himself up in an attempt to rig a suicide bomb vest. His final destination? The Gatun locks—long an expected terrorist target.

The plot was foiled by American contractors employed by the Beaumont Resort Group as counter-terrorism consultants: Carpenter Associates.

The Russians pledged full cooperation. Eighty-four suspected co-plotters were arrested across Chechnya, Dagestan, Ingushetia, South Ossetia; Yemen arrested half a dozen. The Georgians protested. The Chechens protested. The French protested. No one gave a fuck.

The Ramirez Group received a fat contract for border security on the Georgian border with Chechnya.

Barnes Enterprises got a multi-million-dollar counter-insurgency gig in Yemen.

McDonald Consulting cashed in with a contract to train a new Panamanian counter-terrorism force with a U.S. government grant, in return for expanded access to the Gatun Locks for U.S.-flagged shipping during peak times.

I said to Van, "How do you even *know* those names, *vato*?"

Van grinned and nodded proudly at the laughing Trixie.

"She's got a Master's in Public Health, *vato*. She's a whiz with the *epidemiology*."

☠

The video was gone, but rumors of it continued. Some people had bootlegs. They uploaded. Inexplicable outages followed the video around the net like a bad smell.

A few days later, it showed up again—but it was different. It wasn't what Van and Trixie remembered seeing. It wasn't what the Purgatorio people had seen. It had been changed, and there were dozens more like it.

The Dante Bogart Project.

An avalanche of sock puppets posted the three-to-five-minute videos on conspiracy sites worldwide.

Van asked, "Did you know my Mom used to be in movies?"

I growled, "I was too polite to say anything."

Van sneered, "Not those kind of movies, Bubba. She was a makeup artist on sci-fi flicks… acted a little, too. I know a little something about filmmaking, and I gotta say, I think it'll be hard for you to see, but there's some decent production values in these ones."

I said, "Yeah. I think it'll be hard for me to see."

The craze caught fire. I went viral.

Soon everyone was watching them and leaving comments like "LOL!" and "LMFAO" and "ROFL" and "spooky!" and "awesum!" and "Iz this sh*t real?"

The videos were shot in hotel rooms, caves, basements. At first they featured me, dolled up in Living Dead drag and shot like up close at my eyes in a fish-lensed, bleating Blair Witch proclamations of certain death, my voice distorted.

"Here," said Van, dragging over Trixie's laptop. "She's got 'em book-marked. Watch."

There I was, in the Beaumont, in a noise-choked video, fuzzy, choppy. Like this:

I said: "My name is Dante Bogart. I used to be a military contractor…

For the last five years, I have been employed on a project to acquire exotic viral and bacterial agents and advanced biological warfare materials from third-world sites, foreign research facilities and terrorist paragovernmental black sites facilities with the intention of developing viral-based radical life extension technology for both offensive and defensive military application—"

The video fuzzed. I started laughing insanely, spewing ragged distorted fragments of the Panama Laugh.

I yowled: "... on behalf of a US-owned shell corporation owned by the Japanese Aum Shinrikyo Buddhist syncretistic terrorist cult, in an attempt to exterminate the human race. I don't have long; I'm sick with the creeping death... soon I will be a monster—a monster, I tell you, a slave to the laughing death—what began as my personal fight against global Islamic terrorism has become an all-out assault not just on the American Way—but on the human race—ha ha ha! I'm going! I'm going! Brains! I need brains!"

More fuzz. More cuts. Screams. My eyes big and bloodshot, my face slick with monster-makeup in the fish-eyed lens, cackling wildly, getting up in the camera's face, huffing and puffing through whiteface and stage blood as I howled out the Panama Laugh.

I vanished. The vid cut to a clean-cut announcer in steampunk togs: *Augie Amaro* smoking a meerschaum pipe.

"Oh, man," I said. "*That* asshole? Add insult to injury, why don't you?"

Augie deadpanned: "The recent attempted terrorist attack on the Panama Canal reminded us that global security is everyone's problem. Nations and administrations that refuse to secure their borders or do their part in fighting the murderous thugs that seek to destroy our world—these can no longer be tolerated. The fight against global religious terrorism is more important than ever. The threat is not restricted to a single ideology, or a set of beliefs. The Axis of Evil we face is that of all nations and groups that seek to oppose global progress, pluralism and peace."

"Oh, for fuck's sake," I said.

Van said, "That's a great clock on his top hat, though."

I glared at him.

Augie said: "My generation will have to face this threat and win. But now we know that the threat may be greater than we have ever imagined, almost like something out of a science fiction movie. What you're about to see is footage of—well, creatures—in the jungles of the Darién Gap along the Panama-Colombia border. Sensitive viewers should probably stop watching now."

The footage cut to sepia children dressed in rags, painted with latex head wounds, laughing hysterically: "*Monstruo! Monstruo! Nosotros somos los muertos que viven! Somos monstruos!*"

The adorable zombie children tucked in to a howling band of extras, complete with crappy latex entrails.

A series of close-ups followed. The kids ate candy disguised to look like guts and faces and brains.

Van said, "See what I mean? Pretty good production values. That's all I'm saying."

☠

Restrained, howling, laughing and sobbing uncontrollably, I yanked at the pale canvas medical restraints so violently I dislocated my shoulders.

They popped back into place and I started all over again.

It's not that I *didn't* feel the pain. It's that the pain was irrelevant compared to my crazy-weeping howling need for flesh, and how fuckin' *funny* this all was.

It came hammering back to me. Memories. I heard Virgil: "It doesn't make medical sense."

Luke: "Dad, none of this makes medical sense."

A third voice, female: "The latest rounds of salivary extractions aren't showing anything. *Anything.*"

Virgil: "That's impossible."

"His body has actually *cleared* the prior strains."

Virgil: "Ava, that's impossible."

She said bitterly: "You may call me *Doctor* Sorzano."

"I'll call you what I want to call you. We isolated the original strain. There's no question that he got this by bite. It's *there*. If it's not in saliva, where is it?"

Luke, sounding annoyed: "Stomach juices?"

Ava: "Viruses don't just skip around the body randomly as they mutate. Besides, we tried that."

Luke, yawning: "Try it again."

Virgil said: "So now you're an infectious disease specialist?"

"You're right," said Luke testily. "I'm not qualified. So… why am I here?"

"Sure. Take off. Go make a movie or something."

Luke made a petulant noise and vanished.

Virgil approached me tentatively. I laughed at him. I *leapt* for him.

My shoulders popped out of their sockets again; I strained against the cuffs and felt my hips going. They popped. I sobbed in pain. I wrenched them harder. My wrists, too: shoulders, neck. Joints popped all over my body. Virgil backed away from me.

The woman said: "Jesus fucking Christ. He's still going."

Virgil whirled on her.

"Watch it. His judgment shall be upon you."

"Dante's?"

"Christ's!" he practically screamed it.

The woman said: "Sorry."

I LOLed.

Virgil said, "I'm paying you well."

The woman said, "I know."

"Then solve the puzzle. Why's he sick? Why's he *alive*?"

"I'm not sure he is."

"Brain activity!" snapped Virgil. "The others don't have it. Bogart's alive, the others are dead. The neurologists say—"

"—damn it, I know what the neurologists say, Virgil—"

"—watch your language! They say he's got *more* brain activity than we do, not less. How else do you define life?"

"But it's not *normal* brain activity. It's selective. Specific responses. Specific emotions. Specific *cravings*. It's not epilepsy, but it seems to be related."

"Are you a epileptologist now?"

"Go to hell."

"Watch your language! Our Mayo contact already ruled out epilepsy."

"Virgil," said the doctor, "This project is not what I signed up for. I'm not trained for this. I'm not emotionally prepared for this. Emotionally, morally, ethically."

"Ethically?" He guffawed. "No problem. We'll just contact the Sonoma County District Attorney and—"

"God damn it! You're really going to play it that way?" she said.

"Yes, and watch your language. Come up with an answer."

"All right," she said. "There's one possibility."

"I'm all ears, Ava."

No more protestations that he could call her *Doctor Sorzano*. She took a deep breath.

"We've already established he's not presenting with exactly the symptoms of the test subjects. The strength, the... extreme... uh... the *difficulty* in killing him, the rapid regeneration. None of the test subjects showed that. They were very durable, but they didn't *regenerate*, as such. If they got cut, they stayed cut. They got gangrene. Their whole bodies got necrotic in a matter of hours. Plus, they weren't aware. They didn't ever *get* aware, no matter how long we kept them on ice…"

Virgil said: "*He's* not aware."

The woman said: "If we define life as brain activity, let's define Dante as… *reactive*, in a way the others weren't. And his condition is changing. He's not deteriorating, he's getting more… complicated."

"Tell me something I don't know."

"He's not infected with a new virus."

Virgil said: "What?"

"We've been looking for a needle in a haystack. All there is… is hay."

"Clearly we just haven't isolated the strain yet."

"I don't think so."

"What are you saying?"

"His DNA's been rewritten."

I screamed at the top of my lungs, cackling, then sobbing.

"That's ridiculous," said Virgil.

I thought so, too; I howled with laughter. I hooted. I sniggered. I chortled. I threw my head back and forth with such violence I could feel a couple of vertebrae slipping. Now *that* was some funny-ass shit.

The stainless steel table groaned beneath me.

"That's ludicrous. His DNA—it can't—he's been—at a cellular level? He's been changed into *this*?"

"There are precedents in nature," said the doctor.

"I seriously doubt that," said Virgil.

"Not direct precedents."

"Or anything *like*, I should think."

The doctor said: "Okay, okay, you're right. I'm stretching the boundaries of documented science, yes. But then, I have a ward full of patients without pulses or brain activity, laughing. This is the best I can come up with."

"We already sequenced him," said Virgil.

"I know."

"Let's sequence him again," said Virgil.

"I agree. That'd be a start. But I doubt we'll find anything we can use," the doctor said. "It's not like we have specific genes to test for. Plus, if my guess turned out to be right, we'd be aiming for a moving target. I'm willing to bet his DNA is still changing."

Virgil said, "If you're right—would it be transmissible?"

"How should I know? The result *has* to be some combination of the strains, though. Possibly in combination with some other virus he had been exposed to—possibly years ago—that the others were not. If the catalyst virus was a common one, then others would be vulnerable to this syndrome—whatever it is. So my guess is that it's an exotic virus. But which one?"

Virgil sounded stunned and depressed.

"I've sent this guy all over the world," he said. "He could have anything. We don't even *know* what emerging diseases he might have been exposed to. It could be something no doctor on Earth is aware of. Maybe not even a virus. A prion."

"I doubt that."

"But it could be anything."

"Not anything," said the doctor. "It has to be something the others have never been exposed to. But with such a small sample size, there is a lot they won't have been exposed to. It's way beyond looking for a needle in a haystack now. We can narrow the possibilities down, but... it'll take months. Years. The chances of finding it are slim. I'd need his travel records."

"Those records are confidential."

"So's my brother's police record, asshole. And if you're trying to close the barn door now, It's a bit late. You think I don't know what kind of crap you're involved in? You'll probably have me killed the second I'm no longer useful."

"Ava, don't talk like that. After what we've shared together?"

"Yes," said the doctor. "Sexual harassment can be so intimate."

OhmiGod, that was fucking hilarious. I'd figured out how to twist my body just so and smack my funny bone against the side of the table, which hurt so good I screamed with laughter.

Then I started sobbing.

"I really wonder if he'll have memories," said the doctor.

"When?" asked Virgil.

"If he recovers."

Virgil thought *that* was hilarious. I joined him, transitioning seamlessly from Crier to Laugher. Like going from an ordnance specialist to a marksman: easy as pie, *vato*.

When Virgil was done laughing, they stood there watching me crack my joints every place they could be cracked; they heard me laugh until I was out of breath and my muscles went slack. I just choked for a while.

"I should aspirate him," said the doctor urgently.

"No," said Virgil. "If this—theory of yours —"

"It's not a theory," the doctor interrupted him. "It's not even a hypothesis. It's barely speculation."

"What is it, then?"

"Crazy," she said.

"Quit splitting hairs," said Virgil. "So… let's assume what's happened to Dante derives from a combination of strains, plus some unknown quantity that existed in his bloodstream. Something rare enough that it doesn't show up in any of our test populations. Would it then be possible to take some other strain and do the reverse?"

"The reverse of what?"

"Use a *common* virus? Something that exists in most of the population already? Reactivate something already there?"

That was a screamer. I howled. I laughed; I popped joints. I went limp and lay there panting, spent.

The doctor said, "Don't be ridiculous. We don't even know what connection between the strains caused what's happening here, to Bogart."

Virgil said, "Not what's happening to him. What's happened to *them*."

There was a big long empty.

When the doctor spoke, her voice was quavering.

"Virgil, you're scaring me."

"That's my job," said Virgil defiantly. "I run a security firm. It's my job to anticipate threats."

"I don't even want to think about it. If that happened—well, what would activate it? It would burn itself out fast—like the Hantaviruses; outbreaks are limited, because mortality is so high. They don't have time to spread. Unless it were—"

"Dormant? Airborne?"

She'd turned her morals off and her brain back on.

She said, "No, not dormant or airborne—it would have to be both. I mean *activated*."

"By a signal?" he said.

"Like a wireless signal? Don't be stupid. Organisms don't act like that. Next thing you know you'll tell me cancer comes from cell phones."

"A seasonal virus?"

"Cold and flu season," said the doctor breathlessly.

"It would hit the world all at once."

"It's not the same season everywhere on the globe. But maybe it wouldn't have to be. One climate zone might be enough. Once the initial disease engine was dispersed worldwide, it would—if it started—it could start in the tropics and—"

Her voice caught; her heart, or her soul, seemed to realize the depth of the nightmare her brain had just contemplated.

"This sounds like a plausible scenario."

"I'm not going to answer," said the doctor.

"Plausible enough for my contact at USAMRIID to front it to DOD. I'll get CDC to take it to Justice and DHS on the domestic front. They won't like it—"

"*I* don't like it," said the doctor.

Virgil talked over her: "—so you'll have to make it good. Write it up, Ava—in detail."

"Virgil, I won't discuss this. It's a nightmare."

Virgil's tone became chiding: "Now, Ava. Would you like terrorists to get hold of something like that?"

There was another long empty, bigger than the last, as Ava thought about that.

I panted and whined, my tortured weeping starting at a very low volume.

"No," said the doctor. "Of course not."

"Then you'd *better* think about that. Think about it with all of your grey matter, doctor, and then you and your team had better figure out *exactly* how it could be done—so we know how to prevent it. Because if *you* can think about it, so can the Iranians or North Koreans. Or weren't you satisfied losing your husband and child in the Towers? You want other wives and mothers to lose their kids to *this*?"

The doctor was crying—softly at first, then a whiny, twisted sob.

"No."

"Then it sounds to me like you'd better write this up. If we don't get that contract, some other idiots will. My contacts at Defense say after Libya they're preparing multiple black-budget RFQs for speculative bioterrorism interdiction. You think you're the smartest person in the world? If you thought it up…"

"You're right," she said softly, weeping. "Of course you're right."

I yanked at my cuffs till my flesh tore.

I thought: *Virgil, right? Now that's a good one.*

☠

Some time later, the doctor said, "Bogart's cleared the virus. All viruses."

Virgil scoffed. "*Cleared*? That seems impossible."

"It is. He's clean."

"What about things he had before? Colds, flu?"

"No."

"No? That's impossible."

The doctor said, "Sorry, Boss. He hasn't got a thing inside him except beneficial bacteria. Want to know the most interesting thing we found in his stool?"

"Not really," said Virgil. "And he's… alive."

The doctor: "Something like that."

"And the others?"

The doctor: "Gone."

"Laughers?"

"Some. Others cried. Others, just… gone. Except the one. That first one. He's also cleared the virus."

"What's different about him?"

"Nothing at all. We can't find *any* element that differentiates him from the others."

"He's the one Bogart threw out the window of the hotel?"

"… onto the pool canopy."

Virgil snapped his fingers. "He head-butted him. Did he do that to anyone else?"

"More like a Glasgow kiss," said the doctor. "I understand the injury was to the patient's upper lip."

There was a big long empty.

And Virgil said, "Kiss?"

☠

What happened next is vague, even now, in my memory. I remember the woman called in two big gents who held me down and I dislocated more joints and popped them back in trying to get free. She found a vein on my thigh that hadn't been turned to meat by needles being repeatedly broken off as I fought.

I went bye-bye.

I wakened later, much later. I stared up into the dark, feeling sad but no longer sobbing. There was some big strapping blonde Russian motherfucker bending over me, sticking his tongue in my mouth.

I knew he was Russian because when he finished saying hello, I saw he had his shirt off. His big burly body was dusted with the tattoos of a made man in the Russian mafia.

He said, "Thanks for the kiss, loverboy."

And I said, "You're welcome, asshole."

And he fell back as if smacked in the face. He went down on one knee and scrambled to his feet and looked down at me like he had seen a ghost. He stumbled back to the heavy metal door of my padded cell.

He started pounding on the door, never turning away from me.

And I said, "Sorry, shitbag. Did I freak you out? Honestly, things have been getting dull between you and me, Ivan. Let me outta bed and give me a crowbar; I'd like to put some spice back in our relationship."

Ivan screamed, "Guard!"

And I mocked, "Guard!"

And he screamed, "Guard!"

And I went, —POP—

—with my wrist bones and—yes, it hurt like hell, in case you're wondering, and—

Ivan screamed, "Guard!"

And I went, —POP—

—with the bones of my other wrist, and—yes, that hurt like hell, too, and there were screams of "Get them! Get the response team!" a woman's voice with a faint accent but nobody opened the door and Ivan screamed, "Guard!"

—and started sobbing uncontrollably, shoved up against the door—the prick was six-foot-five and blonde and Slavic, muscled all over and decorated with turbaned heads bragging how many Mujahedeen he'd killed—and he was not old enough to have done it in the Russian army—

—and I mocked, "Guard!"—

—and got the IV needle out of my arm and into the padlock on my wrist cuff and that wasn't big enough; I broke it off, so I yanked one out of my thigh and that was a larger gauge and slid right in sweet and easy and click-click-click, pins went, and I was out and off and dragging the hospital bed behind me like it was a ball and chain made out of plaster, and Ivan got up and put his dukes up like this was some kind of boxing match. I picked up the IV stand and came at him dragging the hospital bed like it was made out of styrofoam, spinning the IV stand like I was a baton-twirler.

Because Death had not stopped for me, I kindly came for him, howling,

"More kisses *now*, loverboy—"

With the Panama Laugh blasting out of my lungs.

☠

I said to Van, "Tell me about the Inferno."

He said, "When you released that first video, the group started getting worked up about it. They had that attack right away, but the vid was cached. They passed it around; they tried to distribute it. It kept getting taken down. Remember Wikileaks?"

I said, "Dimly."

"Well, Virgil remembered it, apparently. He must have learned from it. He had programs. They were like... I don't know, Dante. I'm not a computer person."

"Me, neither," I said.

"They called them *sniffers*, I guess. Programs that would find the video, based on its actual data signature. So the Inferno people changed the data... they changed the size, they made you different colors."

"Nice," I said.

"They put up transcripts; they translated; Virgil had people tracking the information down relentlessly. The Inferno people were quick, but Virgil was quicker. At first. Then they got smart."

"How?"

He grinned.

"DVDs, vato. Hand that shit out on a streetcorner. That worked pretty good for a little while."

I said, "And then?"

Van shrugged.

"Then the Amaros made better videos," he said. "They outed you as a hoax."

I listened to Trixie chortling in the sickroom.

I said, "Some hoax."

He said, "Look, Dante. I don't mean anything personal by this, but..."

I glared at him.

He said, "Don't blame the messenger, Bubba. But some of it's really a matter of *production values*."

☠

I asked him, "Van, am I evil?"

"Well… Frosty, you do kill people for a living. Is that evil?"

I said, "I don't know."

"Then I rest my case."

I said, "You've been talking to Trixie."

"She's my wife. That's kinda how it works."

I said, "I always told myself I was a soldier. That I was on the right side."

Van said, "Yeah, yeah, yeah, Fros. We've all heard it. So… who's side did you end up on?"

"Mine. Yours. Trixie's. Those Kuna kids. Anyone who doesn't try to fuck other people over. Does that make me evil?"

"From the sound of it," said Van, "It makes you a greeting card."

I told him to fuck off.

Trixie howled. She sobbed and laughed both. Sometimes at the same times. Sometimes we couldn't tell which she was doing.

It was just a few hours before I had to retie her. Van's knots were better than usual, but still crappy. If Trixie had been in her right mind, she probably would have gotten free. But she was not; she was a laugher.

I tied her tighter than before, while she laughed and strained and snapped her teeth at me.

Van wanted to feed her. He wanted to comfort her. He wanted to go in and caress her forehead and tell her he loved her and I was a prick. He got pretty mad at me for putting him through this, but ultimately he understood.

I told him, "Go ahead. Go in and mop her forehead. Just watch your fingers."

He did, and he did—but just once.

He spent three minutes. Trixie went nuts. She laughed. She cried. She tried to eat his face.

He came out pale and shaken.

"If I try to do that again," he said, "shoot me."

☠

"How is Dante cognitively? Is he coherent?"

Ava: "I gave him a gram of thiopental an hour ago. So… no."

"Did you say a *gram*?"

The Doctor: "A gram."

"That's impossible. He's *singing*."

She said tightly, "Of course. It's unheard of."

"What's he singing?"

"I don't know or care."

"Did he say 'The Sky is Crying'?"

"Sounds like it."

Virgil bent down and looked at me, shocked. I couldn't get my eyes to focus on him. The Doc was just a blur of white and smeared brunette with horn-rimmed glasses; I had never laid eyes on her, or at least couldn't have picked her out of a lineup.

Virgil looked in my eyes.

He said, "Bogart, where are you?"

I stopped singing. My head righted itself; my eyes swiveled; one eye open far more than the other, I saw Virgil as a swarm of lights and one frowning, pissed-off old man.

He slapped me. "Dante! Where are you?"

I said, "I'm with Gramps."

"Your grandfather? So you're dead?"

"I didn't say that. You did. Gramps was a *paisan*."

Virgil sneered, "*I'm a paisan.*"

I said, "You're a *pezzonovante* yegg. But Gramps was a gorilla. He served in the war. He was a guerilla. He lived in the jungle. He played the trumpet but he pissed off Glen Miller. They made him a gorilla. He slipped on many a banana."

Virgil said, "Dante, do you remember who I am?"

I said, "You sent me to Mars."

"I sent you to Libya."

"Libya, Mars… it's all red once you rock and roll a bit."

I laughed my ass off.

Dr. Ava Sorzano crouched down, peeled one of my eyelids back and aimed her penlight in my eye. "To answer your question," she said, "yes, it's basically impossible that he's conscious, let alone talking. But he's obviously incoherent."

"I think he's making *lots* of sense," said Virgil.

I surged up against the heavy straps and buckles of my straitjacket.

The doctor uttered a soft mewling whimper of terror and scrambled back. Virgil stayed in my face, glaring, grinning. His nose was within easy biting distance, but I didn't bite.

Virgil said, "When you say they sent you to Mars—you mean the military academy. After you were arrested for grand theft auto."

"Mars Military Academy," I said. "Mars was boring. There were guys with wings there, bad-ass cats, and flying Wolf Women. Sometimes we'd go to Barnard."

"Does pentothal usually cause this kind of confabulation?" Virgil asked.

Ava ignored him, but I responded as if I understood him: "I wish I could share it with this Sasquatch friend of mine."

"Sasquatch?"

"Bigfoot? He'd love this stuff. No more highovers. Bigfoot loves to party. If I'd known him back when they sent me to Mars…"

Virgil said, "He seems very suggestible."

The Doc said, "You think?"

Virgil turned on her, his voice a thunder of anger:

"Get Luke. Now! *Now!*"

The Doctor ran for the door. She buzzed to get out.

The door, opened, closed.

Virgil stood by it, grinning at me.

He said, "Dante, you just solved this week's PR nightmare. I'm gonna make you a star."

Dr. Sorzano came back.

"He really should rest," she said. "He's eventually going to lapse. I need the pentothal to keep him from biting, but—he can't stay awake forever."

Virgil said, "Keep him going."

"How?"

Virgil said, "We're in Colombia, right? Give him cocaine."

Ava said, "That's unethical."

Virgil guffawed: "But the rest of this isn't?"

Ava didn't like that much.

The key grated in the door.

Luke swam before me in a flannel robe, *pissed*.

He snarled, "Dad. It's 3 a.m.!"

Virgil cackled and said, "So have some espresso, George Lucas."

Luke hissed, "Don't call me that!"

Virgil said, "I'll call you whatever I darn well please. You're about to make a movie."

Luke looked pleased with himself. He said, "Finally. What genre?"

And his laughing father responded:

"Inspirational. You're making a recruitment video."

☠

Virgil Amaro died of cancer while I was away. His obituaries sang the praises of a self-made industrialist and American patriot who had championed private security in the third world. There was no specific mention of the events at the Beaumont Colón. Only *The Free Citizen* alluded to it:

> Scandals, including a Congressional inquiry, plagued the last year of Virgil Amaro's life, and he remains popular fodder for conspiracy theorists. But shortly after his death, his four sons succeeded in securing major international security contacts for Bellona subsidiaries with the U.S. Department of Defense and the State Department, as well as the governments of Georgia, Afghanistan, Iraq, Qatar, Panama, and Colombia.

Four sons? That had to be a typo.

Trixie'd written a big note on a printed-out copy of Virgil's obit from the *Times*, where she'd highlighted the ending line: "Interment arrangements for Mr. Amaro are being kept confidential."

She'd written, in Sharpie:

"Body?"

I thought about that while, thrashing in her sickbed, Trixie sobbed hysterically. She uttered an incoherent bawling: mourning without words.

I smelled the chemical stink of the marker, looked at her handwriting.

I mourned without words, a little, too.

I peered at Virgil's obit, hawked and spat on it.

Flights of angels, fucker.

In the sickroom, Trixie laughed.

☠

The day after Trixie got bit, I showered in the frigid luxury of Van's solar-powered misery-machine. Only Van Fish could build a solar-powered shower in the Caribbean islands of Panama and have the water come out colder than it started.

Van and I stacked bodies on the beach. We burned them with lighter fluid. Prevailing winds blew the barbecue stink north toward Jamaica, but plenty still swirled all around us.

Some people say it smells like pork. I'm not so sure about that. After a while, it's just another stink to stay upwind of—like *Chang'a* stills in Nairobi or open-pit toilets in Calcutta.

The Kuna kids, a dozen of them, came by for lunch—or, at least, that was their excuse. They really wanted to know if Van and I were still pointing guns at each other. We weren't. Van headed them off at the pass. He kept them on the beach on the far side, grilling fish that they'd caught. The smell of the burning laughers still permeated. He pointed at the oily smoke and said: "*Fuego. Desinfección.*"

Sia, a girl of about twelve, aimed her scared trembling finger at the oily black column and said, "*Monstruo?*"

Alei, her brother, told her, "*Si. Monstruo.* Don't worry, Dollface. *De nada.*"

Alei was the oldest of the Kuna kids—a boy of about fourteen. I noticed the first time I saw him that he had somewhat odd taste in clothes, wearing a narrow-brimmed yellow straw porkpie and a Demonio Azul T-shirt.

The "Blue Demon" was the world's greatest Luchadore, or Mexican Westler, so I figured the whole ensemble as a Van Fish selection. Van thought the biggest problem with Lucha Libre was that there was no practical way to incorporate monster trucks into it.

In addition to teaching him bad gangster slang, Van had given Alei a video-equipped handheld and the boy was forever making videos of himself and the other Kuna kids staging half-assed Lucha matches on the turf of Casa Fish.

Van thoroughly approved of such behavior, but predictably Trixie did not. She made them agree to adhere to a complex series of rules that made them learn respect for sportsmanship over violence. The resultant struggles of good vs. evil looked more like interpretive dance than serious fighting.

I laughed my ass off at that one. Good old Trixie.

As we burned the *Monstruos* on the beach, Alei asked me:

"Doctor Dollface okay, Bubba?"

Van tried to say something brave; he couldn't.

He finally said, "*No sé.*" *I don't know.*

Alei said, "She *gonna be* okay?"

"*No sé,*" Van repeated.

A minute later, Van excused himself, mumbling: "I'll go check on her."

I was left staring at a quartet of Kuna boys awkwardly.

I grumbled, "*Hola!*"

Alei jerked his head toward Casa Fish. He said sadly, "Bubba dizzy with the sawbones, *vato.*"

I said, "Huh?"

"Van loves Doctor Trixie very much," he said. He had trouble with the X in her name.

"*Claro*," I growled. "He's funny that way."

We frowned at each other.

Alei brightened. He said, "Hey, that was a pretty good Lucha earlier."

I thought he meant with the pirates. I said, "Huh?"

He mocked punches. "I love her! I love her more! Take that! And that! *Como esta*, Bubba? *Como esta* this, douchebag!"

Alei's four or five friends giggled and tittered.

I said, "Kid, don't even start with me."

He held up his handheld. "I shot some video, want to see?"

"I don't think so," I said.

His friends did; they crowded around and watched it on his handheld for a few minutes while I sat there at Van's picnic table and drained my Balboa. I listened to myself saying "*What, no buenos dias?*" and thought, "Do I really sound that nasal?"

When the video was over they laughed and mocked punches at each other, faking hits and yowling "*Como esta!*" as they went down. They spoke some Spanish, but no English. Maybe when they got older, Alei could teach them the Douchebag dialect, which apparently was what Van had taught him.

Still laughing, Alei said, "You and Mister Van fight over Dollface?"

I said, "Eh?"

"Doctor Trixie." He had trouble with the X again.

I said, "Si. Kind of. I was being an assh—uh… I was being *loco*."

"*Gringo loco*?" asked Alei. "Maybe you need a head shrinker?" He looked pleased with himself.

I said, "Maybe."

"Dollface doesn't let us fight like that."

"Good for her," I growled. "You shouldn't fight. That's how guys get messed up."

Alei said, "Aw, don't be a daisy! You and Bubba made it through okay."

I deadpanned, "Yeah, but we were messed up to begin with."

Alei laughed his ass off and said: "*Claro!*"

His friends mocked punches and pratfalls and giggled: "*Como esta!*"

☠

Trixie laughed louder than ever. When I looked in on her, she busted a gut and tried to break her own bones to get to me.

Her body grew filthy. We couldn't risk changing her clothes or cleaning her. Her teeth were sharp, and she was hungry.

It hurt to look at her.

But then, it hurt her to look at *me*, because every time she did she popped her shoulders out of their sockets, trying to rip herself free and kill me. I got nauseous just watching it happen, because every time she did I remembered another long sequence of pop-ow-pop-ow-pop-ow when I'd howled out the same dark Panama Sob as Trixie Fish was doing right now.

Crying came easy to me now.

So I gave it a whirl, and ended up laughing.

Like Grampa Bogart told me in one of his many pointless lectures on comedy: *Laugh till you cry; cry till you laugh. Sometimes it bends that way, Danny Boy.*

And sometimes it breaks.

☠

Tortured by the sound of Trixie's suffering, Van asked about gagging her.

I got it in a flash. I remembered, distant through pentothal and LOLs: "*Disease progression was arrested at the acute stage in vocal cordectomized patients. Such patients did not clear any portion of any strain and did not progress to systemic non-cephalic necrosis as seen in other patients. Similar but less pronounced results were observed with intubated patients, though effects were less pronounced. Etiology of this effect is unknown. It is surmised, based on brain scans, cephalic vivisections of cacchinating patients and autopsies of the euthanized that the aforementioned otoneurological component requires generating the vocalizations and processing of same as auditory input in order to progress to subsequent disease states including systemic or necrosis or, in the case of Patient Zero, recovery—*"

Ava Sorzano, deadpan into a digital recorder.

She stumbled slightly over the words "cephalic vivisections of cacchinating patients"... but not over "euthanized."

I told Van: "No, don't gag Trixie."

"But the noise, Dante..."

"Play some jazz. You got Trane?"

Under comforting auditory cover of "A Love Supreme" with not so comforting laughter as accompaniment, I scavenged in Van's closet for clothes. I figured I'd find lots of my crap here. I'd spent enough weekends at Casa Fish, and Van never cleaned anything. Trixie did, however. All I found was a swimsuit and a single pair of cargo pants I'd picked up in the $9.95 discount bin at *¡Ropa Alegre!* in El Cangrejo.

Van's shirts were on the big side, plus they all had hippie bands on them. Lynyrd Skynyrd was the best I could do, so I stuck with Felonious Monk.

I got one good piece of news, however; last time I'd stayed at Casa Fish, apparently, I'd left a pair of steel-toed engineer boots I remembered picking up in a street market on a weekend trip to Caracas. If the mercy came down from heaven again, at least I wouldn't face it wearing huaraches.

No sign of pirates.

Van tinkered with the Mobile Display Terminal, rigging it to a maritime battery he dragged in from the shed packed with crap near the dock. He used a completely jackassed setup with jerry-rigged wires stripped and re-wrapped with electrical tape. It was bonkers.

He paused before he connected the jumper cables.

He said, "This is a secure device; it's designed so that enemy combatants can't get a fix on your location. But there's a chance that the person on the other end will."

I said, "That would be bad. You think it's a real possibility?"

He shrugged. "I wouldn't have mentioned it if I didn't."

"Then we'd better leave the juice off for now."

He jerked his head toward the guest room, where Trixie was screaming and sobbing.

His voice caught, "How long is this going to go on?"

I said, "I don't remember all that clearly. I'm not always sure what's reality and what's YouTube. They kept me pretty blasted most of the time. And... well, you saw the videos. They egged me on. I don't know how long it took them to get that much material. The timeframe is unclear. Days, weeks... months. I don't know."

He said, "Way to tell me that *now*."

I said, "Well, since you were going to put a .44 slug in her brainpan, I feel fairly confident that a certain amount of speculation is allowed in *my* plan."

He said, "Whatever. Make an educated guess."

I said, "Once I started this phase—with the laughing and the crying alternately—it wasn't long. A few days. But, Van, you've gotta understand... I'm guessing, here. For all I know, she might not get better at all."

I went to say some more, but my voice caught. I shut my eyes tight.

I said, "God damn it" through tears; I hunched over and shook. I trembled all over. I puked great wrenching sobs, mirroring Trixie's screams of agony, her inconsolable and violent weeping from just beyond a too-narrow door. I clutched my hands to my shoulders and rocked like an autistic kid. It went on for some time. I couldn't bear to look at Van.

Which was probably good, because when I finally quieted down, I stared into the gaping maw of Van's .44.

I said, "Not quite as appreciated as a hand on my shoulder or a pat on the back. But comforting in its own way."

He said, "If it comes to that."

I said, "If it comes to *what*?"

"If you're bit. Will you turn?"

"I don't know."

"Or will you turn back, like you did? Are you inoculated or something?"

"Yeah," I said. "You'll just have to stash me in a cell and make dumb viral sci-fi videos with me. That'll fix me right up… just like the last time."

☠

"Shit," Van said. "San Francisco's gone dark."

I said, "I beg your pardon?"

We were drinking Scotch and warm Balboa. We had Albert Collins turned up high to drown out the laughter and sobs.

Van said urgently, "No communications at all, Frosty. Servers offline."

"The whole city?"

"No, pal. The *cult*."

"You said they were a commune."

"Yeah, well… I might need to revise my view, given recent events. The news says they've sealed off the building. SFPD's got them surrounded. Police copters and everything. Looks like the Feds are getting involved. It doesn't say who—could be FBI, DEA, ATF, DHS, FEMA, FCC—"

I said: "FCC?"

"Seems they may have been operating a teeny tiny pirate radio station. The Voice of the Inferno—Conspiracy shit, natch."

I said, "Natch. They put you in jail for that?"

"Beats me, but they've also got guns, bootleg meds, illegal drugs, explosives—"

"Who doesn't?"

"—There's rumors of underground AIDS therapies… illegal immigration… even organ farming."

"Aw, come on. I'm sure they wouldn't do something really evil, like sell frozen bodies."

"This explains why they haven't been returning my emails about your frozen suitcase from Darién." He rubbed his eyes and made a miserable sound; he hadn't been sleeping much. "This could be bad, Dante. Some of the shit they've been posting makes more sense now. They said a few weeks ago they have the cure to what ails the planet. Got it? The *planet*, not the human race. But now they're locked up. They're not even sure anyone's alive in there."

I got the chills. "Is it a suicide cult?"

He said, "I'm not sure. I'm putting it all together, Dante, and… maybe I was giving them too much credit. Sometimes crazy seems like genius."

I said, "You think there's been an outbreak inside?"

He turned Trixie's laptop around and aimed it at me.

"Maybe not inside," he said.

I read the news story, from the San Francisco *Call*:

The 96-hour standoff between local police and firefighters and a so-called "hacker cult" escalated today, as Acting Mayor Danielle Garmon admitted that she has been in contact with Federal officials over the crisis.

The standoff reportedly began in response to an internet posting by a local blogger known to have lived and possibly worked in the facility. The blogger claimed that the so-called "Inferno" was trafficking in dangerous substances that she claimed were related to the group's disaster preparedness consulting business, and possibly to bioterrorism.

Tenants allegedly refused the officers entry and may have taken the blogger hostage, lowering the fortified steel barriers over the building's windows and doors, which were installed during the historic building's controversial anti-terrorism refit last year.

The building was previously the site of the Paradise Life Extension foundation, which was cited several years ago by the Department of Health for improper procedures with human remains, and of Purgatorio, an adult internet company that was cited last year for violations of federal paperwork requirements. The site was the source of controversy after a public event by one of the group's foundations, known as DePop Art, a group advocating "the radical reduction of the human population by any moral and ethical means possible."

The San Francisco Armory is a 200,000-square-foot building built in the early 1900s as a National Guard Base. The former military facility is now the site of a mixed-use co-operative real estate venture that includes sixteen commercial tenants and over 50 permanent residents. Infernonet, an alternative satellite-based internet service provider that made headlines both with its innovative technology and its financial problems, is probably the most widely-known business operating out of the Armory. Other commercial tenants include a so-called "bondage bed & breakfast," a widely-read message board on paranormal topics, an "urban agriculture" supplier, an alternative community health clinic and several green-energy startups, in addition to the adult entertainment production facility.

Infernonet has reportedly been offline since just before the crisis started. Local blogs showed a screen capture claimed to be the page displayed briefly by the site about ten minutes before the crisis began.

The story didn't feature a link to the screencap. It was easy enough to find, though. An image search later, I stared at the image: a black screen with three big letters.

"LOL."

I said, "L-O-L? Sounds like what you'd put up if you'd just hacked a site."

"Or are they trying to hack the planet?" said Van.

"So... did someone take The Inferno over? Or... wait, what?"

He shrugged and looked very uncomfortable.

"Dante... people post a lot of shit online. This Inferno group, they're like a... commune."

I growled: "*Cult*, I thought."

He said: "Nah, see, I think that's the problem. They all have different agendas. You never know who's really posting, or what they really represent. If they were a cult, they'd be more organized. But some of them… they post stuff about that DePop Art movement. You know, 'Mother Earth is crying'—shit like that. I'd show you, but it's all been taken down. Mirrors, archives, the Wayback Machine, it's all gone. Even my local cache has been cleared."

"I thought you weren't a computer person."

He shrugged.

I said, "Do you have any other way to get in touch with them? Radio… text… anything?"

"Just email and the forums, Frosty. Forums have been down all week—I didn't know why. And as for email… the last couple days, I get bounces. And as for anyone posting remotely, everything's been anonymized from the start. They don't know me, I don't know them."

I looked at the screen: "LOL."

"The thing is, these guys *hate* people like the Amaros. They're, like, Wikileaks types. They're the ones who spread your original video—*before* your employers sanitized it."

I said, "Yeah, well, Hell hath no fury like a lover scorned."

Van said, "That's *woman*, and that's sexist."

I said, "You spend too much time around your wife. Sounds like she gave you one of those *diversity trainings*."

"Nah," said Van. "I was always a sensitive guy."

In the sickroom, Trixie howled with laughter.

Van's lips tightened; his eyes shut tight. He hated to hear her like that. The big prick *was* a sensitive guy.

☠

My epitaph haunted me.

There in the Beaumont Colón, I had struggled with the last words of my dispatch. What should they be? I wondered that the entire time I was speaking. How does one terminate the world's weirdest snuff film?

In the end, it just came to me, like Trane's last note in his very last solo.

And what I told the future was this: "My name is Dante Bogart."

I said, "I'm not a soldier."

I said, "That probably doesn't matter to the rest of you mopes, but it matters to me. I thought I was a soldier. Virgil Amaro thought I was a grunt. But we were both wrong. I was just another killer."

I said, "As of this morning, I'm something new, and it feels *good*."

I said, "Wanna know what I am now, Virgil?"

I got all up in the webcam's shit.

I said, "I'm *viral*, fucker. Open up and say Ahhhh."

☠

I've never bought midnight as the time when night becomes day. Dawn doesn't work either, because I've been up too many days before dawn to do things so horrible they would ensure, in any reasonable universe, that the sun never came up again.

To my way of thinking, the passage from night to morning occurs sometime between those two occurrences, local time, with each break happening on an individual basis: individual to each person, individual to each night. Individual to each morning. You don't always know which one you've passed into, night or morning. When you wake up in the night and see your wife and level a shotgun at her thinking she's a burglar, you've mistaken morning for night. Similarly, when you say "I'll be right back" to go to the store and never get back because you're smeared across the pavement, perhaps you've called "morning" when, in fact it's blackest night.

So I wasn't sure where I was or what time it was or who I was aiming at when I woke up in the night and heard Van sobbing.

The tricky thing about the viral brand of Cry is that, out of context, it's indistinguishable from the real thing.

The same with the Panama Laugh. It chills my bones because it sounds like children having a hell of a time. Hearing that Laugh, I feel my hindbrain jump to the conclusion someone's busting a gut to a Cheech and Chong movie. My forebrain hopes that's what they're doing.

And my limbic system, the mammalian system that's the source of the cuddle impulse and the craving to play?

That part of me wants every laugher from Airborne on down to be busting a gut to a half-remembered gag from an episode of *I Love Lucy*. *Assembly line! They're eating chocolates! Bwa-ha*! Like that.

The part of me that cuddles and cries needs every LOL to be a dream, not a nightmare. In the night, I dream of morning.

But telling the real laughter from the Panama Laugh is harder than sorting out kids from insurgents in Fallujah.

So when I jerked out of a dead violent sleep and I heard Van sobbing…

… I whispered, "*Crap*."

I had crashed out on the couch with Trixie's laptop on my chest, reading news. Mandelbrot's fractals did things to my eyeballs.

As I heard Van's weeping, I reached under the worn-out couch and pulled out my five-sev. It was cocked and loaded. I took the safety off and sat up.

The laptop jiggled.

The Panama Post, freshly loading.

The pictures, the headlines blasted up. The sudden ba-bing! In my ears mixed up with the sound of Van's weeping and my strangled gulp of terror:

La Guerra!

Monstruos en Panamá—el mal de risa!

Contagio reportados en Cali, Medellín, San Salvador, Managua, Guatemala...

The picture was a nighttime shot of a crowd of laughers on the Via España.

Panama City.

I stood there and gaped at the screen. I breathed hard.

I dumped the laptop on the couch and got up. I heard Van laughing, then crying again. I stood in sweat-soaked boxers I'd jacked from Augie Amaro (cocaine and dollars), and a soaked-through wifebeater (The Indigo Girls—one of Trixie's). The Panama breeze came in through on wide-open windows.

I crept to the door of the sickroom. Van knelt beside the bed. His inconsolable weeping covered the creak of the floorboards as I crept by inches up behind him.

I aimed my pistol at the base of his skull.

I said, "Van?"

Trixie said, "Put the gun down."

Van sobbed. "She's okay," he said. "My baby's okay."

I let out a long, slow breath.

Trixie said weakly, "Thanks for not shooting me, Frosty."

I said, "No problem, and don't call me that. And we've got problems."

"No shit," they said at once.

"No," I said. "We've got *problems*. Laughers on the Via España."

Van gaped.

I heard an airhorn outside.

Trixie said, "Will one of you please untie me?"

☠

Barefoot, I took Van's thirty-thirty off its pegs. I jacked a round gingerly into the chamber. I crouched down in the darkness by the door clutching the rifle.

I crept out on the porch in a crouch.

I saw Alei approaching in the darkness—coming at a dead run, clutching his lemon-yellow porkpie to his head and waving his airhorn. He trailed three of his younger buddies behind him, all sobbing hysterically.

I hoisted the thirty-thirty and aimed.

Alei screamed: "*No disparar*! Señor Frosty! Don't shoot!"

I lowered the rifle. I said, "Shouldn't you be home in bed?"

It took him a moment to get the word out: "Monsters!"

I said, "—I know, and—"

He said, "Los piratas!"

I said, "Pirates?"

Alei was shaking all over, scared shitless. He clutched his hat and put on a brave, cocky face. He said in a tortured moan:

"Mister Frosty, did I stutter?"

☠

When it rains, it pours.

Alei was terrified to the point of incoherence. He explained he'd sneaked over and "borrowed" the *Speedy Gonzales*, which he tried to apologize for. (Van told him to save it—where he came from, a little vehicle theft between friends was no big deal.) It was a very clear night out there, full moon and everything. He and his friends took the *Speedy* about twenty minutes from Isla Pescado, where they spotted a pirate fleet of about thirty boats, going nuts, zigzagging. They were tossing laughers off the back. At first Alei thought it was just a pirate game—"These are not good people," he said. The pirates had been known to use their ordnance for target practice.

But the survivors weren't shooting at the things in the water. They were shooting at the things on their boats. Shooting with guns and hacking with machetes, apparently. He said he saw one boat take out another boat with what sounded, from his description, like a rocket-propelled grenade.

Alei said, "They are killing each other," he said. "Some are turning to laughers. The survivors are heading for Isla Pescado."

I remembered hearing Doctor Sorzano: *It would hit the whole world at once. It could start in the tropics and...*

Alei gritted his teeth, trying hard to look brave. He clutched his hat to his head.

"Then they see us. I really open it up, Mister Van. That Fokker is *fast*."

"Watch your language," grinned Van. "You've got brass kid. How far behind you are they?"

Alei said, "Not far. But they were still fighting. Zig-zagging. *Loco*."

Van turned the shortwave on.

There were some screams in Spanish, but there was so much static it was hard to get anything.

And over it all, or maybe *under* it all, a weird, high-pitched resonant kind of interference had erupted—a humming sound, like Tibetan bells. It cut across all frequencies, and it set my teeth on edge.

"What the hell is that *sound*?"

Van shrugged. "We get weird interference here some days, Frosty. Some people say it's the Bermuda Triangle; others think it's all the way from Easter Island."

"How many of them think you're a douchebag?"

"Most of them," he said. Under the humming, there were squalling howls in Spanish. His eyes narrowed, picking out bits of Spanish sentences. "They're talking about—'plaga.' That's, uh…"

Alei said, "'Plague,' Bubba."

Van scowled, "Thanks, Bubba."

The resonant sound was still there. I grimaced, "What the hell is that interference?"

Van asked Alei, "Is there a storm out there?"

Alei mocked a fake redneck accent: "Ten-four, dude—*tempestad de pirata*. But no, like, rain. GPS, she's down, though. And the birds—" He looked like he didn't want to say it. "It's *loco*, but—the birds. Going crazy."

Van said, "GPS is down? "

"Did I stutter?"

I asked Alei, "Birds—going crazy how?"

"All over the place. Big groups. I don't know what you call it. Like bugs."

"Swarming?"

He nodded. "Flying into each other. Sometimes they hit the water."

He shrugged. Van and I looked at each other.

Van said dryly, "Were they laughing?"

Alei shrugged.

Van asked, "This one of yours, Frosty?"

I shrugged. "GPS, yeah. That's a US Air Force operation. If there's a military emergency, it either goes completely down, or it's very inaccurate. But birds going crazy? I never heard of that."

Van glared at me suspiciously.

"Musta been some *other* apocalyptic mercenary cult that caused that one, then."

I said, "Speaking of which…"

☠

Trixie was starving and filthy, and having trouble getting her bearings. While we built a plan of attack, she took a cold shower—the only kind you could get at night at Casa Fish.

I booted up Little Augie's cell phone—nothing. No reception at all. That was not surprising—satphone, radio and satellite internet were the sum total of communications on Isla Pescado.

Van zapped the jumper cables to the Bellona mobile display terminal I'd jacked from the Toyota SUV in the Darién Gap.

The MDT bleeped and flashed; it made sizzling sounds. Long coils of smoke began to erupt from its corners.

Van said, "Is that bad?"

I said, "I was hoping you knew."

"Who do I look like? Lieutenant Uhura?"

Van scratched his head while more smoke rose; there was an acrid smell. "Well," he finally said. "I doubt it's good."

But then the screen brightened and flashed on. I breathed out easy and started punching buttons. There were several messages waiting.

Uno: **ALL OPERATORS URGENT: UNEXPECTED BIOEVENT CONFIRMED. AIRBORNE CATALYST DETECTED IN MEXICO CITY MAY HAVE ORIGINATED FROM DARIEN FACILITY. UTILIZE LEVEL 4 BIOHAZARD PROCEDURES.** Timestamped fourteen hours ago.

Dos: **RIOHACHA AND SOLEDAD OPERATORS URGENT: USAMRIID TEAM EN ROUTE TO DARIEN. ALL PERSONNEL REMINDED THEY ARE UNDER CONTRACTUAL GAG ORDER. ALL PERSONNEL REMINDED THAT US GOVT HAS NO JURISDICTION IN PANAMA AND COLOMBIA. PLEASE REFER ALL USAMRIID QUESTIONS TO BELLONA PR OFFICE MIRAFLORES TOWERS PANAMA CITY.** Thirteen and a half hours ago.

Tres: **URGENT ALL OPERATORS: CONFIRM RENDEZVOUS IN COLON IN 12 HOURS THEREAFTER TO HOLY LAND VIA**

CYPRUS. Ten hours ago.

Quatro: **URGENT PALE BIRD SQUADRON URGENT CANAL SECURITY COMPROMISED—CANAL SEALED—GODS MERCY NEEDS AIR SUPPORT—ARMED ESCORT THROUGH MIRAFLORES LOCKS—PROCEED THERE AFTER COMPLETING KUNA YALA MISSION**. An hour ago.

Van and I blinked at each other. He said, "I think you missed one."

I said, "Hm."

I paged back up.

Cinco—two hours ago: **PALE BIRD SQUADRON URGENT. DOD AND PDF CLEARANCE FOR OPERATION WARMUP STRIKE ORDERED ON MONTERIA CARTEL COCA PROCESSING LAB SOUTHERN SAN BLAS ISLANDS. NO KNOCK WARRANT DOD CLEARANCE DO NOT ATTEMPT ARREST OR CAPTURE. SUICIDE BOMBERS SUSPECTED.** The hairs on the back of my neck did things no hairs should do.

DOD and PDF: The U.S. Department of Defense and the Panamanian Defense Forces.

Coca processing lab in the San Blas Islands… okay. Maybe.

But *suicide bombers*? These asshats had obviously never met a Colombian drug dealer.

The MDT made a wheezing sound.

Van asked, "Gee, is this bad, Frosty?"

I scratched my head. "I'm looking for the bright side. It's not really presenting itself."

Van and I looked at each other gravely.

"Is this about you?" Van asked.

I said, "I hate to get all narcissistic and shit, but…"

I Googled myself. I got a video hit almost instantly: footage of me and Van fighting, crunching Holy Ghost orchids in the garden.

The title said, "Buena Lucha! Dos Gringos Locos!" The poster's username was "MoochALucha"—location San Blas Islands, Panama.

I heard myself say, tinny and distant: "What, no *buenos dias* this time?"—then I let Van have it. Did I always look pasty like that?

Behind us, Alei gulped.

"Did I do bad, Mister Frosty?" asked Alei.

Van's face went red with fury; Alei looked scared. Van checked himself.

I said, "Don't call me that, and don't worry about the video."

Van took a deep breath and clapped Alei on the shoulder. He said through gritted teeth:

"*No problemo,* buddy. We've already got pirates. What's an attack helicopter or two?"

Alei looked sheepish. He said, "*Lo siento.* Steamed, Bubba?"

Van said, "Hell, no. At least you got my good side!"

☠

Options for departure were limited.

The *Speedy Gonzales* was the only boat that could conceivably outrun the pirates, but it was on the small side. It had a limited range.

The *Jerry Bear* was a skiff at best—it'd make fifteen or twenty knots, tops. It wouldn't get the three of us very far. If Alei took it and his friends encountered pirates again, they'd never outrun them in the *Jerry.*

And as for the *When She Was Bad?* Van was a mediocre sailboat captain at best—as I mentioned before, he can't tie a knot for shit—and the only thing I knew how to do on a sailboat was drink beer. We could run on it, and three people could live on it. But if these pirates, any other pirates, or anyone from Bellona gave chase, we'd be sitting ducks even with a favorable wind. Catching up to the *God's Mercy* would be impossible.

It looked like we were traveling by air.

Van and I had been right about what Trixie would say next.

It was a simple question. Run like hell for another hideout in the San Blas Islands, and wait this shit out? Or intercept Luke, get the case open, maybe find the cure, maybe save the world?

The girl passed up a six-figure public health job at a Las Vegas hospital to treat the indigent of three continents. It could never be a serious question, even being fresh out of the Laughing Academy.

Of course, I'd told Van she'd be pissed we had to ask. He disagreed. That bet won me $5. Or five Balboas, as they call them in Panama, where the U.S. Dollar takes on a local name as one of the nation's minor but culturally important kissoffs to Uncle Sam.

A nation, we would soon discover, that was already in flames.

So I'd never get to spend that five bucks.

☠

While Van fed Trixie some Cream of Wheat, Alei went up to the tower and used the field glasses to hunt for pirates by the light of the full moon and I got Van's Cessna 172 loaded and fueled.

The walkie crackled, pouring out static and whines with the intel. Finally Alei got through: The pirates were close, approaching the West side of the island—the opposite side from their last assault. From the sound of it, this wasn't a calculated tactical decision, just chance borne out of blind panic. They left a trail of laughers in the moonlight, many wearing life jackets.

Alei didn't know how many boats—ten at least.

He said, "And the birds are—what did you call it, Fros—"

I stepped on his lines.

Crackle: "Swarming," I growled.

Isla Pescado is not a large island. Once the pirates landed on the the far side, they could hike over here and make an assault. How many combatants? No way to tell at the moment. Enough to make our last moments on Isla Pescado far more interesting than we cared for them to become.

I hauled ass to get the Cessna ready.

In the eccentric tradition Van has of naming everything from his thirty-thirty ("*Old Smokey*") to his .44 Magnum ("*Lucky?*") to his largest bong ("*The Gurgoyle*") to his penis ("*Mister Jehosaphat*"), he had mail-ordered a decal of a classic Maggie Billman illustration from the pulp days: a curvy '40s girl in a bikini with poofy red hair, slightly spread legs, green skin and fangs—and, beneath it, he'd stenciled the name of our sky chariot: the *Bush Soaker*. Classy. Planes don't usually have names, but then, neither do rifles or antique male equipment of questionable utility for anything other than scaring the local minister.

The Cessna was small. With three armed passengers and the metal Salvation suitcase, plus the scavenged float kit Van had installed himself—which added significant weight and drag to the aircraft—it was already kinda pushing its weight limit. I didn't own much nowadays, and Trixie had always traveled light. Van was the pack rat. Isla Pescado was littered with the vague obsessions of a guy who loved to tinker. He said, "It feels good to leave it all behind."

I said, "I'm proud of you, Bubba."

Trixie and I carried scavenged AKs. Van preferred Old Smokey his thirty-thirty and wouldn't give up his uncle's .308; Trixie's Mossberg was the only scattergun we had, so we brought that. I have no idea how many pistols Van stuffed into his garish Hawaiian-print board shorts, but with Van there's a lot of board shorts to stuff things into, so it was likely in the double digits if not triple. He looked like a jackass wearing shorts and combat boots, but I had long since given up trying to give Van fashion advice.

We left the firearms cases scattered across the dock, to save on space and weight. Alei wouldn't even consider coming with us—he wouldn't abandon his friends and family. So Van and I piled the extra guns—scavenged pirate AKs plus Van's old pistols and long guns—onto the *Speedy*. "You'll get the boat hidden somewhere?" Van said chidingly. "The piratas might come and try to steal it."

Alei tipped his porkpie and said with a very brave grin, *"Sólo si los piratas son masoquistas!"* Only if they're masochists.

I laughed like a bastard at that one. So did Trix, through her chattering teeth. Van shot her Trixie a glare, but she said, "Don't look at me, I didn't teach it to him."

I said, "I haven't been here long enough to teach him bad habits."

Van finally gave in and took the ball-busting in stride. He grinned and hugged Alei and the other kids. So did Trixie, who couldn't stop crying.

It was scary as hell to see her do that.

Van told Alei, "Whatever you do, don't come back here for a while. Even after these piratas are dealt with... *things* might be here."

Alei said, *"Monstruo?"*

And Van said, *"Si, Monstruo."*

And Alei and all three of his younger buddies nodded furiously and made stiff-armed clawing gestures and said, "Huh. Huh. Huh. Huh. Huh."

I didn't like that much.

They gave us scared and brave looks, like twelve-year-old bad-asses. Van shadow-boxed with them.

I growled, "Shake a tail feather, Amelia Earhart. It's almost 6 a.m."

He said, "Don't you mean zero-six-hundred?"

I said, "That, too."

Of all the memories I've got that can slam a man out of the blue and give him nightmares, for some reason four Kuna kids saying Huh huh huh huh huh does it every time.

That shit's ugly as sin in any language.

But the ugly was just getting started.

☠

The water was rough, but Van was a pro. By which I mean he had no idea what he was doing, but had phenomenal luck sometimes. He pointed the Soaker into the wind and got her up before Trixie and I even had time to puke or shit our pants very much.

The sun pinkened the sky, lurking just below the horizon. We saw the wake of the Speedy heading off from the East side of the island. Because of the wind, we took off pointing West.

As the floats left the water, Van pointed off to the south.

"Damn it," I said. "I hate running into coworkers when I'm on vacation."

Little Birds—six of them, egg-shaped and black, lined up against the pink sky and loaded with rockets. The copters were coming in low. *Too* low.

"Why the hell are they so low?" I asked.

The morning wind at Isla Pescado means that if you leave early, then the only protected enough stretch of water to safely lift off from—which Van had just used—aims you right at the jagged rocks on the west side. I knew this phenomenon well from many an early-morning fishing trip with Van; he cuts it close not because he likes to scare the living shit out of me, but because there is no other way to safely get airborne from Isla Pescado, "safely" being a relative term here. But most mornings, the beach you therefore passed over wasn't infested with pirates.

Throttles opened, the boats had been run aground at full speed as if chased by the devil. In the pink light of the rising sun, we saw the trails of writhing laughers behind the boats; some glugged and went down. Others were being gunned down by the AK-armed survivors on the beach. They saw us and pointed, fucking with duffel bags in the sand. Laughers came at them splashing and lumbering, or crawling over the sands, over the rocks. Some of the pirates opened up at us with AKs, while others got the duffel bags open. Hadn't Alei said something about RPGs?

He had; there were several of them, long and deadly and aimed at us fast.

"Don't look down," I said.

"I already did," shouted Van. He was climbing fast—too fast. Much too fast. The *Soaker* shuddered violently.

I howled: "Don't stall it, fucker!"

He screamed: "I know what I'm doing, fucker!"

He leaned on the wheel and the *Bush Soaker* plunged toward the water. I screamed, "What the fuck?" and Trixie let out an incoherent string of obscenities, her voice rough from the Panama Laugh.

The RPG hissed over the Soaker's high wing and spiraled off into the sky. We plunged. Van pulled back. We practically skimmed the waves.

Then we were up, and climbing again, and Van banked to put the cliffs on the beach between the pirates and us.

"Any more rockets?"

I said, "I'll tell you as soon as I open my eyes."

"Don't fuck with me, Frosty! Any more rockets?"

I craned my neck as Van took the *Soaker* up. Maybe a minute from takeoff, we came above the cliffs and I saw it—

The copters were making a run for the beach—low. Very low. The RPG had gotten John Amaro's attention. Meanwhile, the pirates had gotten more interested in the copters than in us. They were aiming their RPGs at Johnny Boy's birds, and I realized at least one of the weapons wasn't an RPG—it was a shoulder-fired surface-to-air missile. A Stinger, or something like it.

Flame belched from the pods on the side of two Little Birds. Both copters peeled off and two more fired. I saw a bright flash behind the cliffs, then smoke—and the hiss of rockets from the beach.

I craned my head to see what I could on the beach. The Birds were flying so low it was virtually impossible to miss them. Even AK fire was a hazard at that altitude. What's more, it's not at all prudent to fire Hydras with high-explosive warheads at that kind of angle. The Cubans got a hit, and a Little Bird erupted into a ball of flame. It headed for the water. The Hydras hit, but I couldn't see that part—it was behind the cliffs. I could, however, see two more Birds coming in for a low-level run, as two more rockets hissed off the beach as the Birds fired their salvos. The first of the two Birds ran for the horizon. But in the middle-distance three apparently intact black pirate boats made for the beach at top speed, raking the water with blasts from the thirty-caliber machine guns to clear off the laughers.

I saw the barrels of the thirties swing toward the Bird; the gunners opened up.

Then it was all behind smoke, clouds and distance—pirates, laughers, copters and presumably John Amaro mashed together in a smoking, Grade A clusterfuck.

On the opposite side of the island, I saw the wake of the *Speedy* as Alei ran full-out for home—the islands of the San Blas Kuna, thirty miles distant.

I said, "Why the hell did John bring those copters in so low?"

Van said, "Let's get some air," and took the *Soaker* up.

Which is when we hit the swarm.

☠

Because of its geographic location, Panama has an unusual number and variety of bird species. They were swarming, all right—going *crazy*, heading right for us as if they were chasing us down. Half a dozen small ones smacked into the *Bush Soaker;* blood sprayed. Trixie yelped behind her hand. My muscles jammed up jaw-to-toe in abject terror. I've flown on airplanes and copters all over the world, but this topped them all.

Above us, and not very *far* above us, the "swarm" of birds went from a potential danger to a nightmare—so dense they were practically black.

I asked Van, "What do we do?"

Van eased the Bush Soaker down.

"Hump the waves," he said. "What do you see back there? Any copters after us?"

Trixie and I tried to peer out the window.

"Well?" asked Van.

I saw black smoke rising from the island.

I said, "Someone's having a barbecue on the beach."

Van said, "That's what they get for fucking up our vacation."

☠

We made the coast.

The pale, lovely beach quickly gave way to jungle and swamp. We crossed the narrow mainland strip of the Kuna Yala *comarca*, then passed over the Rio Chucunaque into the northeast end of Darién Province. As Alei had warned us, GPS was down, so we picked up the Pan-American highway just east of Cañita, for the purposes of navigation.

The sun cleared the horizon. The rainforest steamed, dappled with glorious light.

Trixie stared at the landscape, touched by its beauty.

She wept softly, stunned.

She was a different woman, as I was a different man. I didn't want to think about the nightmare we'd shared.

But the future doesn't always ask if you wanna party.

I broke out the field glasses.

☠

We made the Highway.

We skimmed close over chaos, a hundred feet above hell. Hugging the contours of the flat swamps and rainforest, we saw the Pan-American highway jammed with abandoned cars, left to idle when the owners went chuckleheaded and threw themselves into the hunt for live flesh.

We made Cañita, a town of tin-roofed shacks and perhaps two thousand souls.

The laughers were *everywhere*.

In the early-morning light, Cañita was slaughtered. Masses of things that had been human swarmed around the few living Panameños. Illumined by the rising sun, concentric circles of laughing things descended, ten to one, on the serious folk. They clawed violently to get purchase and take laughing mouthfuls of flesh. The things grouped together randomly—three, five, ten, twenty at a time, crowding in pouring out the LOLZ as they tucked in to a single screaming human. From the air, we couldn't hear it, but we didn't need to.

The laughers held the live ones down and *fed*. They took big bloody laughing oozing bites of the screamer's flesh—until the light went out of the screamer's eyes.

Then screamer became laugher, and that one's flesh was no longer tasty. The new laugher joined and the circle of fresh laughers lumbered off as one to find another runner. Some groups staggered into the jungle after those who had fled.

From the air, it looked like schools of fish feeding on shrimp cakes.

Cañita disappeared behind us, laughing.

☠

Ever start laughing, and find you can't stop?

Imagine you *don't* stop.

If you don't know what's happening, then at first it feels good.

But then you laugh harder and harder. Past the point where you get heartburn. Past the point where you can't breathe. Past the point where you think for sure if you laugh any more you crack ribs. Lucky for you, you don't crack ribs; instead you laugh louder, still louder, till you're screaming and the muscles of your stomach and chest hurt like hell; they feel like they're atrophied. You can't get air; you can't breathe, because you're laughing so hard. You know you'll just have to pass out, but you can't; you know your abdominal muscles will have to cramp up or give way. But you know what? Those laughing muscles have inexplicably become strong beyond reason—as if you'd just gone to open your car door and, without effort, just ripped it off its hinges.

You don't remember what was so funny, but then, it doesn't really matter.

Imagine, from the first chuckle, you've felt your brain dying, dying, dying, brain cells popping, IQ points sloughing off with every hilarious bray. You think less clearly with every second, getting more confused even over and above the question you keep asking—assuming you don't already know. "Wait... why am I laughing?"

Then you get *hungry*.

No, not as hungry as you've ever been in your life. Much, much hungrier. You've got no brain left to rationalize "Oh, I need to eat." It's just a primal urge, built even deeper into you than the impulse to laugh.

Which, incidentally, at this point you can't stop, no matter how much physical pain it causes you, or how convinced you become that it's the laugh that's killing your brain.

Is it what kills your brain? The cacchination, the vocalization? Or, as I remembered the doctor saying, do you have to hear your own Laugh to ensure "disease progression?"

Surely, further research is necessary.

Assuming you get a chance to sink your teeth into what you really want, then the Laugh comes and goes—louder, softer, chuckle to howl to scream. You don't stop, unless you're one of the criers. You never stop laughing, but you aren't always laughing quite as hard as you did at the start and for the first few days.

Of course, you don't care, because you went dark long before that.

Unless you're like me, or like Trixie. Then you wake up one morning and remember every chuckle. And the bad news is, it isn't very funny.

☠

I cycled through channels on the shortwave; nothing good was on. There were screams. There was laughter. There was lots of static. But worst of all, we were still picking up that weird resonant interference that set my fillings on edge.

I said, "Solar flares?"

Van said, "I'm with the Easter Island hypothesis, myself. See, my view is that when it comes to the Bermuda Triangle—"

I said, "Stuff a sock in it, Sylvia Browne."

He shrugged. "Truth's out there, Frosty. Deal with it."

I knew the frequencies used by deployed Bellona forces, but they were useless, as was everything else. It didn't make any difference what channels I accessed; too many panicked operators, many of them with little experience, merged everything into a howling mass of nothing even before accounting for the weird interference. When there did turn out to be a single operator on a channel, we heard only rapid-fire, incoherent pleas for help in Spanish. Channels were left open as the operators died, pleading for help while laughers sank their teeth in. We heard a boy bleating in Spanish: "*Mi madre! Mi madre!*" until the plea merged into the Laugh. Far more often, there was nothing but deafening static and the strange hum of the new interference.

☠

The highway threaded west through rainforest and swamp. The canopies of green soon gave way to towns that burned.

Laughers don't remember to turn off the stove.

Houses belched smoke and flame. Damp forests smoldered. The cracked asphalt and cobblestone of local roads bubbled wet with blood. Laughers swarmed. Screamers ran, fell, were torn apart. Then they rose up, ruined and writhing. A smile on every bloody face.

We roared overhead at a the speed of a sports car. Laughers howled and clawed after us, faces half-pulped or just bloody from feeding. The *Bush Soaker* shuddered and weaved and fishtailed, buffeted on a black-smoke wind that stank of bodies.

Above us: The birds.

Below us: The Laugh.

I saw Trixie crying softly.

Trying to make her feel better, I attempted to engage her:

"Any idea about the birds, doctor?"

She fought down her sobs and told me:

"Sorry, Frosty. I skipped that year of medical school."

☠

We made for Panama City and the Miraflores locks.

Every klick we covered saw less green, more blacktop. More cars, more buildings, more flames, more people. More laughers, flooding out of homes and swarming cars on the Highway. It happened overnight, so the homes were where most people got the joke. The as-yet uninfected must have awakened to the sound of late-night laughter, pinned by their loved ones and about to be eaten.

Every mile logged between Kuna Yala and Panama City saw things going from bad to worse.

☠

The approach to Panama City is a tangle of highways. The air corridors are much more heavily traveled, and the sheer number of wrecked aircraft was stunning. We saw airliners, small planes, copters. They'd gone down at full speed when their pilots got the joke. They'd hit highways, forests, buildings. Burning airplanes dotted the wet rainforest with sputtering orange flames, the sky above it with black smoke. Roads were jammed. Cars were dead.

Smoke swirled everywhere. The great gleaming towers of Panama City loomed up ahead of us.

Van crossed the shipping channels.

Vessels lay strewn below us—in pieces, in flames.

The Panama Canal operates at a brisk pace, twenty-four hours a day. Overnight, as this had happened, there were plenty of ships in transit. What's more, as the predawn panic spread, there was a desperate rush to transit the canal. It caused carnage.

We approached the Miraflores locks. This was the Pacific entrance to the canal, adjacent to Panama Bay.

Boats and ships had wrecked on the rocks nearby—or on each other. Broken across the approach to the locks, the vessels burned and listed. Antlike crews set upon each other like laughing pirates on sinking barquentines. Others just drifted, decks dotted with ravenous laughers. The waters teemed with cockeyed fishing trawlers, yachts, tour boats, all making for the Canal in a desperate bid to get home or get away.

Two container ships had struck each other just outside the locks; five-high stacks of oceangoing rail containers had tipped and spilled everywhere, crushing crew members under twisted metal.

Laughing faces peered from pulped-up piles of ruptured flesh and broken bones.

As we passed Isla Flamenco, I saw a cruise ship called the *Panama Pleasure* had run aground at full speed, half-crumbling into the Playa Palacio and the Hotel Hermosa. Black smoke poured from her stacks, spreading above the beachside ruins and shading the scene.

Swarms of laughers breakfasted in the shadows.

☠

While Trixie and Van gaped at the destruction below, Augie's cell phone played "Little Johnny Jewel." It was telling me it had a signal.

I took it out of my pocket. I opened the address book.

My thumb hovered over D for Dad. I stopped.

I hit J.

Jason, Jackson, Jeremiah, Jordan, Jordaan, Jordana, Jordin, Jordyn, Jordyyn, Jorrdan—

Not a single "John." Kids today...

I hit U.

Uerdunn, Uirdun—

Uncle John.

I texted: **hey unc we gonna meetup?**

Nothing from John Amaro, commander, Pale Bird Squadron.

I growled, "Welcome to Panama, John."

I hit D again. Dad. My thumbs worked fast: **dad where r u?**

The phone started going nuts, spewing out bleating sounds. There were a dozen messages waiting—all from Luke, starting 12 hours ago.

augie dante bogart wuz spotted on panama islands on internet video file is tieemstampd after Darien... didn't u saw him killed? :-(

Oops. Sounded like Dad was pissed.

But then the more recent messages came on *fast*:

augie change of plans we cannot wait in panama city :-(
augie we are transit canal erly than plnned contct unc john for copter extract
augie confirm colon meeting with gods grace this am
cleared locks early refugees tryin 2 board from canal fences
we are repelling borders :-(
have 2 meet u in colon pls confirm u still have salvation
transiting lago gatun now
augie colon ok?

There were more like it: **pls confirm, augie confirm, son where r u, augie help me, augie where r u help**—like that.

I thought: *Sure, Luke. I'll be happy to confirm my meeting with your colon.*

I texted Luke: **lol no way dante alive? He must be immortal rofl**

I got an immediate response—and they just kept coming.

AUGIE
HELP AUGIE WHERE R u
gods grace not respondding
copter extract out all copters down avian strain birds going crazy
flight not safe above 30 meters
CONFIRM YOU HAVE TH EPACKAGE
NEED PKG
I am trapped
crew infecteDD i am trapped
help me I am in aft bilge
help me

"Hey, asshole! You want me to keep circling?" It was Van, of course.

Trixie gaped down at the carnage below—the laughing streets that had been Panama City and its vicinity.

Panama City proper is not immediately on Bahía de Panamá, or on the the Miraflores Locks, the Pacific entrance to the Panama Canal. But it may as well be; the distance is only far if you're being quoted a price by an unscrupulous cab driver outside the Hotel Panama. With one slow circuit of the bay, Van had given us a panoramic view of the city that had been *Ciudad de Panamá*. Great masses of the dead could be seen lumbering up the yawning valleys between skyscrapers; the presidential palace was afire.

I picked out the Miraflores Tower, where I'd once threatened to ram my fist down Mark Amaro's throat.

It was aflame.

A copter had plowed into it at what must have been high speed. It had ripped a big chunk in the middle; the tower burned.

I looked down. I saw the squirming bodies wedged between colonial buildings and skyscrapers. There were buildings on fire everywhere; the streets moved like rivers. I stared down in horror and saw the Via España threading through town, a laughing ribbon of—

Van smacked me in the side of the head.

"*Buenos dias,* douchebag! Fuel ain't free, you know! These floats kill my mileage!"

I shouted back, "The *God's Mercy* is in Colón."

"And the *God's Mercy* is the garbage scow with Dick McAsshole on it?"
I nodded.

"Colón, that's southwest, right?"

Colón was northeast; he saw my glare.

"Jesus, Frosty, chill out! Can't a guy cop a laugh now and then?"

☠

Too many of the skyscrapers of Panama City were dotted with huge black holes and masses of pouring smoke and flame. It couldn't all be explained by the birds.

I said, "Why did so many planes hit so many buildings?"

Van said, "Trixie and I worked out a theory for that."

I said, "Already?"

Van said, "No. Earlier. Something like it happened before. The first time the pirates came at us, they didn't have their plan all that worked out. It was two guys in a speedboat. They had laughers in back. You know, tied up, but still laughing. I guess the plan was to land on the beach and let 'em loose on us. Then, you know, come for our bones in the morning."

"That's not a great plan," I said.

He said, "Yeah, well, that's probably one of the many reasons Trix and I are still here. But... uh... I was watching from the sniper tower, with field glasses, so... I can't be totally sure, but I think I saw most of it. It looked like before they even reached shore, one of the dead things broke away, and... uh... well, they got him thrown him overboard. One of the pirates must have been bit. His buddy shot him. Then he tossed the other laughers overboard. Then he ran for home."

"Nice," I said.

"A minute later he turned around."

I said, "He wanted help from you?"

Van said, "Frosty... no. He *turned around*."

I said, "You said that."

He said, "Frosty, *he turned around*."

I got a cold feeling.

Trixie said, "He headed for the shore. He had *already turned*, Dante. He couldn't smell us. It's physically impossible."

I got pale.

I said, "A male bee can smell a queen bee at, like..." I lost momentum. "A thousand miles or something."

Van said, "No shit? Thanks, Marlin Perkins."

Trixie said, "He didn't smell us. He just *knew*. He knew we were the closest living things."

I said, "How far out was he when he turned?"

Trix said, "A half a mile. He couldn't smell us."

Van said, "He couldn't smell us, he couldn't see us... and he was moving. It wasn't just, you know, a random turn. He was standing at the helm, piloting the boat into shore... to get us."

I said, "So that's why all the planes flew into buildings."

He said, "That's my thought. Same with the ships ramming into shore— and other ships. They turn laugher at the helm, or the wheel, and they don't know what they're doing. It's the rote action they've been trained for. They *sense* people. They go for them. They aim whatever they're piloting at what they want—*us*. The living. But then, you might say, the whole *landing* part presents a minor complication they seem unprepared to address."

In the back, Trixie looked pale.

She asked, "How did it happen so *fast?*"

I said, "Good fucking question. Let's get some answers."

☠

In international shipping and strategic terms, the Canal had ceased to be the critical choke point it was during World War II. The Canal's cession to the Panamanians in the Carter years and the 1989 U.S. invasion punctuated a series of migrations from the first world to the third world.

Not of *people*, but of *widgets*. Manufacturing: T-shirts, hairbrushes, casserole dishes. Meanwhile, cargo ships got bigger. So did military ones—until the only really important naval weapon in global terms, the aircraft carrier, could no longer transit the canal. Nor did it need to—the U.S.S. *Enterprise* can top thirty knots.

The Canal went from being an absolutely critical global strategic choke point to being a matter of predominantly convenient business interest, the subject of fantastically complicated calculations conducted by bean counters adding up huge strings of numbers in cubicles buried in city-sized skyscrapers in Hamburg and Tokyo and Beijing. The number-crunchers turned the container capacity of a Panamax vessel into a spreadsheet, added up fuel efficiency and transit time figured, month by month, for the rapidly plummeting salaries of maritime personnel as the expensive American-trained crews gave way to more cost-efficient Soviet-trained crews, who then gave way to more cost-efficient Central and South Asian crews, then to still-cheaper Philippinos, even-cheaper Indonesians, ever-cheaper Chinese crews. By the time supertankers from Dubai reached half again the Panamax size and the 30-man crew of a supertanker made less than a shift at the Starbucks on Hollywood Boulevard, it became often cheaper to go around the Cape.

But that's not to say the Canal ever needed to look for a date. The competing arguments for transiting Panama instead of Tierra Del Fuego are legion, especially for ships shorter than a thousand feet. Everything from cruise ships to container ships to sailboats transited the Canal, and the Canal was always considered a prime target for terrorism, both by cops and crooks. And people like me, who fall somewhere in between. The dense jungle surrounding Lago Gatun proves a reliable defense for the dam, which is the system's most vulnerable strategic point, but the locks are still closely controlled for security reasons. A certain number of PDF spotter planes would always be in evidence overhead, if you knew to look for them. Other than that, aircraft were not allowed to approach the canal, let alone fly over it.

In a security emergency, the canal closed down to shipping traffic. The result was a cessation of all traffic between the Pacific and the Atlantic oceans from Tierra del Fuego to the Arctic Ocean.

In order to transit the locks, a vessel needed have a reservation in the queue and its fee paid by credit card. The fee starts at around $600 for a small-ish boat like the *When She Was Bad*; Van and I had transited several times to fish off the coast of the Galapagos (I always paid). A vessel pushing the "Panamax" size of nearly a thousand feet paid tens of thousands of dollars. Boats unaffiliated with shipping or cruise companies and without existing spaces in the queue could spend a month waiting for passage.

There was physically no way to "run" the canal. The locks were controlled from towers; unless you were to assault and take the towers in a manner that somehow—inexplicably—allowed you to gain access to the controls but prevented security forces outside from cutting power to the locks, you would never get anywhere. If you were within the final lock on either side and power was cut, a sufficient quantity of explosives might get your vessel free.

Or you could ram the lock. That would probably be the very worst idea in the world. If your ship was big enough to destroy the locks and heavy enough of construction not to be seriously damaged in the process—a virtual impossibility—you would spill violently out into either Bahia de

Panamá or Bahia Limon, depending on which side you ran. On the other hand, if your boat was small enough for you to use explosives to detonate the locks without destroying the boat—by mooring your boat on the far side before you blew the charges—then you'd better be prepared for your vessel to become the world's scariest log ride for a while.

All of this ignores the fact that you would have to already have transited the canal to be making a run for the ocean. One does not *flee* through the Panama Canal.

But it looked like ships had attempted to do exactly that.

The two-stage Miraflores Locks are eight miles from the Gulf of Panama. The single stage of the Pedro Miguel lock is a mile or so past that. From the air, they look something like metal bathtubs with doors that hold the water in, allowing an inbound vessel to be raised to the level of the next body of water. Outbound, the water is evacuated into the Gulf of Panama (or, on the Colón side, into Bahia Limon).

All three sets of parallel locks were destroyed. Whether there had been ordnance involved or the damage to the locks came merely from the impact of the giant container ship that had struck the metal doors, busted partway through and tipped over, I didn't know. Someone had panicked and gone for it. Or maybe the Panamanian pilot had gone dark while transiting. Or, or, or. We couldn't tell; given the lack of communications, there was no way to guess.

All that was clear is that Miraflores and Pedro Miguel would be out of commission for a very long time.

Welcome back to the nineteenth century.

☠

Van leaned over and said, "I've been thinking about Frisco, Frosty. I'd like to know what they're doing."

"Probably smoking weed and fist-fucking each other, same as always. And don't call it Frisco. And don't call me Frosty. And—why? Aren't you kind of busy thinking about Panama?"

Van said, "I can't help but think... if the Inferno did this—"

I said, "Virgil Amaro did this."

"I thought Virgil was dead."

"There's still Mark Amaro and Luke Amaro and John Amaro—the whole sick batch of them. They built this virus out of crap I brought them from Libya and the Philippines and the Hindu Kush and—what the hell kind of smoking gun do you need?" I panted. After that long a speech I was winded; yelling over the sound of the plane was exhausting.

Van glanced back at Trixie, who leaned forward in her seat and planted her red-capped head between us. Van shouted: "I don't know, Frosty. Those Inferno people are into some pretty weird shit. Like I said, there's competing factions within the group. Some of them are what you'd call extremists. I've seen things posted about the environment. Global depopulation. The transhumanist movement. Mass slaughter as a way to kickstart evolution again. See, just a few weeks ago some guy named DePop ChokeYa was on the Inferno boards flaming this guy named NotYa Ghandi—"

I interrupted, "Gee, these guys sound like real bad-asses. I wonder, do they have any secret bioterrorism labs in the jungle?"

Van got pissed. He yelled, "No, asshole. They have secret bioterrorism labs in San Francisco! Fucked up shit happens everywhere!"

I shouted: "I know. I've slipped in their lube."

Trixie chimed in: "Yeah, Frosty. You think it takes government defense contracts to build the ultimate weapon?"

I glared. "Let's not make this political. Let's just agree that slaughtering entire populations is my department. I'll be happy to blame you assholes for the Federal Backrub Program, though."

"Eat shit!" shouted Van. "All I'm saying is, these pricks at Bellona might not be solely responsible for what's happening."

I shouted back, "Solely?"

Van yelled, "Yeah, dick, solely. As in, maybe the Inferno got the Laugh from your paramilitary friends—bought it, stole it, stole the plans, whatever—and took matters into their own hands. You think Aum Shinrikyo invented sarin? All I'm saying is maybe these assholes at the Inferno were working with your military friends to develop—"

Trixie put her hand up. "Hold on, baby, hold on. As far as we know, there is no direct connection between the Inferno and the Amaros, right? I mean, sure, you uploaded the videos to the San Francisco server, but it's not like the two groups actually did business together... right?"

Van and I looked at each other grimly. Trixie had been out laughing when I told Van about my trip to San Francisco to pick up bodies for Virgil's research.

So I asked him, "How far to Colón?"

"Twenty minutes."

I told them: "Hold that thought," and grabbed the handset.

☠

I knew the ship well. I had served on her more times than I could count.

The *God's Mercy* was about 330 feet long and displaced a little over 2,000 tons. It was acquired and refitted in the early days of the Bellona Industries empire; it served in humanitarian, consultant transport and pirate-, drug- and smuggler-interdiction capacities.

She was originally a Vice President class high-endurance cutter, the USS *Aaron Burr*, home-ported Treasure Island, California. Decommissioned around the time I took my first job with a Bellona affiliate, the *Aaron Burr* was obtained at auction by Virgil Amaro and refitted to be both a company flagship and family yacht. It supplemented Bellona's then-small fleet of fast patrol boats and transports, which were then in the process of cornering the market for private pirate interdiction in the Gulf of Aden and Somali waters, and in conducting escort operations through areas of extreme civil disruption in the region. The *Mercy* had also been used for humanitarian missions off Sumatra and in the Philippines.

But they didn't usually call me for the humanitarian gigs.

From her decks, I had witnessed the slaughter of the innocent; it was only mildly less disturbing than the slaughter of the guilty, which I usually watched from up close. On the *Mercy*, I had transited the river Niger, from the Gulf of Guinea and the Niger Delta, the Delta of the Oil Rivers, upriver to the Sahara into the land where there were legends of sickness unknown to science, incurable.

Disembarking from the *Mercy*, years ago, I'd faced down something much like laughers—but not enough like them that I was smart enough to get the fuck out of the business. Or maybe the money was just too good.

The *Mercy* had also hosted the first Amaro Christmas party I'd attended—where, while *Twitter Epistle* and *The Sätän Häterz* played Jesus Rock to bewildered Israeli functionaries, I met the Secretary of State and an Archbishop and two former Secretaries of Defense and three columnists for *National Policy* and two Wolf News commentators, one of whom tried to make a pass at me. I'd turned him down politely, but that was the moment I knew I'd arrived; I was no longer a soldier. I was a *policy maker*.

Me and *God's Mercy* went way back; she now lay sprawled across the sands of Bahía Limón, bleeding oil, smoke, and laughers.

It was nice to see her in such good shape.

☠

Back before Virgil sent me away, I'd watched him start the transformation of Bellona from a principally American group to a truly multinational force. He'd been hiring up paramilitaries in Latin America from Pinochet-era torturers to Honduran Special Forces and the members of Salvadoran gangs. I knew for a fact he'd hired at least a dozen documented members of Los Zetas, the drug gang in Mexico that enforced its will with AK-47s, Apaches and Hellfire missiles whenever the government got uppity. They tended to run a little shorter than corn-fed American farm boys, so the crew's quarters amidships had been ripped out and re-installed with 70-inch bunks instead of 78. This was done to enable the *God's Mercy* to cram in more bunks, raising the ship's complement from 120 to 145.

The intention, however, was not to evacuate more personnel. It was to provide more troops to cover the Amaro Family's evacuation for the Holy Land when the Rapture came. If it ever came to that.

It had, so I had no doubt that Luke had brought 145 soldiers with him from Valparaiso. But did his hysterical plea for help mean those troops were dead and devoured—or just dead and dead? Or did it mean they'd abandoned ship or never showed up for work that morning?

Or did it mean they were laughers?

None of those options sounded pretty.

☠

The screams, static, noise on the radio had died out a bit. Many channels were overloaded. There was still the weird ringing sound, but it had faded slightly. The distress frequencies pumped out nothing but static. Not even gunshots... not even screams.

But when I cycled over to the three Bellona frequencies, they were empty.

No one was broadcasting, and there was none of the weird Tibetan-singing-bell interference.

I clicked from one Bellona channel to the other—empty, empty, empty, then back again—then a blast of static. I heard a sound—

The sound of weeping.

Luke said, "Oh God, they're at the door. They're almost in!"

I punched the button and improvised a bad Southern accent: J.R. Ewing drunk on Sterno, rehearsing for a bit part in a Broadway-musical remake of *Deliverance*.

I said: "This is the U.S. Coast Guard cutter *Point Esteban*, seeking the private vessel *God's Mercy*. *God's Mercy*, do you copy?"

There was a scream.

"Help me!"

Van and me looked at each other.

"Vessel, please acknowledge. Is this *God's Mercy*?"

"Help me!"

"*God's Mercy*, do you copy?"

"This is *God's Mercy*! Help me! Help me! I won't last long!"

I said: "Operator, identify yourself."

I don't think Van had ever heard the voice before. Trixie probably had. She was the conspiracy freak nowadays—she could have heard it on podcasts, interviews, found footage. Maybe surveillance; I don't know just how bad-ass these cats in San Francisco were. Luke Amaro has that unmistakable reedy nasal whine to his voice. Hear it once, you'll always know that's who you're listening to. That's why Trixie had that look on her face, like she was listening to the Devil.

Van got it though; something was up. Nobody could lay down that same tone of sanctimonious self-satisfaction while screaming for help.

Or maybe it was just the cold set of my eyes gone black with hate that told Van and Trixie both who it was. They knew before he said it.

"This is Luke Amaro, Bellona Industries Maritime Consulting, I'm a U.S. Citizen! They're at the door! I can't last long! They're laughing!"

I punched the handset and said, "Sir, what is the status of your crew?"

"Fuck the crew! They're dead! *Come get me!*"

"Roger that. Sir, what is your location?"

"Bahia Limón, asshole—The ship's going down! They're at the door—*Come get me!*" The shortwave whined out feedback.

I said, "Roger that, Sir. We'll be there in ten."

"I won't last ten minutes!"

"Fifteen," Van corrected me.

I said, "Fifteen."

He screamed, "I won't last ten!"

I said, "Sir, Can you please stay on the line?"

He bleated "The power's going down! Oh, God, they ripped off her ass!"

Luke was gone.

I said: "*Point Esteban* calling *God's Mercy*! *Point Esteban* calling Luke

Amaro! Please acknowledge!" I got silence and static.

I cursed. There was a big long empty as we cruised over the long ribbon of the Canal, skimming smoke, flame, and laughers.

The radio flared to life.

"*Point Esteban*, this is the private vessel *God's Grace*, Bellona Industries. We are en route to Bahía Limón, ETA two hours. We a fully armed crew trained in piracy interdiction. We will rendezvous with you and assist with the rescue of personnel from the *God's Mercy*. *Point Esteban*, what is your location, over?"

Trixie said, "Did he say *God's Grace*?"

I paled and said, "Um."

The radio crackled again: "Repeat: *Point Esteban*, this is the Bellona Industries vessel *God's Grace*. We are en route to Bahía Limón from Malta, ETA two hours. At your service, Guardians. The marines are coming home, Coasties. Boo-yah!"

I had paled at the mention of the *Grace*. Trixie saw me pale; *she* paled. Then it hit her what it was, and where she had read about it.

Trixie leaned forward and got all up in my shit.

"The *God's Grace* is the nuclear—"

"I know," I cut her off. "The last thing I want is for that thing to catch us in the air. There's no bird on the planet wants to play with that kitty, and this ain't exactly an F-15."

Van growled, "Thanks, Frosty. I love you too."

"We've got exactly two hours from now to find Luke, get the case open, and get gone."

Trixie put her lips to my ear and said, "What's boo-yah?"

I asked her, "Wasn't your Dad in the Army?"

"Yeah, but he never said 'boo-yah.'"

"It means 'woot,'" I told her.

"Forget I asked."

"Must be a new thing," I told her. "In my day, the Bellona battle cry was always 'cha-ching.'"

I killed the radio.

☠

The Gatun Locks came into view. Van circled over them. We all stared in utter horror.

The locks were wrecked.

It wasn't as pretty as the way they'd been wrecked at Miraflores. This was... ugly. Ugly as sin.

The locks at either end are—*were*—essentially large chambers of water contained within concrete walls, fed by pumps that fill said chambers with fresh water collected from Panama's rainy season. They lift a vessel heading inland from Bahía Limón to the water level of the lock above, allowing it to proceed. Coming from the Pacific, eventually the thing reaches the level of the Gaillard Cut and the Lago Gatun, allowing it to cross the mountainous interior of the Panamanian isthmus across what was once a rich jungle valley and is now a helluva place to fish for Cichla Pleiozon, a kind of Peacock Bass that's dandy with a little lemon twist. Or, going the other direction—that is to say, *down*, rather than up—the locks lower such vessels from the continental crossing over Lago Gatun and Rio Chagres, to the level of the Caribbean or the Pacific, respectively.

In one set of locks, apparently two cruise ships and what looked like a Colombian destroyer had played chicken. Desperate to escape the massacres on the coast, they wrecked racing each other to get in, while a fourth vessel had changed its mind when the dead started dropping on deck; it had tried to back up. Some sort of research vessel, from the name of it of it: *The Ends of the Earth*. The gates were jammed open around *The Ends of the Earth*, and all four ships were mired in the shallows. Water still poured from the outlets.

One of the cruise ships had tipped on its side; its name glared, cut into the expansive white side: *Panama Paradise*.

Both sets of locks were now disabled. In the second set, a container ship had rammed the lock—for what reason, I couldn't guess. Maybe the navigator went dark and started laughing as the thing moved. In any event, both sets of locks were ruined. The Canal was down for the count.

Wrecked sailboats and small skiffs had been crushed in the incident; shattered wood, metal, fiberglass was scattered in pieces across the locks.

We flew through coiling tangles of thin grey smoke. Beneath it was more smoke, black—oily and viscous, dancing in loops knotted up like snakes.

Trixie wasn't as used to me as seeing burning cities from the air.

She shouted: "That can't be—"

We through the smoke and the city sprawled out behind us.

Van glanced over his shoulder at her. "That's Colón."

We hit an updraft, and everything *bounced*.

☠

Colón burned. The city, to speak of, was gone. On the southernmost of the two peninsulas that encompass Lemon Bay, Colón was a city of midget skyscrapers and colonial buildings—or, rather, it *had been*. Now it was a city of flames. Streets could be glimpsed only periodically when the wind ripped chasms in the smoke. People, now things, had taken to the streets *en masse*, swarming beneath blazing multistory hotels and jungle-choked colonial resorts. Wave after wave of laughers surged against each other, seeking the very few living who still didn't get the joke. They spilled out of Colón and over the beaches, marshes, the shores of Bahía Limón, swarming the docks, mounting wrecked ships and moored hulks alike. Ships lay broken, everywhere—run aground when their masters went dark, or—there were lots of these, too—when small planes hit them.

Vessels burned, tipped and broken, wrecked on each other or run aground. They lay sprawled and sectioned, half-sunk, half-mired, rendering Bahia Limón virtually impassable. It was a graveyard.

Distantly, I saw the Beaumont Colón.

The towers were burning.

☠

The Cessna shuddered, choked and pinged. It knocked. It fishtailed. Birds hit us all over; one clipped the propeller and the whole plane shuddered. Van struggled to regain control. He cursed. "The birds are getting worse," he shouted.

We broke through another cloud of smoke; birds rattled on our wings. The Cessna jerked violently.

Beneath, Bahía Limón sprawled. It was clogged with ships, laughers and people.

The place was a slaughterhouse… a twisted graveyard of iron, wood and fiberglass. The entry channel was a mass of ships swarming with laughers. Vessels had been overtaken while waiting to be cleared for the locks.

But the exit channel was even worse. Here, vessels had tried to escape Lemon Bay to the Caribbean, but by the time they made it through the locks the contagion had spread to them. I could see how it happened: Those that made it into the locks had been overtaken by the laughers, who crawled over concrete embankments and leapt from towers and walls onto the decks of each vessel. The laughter had spread as the pilots had tried to escape. They'd run aground or struck each other.

Trying to navigate in too-tight quarters with other ships already abandoned and wandering, more boats and ships had piled up, striking shore and docks and buoys until Lemon Bay was a mass of ruined vessels ranging from ten feet to a thousand. Great listing hulks jutted out of the water, swarmed with corpses moving and unmoving. People writhed and squirmed and screamed in the water. Small powerboats flying handmade flags cruised back and forth. Crews shot *things* in the water, scavenging goods and rescuing survivors, or sometimes shooting those, too.

Some flags had red crosses. Others had skulls-and-crossbones. At least one flew the flag of the FARC, the main Colombian rebel group. I didn't see a Panamanian flag anywhere on a moving vessel. The only military ships were sinking or listing, sometimes burning. There were no Panamanian cops. No planes. No copters.

Colón had been abandoned.

☠

The *Bush Soaker* was coughing. Van looked at me.

He shouted, "We're low on fuel."

I said, "Can you land?"

He gestured in horror and said, "On this?"

I said, "You had another bay in mind?"

☠

Debris was everywhere, some of it burning. A few heads bobbed in the water, laughing wildly between shoulder-shaped lumps of safety-orange life jackets. Some of those dogpaddled. On the shore by the Beaumont, we saw dripping, bloated laughing things lurch out of the water, spewing Lemon Bay from their lungs. Had they *sunk and walked along the bottom*?

He said, "I'll get us down. But as for getting in the air again?" He shook his head.

I glanced at Trixie.

I said, "You still on board?"

She said, "Let's go viral."

☠

I took out Augie's cell phone.

I punched up Luke's number and typed:
dad where r u?

Luke came back with an incoherent mess:

AUGGiie helpp QTWRJH

Holy crap, was this asshat texting as he *turned*? If I got a "LOL" I was going to shit myself.

But there was almost immediately a follow-up:

augie come get me

I typed:

where r u dad

Luke: **bahia limon**

Me: **no shit dad where on Bahia Limon**

Luke: **r u in gods grace?**

Oh, shit. I wasn't sure how to answer that one.

no, I typed.

Luke: **copter?**

I figured it was better to tell a half-truth than make something up entirely.

no way dad. hijacked seaplane. lol!!
where is gods mercy??

Luke answered:
don't know...
struck by container ship
I see the old airbase

I whacked Van on the shoulder and pointed at the Beaumont's two burning towers. Ships had run aground there on the beach. On the pale sand where tourists had once sprawled on chaise lounges to devour margaritas, hors d'oeuvres and pool boys, there was a tangle of them.

I felt a chill of recognition, as if I'd been looking for her my whole life.

In the shadow of the place where I went viral, I saw the slaughtered remains of *God's Mercy*.

We went *down*.

☠

The *God's Mercy* had run aground into a beached tugboat. It had then been plowed into by a Panamax container ship, which had pulped the stern of the *God's Mercy* as it ran aground itself, tipping over at an angle until oceangoing rail containers spilled everywhere—onto the beach, over the tugboat, over various other wrecked craft that had beached.

The container ship must not have been going very quickly—she may not even have been under power. The massive ship would have done far worse than pulp the Mercy's stern had it been going anything close to cruising speed. But then, in Bahía Limón, speeds were heavily restricted, though I doubt anyone was handing out speeding tickets.

As it was, the collision had spilled the vessel's cargo of oceangoing rail containers, probably stacked ten or twenty high. Other containers tipped and swayed over the *Mercy* at terrifying angles, threatening to fall any second.

As Van brought the Cessna around, I could see the name on the stern of the cargo ship: KSM *Tagore*, Calcutta.

The three vessels sat half-atop each other at a cockeyed angles in the shallows of Bahía Limón, the mud and their mutual tangle the only thing keeping them from sinking. Long black streams of fuel trailed from the ruined stern. The diesel engines still ran, coughing and choking, shrouding the deck in smoke. Its twin Little Bird helicopters had been upset from their moorings on deck; both sat at twisted angles, folded rotors clearly damaged. Those Birds were being transported with their rocket pods visible. That would have been strictly forbidden while transiting the Canal, and completely improper for a privately-owned vessel anywhere other than a war zone. So I guess Luke thought we were at war, which was a little hard to miss at this point.

On the remains of what had been the stern of the *Mercy* fifty or sixty yards away, there was a nautical-grey plate riveted temporarily over the ship's designation—she'd been traveling incognito. It now hung in shards from a single rivet in the corner of what had been the Mercy's stern: *VS Leonardo, Liberia.* Visible beneath it was the real designation, one it had borne since I served on her during pirate interdiction in the Malaga Strait: *BMC God's Mercy, Panama City.*

Oil trailed from the back.

God's Mercy lay dead.

Van had to take a couple circuits before he found a strip he could land on nearby.

"We're flying on fumes, Frosty."

I growled, "So quit flying."

After we committed to the landing, he spotted laughing heads in the water, cushioned by safety-orange life jackets.

We plowed dead things under as we landed, salt spray rising behind us. We glided through the water. Laughers in life jackets writhed and squirmed. They reached up to us as we passed; some tried to haul themselves onto the back of the floats, laughing as they groped the struts. One got some purchase and started climbing.

I drew a five-sev and thumbed off the safety. I opened the door.

I looked guiltily at Trixie, who said, "What are you looking at me for?"

I hopped onto the float. The little Cessna tipped wildly in the water and Van bleated, "Hey, Frosty! Center of gravity!" as I aimed.

I said "Center this, Bubba," and started pulling the trigger.

The life-jacket laugher went down wet. Two more were behind him, sniggering. Their laughs drifted on the wind with a bright spray of red. A chortling septuagenarian lady with a nightdress under her vest hauled herself onto the driver's-side float. I ducked down clutching the strut of the float I stood on and straightarmed it just under the *Soaker.* I barely got her before her head would have been above the floatplane's body.

I found three more jacketed chuckleheads in the water up ahead, braying salt water and diesel.

I played killjoy with five-sev rounds.

Suddenly a gunshot deafened me—inches away, in the cabin of the Cessna. I looked up, shocked; Van held his silver .45 straightarmed before him, aimed ahead and to the left. The spent brass cartridge ricocheted and rattled—ceiling, window, windshield. It landed, smoking, between the ukulele and knockers of Van's hula girl.

Van breathed hard, eyes wide, struggling for breath as he stared. The windshield of the Cessna had become a spiderweb, a fat half-inch hole the fly in its parlor.

I looked back over my shoulder; a soft brown-skinned guy in Bermuda shorts and a Jimmy Buffett T-shirt tottered on the front of the float just behind me dripping seawater and gore.

He looked like he'd been crying.

Bile poured down the Parrothead's chin and glopped in thick streams across a lemon-yellow Telecaster. He jerked and swayed and went down, falling into the water with a splash. The float hit and plowed him under, but there wasn't far for him to go—we were in the shallows.

Van said, "Put your seatbelts on."

"Why?" Trixie and I asked at once.

Van growled, "Fine. Don't." He opened the throttle; Trixie and I both groped for our belts and locked them only seconds before Van ran the *Soaker* up hard onto the sand. It made a hell of a sound—a bestial scream of tortured baling wire.

He said, "Seemed a hell of a lot easier than tying off."

Up above us loomed the vast grey bulk of the *God's Mercy*.

☠

We stepped out onto the sand to saddle up.

I watched as Van duct-taped a flashlight to the front of his lever-action rifle.

I said, "What the fuck is that?"

He said sheepishly, "I like the thirty-thirty, Frosty. They don't make a rail for it."

I said, "Stratton Industries, St. Louis, Missouri. Christ, Van, pick up a gun magazine now and then, will you?"

"No shit, for the Winchester?"

I said, "Yeah. I mean, it's a little complicated to install, but once it's on it'll do—shit, it'll do lights, scope, laser—it'll even do a bayonet."

Van said, "No shit!"

Trixie said, "Are you two gonna kiss or something?"

She was slinging an ammo belt over her black Patti Smith T-shirt. She clipped her walkie to the belt, as had Van and I, and threaded the wire to the earpiece up under the shirt and into her ear. The mic was integrated. I would find out later that this somewhat expensive purchase—five of them, total—had been purchased mail-order to Van's box in Coetupo, at Trixie's insistence. Van was a cheapskate when it came to everything but guns. If he'd been in charge, we would have been using soup cans and string.

I said, "Let's try channel 5." We did; it was clear. I said, "Only use the walkies if we get separated. Don't use names."

Trixie said, "Does that mean we get cool call signs?"

Van said, "I'm good at that part—you can be Agent Bubba, and I'll be—"
"For fuck's sake," I said. "There's only three of us. Just don't talk unless absolutely necessary."

"I've been telling him that for years," said Trixie. She slid mags into her ammo belt.

I asked her, "Do you feel strong enough to do this?"

She looked at me like I was crazy.

She said, "You mean, like, *emotionally?*"

It was a Van-ism. It hurt my brain to hear her use it.

I said, "No, physically. You were pretty sick a few hours ago."

She shrugged.

She said, "I feel remarkably well. I think my dopamine's off the charts."

I said, "Huh?"

Van propped Old Smokey on his shoulder and whined around his freshly-lit Cuban: "Well, *my* dopamine's in the shitter, Frosty. You mind if I kick back with a beer and watch the game on my cell phone? Air Force is playing Navy." He jerked his big hairy chin toward the *Mercy* and snarled, "In fact, I think the Kuna Yala Air Force is about to *kick the Navy's ass.* Wanna play, or would you rather go make a video about it?"

Sasquatch and Trixie high-fived and bumped hips. They marched across the sand.

Trixie said, "Boo-yah!"

Van said, "Huh?" and she punched him on the arm.

I stared after them. It'd been an awfully long time since I'd left her on the beach at Vuelo Puente. I thought, *Who are these people, again?*

☠

We hoofed it from the *Soaker* about fifty meters to the forward ladder of the *God's Mercy*, crunching sand under our boots. Run aground, it'd pulped a set of metal stairs that had provided access to the beach. Finding the stairs free from laughers—as the beach had been—we used them to climb to the lowest of the metal rungs that led up to the deck of the *Mercy*. It was a bitch of a climb.

I was glad Salvation had backpack straps; that damn metal suitcase was a boulder. I thought again about how Little Augie might still be walking around if, back in Darién, he'd thought to wear it instead of drag it. Wouldn't that be a gas? Then I wouldn't have the case, and for all I know Augie mighta whacked my ass.

Carrying the backpack meant I couldn't carry a rifle, so I holstered both five-sevs at my belt.

Van took lead, because he didn't have the backpack. I came after.

Just before we reached the deck, Van drew his .44 and took deep breaths before he went over. I held my breath, but there were no troops waiting to repel boarders.

Turned out the crew was at mess.

☠

Seconds after he cleared the rail, Van said, "Dante, get the fuck up here." Then I heard three shots; then Van said, "Jesus fucking Christ."

I scrambled. I climbed.

I cleared the railing with my pistol ready.

Gunsmoke swirled on the Panama breeze, mingling with the black stink of burning oil. I stared, wide-eyed through the smoky effluence of the .44.

I said, "Jesus fucking Christ."

Trixie joined us.

She said, "Jesus fucking Christ," and raised her AK.

☠

The *God's Mercy* writhed. Its deck was a sea of flesh.

It took a long, slow moment of horror for Van and Trix me to piece together what happened. We'd seen from the air that the container ship *Tagore* had struck *God's Mercy* at a relatively slow speed—not enough to rip the *Mercy* in two, but enough to dislodge its cargo of oceangoing rail containers probably stacked five or ten deep. It seemed likely that in the haste to depart, the containers had not been properly secured.

The multi-ton containers had spilled over the *God's Mercy* in a heap, pinning Bellona consultants underneath. The Bellona guys must have been massed on the deck, preparing to repel boarders. Those killed or incapacitated in the collision were the lucky ones. Any of them pinned beneath containers or trapped by the avalanche of metal were then set upon by laughers from the *Tagore*, all of whom probably looked worse for wear to begin with.

Here on the bow, we could make out the flow from the *Tagore* as laughers mingled and interchanged, the chuckleheads devouring Bellona "consultants" at their leisure… eating them alive… tucking into men with mangled limbs and broken backs and concussions. Devouring them as they lay unconscious or half-conscious, bones broken, bleeding.

There were two distinct populations from the container ship. There'd been the *Tagore*'s crewmembers: South Asians, their flesh the deep hue of the Bengali people. There were perhaps thirty of them, forty, maybe more—laughing already when the ships collided, which was probably why they'd collided in the first place.

A crew of Bengali laughers was bad enough news for the Bellona troops, but nothing to cry about; after all, these were trained killers.

But several of the rail containers—it was impossible to tell how many— had been filled with *people*.

This was, of course, far from unheard of in the vast universe of international shipping. The men were Asian, in their twenties and thirties. I knew what that probably meant. I'd once intercepted women being trafficked from Xinjiang to Dubai via Singapore, but they were shipped in more secure facilities. That's because, for the cartels that run trafficking operations, one escape or discovery means the potential interest of the press, and that's bad for biz.

But Chinese guys looking for construction work in Bermuda or Argentina? They were the ones who went of their own accord, at prices exorbitant enough to put them in debt for years. These were the ones who mortgaged themselves to the trans-Pacific Coyotes of the container ship industry. They were the poorest, or the most desperate—occasionally, the ones fleeing potential police investigations.

These guys lived in shipping containers like this one for months on end while *en route*.

In recent years, the doors on containers that carried people were not secured as tightly as those on other containers. This had been a trend among traffickers ever since the discovery a few years back of a container on which scores of Chinese migrants had suffocated, many of them *after* the discovery that humans were being trafficked inside. They had died while customs workers debated how to get them out. It caused public outcry and law enforcement attention—even worse for biz than just having a "shipment" discovered. The cartels that ran smuggling ops, thereafter, started hacksawing off a bolt or two to make sure the doors could be opened if absolutely necessary.

So when those containers hit the deck of the *Mercy* hard; the doors broke open... and laughers spilled out.

The Bellona combatants left walking or, if unable to walk, with weapons still close at hand, had dispatched some of the laughers while they were trying to exit the container. Those things still lay, their heads blown open and their bodies across the open mouth of the container, trails of gore streaming back to mingle with the bones.

Others made it out of the containers and assaulted the trapped and injured Bellona troops. But the laughers' bones had been fractured—all but pulped—by the impact.

They probably didn't move fast—but there were a *lot* of them. Hundreds.

They'd writhed across the deck like boneless worms and eaten the Bellona consultants alive.

Now, the deck was covered in every color of nightmare. Bengali sailors and trafficked Chinese were all tangled up with the half-eaten remains of white, black, Asian and Latino Bellona troops.

Some of them laughed, but there was not a living soul, and not a laughing walker among them.

It seemed obvious that, with all the living ones either dead and laughing or dead and dead, any chuckleheads with the capability to get upright and mobile had gone away looking for warm flesh—into the water, onto the shore, or—

Van and I looked at each other—

Below deck.

The ones left topside were ruined, their limbs and torsos mutilated till they couldn't support their own weight. Some could crawl; many couldn't even do that. And they all reached toward us, muscles vainly working soft pulpy arms with nothing of bone structure left... as they puked out wet strains of the Panama Laugh.

Van said, "What do we do?"

Trixie racked her AK.

☠

Their pulped forms writhed and oozed, jutting pieces.

You could tell the dead from the undead because the latter howled out laughter, ranging from chuckles to guffaws.

I motioned Trixie and Van back.

I said sharply, "*Point!*" Neither one asked what I meant.

I took point, with Salvation on my back; I used the five-sevs, both of them, left-right, right-left, killing as needed. I carved us a path across the deck, putting down laughers. Van aimed the thirty-thirty and took down any I missed, or any who crawled after us. Trixie used her AK.

Coming around a container, I almost walked right into a Chinese guy, maybe twenty years old. He'd been torn in half. He was making better time than some of the others, because he only had half a body to pull on his arms.

His guts trailed behind him about eighteen feet.

His teeth clacked and chattered. He made rasping noises, mouthing empty chunks of laughter. But the integrity of his lungs had been compromised; they'd probably been pulled half-out of his torso. Every laugh made a hiss and a slurp in his guts, and a wet, sick, open sound from his gore-covered mouth. Pieces of gut lung, bone and blood, had migrated mouthward; they spilled out as he tried to speak.

I stopped and stared at him, gape-mouthed, five-sevs smoking. He was maybe five feet away.

Trixie and Van stopped behind me. Van aimed the thirty-thirty.

Trixie said, "Frosty—you okay?"

Three feet. The Chinese guy reached for me.

I blew his brains out.

He jerked and went still.

"No," I told her. "I'm pretty fuckin' far from okay."

☠

I knew the layout of the ship like the back of my hand.

When it was the *Aaron Burr*, the aft bilge could only be accessed through a hatch in the aft of Deck 5. Decks 1 through 3 were accessible only via the forward ladders, heavy-duty spiral numbers hewn from plate steel. The front of the *Mercy* had been refitted to include the Amaro family suites near the bow, which meant Deck 5 would have been accessible only through the stern ladder—if there *was* a Deck 5, per se.

But the *God's Mercy* was the Amaro family yacht as well as an operational ship. Decks 3, 4, and 5 on the *Burr* had been gutted. Those levels were now the ballroom. There, every Christmas former Secretaries of State had listened to very bad rock bands telling them they could say "screw you" to

Satan if they'd just say "word up" to God.

We would reach Deck 4 from the forward ladders; there was no other way to do it. The power plant was dead; electric power had shorted out in the accident. There were no lights below deck.

That meant we'd have to cross the ballroom in the dark.

I copped a couple of tactical lights and laser sights from the two of the Bellona laughers we euthanized, and fixed them to the standard rails on the five-sevs.

The lights cut the gloom—but only a little.

☠

We reached the forward access door.

I handed Trixie and Van earplugs.

"AK's are loud in closed spaces," I told them. "Ditto with Old Smokey."

Trixie put hers in.

Van shrugged and said, "All those years of rock shows, Frosty. I'm already deaf." He jerked his head toward a pile of gooey laughers and added grimly, "Besides, I wanna hear the music."

I said, "*Claro*," and stuffed my earplugs in.

☠

I unslung the suitcase. It felt mighty nice to get that monster off my back.

I texted Luke:

dad? still among teh livingg? lol

Luke texted back immediately:

augie help me

I texted:

I have the package

Immediately:

YES!!! BRING IT!!!

Urgent, apparently, but not so urgent he couldn't hit CAPS LOCK.

I pointed at the suitcase, then at Van.

"Can you carry that?"

He frowned. "Only if I have to."

"Bring up the rear. Walkies on?"

I freshened up the five-sevs and took the ladder.

☠

We went *down*.

When the *Aaron Burr* had been refitted, the electronics had been completely redone, but most of the Coast Guard furnishings had been kept as long as they did not bear currently active insignia. The result was that the entire ship, commissioned in the early '60s, had an antique, utilitarian feel about it.

As a vessel, she'd always been one of my favorites.

I felt kinda bad for her.

☠

Stairs on a military ship are always called "ladders." That suits them; they are as close to up-and-down as you can get without being totally vertical. They are therefore a pain in the ass to descend while shooting any kind of weapon.

The good news is, laughers have a hell of a time ascending them, too. They can navigate stairs all right—*real* stairs—but not these. I stood at the top of the forward-starboard ladder and watched a dozen of the laughers, sensing us, try to come up to munch. They'd spilled down through the hatches to consume whoever was below deck. Now, they tried to come for us, but it was like watching a horde of maggots try to climb up a rope. If maggots could laugh.

They crawled, white and swollen, over each other, tittering, chuckling, guffawing.

Their lips peeled back in hysteria, showing teeth bloody with strips of flesh as their gums and tongues worked.

The crews of both ships had mingled with the laughers from the containers. Male without exception, these guys were Chinese and Bengali,

Caucasian, Latino. Liquid spilled from open wounds, strings of skin and muscle dangling. Some had limbs that had clearly been broken in falls down the ladders—they hung at deeply wrong angles.

They couldn't get up the ladder—but there were *many* of them. They piled on each other so fast that before too much longer their slippery, decaying bodies would form a mound, and whichever laughers came later would be able to make the hatch, no matter how many bones they had broken or how rubbery their swollen limbs were.

My eyes went wide; my skin crawled; I fought an urge to puke.

They gained by inches, mounting the ladder atop writhing bodies.

I gave 'em Panama kisses with a five-sev, their laughs bleeding through my earplugs.

I descended the ladder, kicking ruined faces out of the way.

I hit the Deck Three landing and kicked bodies out of the way. I played the tac light around. I shouted, "Clear!"

Trixie shouted, "Huh?"

Above her, Van shouted: "That's what he says when it's okay to proceed. It's a military thing."

Trixie shouted, "What?"

I screamed, "Get down here!"

She started climbing while I kicked more dead things out of the way. She hit the landing. Van grunted his way down the ladder, lugging the suitcase.

He said, "That shit is heavy."

There were a few writhing laughers damaged enough that they were no longer upright—but still chuckling.

I drew my second five-sev and went around double-tapping them.

Trixie took a few with her AK-47. Van complained about the noise; I offered him earplugs again and he waved them off. I'd offered. He held the thirty-thirty in a waist-high grip. He emptied the rifle meticulously into laughers. Cartridges rattled on the the metal deck.

"Fuck's sake," said Van as we swept our lights to make sure none of them were moving. "It didn't seem like that big a job when we started."

I told Van, "I've been feeling like that about a lot of shit lately."

I put fresh mags in both five-sevs.

Van clicked his lighter, lit a fresh cigar. He set the thirty-thirty on a nearby sink and inserted rounds into its tube magazine one-handed.

Trixie took her earplugs out. "What's that noise?"

I cocked my head.

There was more laughing, mixed with sobbing.

From below? Who could tell, in this black-inky empty? I couldn't tell which way was up, but then, there was a shitload of that going around.

"That can't be good," I said, peering down the next hatch.

For a moment, past the hatch there was nothing black beyond as I looked.

Then dead things flooded into view like rats, howling out laughter.

I screamed and lurched back.

Van said, "Hell of a soprano, Buttercup."

I glared. I holstered one five-sev and aimed the other at the laughers below.

These ones weren't soldiers or sailors. They weren't Chinese. They weren't Bengali. They weren't all one thing; they were everything. They were too young for military service, too small for bodyguard work by a long shot. They were twelve, fourteen, fifteen. These weren't any of the flavors of dead we'd encountered so far on the *God's Mercy*. They didn't have fatigues on. They were in underwear, shorts… medical gowns. *Medical gowns.* The kids spewed out goo, drooling, laughing.

I aimed into the mound of laughing adolescents and opened up with pistol fire.

Laughers went down.

Van took over with the thirty-thirty while I reloaded.

It took a while. There were a lot of them. We double-tapped them, descended to the forward landing, adjacent to the ballroom.

The double doors to the ballroom were carved oak; they'd been splintered.

There were char marks around the edges. Someone had used charges to blow this door.

Beyond, I heard laughing.

I stood there staring into the darkness, not wanting to aim the tac light.

Trixie stood behind me, breathing hard, and said, "What's through that door?"

I backed away, looked at her, and said, "The ballroom."

She said, "It's got a ballroom?"

I said, "Don't blame me, sister. I only jitterbug." But it wasn't very funny

I looked at her, weighing what to tell her—what I knew, and what I'd guessed. *Medical gowns.* She musta seen my look. She got pale; she grimaced. Then she nodded.

Van kicked the fresh laughers out of the way.

He said in a growl, "These aren't Chinese."

I said, "I know."

Van said, "Or Indian."

I said, "I know."

Van said, "They aren't Bellona, either."

I said, "Van, I *know*."

Van said, "Some of them have scrubs on. Slippers, paper—medical gowns. They've got *bracelets*."

Trixie said flatly, "That's 'cause they're patients."

Van breathed hard. Trixie and I shared a look. I said, "They're doing experiments."

I stared through the gaping hole that had been the carved oak double doors.

There were laughers beyond.

We could hear them.

In the inky black of the ballroom, there were things that chuckled and chortled and cackled.

There were criers, too, sobbing disconsolately. And there were tweeters and whoopers—and things that moaned or screamed or whimpered or made buzzing sounds.

But not like schizophrenics. Not like garden-variety Laughing Academy graduates. Not like crazy people.

The noises they made came out robotic. Spaztic. Involuntary.

They didn't moan or whimper because they were in pain. They didn't buzz because they thought they were bees.

They did it because that was their *strain*.

Beyond that splintered oak, I knew there was two hundred feet of open space. But it wasn't a ballroom anymore.

The *God's Mercy* was a prison ship.

☠

I carried both the five-sevs, with their tac lights activated.

I crouched and crept through the blasted-open door into the ballroom.

The deck was lined with cells with bars—steel bars. Behind them, things moved and made noises.

Things beyond description.

The ruined massacres of human flesh that had lined the deck under the blazing grey light of the Panama sun with smoke from burned Colón filtering everything to shit grey—those were nothing compared to the obscenities we saw squirming inches away, locked in cages, shackled to the walls and howling: laughing, sobbing, screaming, mewling, laughing.

Pieces of people. Not living, but not dead. Moving.

There were thirty, forty, maybe fifty of them in cages, lining the big open ballroom. There were whole laughers, strapped to tables; there were others missing limbs and chained into cages, chittering and sobbing.

But there were more; there was worse. Ruined torsos. Legless beasts. Severed heads.

I said, "I don't feel so good."

Van said, "Are those *people*?"

I said, "Prisoners," I said. "Guests."

Trixie said flatly, "They're patients."

Van puffed his cigar. He played his light around, cradling the thirty-thirty. His hands were shaking.

He said, "What do we do?"

The path between cages looked just big enough to give us clearance.

Van started walking, thirty-thirty at his shoulder, the flashlight carving him a path through the dark.

Trixie said, "Oh, so now I get to bring the suitcase?"

I said, "You mind?"

She made an exaggerated coughing sound. Frowning, I holstered one of the pistols, got the suitcase and rolled it behind us. Trix and I brought up the rear, but every step we took made us stop and stare at the horrors in the cages.

We both got distracted. We stopped, and Van got way ahead of us.

From out in the darkness, I heard Van yell, "Oh, shit."

There was laughing.

I started running. Van's thirty-thirty blasted; I heard him running. I had both the five-sevs ready; I outpaced Trixie. I swept the light, but couldn't find him. I heard Van's thirty-thirty barking again and again, brass cartridges hitting the deck. I heard wet sounds.

Then I heard the louder blast of his forty-four.

I heard him yell, "Welcome to Panama, fuckers!"

From the end of the corridor came a scream.

"Don't shoot! Don't shoot!"

For a split-second, I thought it was Luke.

But it was a woman's voice.

It made the back of my neck go bumpy.

I caught up with Van. He stood surrounded by the laughers—ones he'd just put down, and others who looked far less fresh. Nothing moved. Van had his rifle cradled and was holding his .44 magnum. He aimed it into one of the cages.

I heard a woman scream, "Put the gun down!"

He said, "Eat shit, lady."

Trixie came behind me. I motioned her back.

I said, "Van? What's up?"

The woman in the cage said: "Don't come any closer or I'll kill him!"

"You'll kill him anyway!"

I kept coming. My flesh crawled as ruined things in the cages reached out for me. Van motioned me back. He hissed, "Give her some room."

She screamed, "Put the gun down! Both of you—all of you! Put the gun down! Don't come any closer! I'll kill him!"

Van said, "Then where would you be? You're locked in."

She screamed: "I locked myself in! I'll shoot!"

Van said, "What are you shooting?"

She said, "What? It's a gun! I'll shoot!"

Van aimed his gun and said, "That looks like a mousegun. Thirty-two? Twenty-five?"

She said, "What? Put the gun down!"

"Kel-Tec? Beretta Bobcat?"

She said, "I—I don't know! I'll shoot!"

Van fondled his revolver.

He said, "Here's my point, Ma'am. Forty-four magnum, etc., etc. I'm sure you've seen the movie. Do you feel lucky? Et cetera. Put the gun down."

She cracked. She started weeping. She let out a soft keening wail and said, "You won't rape me?"

"Lady, my *wife* is present. Watch your fucking language."

The woman in the cage let out an easy breath.

I heard the gun hit the floor, heard Van told her, "Back away slowly."

He kept his .44 on her; he bent down on one knee and said reached through the bars and picked up the gun.

He said, "Twenty-two. Wow, lady. I'm glad I didn't pee myself."

He tucked the gun in the pocket of his beach shorts, never lowering his own.

I caught up with him.

I saw her: pale-skinned, Iberian-nosed in a filthy denim-blue prison-style dress and combat boots, her bleached-out hair showing black roots. She glared at me through the thick bars of a cell.

It wasn't a good moment, when we recognized each other.

She was wishing she hadn't put down the gun.

I said, "Hello, *Doctor*."

☠

She recoiled as if some deeply motile force had arisen between us. She was not in good shape to begin with; the events on *God's Mercy* had pretty clearly caused her great emotional distress.

She looked drained and pale and haunted and terrified and broken. She also looked dehydrated; it was *hot* in the makeshift prison. The things did not put out heat; in fact they had no vital signs and no natural functions to speak of, at least not in the way we understand them. But there was also no ventilation—and, at least until the container ship had ripped the stern off, the *God's Mercy's* engines had been pumping out plenty of heat one deck below trying to make the mouth of Bahía Limón and the Caribbean beyond.

Thirty or thirty-five, she still looked like a petulant punk girl gone slightly rough. Her bad bleach job was grown half-out in a ruined mass on her head. Her heavy eye makeup formed mangled smears from one side of her face sort of, diagonally at about thirty degrees, like she'd been sobbing on her side, maybe trying to get up the courage to end it. It was a good thing she hadn't; suicides with .22s never go well.

She had been crying. She was disintegrating under the relentless force of nightmare.

And it couldn't have happened to a nicer girl.

I said, "Do you remember me?"

She said, "What do you think?"

I said, "I remember you. Dr. Ava Sorzano, right? You're quite a kisser."

Behind me in the gloom, I heard Trixie say, "Huh?"

Ava's voice trembled, her face a mask of horror. She stared at me, waiting for the bullet.

Van said, "You know this dame?"

Trix said, "You know this— gaaah!"

A severed head in a nearby cage had lurched at her, some part of its neck muscles or jaw being intact and leaving it able to launch itself.

If there hadn't been bolts shot through the cranium, securing it to the wall of the cell, it might have made some progress.

Trixie backed away from it and shook all over.

I told her and Van, "I met Ava in the Darién Gap."

Van and Trixie made shocked sounds.

Around us, body parts jerked and writhed.

Dr. Sorzano said, "Are you going to kill me?"

I said, "Did you do this?"

Ava shook her head crazily. "No, no, no." The volume rose every time she said it. "No, no, no." She just kept saying "No," like saying it often enough would convince me.

I said, "I heard you the first time. Not just this—" I gestured at the things in the cages. "I mean—*this*." I made a wider, sweeping gesture. "You know what's happening out there, right?" She nodded furtively. "Did you help them release this virus?"

She shook her head wildly. She sputtered: "After Virgil died, Luke brought in experts—all sorts of experts, and not good people. Not good at all. I didn't do this. These things—these *things*—they're not—I didn't—"

Her claim was lost in a mass of sobs that mingled with the sounds from the other cages.

Van and Trixie were lost, their eyes roving from the sobbing Ava to the gooey things in the cages. Neither seemed to be able to believe what they were seeing. Trixie had also started to weep, though more softly than Ava. Van just kept cursing… yeesh, the *mouth* on that guy.

I said, "Did the Amaros release it?"

Ava got deep gulping breaths into her lungs and managed to say, "I don't know. I really don't. You have to believe me. Luke says no. Luke says they didn't. Luke says it was somebody in San Francisco."

Van and Trixie were far enough away that they didn't hear it. I heard them arguing over whether to start euthanizing the patients… or what was left of them.

I said, "Do you think that's plausible?"

Ava nodded. "Maybe. I know we bought vaccines from them."

"And bodies."

She nodded. "That was before my time, but… yes. They needed ones that had been cryopreserved. It's… technical. And I also know someone from San Francisco cracked our database and posted the gene sequences on the web. I'm not a computer person."

I said, "People keep saying that."

"I know Luke and Mark were both convinced the hackers were the Inferno people."

I said, "Were?"

She said, "Are, as far as I know. Luke's—" she nodded her head toward the bilge hatch.

I said, "How about John?"

She said, "Luke thinks he was killed this morning—a few hours ago. I didn't get where... in Colombia, I think."

I asked her, "And Mark Amaro?"

She told me, "In Malta. The plan is to travel to the Holy Land."

I growled, "So they knew the End Times were coming?"

She made a sad little shrug. "I've been in prison in Argentina."

I said, "Huh?"

She said, "That's a very long story. I'm sorry. I'll tell you everything, but we've got to get out of here. I can't take it anymore."

"Oh," I said. "Do the neighbors make too much noise?"

She finally moaned: "I'll help you. I'll help you. I'll help you to stop it! I don't know how, but I'll figure out a way. I can figure it out, I'll figure it out, there has to be a way, if we found a rhinovirus that—if we—see, there's a sequence in Marburg that—" She made a series of choking sounds, grasping the bars of her cage. She looked like she was about to faint.

Van broke in, "You know, Frosty, I love the Discovery Channel as much as any other pothead, but... "

Trixie said, "Frosty?"

I ignored them. I asked Ava: "Are you contagious?"

She said, "No more than you."

I asked her, "Do you have the cure?"

Ava shook her head. "No."

I asked, "Does anyone?"

She said, "I don't know. I don't think so."

I snapped my fingers, pointing wildly at the suitcase. Van obediently grabbed it and rolled it up.

"Then what the hell is this?"

Ava looked at the suitcase blankly.

She sniffled and said, "I have no idea. But it's defrosting."

I said, "Yeah, no shit. My back is still wet from carrying it. It was on ice. Liquid nitrogen. It's a secure case. Requires thumbprints to open. Luke kept calling it 'Salvation.'"

"Well, I've never seen it before. For all I know they could have thought it was the cure, then found out it wasn't. I know they don't have the cure. Or a vaccine that works." She was starting to break down again. "Please let me out. I'm sorry for my part in this... I'm sorry, I'm sorry, I'm sorry..."

I reached through the bars, grabbed her by the hair and growled, "Save it. Siouxsie. Where's Luke Amaro?"

She jerked her head against my grasp—to the back of the ballroom.

I let go of her hair. I said, "Give me your key."

Ava started sobbing. Our faces were close.

She wept miserably, "If I do, are you going to leave me?"

I fondled the five-sev and said, "If you don't give it to me, you'll never know, will you?"

She started unbuttoning her dress.

☠

The key was on a slender chain around her slender neck.

She might have unbuttoned one or two more buttons than she needed to, strictly, in order to get to the key. She looked at me rough, like she was trying to remind me why I might want her along, rather than starving to death or slowly going laughie in this cell. I glared back at her so furiously that she looked away and buttoned them back up while I opened her cage.

I gave her to Van and Trixie and said, "Take her topside. Tie her up." See if you can find a boat. Like an RHIB."

Van explained to his wife: "Rigid-hulled inflatable—"

Trixie cut him off: "*Whatever*."

Van said, "What are you gonna do, Frosty?"

I looked Van in the eye, held my hand out and growled: "Scalpel."

Van knew what I meant. He gave me the mousegun.

In the cages, things grabbed at us.

☠

The hatch to the aft bilge was gooey with blood and pieces of finger. The laughers Van had put down had fingers ruined right down to the bone. They'd been clawing for Luke, trying to get through the hatch. Why not for Ava, the cage, so much closer? Was that a puzzle-piece?

Fuck it, I thought. *All cats are grey in the dark.*

I holstered my five-sev. I dragged the suitcase down and planted it about halfway down the hall between the nightmares. Things writhed and groped through the bars, reaching for me. Tongues lolled. Teeth clacked. So did gumless mouths.

I took out Augie's cell phone and checked the action of the .22. It was a Colt, antique, pearl grips.

I took the tac light off the five-sev and propped it in the hallway, aimed up and away, toward the suitcase and away from Ava's cage.

I got in Ava's cage.

I texted: **LOL**

☠

Luke responded immediately: **augie where r u!**

Me as Augie: **come on out, dad, copter waiting lol!**

Luke: **god b praised :-)**

The hatch lock turned with a scrape.

The hatch opened.

☠

Luke poked his head out of the hatch.

He said, "Augie?"

He came sliming out of the hatch into total darkness.

He stank of bilge, which is a very special kind of foul.

In the slanted glare from the flashlight, I saw he held a silver pistol.

I lowered Ava's pistol.

Luke Amaro saw the suitcase and started crawling crazily.

He shrieked, "Augie! Augie! Bring him here! Bring him!"

Luke crawled by, reaching for the suitcase.

I shot him in the ass.

☠

I was out the cage door and on him and over him in a second, stepping hard on his gun hand with one big booted foot. It was a little .380 pocket gun, and when he wouldn't let go I kicked him once in the face. He let go. I kicked it away into the darkness, leaned down and flipped Luke over.

I shoved the .22 so far up his nose I was pretty much dipsticking his brain. It was at least a quart low.

I said, "Welcome to the jungle, fuckface."

☠

You know the first rule of combat engagements? Don't shoot if you're not prepared to kill. Shooting someone in the ass is two things: indulgent and stupid. It's easy as hell to miss and take out a femoral artery. If might even have returned fire, though I doubt that prick could hit anything. Whatever. I was over it. I figured… ass? Sure. Why not. Ass. He'll know I'm serious, but not, like, as serious as if I just up and started extracting major organ systems from three meters away. He might imagine I could be reasoned with. Which probably wasn't the best conclusion for him—but then, these are miraculous times.

✠

He screamed. He writhed in pain. He jacked and thrashed and fishtailed. I put my boot on his throat and leaned *hard*: this was hit man yoga.

I pulled the gun out of his nose, shoved it in his mouth. He stopped screaming; his eyes went crazed in the off-kilter glow of the flashlight. He started drooling; I frowned. I took the .22 out and shoved the five-sev where it had been before Luke could make much more than a bleating wail.

Much better; when a man can drool or bleed on you, doesn't he have half the power?

I said, "Luke, you're probably afraid of dying. Is that right?"

He nodded.

I said, "That burning sensation in your buttock? That's as good as your ass gets for the rest of your very short life, and no other part of you will spend much of that time even remotely as good as your ass feels right now. Remember how you made me a hero?"

He stared blankly.

I said, "You might not have heard the stories about what I did in Fallujah."

His eyes went wide. He nodded. He'd heard them.

I said, "Well, Luke, I've had a change of heart, Luke. I'm still a monster… but I'm not that kind of monster. Problem is, in times such as these, guys, like, *revert*. Wanna meet the man or the monster?"

He gulped, or tried to.

I said, "Okay, monster, then. Let's see, which cellmate would you get along with? Hm… how 'bout the one with the dancing intestines? He seems friendly." I holstered the five-sev.

Luke howled, "I didn't do it! I didn't! We didn't! I swear! We tried to stop it!"

I said, "Now we're getting somewhere. You're trying to make friends with me. Creating the illusion of friendship is very important with interrogation. Would you like a cigarette, Luke?"

I smacked him hard across the face.

"Ooops! I'm out of smokes. How about some bubblegum?" I smacked him again. "Damn! I'm all out of bubblegum, too!"

Luke yowled, "No, I didn't, I didn't! We didn't do it! We researched it, yes—it was—speculative—nothing—we didn't —"

He was completely incoherent.

I drew my five-sev again and shoved it in his mouth.

I said, "I didn't kill your son, Luke. But I *will* kill you. And not with a bullet. I feel kind of icky saying it, but, you know, I'm kind of an icky guy."

Luke slurred wetly around the barrel of the five-sev: "The suitcase! The suitcase!"

I pulled the pistol back slightly and said, "What about it?"

He said, "Let me open it!"

"What's in it?"

He sobbed, "Dad. Dad, Dad, Dad, Dad!"

I said, "Huh?"

He sobbed, "Dad. Virgil. Dad."

I said, "Huh?"

"Please?"

"Is it a treatment? Is it a cure?"

He nodded furiously, sobbing. "It can help us find the cure. Please, Frosty, please?"

I shoved the gun back in Luke's mouth and screamed, "Don't call me that!"

☠

Luke sat on the floor in front of the suitcase.

He said, "Dante, I'm sorry."

I said, "Save it. What's in the suitcase?"

"My father," he said.

I thought he'd cracked.

I said, "Who's the third thumbprint?"

He said, "It's in my jacket pocket."

I put the gun against his skull and said, "Get it out. Slowly, with two fingers."

He did—very slowly, as I looked in his eyes for any hint of a thought of a furtive gesture.

He said, "Here."

I stepped back slightly; I looked down.

He held a hand.

It was an old one—old in that the guy it had come from was old; it was also old in the sense that it had for some time been dead, though it barely looked fleshy. It could have been a plastic replica, except that there's some creepy trait to actual human body parts that just can't be duplicated; that's why horror movies don't creep me out.

I said, "Um."

He looked apologetic, "It's my father's. It's been preserved by plastination."

"Exfuckingscuseme?"

He said, "It's not as secure as a retina scan, but that would have cost $108,000."

I said, "Wow, you are a really huge douchebag, you know that?"

He said, "He knew he might die before us."

I said, "It's not a suitcase nuke?"

He said, "I don't want to die, Dante. No."

"Open it."

He nodded.

He aimed one last look at me. His face was drawn but he'd borne no wounds, apparently, until I blew a hole in his buttock. The little whiner; I'd really just clipped him.

The suitcase had three places for thumbprints.

Luke said, "You have to hold my father's hand."

I said, "I don't think so."

He said, "You have to. It has to be at the same time. Both my thumbs—or both of Mark's—and one of my father's. Mark has the other one."

I said, "I never hold hands on a first date."

He said, "There has to be pressure. Dante, please."

I said, "What's in it?"

"He is."

"What, his *ashes*?"

"No, he wasn't cremated."

I snatched up the hard plastic hand and rammed the five-sev in Luke's kidneys.

I said, "Go."

"When I press, press."

He did. I did. The suitcase gave off a hiss.

It popped.

I grabbed Luke by the hair.

I said, "Open."

He raised the lid.

White smoke poured everywhere.

I started screaming.

I mean, nobody wants to run into their old boss when you're working a new job, right?

Especially since I'd never got it straight whether I had quit or I was fired. I think I'll just say *quit*. Like... for my pride, y'know?

☠

Like I said, horror movies don't freak me out. I've seen too much shit that made horror movies look like jokes. They just don't scare me.

But there are a few things that do. I'm gonna have to say... they tend toward, like, the *esoteric*.

And I'm sorry to say they get more esoteric every time I meet an Amaro. Someone had frozen Virgil Amaro's head.

The suitcase that held his remains, apparently had not been designed to get dragged from the Darién Gap to the Colombian coast to the San Blas Islands to Panama City and then flown the fuck across the Panama Canal. At some point its liquid nitrogen boiled off or its structural integrity was lost.

Virgil had *thawed*.

What crap had this prick played around with? Had he been seeking eternal life, so he could live through the End Times and—if you believed a Candy Commando blogger from San Francisco—profit from them?

Well, that radical life-extension garbage wasn't quite the asshattery it appeared to be.

He was alive now, or something like it. He sucked air in through what was left of the tissues of his neck—and belched it out with wet crackling sounds.

Virgil bleated, "Dante! Dante! What are you doing here? Is it Easter yet?"

I screamed at the top of my lungs.

Virgil said, "Luke! Luke! Is it over? Is it over? Is He here? Is God here? Is He here?"

I stumbled back; I lost hold of Luke's hair. I went scrambling back down the hallway with old broken half-things clawing after me, tongues extruding, empty gums slapping together.

I screamed.

Luke seized his father's head and howled in pain. The clear container housing it was frosted thick with snowflake shapes. His fingers froze to it instantly; he got up and started lurching for the ladder, trailing the metal-Lucite cylinder after him as he screamed in pain. He didn't move very fast with a slug in his ass and a ten-pound container of howling human head Superglued to his fingers. He left a trail of blood and sobs.

I grabbed the tac light and limped down the corridor, stiff-limbed from fright and half-hyperventilating.

I aimed the five-sev and the light. I howled, "Freeze, motherfucker! Luke, freeze! Get the fuck back here!" I went after him, sweeping the light from side to side. I swept the light and found only shadows.

Was he hiding?

I swept from one end of the ballroom to the other.

I swept the cages. That was not fun. He wasn't in there.

Things reached at me from the cages.

Something toothless puked bile on the ground from its laughing mouth.

The walkie crackled in my ear.

Van said, "Agent Bubba! We got company!"

I howled, "In a minute!"

Van said, "Not really, Dante—*now!*"

I ran.

☠

I made the deck.

As I exited the forward-starboard access door, I heard a "Pssst!"

Trix and Van hid in the shadows of an empty shipping container—one of the ones that had once held laughers. Their eyes were like saucers.

Van held the thirty-thirty, Trixie her AK.

Van jerked his head skyward, behind the container.

I said, "What?"

He said: "Panama, Panama, God shit his grace on thee, Agent Bubba."

I said, "Don't call me that! And… Huh?"

Trixie said, "It's the warship."

"The *God's Grace*? They said two hours!"

"It's *been* two hours!"

I crept up to the edge of the container they were hiding in… and stuck my head out.

It was only maybe nine o'clock. The sun was low enough in the East that

The vessel cast a loooooooooooong shadow.

I'd only seen her press photos in Trixie's bookmarked files. But the *God's Grace* had since been loaded for bear.

She had been Virgil's pet project before his death, but she'd proven so expensive that it was not until now, years after his death, that she was being delivered. Checking out her technical specs had provided me with a comforting sideline while taking a break from listening to Trixie's sick chortle over the last few days.

Manufactured in the shipyard at Papenburg, Lower Saxony, the *God's Grace* ran on two mini-nuke power plants. The thing pumped out twenty megawatts and could top forty knots if it came to it—and do it for *two years* without wiping her ass. From her deck projected chain guns, Gatlings, grenade launchers, and an 81mm mortar. She carried six RHIBs, four 175cc scout bikes and a pair of unmanned aerial vehicles for reconnaissance. She was rigged to carry two Little Bird helicopters, but when the *Grace* arrived in Bahía Limón they were not at their stations. The Bellona site used all the toys of the *Grace* as a recruiting tool for new contractors; they even had an exploded PDF spec sheet that proclaimed to potential employees: "Join Bellona Industries, and someday you might serve on the *God's Grace*, the smallest and most potent nuclear warship ever built!"

That was hot air; the *Grace* was not the world's most potent nuclear warship—you'd have to lay those laurels on the U.S. aircraft carrier fleet—but it was the smallest. And ton for ton, nuclear propulsion and state-of-the-art engineering made her the equal of anything in her class, including the ships of most militaries.

From what Trixie's files held, the *God's Grace* got the conspiracy freaks awfully hot and bothered over what exactly it meant that the Amaros wanted such an impregnable ship. Those cats lose their shit over anything that glows.

But now that I actually got a chance to see the formidable vessel, it occurred to me just how reasonable a question it was: Why would it be cost-effective for a a private military contractor providing pirate interdiction and counter-insurgency services to third-world governments to build a nuclear-powered surface vessel using state-of-the-art mini-nuke power plant technology and arm it with 25-mm chain guns, 30-mm Gatlings, crew-manned thirty-calibers and autofeeding grenade launchers? So they can cruise around using high-tech weapons to whack Indonesian pirates with twenty-foot speedboats and AK-47s that haven't been field stripped since Stalin delivered them?

Or did they have bigger game in mind?

Van whispered, "What do we do?"

Still staring at the *Grace*, I said, "Where's the doctor?"

Trixie said, "Um… right here, dipshit?"

I turned around and whispered, "The other doctor!"

"Oh." Trixie turned on her tac light and aimed it back into the shadows of the rail container; there sat Ava, looking miserable. Her face was ruined from the crying. She'd been tied up, wrists and ankles—apparently by Van. He did a shit job; the knots were all lumpy.

Van said, "Where's what's-is-name?"

I said, "I don't know."

"You don't *know*?"

"He escaped. I was distracted."

Trixie hissed: "You were distracted? How did you let yourself get distracted?"

I said, "It was kind of an unusual situation."

Van cut her off: "Who cares about him? What do we do about the nuclear warship?"

I whispered, "I don't know."

Trixie whispered, "Dante, what do we do?"

I hissed, "I don't know!"

Van begged, "Dante, tell us what to do."

I said, "Surrender."

Van said, "After what they did to you for five years?"

I said dourly, "You don't know the half of it."

"I get the sense I don't know the *tenth* of it," said Van. "And I'd rather not."

I said, "Fine. You wanna go down fighting?"

Trixie said, "Not particularly."

I said, "Then we've gotta run. Are there Zodiacs?"

"Sure, Frosty, four enclosed RHIBs—that way," said Van. He jerked his head in the direction of the *Grace*, which had pulled up to the ruined stern of the *God's Mercy*. "We could get to that one, on the port side, but we'd walk right across their line of sight. There's one more at the bow, but it has laughers."

I said, "There are still laughers?"

Van said, "Someone apparently locked them inside. Smart move. Besides, even if we could clear it without attracting attention, we can't get her launched from the bow. We'd have to crane it to the sand and hump it to the water—and as for craning it, there's no power."

I said, "The plane's on the sand."

"We're out of fuel. I might get her airborne, but we won't get far. Besides, gee, Frosty—I'm not sure, you're the expert here. Do you think that thing could shoot us down?"

I flipped him off. "Hide, then."

"With her?" He jerked his thumb at Ava. "I thought she was theirs. She'll shout."

"Gag her."

Trixie said, "Have you ever tried to gag someone, Frosty?" I gave her a piteous look, as in, *What do* you *think*? She went on, "It's not as easy as it seems. She could still make noise. Kick or something. Get their attention."

In the back, Ava said, "I won't!" I think she'd decided we were about to slit her throat, which… it wasn't a bad idea, but we needed her.

So I said, "She won't make a peep. Those fuckers sent her to prison." I shined the light back at her. I added, "She *claims*…"

Ava nodded furiously.

"Well," said Trixie, pleased with herself. "Unfortunately somebody just got finished threatening to torture her."

That pissed me off. "I did not! I never once threatened to torture her." I racked my brains. "Maybe a little. Barely. I barely threatened to torture her."

Trixie said, "Well, she thinks you're going to torture her. The whole time Van was trying to tie her up, she was sobbing and saying how did we really want you torturing her on our conscience, and I was like—"

I said, "*Trying* to tie her up?"

Van said, "Don't worry, Frosty. I tied her up. Christ, I'm a sailboat captain."

I stuck my head around the edge of the rail container.

I said, "Fuck it."

"Huh?"

I said, "Wait till I get clear. Then run there, there, there." I gestured, pointing at a path between containers and over to the opposite side of the ship from the *God's Grace*. "Get to the port amidships RHIB. Reach under the rig and you'll find an emergency lever. Pull it. Then once the shooting starts, hit the red RELEASE button. You'll have to climb down the amidships ladder, so climb fast. If it's not already fueled, you'll have to fuel it; there are jerry cans by the outboard."

Van said, "Did you just say once the shooting starts?"

I pointed the tac light at Ava. "She gets left for the marines… or the chuckleheads." She gaped in fear. I said, "Sorry."

Trixie said, "Frosty, did you say 'When the shooting starts'?"
I snatched the AK out of her hands and ran for it.

☠

I ignored the hissed pleas of *Get the fuck back here!*, and the subsequent hurled growls alluding to the improper personal conduct of my ancestors going several generations back.

Then there were tears, but I was getting used to that shit.

I made it through the open area without getting spotted. Now I was behind a rail container on the far side; it would be an easy climb to the roof of the bridge.

About twenty Bellona troops in body armor were crossing onto the *Mercy*.

I looked back at Trixie and Van; they gestured at me desperately.

I blew 'em an air kiss and hopped on the bridge ladder.

☠

I took the ladder to the sniper's nest in front of the bridge.

This was a rig designed specifically for what I planned to do—and I had used it many times before. The railing in front of the bridge was fitted with bulletproof plates; railing and plates alike could be removed to provide line-of-sight to a target. In this case, it was amidships. I removed the plate gingerly and set it aside.

I was almost at the highest point on the *Mercy*. The only thing higher was the flying bridge, which Luke had used for cocktails and hitting golf balls into the Indian Ocean.

Cradling Trixie's AK, I stretched out on the no-slip rubber.

I had the field glasses.

I peered through them.

I watched the Bellona marines argue for a while, then split up into four teams of five and start picking out paths through the things that had once been human.

The marines didn't like what they saw.

I got the impression that while they may have seen the news stories about Cuba and the other outbreaks, none of them had seen laughers in the flesh. And certainly not this many of them.

Before long, the Bellona teams were yelling so loud I could hear them from my perch—even make out words.

It wasn't pretty.

☠

The word "marines," in the generic, indicates something very different than "Marines," with a capital M. Capitalize that M (at least if you're an American) and you get centuries of service, a dose of *Semper Fi*, and arcane rituals like naming your rifle something creepily erotic like "Lucille," instead of something reasonable like "Old Smokey."

But in the world of contractors, a marine is merely a combat-capable contractor trained to deploy from ships and/or serve in an interdiction force for maritime activities, over and above what the typical sailor would be able to provide. It becomes a bit more complicated if you're talking about ground deployments from ships, boats or ship-based copters, but if you're operating a privately-financed campaign against, say, an uppity group of pirates, then marines, lower-case m, are the mopes who climb down the rope ladder and start cracking pirate skulls.

I could see from my perch that this force contained both women and men. That was my first hint that something was unusual. In the old days, Virgil and his sons were such raging sexist pigs that they'd literally *never* hired women for combat roles. Technical ones, yes, but not combat.

Mark Amaro, who oversaw all Bellona recruitment—in concert with his father, when he was alive—would *never* have hired women for the elite staff of the *God's Grace*. Certainly not to escort Luke Amaro from burning Colón to the Holy Land under this kind of danger.

Had time made Mark less of a sexist jackass?

Anything was possible—after all, the dead were walking.

But Mark Amaro no longer a prick? That woulda been a stretch.

But there was far more messed up in their behavior than just the constitution of the group.

Out of the twenty who had boarded the *Mercy*, in addition to the five or so female faces, there were another few who were so fucking young you coulda slapped lipstick on them and never known the difference. These kids were twenty-two, twenty-three, maybe some of them twenty-four. They were younger than typical deployed Bellona contractors—who usually had military experience to begin with.

These cats were young. They were raw. These weren't killers.

It wasn't that they did anything wrong on technical terms; they knew how to clear a deck, by the book.

They knew what to do, and they tried to do it. But they *couldn't*.

Frankly, I had just about lost it when I'd seen the deck of the *Mercy*.

And I'd seen a lot more than these schmoes had.

Even if they'd been the seasoned killers I expected, it probably wouldn't have made that much difference.

This was well beyond killers' ken.

Seeing them react to it was beyond mine.

☠

The twenty or so marines had split into four squads to clear the deck. In my sniper's nest, I was not far above one group of five—two women and three men. One woman had a pistol; the rest had M-4s.

The wind caught their voices; I heard pieces of conversation and ranting—distantly:

"Oh God, oh God, oh God..."

"His name was Pedro—"

"I knew him..."

"Oh, for fuck's sake, they ate him alive..."

"Fuck! Fuck! Fuck!" The pop of gunfire as one put down a laugher.

"Oh God, he's still moving..."

"It's still moving!"

"It's still moving!"

"Get it! Get it! Get it!"

"It's still moving!"

Gunfire, gunfire, gunfire. They must have put out seventy rounds to take down one laugher.

Then the recriminations started.

"Did the fuckers who sent us here know about this shit?"

"Those fuckers write our paychecks, asshole!" The guy who said that last thing was sobbing. The other guy took a swing at him. He missed. The crying guy danced away, waving his rifle in wild-eyed paranoia.

"Fuck that!" someone else snapped. "I heard a rumor they—"

"Don't even fucking say it!"

Someone else: "I heard they're into that apocalyptic—"

Someone screamed and started firing wildly into a Bengali laugher who'd crawled up behind them.

I watched the group go further to shit. No one seemed to be in charge.

No one said "*Pipe down!*" or "*Watch your six!*" or "*Hold it together, marines!*" or any of that shit R. Lee Ermey says on *Mail Call*, let alone anything that made any actual operational sense in this case, like "*You mind shooting that laugher, dipshit?*"

I got to my knees and craned my neck, looking behind me and to the port, to where Trixie and Van were running for the RHIB's; as it turned out, the *Mercy* itself had provided all the distraction they needed. For now.

But when Van and Trixie hit the emergency release and their lifeboat started to crane its way down, it would make a joyous sound unto the Lord. I'd heard it; it was not unlike a chainsaw.

They'd need minutes—many of them—to get down into the water, climb into the boat—hopefully without getting caught by laughers—and, if the boat wasn't fueled, to fuel it from the jerry cans.

To get clear, Van and Trixie would still need a distraction. The marines would have to be occupied.

I put my eye to the AK's iron sights.

I picked out a head.

The marine who owned it dropped to her knees, grabbing pieces of what had been face. She wailed ceaselessly.

Another guy dropped his rifle and puked his guts onto shredded fragments of a Bengali all mixed up with the crushed remains of a Bellona industries beer cooler, shattered bottles wet with puke and blood and beer and melted ice, the mangled front of the cooler still bearing the in-joke Bellona industries "motto" for Panama pool parties and Harper's Ferry recruitment events and Tikrit rooftop barbecues:

War gets hot. We'll bring the ice.

The cooler had mostly bisected a Bellona consultant's torso; he didn't have much use for it, though, because Van or Trixie or I had put two slugs in his forehead an hour ago.

One of the marines screamed, "Keep it together!" with a trembling voice. He was no older than the others, but had the bearing and fury of a man with a Master's degree. He was Harvard, Yale, Princeton. He was the kind of guy whose dad was a soldier and his dad was a soldier and his dad was a soldier and some big percentage of them had been cops for thirty years after and spent their waning years grilling chicken on the porch and swapping stories about Korea. This guy dreamt of glory but flunked his drug test. He thought he was an officer.

Far as I was concerned, he was a corpse.

I thought that just as his face broke apart.

He lost it.

Tears poured down his face.

Christ, he looked about *twelve*.

I put down the AK and took deep breaths and thought: *What the fuck is happening here?*

There was a crackle from the walkie.

Trixie: "Dante! Dante! You've got—"

—which was pretty much when I heard soft weeping above me.

I said, "Oh fuck."

I whirled and raised the AK as the thing tumbled over the railing, hurtling down at me from the flying bridge, its sobs changing to hysterical laughter as his mouth opened wide.

I got the AK at waist-level, pointing straight up. I started firing, crazily, stupidly, without even thinking. Bullets tore through his chest, till I remembered I wasn't a douchebag and tried to aim for his head—but by then it was too late. If I'd had a bayonet fixed, the sailor—a big beefy blonde guy in a Bellona ship crew uniform, not a soldier or marine—would have impaled himself on his belly. I probably would have run him through.

As it was, he hit with enough force to impale himself anyway.

It just wasn't a nice, neat, *pretty* sort of impalement.

☠

He landed on me hard enough that he pinned me. The AK jammed into my guts. The wind was knocked out of me. I started shoving myself back; the laugher screamed at the top of his lungs, have a grand old time.

I heard Trixie's voice in my ear, crackling. "Dante, there's a laugher above—oh. Oh wow. Oh wow. Oh *wow!*"

I thought, *Thanks*, Trix as I struggled with the laugher. It seemed to be everywhere—as in, all over me, goo-wise—and it seemed to be everywhere—as in, pinning my wrist as I tried to pull a five-sev from its holster—it went flying—grabbing at my throat, lunging for my face.

I fought it.

I was out of my mind. The thing had me pinned, its clacking teeth inches from my face. I'm going to be honest; I can't be sure I wasn't screaming, though no one seemed to hold it against me later.

The thing almost had me. I went nuts. I tried to use the AK as leverage, but the laugher had its arms around me and was closing in on getting a taste of my oversized nose.

I let go of the AK, but that only hurt my purchase—because now the laugher was jacked down on top of me, and the butt of the assault rifle was shoved hard into my balls. I tried to shove him off me and get up and crawl, but the fucker was just plain too goddamn big.

So I rolled.

Remember how I told you that staircases on a military ship are always called ladders? How they're mostly up and down, mostly?

That's *mostly* why I didn't break my neck. *Mostly.*

☠

The three of us—me, my rifle, and Laughing Boy—went tumbling down the bridge ladder. The walkway beyond had been pulped by the corner of a rail container, and was cocked at a rakish angle. I landed not on the section of walkway that I'd mounted, from the forward side, but the one facing amidships.

The laugher and I started sliding. The thing was going crazy, wild with hunger and LOLZ.

I wrenched my shoulders against his weight. I struggled. I fought.

I managed to draw my second five-sev, but he got my wrist and bent down to take a bite as we slid and we rolled and we tumbled. I thumbed the safety and pivoted my wrist and started firing wildly; bullets tore through his cheeks. Teeth went rattling out and slid down alongside us.

We slid through the vast, twisted gap in the metal railing.

Me and my three sons—AK, pistol, and laugher—hit the deck *hard*.

We landed amidships.

In a circle of Bellona mercenaries.

☠

I hit with the laugher under me. He cushioned my fall, or I would have been cracked in two. As it was, I was just hurt like hell, as the AK was still shoved through his guts, so I landed on the laugher with the butt shoved up between my legs. Little Dante and the Huevos were not thrilled about that; pain exploded through my guts and up into my throat.

The thing was beneath me, its neck working violently up and down with the sound of scraping vertebrae as it tried to get a bite of my head. But then, I'd just shot most of his teeth out.

In fact, I would find out a moment later, most of his face was gone. His cheeks were wide, pulpy flaps, as his exposed, toothless, fleshless jaw went snapping up behind me.

It happened in seconds—I was about as stunned as a man can be, and had had the wind knocked out of me good. But this was a thing of some importance, so I found the motivation through the screaming pain in my lungs.

I was pinned by his one working arm, but the other was broken in enough places that it lay out alongside me like the tentacle of a jellyfish. My right hand was free, and I got it in my pocket.

It came out holding Ava Sorzano's Colt .22.

Without looking or aiming, I started shooting over my shoulder.

I emptied the clip.

I blew laughing boy's brains out.

☠

The Bellona troops near me—faced with a prone target who'd just fallen from the sky and been smacked in the nuts with a rifle butt—one armed only with an empty .22—finally figured out how to be soldiers.

Four of them stood over me, rifles aimed at my head.

Someone boomed: "Sir! Surrender your weapon!" It was a female voice.

I held up the empty, smoking mousegun. I let it dangle from my trigger finger.

Someone snatched it away.

They kept their their rifles on me. Railed-up M-4s—tac-lights, laser sights.

The smoke from Colón made the laser beams swirl like lightsabers.

I watched the red beams dancing. These cats were *shaking*.

I'm not a big fan of nervous soldiers. When hands start to shake, people get dead. Sometimes soldiers. Sometimes insurgents. Sometimes kids.

I wasn't sure which one I was, so when someone barked, "Nice and easy—on your knees, hands behind your head, fingers laced together—"

—I wanted to be cool.

But I just wasn't. I was pissed. I'd seen too much before breakfast to keep it together.

So I growled, "Whatever you say, Colombo."

But I did it.

I struggled to my knees, which was not a lot of fun. My back hurt like hell. My nuts felt swollen. Four marines half-circled behind me, aiming their rifles.

There was one woman in front of me with a five-sev. She was the one who had spoken.

She said, "Identify yourself!"

I snarled, "I'm viral, fuckers. Open up and say aaah!"

I'd said it without thinking. I'd had a pretty rough morning, and when I climbed that bridge ladder to the sniper's nest, I'd planned to come down in a body bag.

Now, I expected to be dead the second Luke showed up.

Dead, or downstairs, in those cages.

Alongside Trixie. Alongside Van.

The woman got in my face, her gun hand trembling.

She had high cheekbones; her eyes were almond-shaped behind yellow shooting goggles. She had skin that I guessed was usually, probably, the color of a very wet latte at Starbucks on the Via España. Right now it was more like the grey of concrete; she was shaking.

Her jaw dropped. She said: "You're not—"

She'd stepped very close.

That was not her first mistake, but it was going to be her last.

I had it all planned: grab her gun hand, get control, get the gun to her head. If I couldn't get the pistol away, just start breaking her fingers and pulling the trigger.

The marines weren't far away, but they didn't seem to be able to shoot worth shit, and if I couldn't break enough of the woman's fingers to get head shots at three meters… well, the rounds from the five-sev will pierce body armor. With her as a shield, I'd take a few of them with me—and in the confusion, Trixie and Van would be the least of their concerns.

The woman said, "Holy shit—Sir, you're not, Sir, Sir, you're, Sir—"

Her sidearm was back in the holster so fast I didn't know it had ever been out.

She kicked her Bates Tacticals together hard and stood at attention. She saluted me.

"Sorry, Sir! I didn't recognize you, Sir! With all the gore, Sir! Sorry, Sir, we're all very sorry, Sir."

I thought, "?"

I wiped laugher guts out of my face and stared at her.

I got from my knees to my feet. I hurt all over.

I said, "Identify yourself!"

She held the salute. She barked: "Supervising Technical Contractor Second Class Amber Lin, Sir!" she said.

Her hand trembled. She stared at me. He lips were tight. Her yellow-tinted shooting goggles hid nothing of her fear; the sweat stood out on her forehead underneath her flat black helmet. It poured underneath her body armor; I bet she already had heat rash.

That's when I saw Van, up in the sniper's nest. The fucker had started climbing the same moment he saw the laugher fall on me—but, coming from the RHIB, he'd scrambled up the back ladder, so his view had been obscured. He'd had no idea I'd fallen with the laugher atop me—until he got up there.

And by then, I was busy making new friends, as is my wont.

So when I spotted him, Van had Old Smokey aimed at the back of Amber Lin's head. He was maybe half a second from pulling the trigger.

Then someone behind me saw him, too, and uttered a strangled yell of alarm. "In the... thing up there! On the pointy part of the ship!" The marines behind me started waving their rifles wildly, squealing "Who's that?" Who's that!" "Who's that?"

I hit the button on my walkie.

"Van! Hold your fire!"

From the sniper's nest, Van looked at me like I was crazy.

I hit the walkie button and said, "Get down here!"

He disappeared down the back ladder.

Amber still held her salute. I'm a little rusty on my salutes. In my day, contractors would mostly just flip each other off. So when I returned it, I'll admit, it was pretty half-assed, but it seemed to be good enough for Amber.

I said, "Uh... as you were, um... Amber, was it?"

Then Supervising Technical Contractor Second Class Amber Lin said, "It's okay, guys! Don't you recognize him? Everything's going to be okay! It's Dante Bogart! He's in charge! It's Frosty Bogart, guys, it's Frosty!"

Their faces went *zing!* As a group, they trembled all over and let out a soft moan of gratitude. Then they stood at port arms.

I regarded them like they were batshit crazy.

Having heard the screaming and the shooting, the other squads of marines came double-timing it along the deck, threading through the debris and laughers. They saw their fellows standing at port arms and didn't know what to do. They gaped stupidly.

Amber said, "Guys, guys, it's Frosty Bogart. Frosty Bogart, guys!"

Then *those* assholes kicked their stompers together and stood at arms.

One of them, in the back, said, "Who?" and someone smacked 'em on the head and hissed, "From the recruitment videos, dipshit!"

Behind me, I heard Amber say, "Pssst! Sir! Sir! Is she one of yours?"

She pointed at Ava Sorzano, who was double-timing toward us across the deck of the *Mercy*, rubbing her hands. Ropes trailed from her wrists as she picked away the last of Van's crappy knots.

I said, "Um…"

Amber said again, "Pssst! How about her?"

On the far side of the marines, Trixie perched atop a half-crushed shipping container, holding Van's .45.

She'd been about to make a rear assault.

I said, "They're both with me. So's Captain Fish. He's another contractor. He and I go way back. Lower your weapon, Captain. The marines have this under control. Boo-yah!"

Behind me, the consultants shouted awkwardly, "Boo-yah!"

Van reached the deck and ran up to us, puffing, Old Smokey half-cocked, like the rest of him.

I said, "This is Captain Van Fish, and these are Doctors Beatrice Ferguson and Ava Sorzano. Van, Dr. Ferguson, Dr. Sorzano, this is Amber."

Amber looked at Van. "Captain of the *God's Mercy*, right?"

My eyes narrowed. I said, "Well… let's just say he's the captain *now*."

Van said, "Uh… welcome aboard."

Amber said, "Sir, yes, Sir. I had one of those myself, Sir. Our Captain went laugher on us."

"Huh?"

"We had to kill him, Sir. Well… *I* had to kill him." She looked pleased with herself. "I'm sorry, Sir, we weren't briefed on personnel. Just that we'd be escorting some VIPs back to Malta. We got call signs but not names, Sir—Coppola, Brunel… Brunel must be you!" Her face brightened, like she'd figured something out. She gestured at my shirt, which bore the legend "Isambard Kingdom Brunel," and a photo of a Captain Beefheart type in a top hat. Augie's, of course.

I said, "Let's retire that name. Just call me Mr. Bogart."

"Yes, Sir," she said. "Mr. Bogart, Sir, do you know what's going on? The MDTs are down, now, and the radio's crazy. There's this weird interference—like Tibetan bells. SATCOM, BELLOCOM, cellular, internet, GPS —" She looked ashen. Her throat thickened. She couldn't go on. "It's all screwed up, Sir. Do you know what's going on?"

I frowned at her. I said, "Are you in command?"

Amber said sheepishly, "No."

I said, "Then who the hell is?"

Amber's mouth hung open silently.

Someone behind me said, "Um, Sir, Jason, Sir."

It turned out Jason was the ten-year-old who'd screamed at his buddies to keep it together, then lost it. He was sprawled out on the deck twitching in his sleep while three of the marines surrounded him with their rifles aimed at his head. They were waiting for him to start laughing.

Amber said, "Um."

I said, "Supervising Marine Second Class Lin, did you have something to add?"

"Sir, there were conflicting memos."

I blinked. "Did you say *memos*?"

Amber said, "I'm sorry, Sir, we're not very good at this. We were all training in Hamburg, but, like, almost none of us with the same companies, Sir. See, I didn't even know I was signing up with Bellona; I thought I was signing a contract with Maddaloni Security Systems, and Jean over there is a cryptography trainee with Samson Computer Security, and Susan works for Schleimer Retail Shrinkage Prevention, and—"

I whirled and howled, "You're a mall cop?"

From the back, Susan bleated, "Sorry, Sir!" and saluted.

Amber kept trying to explain, her voice uneven but clear. "And, see, we all got this order, to serve as security to deliver the *God's Grace* to Malta—I mean, she's fresh out of the shipyard, Sir, but there's this German law about nuclear vessels, Sir, and, see, after what happened in Japan there are requirements for armed security—but, well, Sir, none of us finished our training so we're not that sure exactly who's in charge of whom. See, Jason's a Supervising Interdiction Agent First Class with Giorno Border Systems, and I'm only a *second* class with but now it's with Ringuette Interdiction, which as far as I can tell from Wikipedia is a wholly-owned subsidiary of TDT GMBH, which is Bellona's name in Germany, whereas Giorno is part-owned by the Israeli company—see, Sir, we're in the process of—"

I lost it. I went ballistic.

I got in Amber's face, spewing spit and turning seven shades of thermonuclear.

I channeled every jacked-up weekend-warrior asshole I ever knew who wanted to be George Patton but didn't have the necessary brains, balls, experience, knowledge, right hook, left hook, general vicious meanness or commensurate mental illness.

I screamed at the top of my lungs:

"Supervising Technical Contractor Second Class Lin, I asked a simple question! Who is in command of you freaks?"

Amber said it the same instant that all twenty marines behind me said it: "You are, Sir!"

I screamed, "I can't hear you! Who's in command of you worthless shits?"

They screamed: "You are, Sir!"

I got Robert Mitchum-sized goosebumps.

I did it again, maybe seven times, with fresh invective and insults hurled with each new iteration of the mantra. Van looked like he was about to suggest a few more, but Trixie motioned him silent.

"You are, Sir!"

After years of interdiction, it looked like I'd jumped sides for real.

Piracy was a hell of a lot easier than I thought it'd be.

☠

Amidships, a Bellona guy clacked and wheezed. What had been a Bellona guy. Not from this crew; from the *God's Mercy*. Trix and Van and I had missed him on our way in. His chest had been crushed by a falling piece of the Tagore's onboard crane. He had no air in his lungs, so his Panama Laugh was much more like a squirt, or a gurgle. Like the gasp of a goldfish for air.

I looked at him; my guts went *ow*. My hackles stood at attention.

I yelled at Amber, "Supervising Technical Consultant Lin!"

I snapped my fingers.

She said, "Sir?"

I snapped my fingers.

She said, "Sir. Sir? Sir. Sir?"

I said, "Sidearm, Amber."

She said, "Of course, Sir," and handed it over.

I put him down.

"That's how it's done," I told the marines. "These things are not your friends. These things have *never* been your friends. Your friends are dead. I'm very sorry. These things inhabit the bodies your friends used to inhabit. And if someone tries to keep you from shooting one? Well, that person's not your friend, either. Is that clear?"

It was.

I screamed, "I said, is that clear?"

It was clear.

I said jump; they said "How high?"

I got *John Wayne* sized goosebumps and an Elvis-sized head.

I was doing pretty good for my first time ever.

☠

I said, "What happened to the captain again?"

Amber said, "Sir, er... unfortunate accident, Sir. Lost at sea."

I said, "You *accidentally* killed him?"

She said, "No, Sir. He'd accidentally *turned*."

I said, "Navigator?"

She said, "Sir, he's dead, too, Sir. All the bridge officers are dead."

"Did you kill them all, Consultant Lin?"

"Not all, Sir. LaTeisha over there killed a few. After I killed the captain, the XO locked the bridge, see. And then, well... we heard laughing. A few of us suited up and ingressed. They'd all turned, Sir. I don't know if you noticed, but that's why we came in so hot. We couldn't figure out how to stop. We finally had the nuclear engineers insert the control rods."

I said, "Good thinking. Lucky you didn't kill *them*. You didn't, did you?"

"No, Sir. They're still on duty. They're not laughers. In fact... they're Russian. I don't know if they *can* laugh." She looked pleased with herself.

I said, "Are you bucking for promotion, Amber?"

"Sorry, Sir."

"Do you have a brig on the *God's Grace*?"

She said, "Of course, Sir. It's not very big, but it'll hold a few prisoners."

I said, "I'm afraid that Dr. Sorzano had a slight misunderstanding with the Argentinean authorities. It's purely a technicality, but I'm under legal obligation to have her securely interned until we sort it out. I'm sure she'll understand."

Ava frowned bitterly. "Of course, Mr. Bogart. I completely understand."

Amber brightened. "Sir, *are* there Argentinean authorities? Before communications went out... it sounded pretty bad down there."

I said, "I guess we'll find out. Inform the crew we're putting to sea."

She said, "Yes, Sir. Um... sir, can I ask... who's piloting?"

I ran my uncle's eight-foot fishing boat aground when I was twelve. I'd once attempted to take the *Speedy Gonzales* from Casa Pescado to Señor Mike's for a poker party. Van had to come get me in the *Jerry Bear*—in Colombian waters. Want someone shot from a sniper's perch? I'm your man. Want your skiff piloted from Natchez to New Orleans on the Mississippi? Put me in charge and I hope you like sushi.

So I said, "Captain Fish will be in command."

She said, "Oh, Sir. That's a huge relief, Sir. Very good news, Sir."

I smiled at Van and muttered, "Is it?"

Van, wide-eyed, muttered back at me: "Not really."

Amber asked, "Where are we deploying, Sir? Er... departing. Are we deploying?"

I said, "San Francisco."

She asked, "What's our mission?"

I said, "Classified."

She said breathlessly, "Oh, wow. I'm from Berkeley, Sir."

I jerked a thumb at my chest and said, "Oakland."

She said, "Oh, Oakland, Sir. I love Oakland," with the sad, soft voice that people from Berkeley give you when you tell them you're from Oakland. It's matched by the sneer we give them when we hear they're from Berkeley.

She said: "I've got family. Is it bad there?"

I said, "I guess we'll find out."

☠

The *Grace* was a small vessel—lighter, quicker, more agile, more deadly than the *Mercy*. The *Mercy* had no integrated weapons systems. The *Grace* was nothing *but* integrated weapons systems. It was supposed to have twelve crew and carry forty marines. At the time of its shakedown to Malta, it had six and twenty, respectively. Now, the only crew were a Serbian crane operator and a pair of Russian nuclear engineers, one of whom didn't speak English. Amber summoned them to the deck of the Mercy to introduce me while I toweled the goo off my face. Neither of the Russians had the faintest idea how to pilot, but the one who spoke English told me reassuringly, "Don't worry, Sir, we can definitely keep her from melting down."

I told them, "I'd appreciate that."

☠

The marines cleared the deck, using shots to the head. The sound of laughing slowly dwindled.

Overhead, birds whirled and screeched. Colón burned. Smoke rose on the morning. Through the birds and the burning, the sun had gone black-greyish-bloody.

I told them, "If you find any criers, watch it. When they turn, they're faster than the others."

Amber said she could ask for volunteers to clear the lower decks and search for survivors.

I told them no. Chances were too good that they'd find Luke down there, bleeding from his ass but alive, ready to re-assume command.

I asked Ava if there was a chance that our "guest from downstairs" knew something we didn't about the laughing sickness—something she, or anyone, could use to find the cure.

She said, "Probably. But, Frosty, he was pretty crazy. You saw what they were doing down there. Luke had completely lost it."

I said, "Did he have other doctors working for him?"

She said, "He killed them all."

"If we found him, would he help us?"

She said, "He'd have us killed."

I jerked my head toward the marines. "Would they follow that order?"

She said, "Do you want to take that chance?"

I said, "Fine. And the patients?"

Her eyes filled with tears. She said, "I'm sorry."

I told her, "That's not what I was asking. Can anything be done to help them?"

She looked at me.

I told Amber no, there were no survivors.

I told Amber I would make one last trip below deck, myself. Alone.

I'd lost both my five-sevs when I took a tumble.

I told Amber, "Find me a sidearm."

☠

She got me one: five-sev, tac light, laser. Five extra mags, thirty rounds each. I wasn't completely sure I could shoot straight in this context, even with the laser sight, so I wanted lots of extra ordnance.

I took the stairs. Excuse me, the ladders.

I went down slow and easy while, up above, Van supervised the hoisting of the *Bush Soaker* up onto one of the *Grace*'s two empty helipads, and Trixie made sure that Ava got locked in the brig without running her mouth.

I didn't tell Trixie and Van what I was about. I didn't tell Ava.

I just went.

I took the stairs. I went down.

We'd missed laughers. I shot them. I swept with the light.
I went *down*.

☠

Why did I go down there alone? Because I wanted to face him? Because I wanted to die? Because I knew if I found him, he would die, I would die, it would be over either way?

And which of my tormenters was I looking for? What was left of Luke? What was left of Virgil? Both? Neither? The things in the cages?

Had I decided, inexplicably, to *trust* Luke? Virgil? The *things*?

On the first landing down I found an emergency kit. It had an airhorn and a megaphone.

On the ballroom level, at the place where the doors had been blown, I hit the airhorn to get his attention.

I fired up the megaphone.

☠

I said, "Luke, you're probably still bleeding. You may not know what it's like out there. You won't survive. Give up. I won't kill you. That's all I'm going to promise you, asshole. But trust me, it's more than you'll get from the laughers." Nothing. Nothing. Nothing. Just the chittering of things in the cages. My heart pounded.

I said, "Last chance, fucko."

Nothing. Nothing. Nothing. Giggle, chitter, chortle, guffaw, sob.

I said, "Fine. Stay here and go meet God. I'm sure he's stoked with you."

I entered the ballroom.

Things reached for me.

The light illuminated writhing heads and torsos, squirming limbs not unlike tentacles. Things that were not human. Had never been human, maybe. Who could know? Who could ever know?

There were a million hiding places on a ship the size of the *Mercy*. Luke could be anywhere, passed out, bleeding to death, or just crazed with fear. Cradling his father to his breast and begging desperately, *Tell me what to do*.

Well, I knew what to do.

I took it easy. I swept from front to back, laying red dots down and ending it for things that should have ended long ago. I looked in their eyes and saw wild, roving crazy. I tried to see something left in them, anything human.

I found I didn't know what that meant.

So, because Death could not stop for me, I kindly stopped for him.

I handed him over a boatload of things that morning... fucker's probably still scratching his head.

☠

I went looking for Luke's office.

I heard laughers in the galley.

Then I smelled something cooking; I heard a hiss beneath the LOLZ.

I entered the galley through the crew's mess. There, I found three of them, non-ambulatory. They reached for me. Why the sailors hadn't sealed the watertight door to the mess, I couldn't fathom. Maybe one of their number tried to flee, and the laughers flooded in as soon as the door was open.

They held the sailors down on the stainless-steel tables and ate them till the sailors got the joke. They ate them in *pieces*.

Then they lost interest, leaving mostly-eaten corpses without much left to laugh about.

The sailors laughed anyway. They reached for me with stumps. They could not crawl for me. They had no limbs. Not much to laugh with, either, which is why I had not heard them. The laughing I heard came from the galley—louder, hysterical, mingled with the sound of sizzling and the smell. It smelled like long-burned meat—a roast left in for too many hours.

I used six easy shots from the five-sev—double taps. I did it while barely paying attention, because I could hear the laughing from the galley.

I did a quick sweep of the mess to make sure nothing was laughing.

Then I entered the galley.

☠

The things in the crew's mess had been dismembered with brute force—I had to guess maybe half a dozen, even a dozen laughers holding their arms and legs down and—I got images in my head I'll never get out.

They hadn't been dismembered by cleavers or knives; those still hung neatly on a magnetic strip next to the grill, which was hot. The power was out but the propane was dandy. Someone must have been cooking breakfast when the laughers made the scene. One guy had been pinned across the grill. He'd been pinned by creatures impervious to the pain—his, or theirs. Strips of their flesh, cooked black, had adhered to the surface. But most of his was gone.

He'd cooked through… or, mostly through.

But something of his lungs still worked.

Staring through the smoke, I raised my pistol.

The cooked thing on the grill yowled and brayed at me.

I said, "Fuck, fuck, fuck, fuck, fuck."

☠

I've done a lot of bad things.

I've done some *really* bad things.

I've done a couple really, really, *really* bad things.

Leaving that laugher there on the grill may have been the very worst.

But sometimes your trigger finger just doesn't work.

☠

I found Luke's stateroom in the bow. Taking up the front twenty feet of Deck 2, it was triangle-shaped and had a giant bed, essentially a huge version of the V-berth on a boat like the *When She Was Bad*.

It was a mess; it had been ransacked.

The office was makeshift at best. There were no paper files, no desktop computers. Just laptop and thumb drive sitting on Luke's cleared-off desk.

The safe hung open, empty.

The *gun* safe hung open, with five long guns lined up in hard cases. There was space for a sixth, and on the floor sat an empty shotgun case marked *Benelli*. There was another case on Luke's desk, marked Smith & Wesson. Empty boxes of Cor-Bon ammo were scattered on the floor, tangled up with a bloody pair of slacks—the ones he'd been wearing when I'd shot him in the ass. I shoulda used Van's .44.

The hibernating laptop was plugged in to the ship's power, but that was long gone. So was the *Mercy*'s satellite internet connection. But there was a little juice left in the laptop. When I ran my thumb over the trackpad, it sprang back to life, displaying a browser window. The laptop battery was almost dead. There was no internet.

I was looking at the Chanel 8 Oakland site, showing a video of a logo over a split-screen showing the Armory, and a mug shot of Ava Sorzano stenciled *EXTRADICIÓN DE ARCHIVOS*.

The headline:

San Francisco Hostages Threatened
Panama Connection?

The local time stamp on the screen was half an hour ago—when I had been upstairs shooting the shit with the mercs.

I hit my walkie.

"Trixie, you up there?"

She said, "Go, Frosty."

"You seen our friend?"

She said, "Who?"

I said, "Any friend. Any of the members of our favorite family?"

She said, "No, of course not. I assumed—by the way, where the hell are you?"

I said, "Just get ready to go. And if you see anyone, think fast and come up with something good. Meantime, keep our prisoner locked down tight."

"You mean Ava?"

I said, "Ava."

She said, "Okay, but she and I talked for a while."

I said, "Well, *stop*. No one talks to her, period."

She said, "Why, Frosty?"

I said, "Don't call me that. I'll be up in a minute."

The TV news footage—Cable News, Washington, DC—was time-stamped early this morning. Luke must have loaded the page just before the laughers got the upper hand.

The video had been cached locally. I saved a copy to the laptop's hard drive.

Then I turned up the speakers and hit PLAY.

The announcer said: "As the public health catastrophe in Florida and Texas spiraled out of control early this morning, Federal officials refused to draw a connection between the reports of sickness in the Continental United States and the suspected pandemic in Latin America and the Caribbean. But News 8's investigative reporter Dan Lundberg has discovered that local officials are asking questions about whether *this* woman, Dr. Ava Sorzano, may be involved, connecting the so-called Panama Laugh and the tense, mysterious hostage drama playing out in San Francisco.

Sorzano is a a former UCSF infectious disease researcher and a former consultant for the Department of Homeland Security who was investigated five years ago for allegedly setting up a Panama-based shell corporation to sell unapproved flu vaccines illegally to clinics in Panama, Colombia, and the Middle East. Investigators are trying to find out if those vaccines might have originated at the so-called Connectome Research Facility in the Armory. However, Federal investigators said again they could not confirm or deny whether the pandemic could be connected in any way to those vaccines, or to the armed standoff now taking place at the Armory. The building is currently owned by a group known as 'The Inferno.' It's said to be a loose cooperative association of commercial and nonprofit ventures. Several of those companies are said to be private security firms involved with disaster preparedness, and at least one of those is a firm related to medical research into bioterrorism. But some commentators are claiming it may actually be a front for a group called DePop Art, an environmental terror group that advocates global depopulation."

A helicopter shot showed three armed men with body armor and what looked like Halloween masks on the roof of the giant San Francisco Armory, illuminated in police klieg lights and surrounded by cranes. The men pointed AKs at a dozen unmasked hostages in street clothes, who had apparently been forced to kneel on the wide stone wall that rimmed the roof.

I got a good look at the masks: they weren't Halloween masks at all. They were the smiling Janus.

Janus: The Roman god of beginnings and transitions... and patron of the drama department at every high school.

These cats only wore the one face, though. I wondered if somewhere in some asshat costume store, there was a pile of weeping Roman gods, waiting for a terrorist cult to adopt them.

The footage zoomed in and crawled over the hostages, who had their fingers laced together at the backs of their heads, while the masked guys behind them jabbed them in the back with their AKs.

I would have recognized one of those hostages anywhere. She was a pissed-looking, raven-haired thirty-something Latina with a nose ring.

She'd helped me move bodies from the Armory to the Port of Oakland.

Guys in smiling masks waved their AKs at her as a news crawl said: "'DE-POP NOW!' GROUP THREATENS TO EXECUTE HOSTAGES—"

And the laptop died.

I looked around for a laptop case; the best I could find was a gym bag.

I spotted a tool box behind Luke's desk.

I popped it open.

I found a pair of wire cutters.

I found a pair of pliers.

I found a claw hammer, and one of those handy little kits they sell at the hardware store that has just a few nails in just about every size you'll ever need.

Except I might need a *lot* of different sizes.

I found some picture wire. I found a small chisel.

I put it all in the gym bag alongside the laptop, which I'd wrapped in one of Luke's sportjackets to keep it from getting dinged. I found a mail cart and loaded up Luke Amaro's long guns.

As I went to leave, I heard a sob: a sick, sad, pathetic, wet noise coming from underneath Luke Amaro's V-berth.

I pulled aside the rumpled 1200-thread-count sheets, cream-colored. They hung down, bloody; Luke had used them to stanch the blood.

There, kicked under the bed, was Virgil Amaro's head. It stared out blankly, slack-jawed and wide-eyed, confused. His son had abandoned him.

He saw me. He clocked who I was. He blinked. He struggled. Air made wet sounds as he sucked it through his neck.

He said, "Dante, is it Easter yet?"

I grabbed Virgil by the hair and stuffed him in a gym bag.

I told him, "Quiet, Boss. Call me Frosty."

☠

Loaded with gym bag and Luke's long guns, I encountered four more laughers on the way out—all, at least, semi-ambulatory.

I didn't go back to the galley.

☠

When I was done punching tickets and collecting heads, I ascended to the *Grace*, thinking, *The ballroom held but just ourselves... and immortality.*

I got myself a stateroom and stashed the gym bag.

The *Soaker* was loaded; the gun locker of the *Mercy* had been raided for spare ammo.

The topside laughers were silent.

The smoke of Colón hovered over us, mingled with the birds.

Van said, "Goodbye, Colombus."

We took the *Grace* to the edge of Lemon Bay and sent a deck-mounted torpedo up into the stern of the *Mercy*.

We left her burning.

☠

Van told me, "I really fucked the *Soaker* up running it up onto the sand like that. I'll need to scavenge some floats before we can use her again." He frowned at me and puffed his stogie. He said, "You know I'm not even remotely licensed for this shit, right?"

I said, "I figured."

He said, "Wanna know the biggest boat I ever piloted?"

I said, "Not really."

He said, "*The When She Was Bad*. Forty feet. Thirty-six if I hack all the algae off the stern before I put to sea. You wanna hear about her propulsion?"

I said, "Not really."

He said, "It wasn't nuclear."

He started laughing hysterically. He said, "Remember that one time off Santa Marta? That swordfish? All season I'm after swordfish, and now, the storm's coming fast. And the fucker finally shows up. *Big* mother—it's goin' *nuts*, goin' crazy, and I'm running all over trying to find my .22 'cause I don't wanna blow a hole in the deck with my .44. You remember that little .22, Frosty? Browning? Anyway, I can't find it, so I get out my .44 and you start bitching, calling me a savage and a nut case and a—"

I said, "That wasn't me."

He puffed his stogie and said, "Oh. Of course not. I only got the .44 three years ago."

"Try not to shoot holes in the deck, Captain."

He said, "No promises. By the way, what was in the case?"

I said sadly, "It didn't have the cure."

He said, "I figured. What was in it? Something medical?"

I said, "Yeah. It was a stool sample."

☠

We couldn't get any information to speak of from shore. Everything was down except GPS, which was wrong. The last reports the *Grace* had received before they arrived in Colón had been that the contagion had reached the

Caribbean and Canada. There were reports of laughers in Africa, Japan, Central and South Asia.

Then everything had gone dark.

The *Grace* had surveillance drones—CS-80 Gypsies. Unmanned Aerial Vehicles. Catapult-launched, net-retrieved. No one on board knew how to fly them.

The *Grace* had surveillance balloons—CS-33 Jellyfish. We launched one. It floated through the clouds of birds, battered but not mobbed. The birds avoided it; they seemed to avoid anything silent.

On the streets of Colón, only laughers moved.

We took a detour to Isla Pescado.

I told Van to keep his bridge crew focused on their instruments and ordered the marines to mess. No one was to look out the window.

We got the rest of the story from the Jellyfish.

On the island that'd been Van's home for years, I saw a beach so littered with wreckage it was impossible to tell how many copters had been downed, how many boats beached and burned.

Van's house was choked with laughers—pirates turned, and one guy in Type III-A body armor. It wasn't John Amaro.

I watched the laughers stepping on the Holy Ghost orchids—the pale souls of Panama. I watched the laughers shamble and laugh in the garden where a few days ago, Van and I had tried to beat the shit out of each other.

I climbed down. I went to the bridge and told him. "Homesick?" I said.

He shrugged and said, "*Sick*, sick."

Van only knew where Alei's family lived in the vaguest terms—he'd been there, but always using GPS. It took us most of the afternoon to find it. I climbed back to the crow's nest and saw, through the field glasses, nothing but abandoned huts. The *Speedy* was nowhere to be seen, nor was a single Kuna.

I asked, "You sure this is the place?"

He said, "Not really."

I said, "We can keep looking."

Van said sadly, "We got global responsibilities now, fucko. If we can help find a cure to this, that's what we do, Frosty. You say the answer might be in Frisco?"

I said, "Don't call me Frosty. And don't call it Frisco. And—" I shrugged.

Van shrugged right back at me. "He's a tough kid. He can fight his own *Lucha*."

But I could tell he didn't like saying it.

There was an ugly sky overhead—the smoke of Colón, the swirl of birds. There were laughers on every shore.

So we made for the Cape, with as few tears as possible.

☠

Just before sundown, as the *God's Grace* made forty knots into the wind, Amber came and visited me at the stern.

We traded salutes and she said, "Captain Fish wishes to inform you that we are passing Suriname, Sir. There's… no signal. No shortwave, no FM, no AM… there should be six television stations. There aren't any."

I said "Did you get a visual of the beach through the scopes?"

She nodded.

She said, "Laughers, Sir. Same as the others."

"All right," I said sadly. "Dismissed."

She waited.

I said, "Something on your mind, Supervising Marine First Class Lin?"

She said, "Sir, I love your videos."

I frowned and said, "*Gracias*. Sorry we couldn't have met under better circumstances. And you don't have to call me Sir. Just call me Frosty."

She said, "Oh, thanks, Sir. It's an honor… Frosty. Wow. Anyway, there was a lot out there in the news about you, Sir. I just want you to know, I don't believe the bad stuff." I shrugged. She continued, "But I just wondered something. If it's not too personal."

I shrugged and nodded.

Amber said, "None of the news stories really seemed clear on what your background is. I mean—there's the two names, of course…"

I said, "Only one, really. Bogardi was my grandfather's name. He was an actor. He switched it late in the vaudeville era. I've always been Bogart."

She said, "But… Daniel T."

I nodded. "Dante started as a nickname in the old days. Because—" I took a big long breath. Why was I telling this?

She cocked her head.

I finished, "Because I always seemed to be in Hell."

She said, "Right, Sir. Of course… Dante also toured Heaven."

I said, "Yeah, I'm looking forward to that one of these days."

"But your background. What I'm trying to ask is, what's your training? What branch of the military were you in?"

I looked at her.

She said, "If it's not too personal."

I said, "Sorry, Amber. That's classified."

She looked happy. She saluted.

She said, "Of course, Sir. Sorry... *Frosty*." She laughed. She looked pleased as punch to be saying it. "*Frosty*. Of course, Sir. No offense meant. Thank you, Sir. Thanks. No offense?"

I said, "Dismissed."

She was gone.

Trix was waiting in the long Atlantic shadows, lurking, hiding.

She came up behind me. And said, "Oh, Sir, Sir, Sir. May I drop my fatigues for you, Sir? I've touched myself to your videos, Sir, and—"

I growled, "Hell's bells, woman. You talk to patients with that mouth? Did I actually *date* you?"

"Yeah," she said. "And I dumped *you*, remember?"

"Right," I said. "But I Tasered you first, so I was asking for it."

She frowned. She said, "You know, I've been wanting to ask the same thing."

"Same thing as what?" I asked.

"Same thing as Amber," said Trixie.

"Whether you could drop your fatigues for me?"

"You wish. I mean what your background is, Dante. I never asked you in the old days, because I was afraid of what I'd hear. I'm not afraid anymore."

I said, "You should be."

She said, "Dante, my Dad spent lots of time in combat. He was older." Our much older fathers—both of whom had died young—was something that had initially bonded Trixie and me.

She said, "Back then, men didn't talk about what they saw... at least, not to their daughters."

I said, "That's probably wise."

"But I kept at him, because I felt like I had to know. He told me stories. Why do you think I'm so fucked up?"

"Oh," I said brightly. "I hoped that was my fault."

"You wish. Why do you think I travel all over the world trying to fix things? You're different than him, Dante. Guys from our generation are different; they might not talk about everything, but they talk about certain things. And even guys from my father's generation still talked about some stuff. But you won't say anything about your twenties. You wouldn't even tell me if you were an officer."

I said, "I wasn't."

She said, "I gathered that. I figured you were a West Point dropout, Annapolis washout, something like that, maybe just a ninety-day wonder. I thought you got court martialled and busted, or something. I know you were in Iraq—in Fallujah."

"Don't say that word."

She said, "I know you were in Helmand—"

I growled, "Don't say *that* word."

She said, "I know something happened in Samarkand—"

I snarled, "Trixie, don't say *that* word, either. In fact, just stop saying place names."

She said, "But that was all when you were already a consultant. Where did you serve, Dante?"

I said, "You shouldn't ask if you don't wanna know."

She said, "If there's one thing I learned while you were away, it's that you can learn anything you want out of books and the internet. How to talk, how to walk, how to be a soldier. Without ever pulling a trigger." She said. "I don't think you're a soldier at all. I don't think you've ever been one. I think you're a con man."

I said, "Can't a guy be both?"

She said, "If you're a con man, you better be a good one."

I said, "I am."

"Tell me about Karen Klein."

I said, "Fuck off, Beatrice."

She kept at me: "Tell me about the rape trial, Dante. Your record was expunged, but I found it in the news archives. Then you *vanish* for ten years. Nowhere, nothing. Ten years you're gone, Dante. Poof. Then suddenly you show up in Somalia. Ten solid years, Dante, and you're getting jobs only experienced military consultants get. What were you? Navy? Marines? Air Force Special Ops? Something foreign?"

I stared at her.

She said, "CIA? Green Beret? French Foreign Legion? Saudi Military? Russian? Israeli?"

I looked at her sadly.

I said, "I was a hit man."

Trixie looked like I had punched her in the face. She put her hand to her mouth and said, "Are you fucking with me?"

I said, "Sure."

But she knew I wasn't.

I said, "Now you tell me something, Beatrice."

She said, "Wow. You never call me that."

I said, "Except when I'm mad. How 'bout Van? Did he tell you how he got all that money? Enough to buy his own island and build Casa Fish?"

She leaned up hard on the rail, still stunned by what I'd told her. She didn't look so good.

She said, "He stole it from a bank in Santiago."

I said, "So he's not a soldier either?"

She said, "He is now."

I nodded.

She said, "Don't tell him I told you. He's scared you won't respect him."

I said, "Whatever. Don't you tell my jarhead babies. They think I'm their Daddy."

She said, "You *are* their Daddy. Like it or not. Dante, are you serious?"

"About what?"

"You weren't military? You were a… ?"

I told her sadly, "Nah, just fucking with you. I was Legion. *Viva le France!*"

She looked at me slow and sad and melted back into the long Atlantic shadows.

I was alone.

☠

After Trixie had gone and Van had sent Amber up to find me and send me up to the helm so he could ask me if I knew whether we had a keel or not, I told her:

"Amber, I'm going to get some shut-eye now. I want no one to disturb me, *Claro?*"

She looked at me blankly.

I said, "Marine, *Claro* means—never mind. Is that clear?"

She said, "Crystal."

I said, "Dr. Sorzano is the same. She's been traumatized by these events, and she's very upset by her trouble with the authorities. She hasn't been sleeping. Inform the crew to keep away from the brig."

She saluted me.

She was gone.

I went to my stateroom.

I got the gym bag.

I got the laptop.

I went to the brig.

💀

The brig was alongside Shaft Alley, where the power train provides impetus to the screws. Electric power is quiet, but the mini-nuke plants on the Grace put out substantial noise due to the coolant pumps, and the screws themselves provide a hell of a shudder just from cavitation.

But Shaft Alley provides the real noise—hot, hard and furious, a big violent throb that fills your soul.

It didn't seem to agree with Ava Sorzano—or maybe she'd just had a long day.

💀

We were still in tropical waters; even now, an hour before midnight, the deck was balmy. Amber hadn't made it far enough into the manual to understand the computer-controlled environmental system, so the temperature throughout the ship was ambient and uncomfortably warm. Add to that the fact that Shaft Alley puts out considerable heat. Ava Sorzano had been cooking alive since this morning. She looked worse for wear.

She sprawled on her rack—listless, ruined. Her blue denim dress hung half-open.

She knew what I was here for. She looked at me, terrified.

I'd come unarmed. Unless you count the pliers and the wire cutters and the claw hammer and the nails and the chisel and the wire.

I unzipped the gym bag and set the tools out on the little bolted-down bedside table, on a copy of *Nautical Times*.

She whimpered, "You said you wouldn't torture me."

I said, "Of course I won't. I only torture women I date, and then it's purely an emotional thing. But there are so many things I *didn't* promise you, Ava."

I took out Virgil. His eyes roved wildly. His lips moved without sound.

Ava looked at him, wide-eyed, disbelieving. Her jaw dropped.

Virgil burbled, his voice wet and hissy: "Is it Easter yet?"

I set up the laptop. I turned it toward her. The flash video was still loaded. I set it, uneven and wobbly, atop the tools on the nightstand.

I hit PLAY.

💀

While the video played, I remembered things I'd tried to forget. I saw Fallujah: the bastard's face, flesh peeled back, teeth gone. I had taken them. Nose, eyes, mouth. He lived. He screamed. He couldn't talk. He couldn't sob. And he definitely couldn't laugh.

Ten years rotten in my brain, that face looked *beautiful*.

Ava's eyes widened as she heard about herself... vaccines... hostages in the Armory. Contagion. Panama. Shell corporations. *Pandemic*. Questions being asked.

When the video finished, Ava's fear had turned to panic.

She weakly, "I can explain."

I said, "You don't have to... not yet. First, I want to make sure that you know who you're dealing with."

She whimpered, "I already know..."

I said, "You *don't*. That's why before I ask any questions about your past... you and I could have a little chat. About *my* past."

Virgil had come to his senses a little; he watched me, eyes wide, blue mouth agape.

I said, "Let's all three talk," I said, "About what really happened at *Fallujah*."

I reached for the pair of pliers.

Ava put her hand to her mouth.

Just then Shaft Alley came alive, and the whole room started to shake.

Virgil said weakly:

"Dante?"

I gave him a big one, with lots of teeth.

I reached for him.

I said, "Call me *Frosty*."

PART 3:

THINGS THE GYPSY TOLD US

We went south.

We made for the Cape.

Like this:

The skies were a maelstrom. Swirling birds made them impassable except at treetop level. Merged together, undifferentiated by species, they uttered a collective chitter than sounded like the Panama Laugh gone avian. At random moments the birds would rocket down screeching and hurl themselves at anything that moved.

We saw more planes falling—flaming, tangled in kestrels or choked with contagion. They crashed into the water, boats, other planes, the ground. They ate shit into cruise ships and reefs. They careened, lost without GPS, lost without radio. They plunged and burned.

They hit buildings.

Amber had a theory about a very large electromagnetic pulse weapon and the reversal of the Earth's magnetic poles.

Van said she was nuts—which was saying something. If he said her theory was bullshit, it must *really* be crazy.

She said, "Sorry, Sir," and saluted him.

☠

We went south.

We made for the Cape.

Like this:

Ships flooded out of collapsing Panama. Cruise ships, cargo ships, survey ships, military vessels. Boats *poured*. Fishing boats, speedboats, tugboats, sailboats, Zodiacs, life rafts.

They crisscrossed the southern Caribbean heading north, east, south.

They made for land. No one told them not to.

They died laughing.

Others heard the warnings, or intuited them from the rampant chaos implied by the *lack* of warnings. They made for open water. They met the *pirates*.

These mothers didn't say "Ahoy."

The war for men's souls had begun, and *Reach for the sky!* was the battle cry on both sides.

Strangely, Trixie and I had debated this very point of speculative human history numerous times, naked in bed or over a Vegan Panameño Scramble and a New York Steak with Eggs and a Side of Bacon, respectively, at the Hotel Siete in El Cangrejo. Given the absolute removal of all enduring social strictures and the stress of impending violence, would humans band together to seek solace and deliverance, or would they start whacking each other with sticks for Power Bars?

We had our answer... maybe not in absolute terms, but in one extreme example.

The *God's Grace* was not a large vessel, and did not look appreciably different than a small survey ship. Designed to operate in both military and humanitarian theaters, it could shroud its weaponry behind steel panels. We did exactly that, and pirates who came at us took hairpin turns when those panels dropped.

Most of them. One decrepit trawler just north of Maracaibo gave the crew its first taste of combat, unless you count Amber's whacking the bridge crew. Late one night, this boat was spotted careening toward us, rifle flashes blasting out on the deck.

Whether they were firing at us or at laughing things on board, we never knew.

It took one burst from the chain guns to sink them.

☠

Raising a particular shortwave station is always a dicey proposition. Raising a distant one? Much less likely. Add mobility to it, and things start to get difficult. Add thousands upon thousands of crazed, untrained operators screaming for help, and the airwaves become unusable.

And that was before you factored in the intermittent hum of interference—which no one could figure. It came and went, but it came more than it went. It got more frequent... louder. It interfered with reception across all frequencies. But we could still hear screamers beneath it, bellowing for help—until they started laughing.

The MDTs were dead. Satphone was spotty, then dead. Satellite internet, dead. GPS was pretty bad to start with; it got progressively less and less accurate. No administrative messages, no weather. When you're at sea, without a weather report you're in grave danger. Even a vessel as advanced as the *Grace* was in deep shit if a serious storm erupted.

We were also cut off from the rest of the Bellona fleet. For me, Trixie and Van—and Ava Sorzano, if I believed her—this was a good thing. If Mark Amaro got a call through to the crew, I'd end up dead.

But for the rest of the crew? It was terrifying to be out of communication.

They turned to me to reassure them, so I did.

Doing it taxed me.

I lost a lot of sleep. Like, all of it.

We sometimes saw laughers in the water—the ones in life jackets, or the ones old enough to have bloated. They came at us dogpaddling in drifts—dozens, sometimes. Flooding out from the island resorts, *sensing* us. Wearing board shorts and shattered sunglasses.

But they were the least of our worries; twenty-megawatt screws could outrun a few paddlers.

What we couldn't outrun was *our* hunger.

Food prices were high in Germany this year, so when the *Grace* left the shipyard, she was not stocked. She had just enough food to get her to the Port of Antwerp, where they took delivery of their small arms and ammunition from Fabrique Nationale d'Herstal, and picked up enough provisions to get them to Malta. We were already short on food.

We went ashore to scavenge at Fortaleza, João Pessoa, Aracaju, São Paulo, Rio de Janeiro.

We stalked beneath the screeches of pirouetting birds, whirling in great airborne drifts and slamming themselves into buildings. Avian corpses littered roofs; the balconies of the colonial buildings in Rio's beachside villas and São Paulo's old quarter were choked with them.

There were, as we could discern, no survivors.

We scavenged food and medicine, fuel for the outboards on the RHIBs.

Everywhere we went, we heard the Panama Laugh.

On the streets Buenos Aires, buildings gave up their dead. They lumbered toward us, snickering.

We gave 'em Panama Kisses as we scavenged. Every kiss is different, but at the end they all taste the same.

☠

We went south.

We made for the Cape.

Like this:

It became very clear right away that Dr. Sorzano planned to tell me everything…or convince me that's what she was doing. At the very least, she was editing events to make herself look as good as she could look, given the circumstances.

And as for the Amaros? Could I hold them responsible? Ava said only partially. They had researched the virus; the idea had certainly occurred to them to hasten the End Times with a genetically engineered contagion.

But Virgil was the true religious fanatic. Once he was gone, his sons were indulgent fuckers. They coasted on their father's contacts and the fact that powerful men from other families in the U.S. were able to use them.

Maybe Luke and Mark and, to a lesser extent, John, were being used in ways that Virgil had foreseen before his death. But Ava did not think they would have intentionally destroyed the world.

Ava seemed to think the most they could be guilty of was possibly—possibly—allowing a release from the Darién facility. But she did not think the virus they had engineered could possibly be as virulent as this one.

Yes, Virgil had been (was?) the true religious fanatic, but Luke was the one most capable of royally fucking up any enterprise to the point of destroying the world. And as for Mark? He didn't give a shit. I felt confident that to Mark Amaro, killing people with a virus just seemed like bad sport. He'd rather kill them with high-tech toys, which was what worried me.

John had always just wanted to kick ass and play beer pong with strippers.

Virgil, for his part, was unable to understand anything. I asked him why they'd frozen his head. He said, "To live forever."

I asked him, "But wouldn't it have made more sense to freeze your whole body?"

To which he directed his eyes downward, his blue mouth open in an expression of horror.

He said, "That son of a bitch!"

He meant Luke, I think. Freezing a body is more expensive than just freezing a head, and Luke had not expected Virgil's "resurrection" to ever be viable. After all, despite all their research into radical life extension through virology, Virgil had died.

And Luke, as was his spoiled, petulant wont, had neither obeyed his father nor *quite* disobeyed him.

He'd just obeyed half-assedly.

That didn't seem like someone who could have pulled the trigger on a global pandemic… just to make his Dad happy.

I got no reasonable intel out of Virgil. Determining whether his group intended to release the virus, or even *could* have released it, was impossible.

But I knew three things for sure:

It was Virgil who wanted to survive the End Times.

It was Virgil who wanted to profit from the End Times.

And it was Virgil who gave the order to euthanize me.

☠

As spotty as were my memories of my tenure as a guest of the Amaro family, I knew there wasn't anything like 1,825 days of them. I hadn't spent five years being experimented on.

At some point, after a dozen videos, a thousand kisses, a hundred thousand milligrams of thiopentone, it was time.

Virgil crouched over me.

His face was drawn, white, crisscrossed with broken blue arteries. His eyes were milky, bloodshot. His lips were almost white. His hair had all but fallen out; what was left swirled empty and fine like a baby's hair around the crown of his head and the temples. He had plenty in his ears, though; it jutted out in great grey bottle-brush tufts.

He looked in pretty poor shape.

He licked his lips and stuck his tongue in my mouth.

When he came up for air, I stared up, eyes swimming, and jerked against the straitjacket. There was no purchase in my muscles. My stomach roiled.

He said, "Euthanize him."

Ava said, "You can't be serious."

He said, "Would you like me to do it?"

Ava said, "Virgil, you're not thinking rationally."

He said, "Are you telling me that I don't pay you enough to kill?"

Ava said, "I'm telling you that you *can't* pay me enough to kill."

He said, "Then maybe I'll kill you, eh?"

Ava said, "Virgil, please don't say that."

He said, "I'll say whatever I damn well please. Freeze him. Euthanize him first."

Ava said, "Why freeze him if we're going to euthanize him first? Why extend his life if—"

Virgil coughed wetly and said, "That's the point. Freeze him so we know if he'll survive it, unlike the others. But don't freeze all of him. Just his head."

Ava said, "You're not thinking rationally."

Virgil growled, "What are you, sweet on *him* now?"

She said calmly, "Virgil, don't be ridiculous. This is about data. This is strictly about data." She thought fast and said, "It makes better scientific sense to freeze the whole specimen, since traumatic compromise of cephalic tissue is almost impossible to avoid—" She started hurling figures, temperatures, chemicals, Kelvins, flash-freezing procedures, bone saws. She lingered on bone saws; she made a ragged sawing motion with her hands and let her tongue loll out, kind of going jiggle-jiggle-jiggle with her chin as she mimicked decapitating herself.

She kept at it until Virgil turned green.

She said, "Virgil, do you need a basin?"

He made a sick sound and said, "Fine. Freeze him *all*. Just euthanize him first."

And Ava said, "Of course, Virgil. Of course I'll euthanize him."

☠

It happened later, much later, after a thousand measurements and a hundred insertions and a few holes drilled into my skull to track the cracking of my brain on a seismometer; I saw my capsule rolled in and looked up at it, eyes swimming, brain going haywire, uncomprehending; I looked up at the Doctor's masked face and watched her hold up a 50cc syringe of clear liquid. I heard her say with her voice shaking, "Virgil, you're sure you want to do this?"

He was snoring.

She blurted, "No! Don't wake him up. I—I need the number 2 bone saw."

A petulant nurse-voice, Russian accented: "I thought we didn't need it for this procedure. It'll have to be sterilized."

She snapped, "Then go do it!"

The nurse left. Sorzano glanced at Virgil. She leaned over and squirted the syringe into a basin; she hiked her gown and her skirt and slipped another syringe out from under. She looked at Virgil furtively. She held the 50cc up and tapped it; she squeezed out bubbles.

Then she looked in my eyes and pulled her mask down.

She said, "Don't get any ideas, Frosty,"

… and kissed me.

A snap of spit went jacking into my eye when she pulled away; more ran down my jaw. She looked furtively at Virgil, who snorted.

She did it again, wiped her mouth, pulled her mask up.

The nurse came back.

"Oh, silly me," said Dr. Sorzano. "I'm such a bubblehead today. I don't need the bone saw after all!"

The nurse groaned, said "For fuck's sake" in a thick Russian accent; Virgil snorted.

He growled wetly, "Watch your language! Why isn't he *dead* yet?"

Sorzano inserted the needle. I twitched.

Virgil chuckled.

He said, "Count backwards from ten, Dante!"

He started laughing.

Sorzano shot him a look.

He laughed louder. He *cackled*. His cancer-wet lungs, pulped with rot, made his laughs sick to the core.

He lost it and started coughing from the wet sodden spurts of his lungs, Ava Sorzano began to tremble; I saw her eyes wet. She howled furiously:

"Jesus Christ, get a mask on him—!"

And then she broke. Her throat closed violently; she whirled on me and grabbed the biggest needle I'd ever seen and said through her mounting violent sobs:

"Count backwards from ten—"

And then she was weeping, her pretty face swimming around me haloed in swirling black hair as Virgil cackled; Ava sobbing, like she was fighting to get through the procedure before she succumbed to her tears—or like she just cried.

Then I went dark.

☠

I lied and said, "I don't remember any of it."

She said, "Then I'm a fool to have told you."

After the first time, I never saw her in her cabin without a five-sev pistol on my lap, cocked and loaded. Sometimes I had the safety off; other times

I flicked it back and forth with my thumb when she pissed me off—a thing that, since she'd seen my tool kit, Ava Sorzano had taken enormous pains to avoid.

I said, "Not really. It makes you look all right. You're the one who saved my life."

"Yes," she said urgently. "I was. I'd lied to Virgil. I knew the new cryonic processing could be survived. Several of our specimens—"

I flicked the safety of the pistol violently on and off about thirty times in two seconds as she looked at me terrified.

Like a deer in the headlights—or a butterfly pinned to a board, and still squirming.

She cleared her throat and said, "Several of our *patients* had survived it. I knew you'd survive."

I said, "Why is that, if only 'several' specimens had?"

She shrugged.

"I don't know why, Dante. I just *knew*."

I said, "Why?"

She said, "Same reason I kissed you."

I cocked my head.

She said, "Because I believe in *God*, genius."

I glared at her and said, "What is that supposed to mean?"

"I believe he tests us. I believe he gave you something."

"Like what… the clap?"

"Not at all like the clap," she said bitterly. "Your kiss cures people. I don't think there's a scientific reason for it. It just happens."

"You're saying it's a miracle?"

She said, "I don't like that word."

I sighed.

"Whatever word you use," I growled, "it's still bullshit. Now quit stalling, and tell me about the vaccines."

☠

Ava's story: The vaccine accusation was a plant. She had been involved in setting up the corporation that provided San Francisco-cultured vaccines to Latin America—but *only* in setting them up, which Virgil had blackmailed her into. She had no idea what the shell corporations had done.

Virgil had made it so easy. She'd signed off on a shell corporation or two—Panama, Vanuatu, the Seychelles. It kept getting easier…

I asked Ava whether the Amaros could have distributed the virus through the vaccines and then planned to activate it with a catalyst... the way I remembered her discussing with Virgil. Could it have been designed and stored at Darién—and released when they blew that site, the day I escaped?

Or could it have been *intentionally* released?

She said, "I don't know. They framed me in Argentina, Dante. I haven't been in the loop for years. But I don't think the Amaros did this."

I said, "Do you think they could have?"

She said, "Do you mean 'could have' as in, constitutionally, emotionally, so-called morally?"

I said, "I mean, scientifically. But sure, so-called morally also works."

She said, "Scientifically, I just don't think so. I can go into detail, but the short version is... no. Morally, I can't say for sure what Luke was capable of."

"Then you think, scientifically, someone else did it."

She nodded. "The Inferno."

I said, "See, everyone keeps saying that. I just don't see it. I know these people. They're douchebags. They couldn't engineer something of this magnitude."

Ava said, "I know they hacked the Bellona server. We know they were involved in the vaccines. And we know they took their website down, locked their building and put up a page a few days before this happened... that strongly suggests they thought what was *about* to happen was pretty cool."

I said, "But that was *after* Darién. They could have had intel about it."

She got agitated. She hissed, "They're the ones who wanted this! I didn't want this! *No one* sane wants this."

I said, "Someone did. As fast as this happened, it's not an accident."

She said, "Then they're crazy."

I thought about fearless, freaky, whack-job Guadalupe Grope on the roof of the castle with an AK to her head, looking about as pissed as when she called me a baby-killer and said, "*The human race must depopulate, if the planet is to survive...*"

I said, "*Claro.*"

☠

We hung a starboard.

We flipped a bitch.

We went north.

We picked up the signal from the Voice of the Inferno—the pirate radio station broadcasting from the Armory.

It was a low-power signal, of course—pirate shit.

Nothing else was broadcasting from the City or its environs. Not radio, not TV. The cell phone towers had ceased functioning when they lost power. Satellite communications were down. The resonant interference had grown until every shortwave frequency was haunted by it. Except for the one on which the Inferno pumped out its private broadcast.

We listened—me and Van, on the bridge with our haphazard deck crew.

We heard voices on the radio. Not talking—laughing.

Pirate radio in San Francisco was playing the Panama Laugh.

☠

In the middle of the night, I heard Virgil, distant:

"Dante, Dante... is it Easter yet?"

I unzipped the bag and looked at Virgil's grey, pulpy flesh.

He was grinning, his teeth yellowed with age and cracked from liquid nitrogen.

His voice a wet, barely-audible vomiting sound, he said:

"That video thing. Going viral."

I said, "What about it?"

"That was smart."

He had to struggle to talk; getting breath was a matter of doing things his throat muscles had never been meant to do. But he could still do it, just barely loud enough to hear.

He said: "It was a hell of a move, Bogart. I was behind the times. Information is viral, but I didn't know that until you taught me. You got Justice up my ass about the USAMRIID contract and you made Defense completely freak out. You almost lost me the contract for the Shiite neighborhoods in Al Qatif. You almost had me, Dante."

I said, "So someone's home in there after all, Shorty?"

Virgil's eyelids sank half-down. He rasped:

"But I learned fast, Dante, didn't I? My next move sank you. Bishop to Queen's... uh... whatever. I really got you, didn't I, Dante?"

I looked at him sadly.

I said, "Yeah, Boss. You got me."

I zipped the gym bag.

I kept it zipped.

☠

Birds plummeted hot and laughing off the Farallones.

The Golden Gate Bridge had come down like a sack of rocks. A container ship and a cruise ship, both clearly being used in attempts at evacuation, had gone out of control—probably when their masters went dark. They must have struck pylons at full speed. The bridge came down. Debris built up. What was left of the bridge and the ships were covered with laughers, guffawing and writhing.

Smaller ships, ferries and boats within the bay had done the same thing. Those underway, or otherwise not tied off when caught laughing, had drifted toward the Gate. Because San Francisco Bay is where the Delta dumps its water, tides tend to migrate things toward the Gate and the ocean beyond. Those tides took with them all the ruined sailboats, skiffs, ferries and rafts on which the bay's would-be water-borne refugees attempted to take flight.

The Gate was an impassable wall of detritus and laughers.

The *Grace* cruised back and forth before it, oceanside.

Like a caged lion we stalked, seeking an opening in our jailer's guard.

But there was none, and the Pacific-side beach from the Presidio to Lake Merced was packed with laughers. All along the shore, the dead were massed, laughing at us. Barefoot and naked, clad in business suits with pieces missing, they lumbered up and down the Great Highway searching for the living. They didn't find them, so they followed us. They reached out for us as we cruised north-south, south-north. They followed us with their hands and their great bleating laughs and their hungry, empty stares.

The fog rolled in every afternoon; it rolled out every morning.

Food was getting scarce, but that was a hell of a lot of dead on the beach. Probably more than we could take. Maybe a small band could slip through, but getting provisions back would be a *bitch*.

And as for the Inferno, where we might find the answer to the mystery of who killed everyone, and why? It was silent, except for pirate radio that pumped out the Panama Laugh. I woulda preferred Ella Fitzgerald.

Was Guadalupe Grope locked in the Armory somewhere, an AK to her head? Was she a hostage? Or was she one of the laughers on the Voice of the Inferno? Was it nothing more than an open channel, fed by solar panels… left open when the whole goddamn castle became a nest?

Or was it all more viral misinformation?

As for Lupe personally, I owed her jack. I had met her once years ago, and been verbally abused by her. She told me I'd be her hero if I ever switched sides. Well… I switched 'em, wolf-woman. Just too late to do any good.

I didn't care to be her abused Messiah. I hadn't been interested in the job when she'd offered it to me in a bread truck with frozen bodies in the back, and I wasn't interested now. But I'd fucked the world up pretty bad. That's a lot of responsibility for one guy. Whether Lupe was the key or just a piece of the puzzle, she was my next witness in the only murder mystery left to solve.

We anchored off Point Lobos and launched the drone.

☠

The Gypsy is remote-controlled unmanned aerial vehicle, or UAV—colloquially called a drone—about the size of a large model airplane. Launched from the stern of the *Grace* by a rocket assist and powered by a turboprop pusher, it can do 100 knots. It's basically similar to, but smaller than, the RQ-7 Shadows and Predators used in Iraq and Afghanistan. It can be guided by any laptop on which you install the software package and the model-specific security key, and feeds you back hi-res video. It's about the cheapest way to get airborne video surveillance without putting any personnel in harm's way.

The official *God's Grace* drone pilot was Command Technical Consultant Josephson, who was also the Communications Officer. Amber Lin had shot Josephson north of Santa Cruz da Gracioca and thrown his body in the ocean, so she got the job. I made her speed-read the manual.

The video output can also be fed via USB cable into essentially any data-capable monitor—like, for instance, the 36-inch TV in the crew lounge of the *Grace*. That made it a lot easier to combine aerial surveillance with enjoying the last few bottles of the case of Cerveza Grassau we'd scavenged from a laugher-choked bar in Coquimbo, Chile, which suited me fine—at that point, I really fuckin' needed a beer.

Trixie and I sat on folding metal chairs on either side of sweating Amber Lin, who had a notebook computer propped on a counter. Her hand shook on the USB joystick. Her controls filled up the laptop screen. It was like watching your niece play a video game.

Using the ship's wired intercom, I gave the order to fire the solid-rocket assist. The Gypsy launched from the stern.

We had observed the birds mobbing anything that buzzed or chugged, including the few power transformers still live—of which there were damned few, and fewer still with every passing day as the birds mobbed them and cooked alive. Anything that flew became a magnet for an avian orgy.

For that reason, I had Amber guide the drone at rooftop level. Power lines and flagpoles came up fast and furious.

Growing up in Oakland, I'd been dragged across the bay to stand-up comedy shows, twelve-step meetings and old showbiz reunions with Grampa Bogart. I knew how to drive when I was thirteen largely because Gramps's twelve-step meetings and his jazz-trumpeter reunions were rarely advantageously placed with the latter preceding the former. I couldn't have walked you through a virtual tour of San Francisco at street-level, but I knew the high points. I was the tour guide.

☠

The Armory is at 14th and Mission Streets. Though it strikes one as a great and monolithic building, it is not as easy as one might think to see from the air. Around it are numerous multi-story warehouses converted to live-work buildings. To the north is a vast freeway overpass, so the Armory is best viewed from the South, on Mission Street once one gets past the taller buildings at 16th Street. We'd have, essentially, two chances at a perfect view.

In order to maximize our reconnaissance of the whole bay, I had Amber guide the drone diagonally south through the City—from the *Grace*'s anchorage at Point Lobos, over the rocks of Seacliff and across the Richmond District, then south toward San Jose. It was on the Gypsy's return voyage, heading north and back to the *Grace* to be caught in a net, that we would surveil the Armory itself.

☠

The Gypsy came in hot and topped the jagged rocks of Seacliff.

"That's Robin Williams's house!" piped Amber.

Trixie said, "No shit?"

I looked at them both like they were crazy.

Then Amber guided the drone south, and we saw it all on the crew's lounge TV screen:

The Richmond District, north of Golden Gate Park, sprawled with three-story early-to-mid-century buildings. Some of them had burned; they'd gone damp and ugly in the fog. Stray dogs roamed. Cars abandoned everywhere choked the streets and alleys, doors open. It was obvious that everyone with a car had hit the streets and slammed together all at once as drivers went dark, sudden laughter slaying busses, bikes, trucks. The major streets would have been impassable to anything wheeled smaller than a bulldozer. Less clogged streets could probably be transited by a small motorcycle.

There were a significant number of laughers—but not a lot. It was pretty sparse.

The Haight-Ashbury district and the Western Addition are to the south and east of the Richmond; geographically, they form the center of the City.

In both neighborhoods, there were very few laughers and very little visible human life. But the streets were still choked with cars, which everyone seemed to have abandoned. The streets would not have been easy to get down in a car. Nobody was driving a Volvo down Haight Street anytime soon. There were bodies, but not many. Where was everyone?

To the south of the Haight are the hills of opulent Buena Vista, with even fewer laughers and almost no cars abandoned. No survivors could be seen. Great packs of dogs wandered; cats could be seen climbing fire escapes and transiting roofs.

The laughing population in the Castro, south of Buena Vista, was similarly sparse. Noe Valley, still further south, was practically empty. Where the hell was everyone?

As the Gypsy headed still further south, toward the hills in the south of the city, we left the realm of tall buildings, and got a much broader view. The things we saw put everything in perspective.

The hills to the south of the SF County-San Mateo County line: burned. Destroyed. Planes downed everywhere. The airport ruined. Great parks burned. Mountainsides blasted, discharging landslides. We saw freeways impassable—buried under massive traffic jams that had stopped mid-honk as drivers turned laugher. We saw the Hayward-San Mateo Bridge—down. Distantly, we saw the Dumbarton bridge, from Fremont to East Palo Alto—down. We saw a bay littered with wreckage—as, with the highways impenetrable, every boat, raft, and jet ski had tried to depart. The wreckage slowly migrated North, toward the Gate.

It looked like the aftermath of an enormous earthquake—with the big exception being that no one was here to clean up. It was a Very Special Episode terminated by tape splice. There was no little kid or schoolteacher to give an inspirational speech about not fucking around with things that laugh when they shouldn't, or stealing crap from Libya. There was no inspirational talk about anything.

South of the City, laughers drifted—grouping together, we surmised, where survivors cowered. The laughers could sense them. They craved them. They came for them.

As we got a broad view, it dawned on us with terrifying certainty.

Humanity was gone.

There was nothing left but the laugh track.

☠

I had Amber guide the Gypsy north, back into the city.

The airspeed indicator said about a hundred knots.

She came screaming over the hills. We saw scattered laughers below us.

Birds were denser over the green spaces. They struck and swirled around us. Pigeons, starlings, bluebirds. At thirty meters, it was like slaloming fast on a dangerous ski run, and Amber was breathing harder and sweating more with every close call—of which it seemed there were several every second.

We had all been wondering where the corpses were. The ones that laughed, or the ones that didn't. There were too few bodies.

As we headed north, we found the laughers.

In fact, we could see them—crammed in tight between the buildings of the Mission, all facing the same direction, and facing one direction. Thousands of them. Tens of thousands. It was a wonder they could move. They mostly didn't—they mostly just howled, and writhed, and laughed. They mostly just seethed against each other, guffawing, seeking to converge on a single point.

The Inferno.

They could sense the survivors.

They were going after them.

That meant two things:

First, there were survivors there—crazy or otherwise.

Second, that was a *lot* of fuckin' laughers. Getting to the Armory on surface streets would be completely impossible.

I racked my brains as I watched the scene on the crew lounge TV. My first thought was that if we could get the *Soaker* rigged to touch down on land, we could utilize that freeway overpass. But it was packed with cars tighter than anywhere else in the City. Even worse, it was packed with laughers.

Even if we'd had wheeled landing gear for the *Soaker*—which we did not—there was nowhere to land. If we could fix the floats, we could get into the bay. But what the hell good would that do? The bay was choked with laughers and debris—and, more importantly, the rim of the bay was just as infested as Ocean Beach. Fixing the *Soaker* and landing her on the bay would be difficult, dangerous, and would get us fuck-all.

But the problems were just beginning.

Without laughers, breaking in to the Armory would have been feasible, but it would have been a *bitch*. With laughers, it was completely impossible. The vast structure was a city block wide, built out of grey stone and built along the lines of a Moorish castle straight outta Spain. I'd heard about it growing up, and I'd looked this shit up after my one visit there years ago, to pick up frozen bodies from the Paradise Life Extension crew. Constructed just before World War I, the Armory housed the local National Guard and was designed to be locked down in the event of a labor riot. It was to be the last rallying point for US troops if an enemy ever took the City. But that hadn't happened; the Armory had never been besieged.

Until now.

Presumably in anticipation of this, the Armory had been secured by its residents, the denizens of the Inferno. The details were hard to get on that first pass, but we logged it all later on the video. They had locked it down—then they had shut it down. The vast, open tarpapered roof with its skylights and its battlements and its fortified towers had been covered with what looked like black plastic sheets—solar panels, I figured. Satellite dishes projected above the panels.

The castle had four huge turrets, complete with battlements. One of them had what looked like a giant radio tower. The other three had flagpoles, flying half-shredded flags. Black fabric and red flaming letters:

LOL!

Steel rollup doors had secured the Armory against the SFPD and the Federal authorities in the last few days before the disaster. Since then, those doors had been augmented by rust-colored shipping containers packed tight against the building and rendered jagged with welded metal spikes jutting out from every corner at a forty-five-degree angle. The spikes, which might have once been the kind of rebar destined to make reinforced concrete, had been ground down sharp, so that even when the laughing corpses piled up deep enough to climb onto the containers, they mostly ended up impaling themselves; poked through with the spikes, the things jerked and spasmed as they laughed hysterically, visible through the swarming mass of their fellows as each laugher tried to crawl over the ones piled under it—and ended up slipping. It was like watching rats try to leave a burning building by crawling up a jagged array of greased poles. The impaled creatures' limbs flailed wildly as they jerked in wet laughter.

We saw it all on the giant TV screen. Amber and Trixie and I stared with horror at the writhing carnage on the walls of the Armory. I think all three of us felt about ready to puke.

I told Amber, "All right. Bring the drone back to the ship. We've seen enough."

Someone else thought so, too.

That's when the airship attacked.

☠

The airship rocketed out of its hiding place in the canyons of stone, looking on the giant lounge TV screen very much like something from an out-take of *District 9*.

The thing looked like a leopard-print sausage. Painted bright, in big-cat colors, it could have been said to espouse an '80s punk esthetic. But this was an '80s punk sausage with fins, and rear elevators, and rear nacelles from which propellers protruded. Those propellers were going full-bore, and the elegant machine tore out of its hiding place at a good clip.

It was evident from first glimpse that it was not a blimp—it was a zeppelin. Sort of the next step, the way one only buys a Porsche after driving a Miata for a while. It was a semi-rigid airship, with its name emblazoned on its side: EO4 *Leopardo*.

The airship turned quickly and pointed down Mission Street—facing the drone head-on.

Then it came for our Gypsy, Gatlings blazing.

They were big fuckers—20mm, at least, the size of Vietnam-era Vulcans. There were two of them—one on each side of the gondola.

The Gatlings were loaded intermittently with tracers; even in the afternoon light, I could see bright hot streams of flame belching out of them. It is no mean feat to shoot down a drone that size with Gatlings. From what I could tell, the Gatlings hit the Gypsy's wing at an oblique angle—but it was enough.

The whole world spun.

The Gypsy twirled and thumped.

A kestrel screamed in our face.

The street rushed up.

A taco truck bloomed before us, mobbed by laughing things, a one-eyed thing in a bloody apron trapped behind a wall of Snapples and Plexiglas, laughing hysterically. The truck said:

Paco's Tacos. Viva Carne!

The last thing I saw on the screen was a closeup as the Gypsy shattered a windowpane stenciled *Nirvana Flowers*; rotting gardenias flew everywhere as the drone careened into the building.

Then the Gypsy went dark.

☠

Whoever did that shit knew what they were up to; they either had helicopter counter-insurgency or counter-terrorism warfare experience. Say, an ex-Army helicopter pilot turned dot-com zillionaire and blimp hobbyist, who ran a porn company and was obsessed with Guadalupe Grope.

Who, incidentally, was either a hostage or a terrorist, possibly both, while her boyfriend purred around town shooting down other peoples' drones.

Or maybe she was a laugher. The only person in San Francisco I *knew* wasn't a laugher was EO4—Ellis Osborne IV, pornographer and zeppelin-endowed motherfucker who was about to get my fist so far down his throat I'd play pattycake with his duodenum, and not in, like, a friendly way.

Trixie said, "Was that a blimp?"

"Zeppelin," I said. "Semi-rigid."

"Yeah, I bet, asshole. Combat does that to guys like you, huh?"

"The airship's semi-rigid," I growled. "This asshole's *last* ship was a blimp. Apparently it gave people motion sickness."

Amber said, "I'm sorry, Sir... *what* asshole, Sir?"

Trixie said suspiciously, "Yeah, Dante. Do you know this blimp? And you're more than semi-rigid, incidentally. You're *grinning*. I think it's a psychosexual thing."

I said, "Let's just say I've heard rumors of lighter-than-air travel enthusiast in the Armory. Apparently he's a cat person."

Amber said, "I thought that was camouflage."

I said, "It is. The kind you wear to blend in at a B-52s reunion."

Amber brightened and said: "Sir, the birds are attracted to noise. I bet it's electric! It wouldn't be totally silent, but it'd be silent enough. Someone in California was developing a company to build airships at a very low cost—*green* airships. Electrics. Deployable solar panels above 10,000 feet. I don't remember the guy's name."

I growled, "Ellis Osborne IV, of the *EO4 Leopardo*." I explained to Trixie, "Commercial ships don't use USS and the like. They use the initials of the company that runs them."

Trixie said, "Fascinating, professor. What the fuck is EO4?"

"Ellis Osborne IV. It's like, his hip nickname."

"Ow," said Trixie. "That makes my brain hurt. Why did he shoot down our drone?"

I shrugged and said, "Guy's name is EO4—don't expect to figure him out. Maybe it's a dot-com thing."

"Sir, I don't know all that much about airships, but I've read a little. You can't fire guns that big from a zeppelin. Unless they're recoilless."

I said, "Those were Gatlings."

"It's impossible. The recoil would knock an airship right over. It'd turn turtle."

The intercom buzzed.

It was Van's voice, blaring out from the bridge. "Dante, get up here before I come down there and beat you to death."

I hit the com button.

I said, "Afternoon, Captain Fish. Get some sleep last night, like I told you to?"

"Eat shit."

"Hey, Van, we're having a debate down here. Can you fire guns from an airship?"

He said, "I sure as hell hope not."

☠

I made the bridge; two scared looking marines underqualified for bridge duty looked like they'd just finished being yelled at.

Van was waving his stogie at the distant hills.

He said, "I know I haven't slept in a while, but am I seeing things? Look—there—wait, it went behind a skyscraper—it's going up—not straight up, it's—wait—you see it? You see it?"

Trixie said, "You're not seeing things. It just shot down our Gypsy."

"There!" he pointed. "That damn thing is coming for us."

The airship was crossing the City. With field glasses, Van and I could see it coming down the west slope of Twin Peaks.

"I'm sick of this shit," said Van. He was getting about as testy as Van gets, which is *testy*.

I growled under my breath, "Are you gonna get some sleep tonight, like I ordered?"

He said, "That depends. Are we about to come under zeppelin attack?"

I looked through the field glasses and said, "Looks like."

"Then... no."

I looked through the glasses.

However much Osborne had bent the laws of physics with the *Leopardo*'s Gatlings, I felt confident in one thing: there was no way that flying sausage could outgun the *God's Grace*. If they came within Gatling range, they'd be down before they got a shot off.

But the problem was that the *Grace* was never designed to operate against offensive aircraft without air cover. Smugglers usually don't fly fighters or bombers, and they don't have torpedoes. At worst, they might fire a rifle at you from a helicopter. On contract with Bellona, I had briefly engaged with drug gangs in Mexico that used helicopter gunships—but in that case, all a ship like the *Grace* had to do was radio for air support, or launch her Little Birds.

But we didn't have our Little Birds. The *Soaker* was not airworthy, and wouldn't have been much of a combat vessel, anyway.

I watched through field glasses as the *Leopardo* came cruising over the city, ducking behind hills and buildings.

It gained altitude.

Wisps of fog shrouded it.

I grabbed the intercom and growled, "Battle stations."

☠

The fog came in.

The Leopardo vanished above it.

We put to sea. We lit out for the Farallones.

The crew put on helmets. The crew gripped their rifles. The crew manned the chain guns. The crew manned the Gatlings.

We watched the skies.

I whispered, "Do we have, transponders or some shit? Anything they can home in on?"

Van said, "Fuck if I know."

I said irritably, "You're the captain, aren't you supposed to know these things?"

He said, "Yeah? Well, Ava Sorzano says you're the Messiah. Walk over there on water and kick its ass."

I frowned.

"Trixie told you about that, huh?"

He said, "No big deal, Frosty. I've always thought of you as Jesus. Especially when I was beating the living crap you of you at Casa Fish."

I said, "Shhh."

He cocked his head.

We heard it coming.

It didn't whistle like you hear in movies.

It made a blatting sort of sickly howl-moan, like a cheap dying trumpet, like the Panama Laugh if it issued from a single half-mashed human lung. It set my teeth on edge.

I grabbed the intercom.

I said, "Incoming!"

The whole world exploded.

☠

The sun had started to go down; cloaked in grey fog, the night was empty.

Then it was full: bright light, fire, waves of heat.

Seawater drenched the deck.

Hot gouts of steam blew everywhere.

Smoke: mingled black and grey, unburned powder tangled up with the fog.

Van said, "What was that thing?"

I said, "I'd guess a pipe bomb of some sort."

He said, "There's another one—you see it?"

I howled, "Turn left!"

He said, "You mean port? Way ahead of you Frosty."

I howled, "Turn! Turn! Why aren't you turning?"

He was furiously clicking his mouse button while talking to me.

I looked at the ship's wheel, a big wood and brass assembly.

He said, "That's for photo ops. What do you think this is, the diesel age? We're running *nuclear*, Frosty."

We heard a deep whining buzz-howl up ahead.

He gritted his teeth.

He said, "And here comes *steam*."

The world exploded.

☠

This time the blast was much closer. I'd gotten a glimpse of it coming down—just a blur of white in the light of the moon.

It was a gravity bomb—though calling it that was probably giving it too much credit. It was more like one of those goofy globe bombs you see in old cartoons about anarchists.

It blew up a few meters above the water, maybe ten meters away. It blew a flaming hole in the Pacific Ocean about the size of a small house, and the deck was swamped. It described a big oblong flash with lingering sparks in the fog. Whatever substance they used as the charge burned unevenly; otherwise the roofing nails that rained all over us might have injured the crew severely. As it was, several of the riflemen crouching at the ready caught jagged slices across their exposed hands, and the cloth outer layers of their body armor was peppered with nail marks.

I said, "Evasive maneuvers?"

Van said, "No shit, Frosty, I watched *The Enemy Below* just like you did. Only I didn't fall asleep. I've been taking us serpentine toward the Farallones, for all the good it's doing. I haven't got the faintest idea how they're tracking us, but they are."

The screaming sound came again.

I punched the speaker, said "Incoming!" miserably—the crew hit the deck.

Louder... louder... louder...

Bam!

The bomb hit hard on the roof above the bridge; they'd scored a direct hit. It made a sound like a cannonball hitting the side of a corrugated metal shed.

It bounced.

It slid.

It smacked into the deck.

I cursed.

I waited.

I said, "It didn't explode."

Van said, "Yeah."

I asked Amber, "Do we have a bomb squad?"

She saluted and said, "No, Sir. Sir, I'd like to volunteer, Sir."

I frowned at Amber and growled, "Eat shit."

☠

I ran out on deck with a Maglite. I screamed at the crew to back the fuck away. I was not wearing body armor, but I didn't give a fuck.

The bomb had smacked into the roof and cracked open; it slid down the metal of the *God's Grace*'s bridge roof in a big wet wad and sat there on the deck, a split-open plastic sheath with a peeling-off label that said:

Preuss Farms 2% Milk
Petaluma, CA
Grass Fed - Organic - Cruelty Free

This Container Is Compostable

Sticking out of the jug was a broom handle and four stabilizer fins carved out of plywood.

Duct-taped to those were four vuvuzelas.

I had worked a job running security for embassy personnel at the World Cup one year. Those fucking vuvuzelas were *never* good news.

A bread-sized loaf of a sloppy black claylike substance had been squashed on impact into a vile smear about a foot across. A glass bulb jiggled ominously in the wind, exposed wires jutting from its back end. Roofing nails had scattered everywhere; they crunched under my boots.

I screamed, "Back off!" and plucked the glass bulb out of the black smear. The substance stank of chemicals.

I threw the glass bulb as hard as I could; it cleared the deck and disappeared.

The airship pirouetted out of the fog, scattering vapor in swirls around us. It hovered thirty feet above the water.

The crew scrambled and raised their rifles; those at the Gatlings and thirties whirled into place.

I screamed, "Hold your fire!"

The zeppelin cruised through the mist, Gatlings trained on us.

I repeated my order.

The thing retreated, pulled up. It started speeding away from us, unfurling a big long banner with a single easy motion.

I screamed, "Searchlights!"

At the very edge of our vision, before it disappeared into the fog, the airship banked hard a-starboard so we could see the banner, on fabric with big drippy spray-paint letters, red-on-black like a *Rocky Horror* poster.

The banner read:

LOL!

The thing vanished into the fog.

I stalked into the bridge.

I said, "Then this bucket's dropping me off on the beach."

Van said, "Huh?"

I told him:, "I'm going in there. *Tonight*."

"Into the City?"

I said, "Yeah, Cap'n. That big one over there, with all the fog?"

Van said, "Are you serious?"

I said, "Do I *look* like I'm laughing?"

☠

I told Amber to assemble the crew.

I went to the brig.

I got Ava Sorzano and told her, "Time for your parole hearing."

I went to my stateroom.

I got my gym bag.

I brought Ava and the gym bag to the crew's mess.

I unzipped it and introduced them.

Virgil was the hands-down attention-getter. Some crew members stared at him in his clear Lucite tube; Every time his haunted eyes moved, ripples ran through them in response. Some looked away, stared again. Others looked once, went green, and never looked back.

Someone asked, "Wh-what is that?"

I told the crew, "This is Virgil Amaro. Well... his head. He's not my friend. As far as I can tell, he either made this happen or helped make this happen. I know you've all seen my dumbass videos; it's a very long story, but some aspects of some of them were factual. Virgil really did send me all over the world looking for viruses to aid his quest to live forever. As you can see, it worked pretty well for him."

Virgil said, "Dante. Dante! Is it Easter yet?"

I growled patronizingly, "It'll be Easter soon, Virgil. As I was saying, I don't know what Virgil's part in this… plague… was. But he definitely isn't innocent. However, technically this is his ship, so if any of you want to hand over command to him, I suggest you discuss it with your colleagues."

They looked at me like I was crazy. They still couldn't believe what they were seeing.

I continued: "Now, this is Ava Sorzano. Before this all happened, she was being sought for questioning about some improper use of vaccines. She claims she was set up by Virgil. I don't know. I know that as far as I can tell, she helped make this thing happen. But as far as I can tell, she didn't mean to. I don't trust her, and you shouldn't either. But I'm letting her out of the brig."

I said in my Sermon at the Mount voice: "You guys got hired to escort Luke Amaro to the Holy Land. But the Amaro family doesn't have a bank account to pay you with, or health insurance to offer you, or a letter of reference to get you when you apply for a cushy job at a defense contractor. You know what Virgil here has? Well, I'll tell you two things he *doesn't* have. *Shoulders.* You know why? Because Virgil Amaro wanted to live forever. He wanted to bring about the End Times—"

I glared at Dr. Sorzano.

"—and survive them, so he could profit from them. He had me retrieve viruses from sites in Libya, Congo, the Philippines; he had—Dr. Sorzano here do medical testing to create military and civilian applications for those viruses, to build super-soldiers and extend life and maybe—just maybe—create the ultimate biological weapon." I howled at the top of my lungs: "Marine! What's so funny, Supervising Marine Third Class Gilden?"

The gawky kid named Gilden saw my displeasure. He kicked into attention and saluted.

"Sorry, Sir."

I screamed: "Stop saluting me!"

He paled, dropped his hand, looked like he didn't know what to do with it. He put his hands behind his head as if he was being arrested.

I got in his face screamed: "What's so funny? Speak your mind."

Gilden trembled. "It's just like the videos, Sir. We're all really big fans. Your videos are a lot of the reason I wanted to become a military contractor." He saw me glaring and tried to backpedal. "Look, Sir, I'm sorry, Sir, Sir, it's just—it's just, you know, it's true what they say, if you don't mind my saying. Good science fiction is *visionary*."

"Talk like that'll get you a knuckle sandwich, marine!"

He paled and saluted me again.

Trixie stepped in. She said: "It's not science fiction. The Amaros are probably responsible for everything that's happening out there. They put Frosty here in prison for five years because he tried to blow the whistle before it happened. That's when he recorded the first video."

"Wh—which one was the first one, Sir?"

"I—I torrented them. The track numbers were all messed up."

"Was the first one the one where he talks about his Grandpa teaching him the spit-take?"

"No, I think it's the one about the wolf women in the bikinis."

"That one with the Ruben Blades tattoo was hot!"

"No way, the first one was the one about Alpha Centauri—wait a minute, Frosty! You're saying these things are aliens?"

I screamed: "Pipe down! Attention!"

They all stood at attention like a class of errant kindergartners.

I said, "Keep a lid on it!" I stalked back and forth, up and down, getting in the crew's faces and watching them piss their pants. I screamed: "This isn't a fucking science fiction movie! This isn't paint ball! This is the end of the world! Your families are dead! Your friends are dead!"

Nobody moved.

Virgil said, "Is it Easter yet?"

I said sadly, "It'll be Easter soon, Virgil." Then, to the crew, I said: "Attention!"

Every last one of them snapped to attention like clean marines. Well... the Russian engineers seemed a little bored by it all, but that was their style.

I told them, "I want each and every one of you to look in my eyes. Personally. My eyes, and promise me that you are one hundred percent loyal to me, to Captain Fish, to Dr. Ferguson, and to your fellow crew members. Into my eyes, people. Mine. You're promising me. Not your commander, not your Boss, but the only idiot stupid enough to try to bring you bunch of lames through this mess alive. Look into my eyes and tell me you will not do one damn thing to hurt your shipmates. Got it? One at a time, people You! *C'mere*."

That took a while, but it was important. I eyefucked every one of them with my R. Lee Ermey glare. Each crew member looked in my eyes and swore loyalty to the *Grace* and his or her shipmates, to Captain Fish, to Dr. Ferguson.

The last cat I eyefucked was Ava Sorzano.

She looked at me *hard*.

I said, "Tell me."

She did.

I said, "Welcome aboard." Then, to the crew, I said: "I know that was dramatic, but I needed that reassurance before I leave you out here in the fog. I'll explain everything when I get back."

They looked at me nervously.

I said, "Which will be either tomorrow morning or never. I'm the only one who's immune to this shit. Dr. Sorzano and Dr. Ferguson might be… but we can't be sure. I know I am, so I'm going. Alone."

Amber, without asking first—she was learning—said, "To do what, Sir?"

I clapped her on the arm and said, "Supervising Technical Consultant Lin, I wanna find out if that goddamn place still knows how to party."

☠

The land maps and atlases on the *Grace* had all been online; CD-ROM copies for the ship's library were supposed to be picked up in Malta. I'd need that shit if I had to get off the main streets, so I brought Augie's cell phone, which had a map of SF saved locally as a PDF. Had he planned to come to San Francisco?

Yet another trip an Amaro would never make.

I mined the *Grace*'s stores for everything I could think I might need. These fuckers knew how to pack, all right. I pulled on a thermal long-sleeve shirt. Over it I put body armor and a load-bearing vest. I threaded the earplug of the walkie up the shirt and into my ear. I carried two holstered five-sevs with extra magazines; across my belly I strung three magazines of .45 rounds for the TDI Vector submachine gun I would need to fire one-handed and left-handed at least part of the time—never fun or easy, no matter what the John Woo movies tell you. On my vest I put flash-bangs, fragmentation and tear gas grenades, knives.

I slung an AR-57 over my back.

As I loaded up the RHIB with the scout bike, Van asked me:

"Isn't Golden Gate Park kind of far from the Armory?"

I said, "It's not Golden Gate Park, douchebag. It's Lake Merced."

"Oh," said Van, puzzled. "But it's green."

"That doesn't make it Golden Gate Park," I said. "There's more than one park in this asshat factory."

"Fine, then. Why so far?"

"It's got to be somewhere with cover."

He said, "Cover?"

I said, "Trees, genius."

"Oh, those."

"In case that airship's still out there. If they see you landing a boat, they'll be after me."

Van said, "What are the chances of that?"

☠

In case you have never heard the famous "Mark Twain" quote that is not by Mark Twain, let me just paraphrase it for you:

The coldest winter I ever spent was the night I pulled a Tom Hanks in San Francisco six weeks after the apocalypse.

In short: I froze my *ass* off before the zodiac even hit the water. That fog gets cold in any month, and midnight is not the time to hotfoot it around San Francisco.

The *God's Grace*'s scout bikes—of which there were four—were just exactly designed to load, one each, into the zodiac—one of the inflatable boats in which personnel from the *God's Grace* were expected to make any excursions ashore when a pier was not available, like, say, in a hot zone. The *Grace* was not a boat; it was a small ship. It was not a landing craft; it did not have a flat bottom and was not expected to make the beach under any circumstances—especially not with that mini-nuke plant, which would make such beaching illegal in just about every jurisdiction. Under rough waters like those that night at Ocean Beach, could not come closer than a hundred meters to shore. Without GPS or a trained ship captain, even that was risky.

They loaded up the 40mm grenade launchers with specialty rounds.

They unshipped the Gatlings and chain guns.

Van brought me in as close as he dared.

The walkie chirped.

Van's voice crackled down from the bridge: "It has to be tonight?"

I said, "We know there are survivors at the Armory."

Van said, "Yeah, but they could be douchebags."

I said, "Or hostages. Plus, that flying kitty could come back any minute. I'm going."

"Then let's get this over with. Over and out, fucko."

I stuffed earplugs in my ears as they craned me down in the RHIB.

I pulled my balaclava up. I settled goggles over my eyes.

The seas were rough.

Fog cloaked everything.

The wind cut me.

I fired up the outboard.

The forties boomed.

The mortar boomed.

The night screamed to Heaven.

I opened it and headed for the beach.

☠

Spray drenched me as the RHIB clipped the waves at fifty knots.

I was perhaps eighty meters from the beach when the flare rounds detonated: Pink lights on parachutes. They burned high above me.

They lit up the beach with pink light.

Thousands lined it, laughing.

The forties boomed again. Fragmentation grenades hit the Great Highway. Laughers went down.

Sixty meters.

More fireworks: frags, HEs, screaming as they plummeted, the vuvuzelas of Normandy. The detonations rumbled through my earplugs. Forty meters. The things looked at me and opened their pie holes: hilarious. I thought: *Mine. Mine, all mine. These laughers are mine. Virgil said, "Congo," I said, "Cha-ching." Virgil said Niger, I said, "Cha-ching." He said, Bring me kisses from Libya: I brought him kisses, from a terrorist camp where killers grew laughing Tuareg kids in rail containers in hundred-and-twenty degree heat; Virgil told me, "Help make the world an ugly place," and I said, "Bank of the Caymans, account number for international wire transfers…"*

I'd brought these people here, to the beach to laugh in the darkness at nothing, to strip the meaning out of all that had ever mattered. I'd humored Virgil's belief that given enough money and cruelty and the willingness to disregard the screams of every child, *any* man can be God: Any man. Any man at all. That he can choose not only the moment of his passing, but the moment of others' passing.

I'd brought back mercy from the darkness: the very last mercy the world had to offer.

But it was the Devil's Mercy.

And the Devil never cries.

I saw more screaming pretties: pink lights on parachutes.

And under them I saw my laughing dead children screaming the Panama Laugh.

Forty meters. Thirty-five. Thirty.

Tears froze on my cheeks.

I saw them holding their spilling guts with their rot-distended fingers.

I saw them laughing.

In the very last instant before the nightmare started, I thought:

Dante, this is by far…

… the dumbest idea…

… you've ever fucking had.

The chain guns opened up wide; sixteen thousand rounds a minute. Laughing faces dissolved before me. They blew back in a red spray and mingled with the fog. Illumined in pink, they went down wet, some dropping and writhing there in pieces, legless, armless, laughing still. Always laughing.

I hit the beach *hard*.

I opened up with the Vector on three-round bursts. I emptied it fast, spilling laugher brains everywhere. I reloaded and pirouetted-till-spent; .45 slugs tore holes in chortling faces until I stood in great clouds of smoke in a circle of empty. Laughers still lumbered toward me, humping down the beach, groping; dancing in the pink. The fog and gunsmoke swirled around them. I slammed in the last 30-round mag for the Vector, switched it to my left hand and aimed the scout bike at the stairs. I hit the starter. The fucker coughed, kicking sparks. I hit it again. The bike started. Laughers closed in. Revving the scout bike, I opened up with the Vector in my left hand.

I drew a half-circle of juicy red spray.

I dropped the submachine gun and let the clutch out.

I dodged laughers and bounced up the stairs that led to the Great Highway. The shocks made yowling sounds.

Laughers came for me, groping; I punched and dodged them and beat them off. I climbed the stairs with my feet high off the foot pegs.

I was through.

The sea of laughers closed tight behind me. They came for me, but I was faster now.

I made for the Big Green.

Before I got there, I saw it hovering over me in the fog, black against the pink flares burning on their parachutes. It was the shadow of a former life, dangerous and deadly.

The *Leopardo*.

It didn't make a sound.

It hovered, silent in the fog. Its Gatling mount tracked me.

I killed my headlight.

I slalomed, expecting a blast of Gatling fire.

The pink flares burned out.

There were no street lamps.

No moon could cut through that fog.

I leaned hard on the throttle and hit the park going forty miles an hour.

Then I was shrouded by the branches of evergreens, flooring it through drifting tides of laughter.

I was in Hell.

☠

Lake Merced was packed. Bloated laughers splashed out of the water. I stuck to the green areas on the edge of the lake, but I was moving fast enough that they didn't come after me until after I'd passed. The fog made it dark. All around me, I heard laughers. Dozens, hundreds, maybe thousands of them.

Their uncanny sense of where their prey was seemed to depend on one's staying in one place. They didn't know enough—didn't have the higher *brain* functions—to step in the road and wait for me.

And I could hear them, if not see them, up ahead.

They wandered in the dense trees; they stumbled across the road and didn't flee from the buzz of the scout bike.

I unsnapped the five-sev on my left, but I resisted drawing it. If you have ever tried to ride a bike one-handed, it is not much fun at any speed. At night, at high speed, in the cold, dodging obstacles, it is even less fun. Shooting left-handed while you do it—even with a five-sev, which has little recoil? I'd give it a pass unless I absolutely had to. I had a suppressor for the fucking thing, and one magazine of subsonic rounds, a necessity when using the five-sev for stealth. But wouldn't you know it? If I wore the damn thing with the suppressor, it didn't fit in the holster. Military intelligence strikes again.

And above me, a shadow through the trees, stalked the almost-silent *Leopardo*.

I say almost-silent 'cause her altitude was low enough now that she *did* make some noise—enough that I could hear, but not enough, it seemed, to summon the attentions of the birds.

There was barely a whine from its engines—like the sound of a Prius running on electric. Mingling with that was the whirring sound of its electric airscrews, starting and stopping at will. It didn't keep them going full-bore—doubtless because of the birds. And it gave off one other sound: the sound of the Gatling mount, tracking me.

It shadowed me as I dodged laughers.

Then she was gone; I heard her swirling away, up high into the fog, leaving a wake as she headed out to sea.

I leaned on the throttle.

☠

The trees, the roads, the fog: silent, dark around me, green in the low-light goggles.

The laughers: dark around me, barely visible, and not silent.

The streetlights didn't even tick and purr soothingly the way they do when they wink out just before dawn.

The fog was the only reason I could still run. If it was a clear night, the *Leopardo* would have had an easier time picking me off the beach. As it was, the killer could be stalking me silently, watching for my telltale trace in the fog.

I punched it *hard*.

☠

I found Portola and made for Twin Peaks. More trees, more fog, more cover.

I chicken-necked the throttle so hard I popped a wheelie and almost went down. I kept it straight and tapped the footbrake; I brought it down hard and hit tight on the asphalt.

With the low-light goggles I could see them waiting up ahead: Laughers. Dense, packed, dozens and dozens and dozens of them. Bits and pieces. Things missing. Faces gone. Open skeletons. Flesh melted off. Puffy faces blue with bruise. Some were silent: their lungs were gone, or the muscles of their throat opened up so wide that all they made was slurping noises. What was left of them chirruped and jiggled and shook, but it didn't laugh.

Others bleated: Screaming uproariously. Packs of hyenas.

I hauled out the five-sev and held it left-handed.

As I neared the group of laughers, I opened up.

I emptied the thirty-round mag; half a dozen went down wet. I dodged around the group and made it through.

Breathing easier, I twisted my head and looked up—had the gunfire tipped off the stalking *Leopardo*, lurking in the fog?

Nothing. I holstered my sidearm, let out a sigh. I leaned on the throttle. I breathed easy.

Then she came for me out of the darkness, hitting me at face-level.

She came for me in black and orange.

She came for me in stripes.

Kitty took me *down*.

☠

One of the chief combatant's skills is recognizing threats; in any given war zone, if you are on the front lines you develop this skill fast or you don't develop it at all, because you're compost. I'd clocked the major threats: Laughers. Check. Criers. Check. Hindenburg, Gatling guns, exploding vuvuzelas, oil slicks, fire hydrants, parked cars, garbage cans, check, check, check, check, check.

But Murphy's law applies even in times like these. And Murphy's a prick. I'd been vigilant, but not vigilant enough.

I hadn't been watching for a Siberian tiger.

☠

Her name's Tatiana; you might know her from the news reports.

I only know about *this* Tatiana because Trixie held forth about it once, over a Seitan Omelette (hers) and a Corned Beef Hash and Eggs at Ali Mento's on the Via España.

Tatiana I rendered in eloquent form the most stirring argument I've ever heard for not shooting slingshots at Siberian tigers. She was then shot by the SFPD, in an incident that made Trixie, who rabidly opposed the death penalty, suggest that feeding some people to tigers might actually be an awesome idea.

Trixie thought it was also an awesome idea when the zoo acquired a female tiger cub and a citizen's coalition banded together to insist that she be called Tatiana II, nicknamed Tatianita—*Little Tatiana*.

The name probably fit her just fine when she was a cub.

Now, she was a tad large for the moniker.

She was also muscled; she'd been getting her exercise.

I knew that because I'd just had my face smashed into those muscles.

It wasn't a surprise that Tati'd been working out. Since the laughers came, she'd had the City to herself, unless you counted all the laughing cat toys.

If you've ever played with a cat—presumably in the five-to-twenty-pound range, instead of the 350 pounds that Tatianita must have been—you know the phenomenon. Drag a piece of yarn slowly along the ground; your cat will go after it.

In terms relative to Tatianita's size, the laughers moved exactly that speed.

The City was now packed with things that moved at the speed of giant cat toys.

And I, as something moving faster, presented a new and pleasing challenge.

Tatianita liked to play with her food.

☠

In case you've never had a Siberian tiger pluck you off your dirt bike at thirty-five miles an hour—or to be wholly accurate, a combined seventy since she was coming at me as I came at her—I'll try to sum up the experience. I hit the vast wall of tiger and you know what? That fur's not even remotely as soft as it seems when you see Paris Hilton's taking shots from the paintball set. That's 'cause there's *muscle* under, and an awful damn lot of it.

Tiger, though, is softer than asphalt; if she hadn't taken me down with such little effort, or if I had not been watching for silent death from the skies, I would have seen her and dodged her, or tried to, and gone down hard and eaten shit, face-first on the sidewalk.

But Tatiana II didn't kill me.

She wanted to *play*.

☠

No matter what kind of whackass shit has happened to you in the six weeks prior—the apocalypse, waking up from being frozen alive, suddenly being in command of a nuclear gunboat—nothing has prepared you for the experience of getting hit by an actual flying tiger at top speed.

The bike went out from under me; it twisted; the rear wheel jacked up into the air and my face hit the handlebars; an errant tooth or my forehead or my nose hit the headlight and it went on.

Bright white light blasted me.

I had the low-light goggles on, it blinded me.

That's bad.

The bike skittered off and screamed across the asphalt. I came down hard, face-first across the roof of an SUV parked square in the middle of the intersection. My goggles went flying.

Tatiana II went pad-pad across the intersection, like the happiest clam in the clam farm. This was her element. Millions of years of tiger evolution had rendered her a perfect killer. She'd been built by God and his minions the carbon molecules, fine-tuned and tweaked with million-year engineering schematics so she could whisper over downed cars in hunt for the Messiah.

She gave a squeal—a *happy* squeal, 'cause this was so much *fun*. A tiger's squeal sounds like a roar—so much that I thought it was one. But a few seconds later she actually roared, and that squeal? It seemed more like a purr.

I panicked. I scrambled. I slid to the ground from the SUV and landed on my ass. I had the strap of the AR-57 over my head before I even knew what I was doing.

I'd done this a thousand times, right?

I had the safety off and the rifle aimed up.

But I couldn't see shit.

Tatiana II was gone.

It was *black*. The dirt bike had hit something hard, far away, and its motor went dead. The headlight was out. The city was nothing but nighttime around me; the bright pink flares of the beach were high-tech things, intended to preserve some hint of my night vision. They hadn't. I couldn't see *shit*.

Just grey fog and shapes, moving.

Shadows.

Shadows.

Shadows.

But a kitty-cat's eyes glow in the dark.

She leapt; she landed on a Muni bus and perched high above me; I knew her only because I saw her eyes.

In the dark.

In the *dark*.

I saw those eyes blooming high above me.

She stood on the bus, silent, peering at me. I could only see her eyes. I had the distinct sense that she could see all of me, and that if she knew what a rifle was, she wasn't especially worried.

She looked down, her eyes catching what little light there was.

I blinked and they were gone.

She vanished silent into darkness.

I looked around.

The fog cloaked Tatiana; without street lights, I saw nothing but grey. And stars; I'd hit my head hard when I came down. I was pretty sure I was bleeding—like I gave a fuck.

Or did I? Could tigers smell blood?

Holy crap. That wasn't a comforting thought.

Bad things laughed all around me.

Something growled in the darkness.

The laughers were ten feet from us, maybe less.

I looked up at the tiger and thought, "pull the trigger?"

Which is something I almost never wonder.

I'm not a hunter. I don't have strong opinions on what I'd use to bring down big game. But I knew a 5.7 round was not my first choice. I would have preferred Van's bloop tube.

What I did know was that if I put a slug in that beast and did not end her tenure on this planet, she would not be my friend.

Faintly, around me, coming closer, I heard the chirrups of the Panama Laugh.

Coming closer.

Closer.

Without once lowering my gaze, I reached up gingerly to fondle my rifle.

I hit my laser sight: nothing. It speared up empty into the fog.

I hit my tac light: nothing. All it did was blind me more, as the halogen-white ricocheted off steamy white wisps and made me squint.

The big shadow far overhead answered the question for me.

The airship loomed above at a height of maybe twenty meters: completely silent.

Not even a whisper of wind through the riggings.

Then the world exploded.

The *Leopardo* blasted her searchlights.

I was blinded again—worse than before.

But I could see Tatiano's shadow: black in the circle of midnight sun.

Five feet away, big and toothsome above me on the big flat roof of the SUV.

Oh, sweet Jesus.

Had the tiger chosen that moment to pounce, it probably could have bypassed my rifle and eaten me alive before I even thought to shoot it. It would have beaten the laughers by only a few seconds; I could hear them closing in on me. They were a few feet away, but I was blinder than ever.

But the tiger didn't jump; it looked up at the airship; it pawed at the air.

I killed my tac light and laser fast; I didn't want to give *The Leopardo* a target. I aimed my rifle.

If I started shooting, the airship would open up; the Gatlings would mulch me.

If I didn't, the laughers would come for me. I could hear them but I couldn't see them. They could see me. Or they could sense me.

There was nowhere I could hide.

The tiger turned toward the searchlight; she pawed at the air.

Then she got on her back and started *rolling*.

It was a cheap, hot searchlight; it *buzzed*. It put out a lot of heat.

Kitty liked the heat.

The SUV rocked and groaned under the weight; she slid around smooth on the roof; no luggage rack.

The Gatlings hummed on their electric mounts.

In the darkness: *Huh, huh, huh, huh, huh.* Close around me. Laughers. Closer, laughers. Closer. Closer.

I was tucked on a side street between two apartment buildings; the airship couldn't get a shot at me with the Gatlings without taking a substantial chance of hitting the tiger.

I guess they were cat people.

There was a soft roaring purr overhead; the propellers started.

The Leopardo rose silently, slowly, disappearing into the mist, until it became just a bright light, then nothing.

The cat was nothing more than a shadow to me in the dwindling searchlight from *The Leopardo.*

The shadow rolled it sat up tight on its haunches and started licking its paw.

Then *The Leopardo* was gone and I was blind again.

Around me: Huh-huh-huh-huh-huh.

I should have fired.

Shoot at the cat, the laughers would take me. Shoot at the laughers, the cat would jump.

Tiger's claws, scraping; footfalls. Heavy, light—everywhere. Tiger, laughers. Tiger, laughers.

I raised the rifle.

If all the liquid in my body hadn't been frozen solid by the infil, I would a left a stinking yellow puddle there on Nineteenth Ave.

I said softly, "Holy Mary, mother of God—"

Then Tatiana came down.

☠

The second I saw those terrible muscles move, I hit the ground hard. It was good that I did; the laughers were reaching.

Their hands swirled over me as Tatiana struck. I saw shadows; I hit my tac light. Laughers everywhere, swept to the side by Tatiana. She took them down like she was playing.

I drew a circle with the laser; faces, lips peeled back, teeth bloody. I started shooting full-auto, blasting wildly around me.

This is quite possibly the stupidest thing I could do in that situation. Even with a light-recoil shoulder-fired weapon like the AR-57, fully-automatic fire is next to impossible to control; you can pour fifty rounds at a target in ten seconds and score far fewer hits than if you'd fired single-shot and aimed each time. Full-auto from a shoulder arm to impress your girlfriend is fine, if she's the kind who gives a shit. Full-auto in warfare is useless except as covering fire. In a close quarters combat situation like this, with targets who must be hit in the head, or you achieve nothing other than making them more disgusting, doing what I did is probably far stupider than it would have been against a close-in crowd of combatants bum-rushing me.

Perhaps someday you'll have the unique opportunity to experience such a thing and correct my tactical error.

The good news is, my idiocy is probably the only thing that saved Tatiana—because in the moments that I fired, I was so shit-scared I would have killed her.

But I didn't. I missed her, and she barely noticed. She was perched atop a pair of laughers, who chirped and squirmed underneath her as she played with them.

Laughers sprayed around me; brains exploded over 19th street in wide wet cones.

At the sound of gunfire and the sight of the muzzle flash, Tatiana froze atop two laughers she had just taken down. She cocked her head, looking very much like a housecat who hears the footfall of the neighbor's dog.

The AR-57 I carried was not suppressed, either for sound or for flash. It made a big bang.

It didn't faze my Tatiana.

The laughers were arrayed out around me in waves, a few of them twitching.

Tatiana looked at me.

She opened her mouth; I thought she was going to roar.

Instead, she *yawned*.

One of the dead things underneath her gave a titter.

Tatiana looked irritated , came down hard with one paw on its head.

The thing didn't laugh again.

I fumbled my pistol out of my thigh holster and backed away.

I hit its tac light and laser and backed away.

I slung my rifle and backed away.

Tatiana *watched*.

For all I knew I could have been backing into giant crowd of silent laughers, or ones I couldn't hear because I'd just blown fifty rounds into the big empty night and the fog and frankly I couldn't have heard a scream. Not even my own.

I could have been backing into laughers, but I just didn't care. Laughers I was used to, and they weren't tigers.

I found the bike. I fumbled it up. My goggles dangled from the clutch lever.

I put them back on, gingerly.

I straightened the bike.

Tatiana cleaned her paw.

I hit the starter; the bike roared to life. The headlight was dead.

Tatiana stopped washing her paw and leaned forward, watching me.

I holstered my sidearm.

Tatiana crept forward.

I twisted that throttle.

Tatiana took a step.

I let out the clutch and hurtled forward without looking back.

When I looked back Tatiana was padding after me—thirty, thirty-five.

I punched it; my front tire left the asphalt.

I eased up, tapped the brake, hit the ground hard.

I punched it again, this time more cautiously.

I roared forward into the night, waiting to hear Tatiana padding after me—or, worse, *not* to hear her.

I didn't. She was gone.

For a time, at least, I felt no longer scared of the laughers.

☠

Portola was a big wide serpentine path through the center of the city, where fewer cars had been at the time of the "incident." It yawned wide open, empty, and scary as shit in the dark. But there were few laughers, and no tigers at all.

The laughers reached for me and cackled. They lumbered at me and brayed.

I dodged them and climbed into the hills.

They chuckled as I passed, leaving my wake in the fog.

Above me, I heard nothing, which was not a good sign.

☠

I am not an expert on streets in San Francisco, and I was taking a circuitous route in an attempt to stick to the trees. I got a bit lost turning off Portola. Luckily, my alter ego Augie Amaro had a local map of San Francisco saved on his smartphone, so I pulled up under a copse of evergreens and consulted that.

I got back on track. I tucked the phone back in my vest. But I was left thinking:

"Why the fuck would Augie Amaro want to come to San Francisco?"

One more piece of the puzzle.

I chicken-necked the throttle and headed up the hill.

☠

I screamed around curves at the base of Twin Peaks.

Branches were down everywhere; I slalomed.

The light-sensitive goggles kept me from wrecking, but barely.

I didn't dare turn on the headlight, a flashlight, a tac light—anything. The *Leopardo* stalked me overhead. To give her a visual target would be to invite disaster.

I raced through fog and blackness.

I felt the airship seething above me; I heard propellers sometimes. Sometimes.

Otherwise: silent, which, like I said, was not a good sign.

But then, there weren't many good signs to be had lately.

☠

Twin Peaks is a double-tipped prong of hills that juts up from the guts of San Francisco; on clear nights you can see seven counties. But there aren't many clear nights, and this wasn't one. If there was, I'd be strewn in chunks across, probably, two of them.

I hugged the curves as fast as I dared; the dirt bike handled beautifully, considering its earlier crash. It is a scary thing to scream through darkness hunted by a silent predator on the other side of a wall that it can breach at any time with a blast from its guns.

I felt the sausage track me through the fog.

Its Gatlings hummed sometimes; electric pushers whirled.

The guns hissed cruelly on their tracks; why didn't the thing shoot me? It didn't need to.

It had known where I was the whole time; it was playing with me.

Like Tatiana, the giant sausage honed its skills by playing with its food.

When they finally took me, I didn't even know they were there.

I thought I would make it.

I'd seen the end.

I'd reached the breaking point; from here on out it was all downhill, to the easy, smooth trip down the hill to the Mission.

And into the heart of the zombies, piled a hundred-deep on every block surrounding the big Moorish castle—but never mind that. I'd come up with a plan.

I was improvising.

I topped the rise and hugged the curves.

The world exploded.

I went blind.

I went down.

I went over.

I went *out*.

☠

I surely described a trail through the fog; the *Leopardo* probably could have skeet-shot me.

I hit the side of the mountain and slid.

Fast and up through a rust-metal fence; it tore like paper, slashing me open. Then faster and down through a wet drape of bushes. Scraping my flesh from my bones.

Then faster than ever into the rocks, and sliding, down, down the side of Twin Peaks.

☠

I saw him, Gramps, three sheets to the wind, cigar smoking.

His El Dorado was parked behind us.

I leaned far over the railing, happily, taking in all the glory of the cityscape spread far below from the glorious vista.

Gramps said:

"But whatever you do, Danny Bogart, are you listing? Are you listening, Danny Boy? Listen to me, Danny: Don't call it Frisco."

I said, "Frisco?"

He said, "You've done it now!"

And he *shoved*.

I screamed at the top of my lungs.

Grandpa caught me.

I screamed.

He felt bad.

I screamed.

He said, "Sorry, kid. That's an old vaudeville routine. Didn't mean nothing. I forgot! You're too young for that shit. Sorry, kid. Let's get an ice cream."

Any sane child would have taken a simple equation away from this: scream and get ice cream.

Instead, I became Frosty Bogart. Never show it, Bubba. Keep your cards to your chest; don't let 'em see your fear.

He kept saying, "I'm sorry, you do that with ex-comics from LA, they laugh their asses off, Danny. 'Specially when you do it in a gorilla suit!" He laughed nervously. He held me tight. He said, "I forgot, you're not old enough for slapstick. You okay? You okay. Let's get some ice cream. Butter brickle."

Oh, I loved that old fuck. If he was here right now, I'd tell Gramps *"Como esta usted?"* and give him a knuckle sandwich. Not old enough for slapstick, Gramps? Slapstick *this*.

I was old enough for slapstick now.

Or, at least, the laughers in the trees thought my pratfall was a *riot*.

☠

I tried hard to move.

I couldn't, at first.

Then I tried *not* to move; I tried to get my bearings.

I saw the sausage swimming, sizzle-hot searchlight scouring the mountainside.

They were looking for me, but they hadn't yet found me; they were looking on the wrong slope. I lay in darkness, buried in bushes up against some rich cat's house. I'd hit the side of the mountain at an oblique angle and slid till I smacked full up into a wall of hydrangeas.

I heard it.

Laughing.

All around me... getting closer.

I couldn't see *shit*.

I had to psych myself up for the pain when I *did* move. I managed it, and even managed not to call out.

The bike was nowhere to be seen—it probably wouldn't be, for the foreseeable future.

The rifle was perhaps fifteen feet away, so I drew my five-sev.

I listened for laughers. They were close, creeping toward me through the underbrush.

I watched the searchlight of the *Leopardo*, sweeping the mountainside.

When it was at its furthest point from me, I hit the laser and the tac light on the five-sev—and swept it.

I saw half a dozen laughers.

I started firing.

☠

The *Leopardo* was up there listening for me. They heard the crack of the five-sev rounds as I sprayed laugher brains. The searchlight swung toward me.

Every joint in my body heart as I wrenched myself to my feet and lunged. I ran, firing, clearing a path through the laughers. I grabbed my rifle as I ran past it, dangling it by the strap as I spotted a copse of trees and lit out for it.

Over me, the Gatlings chattered.

A line of hot lead and burning underbrush lit up behind me.

I dove. I disappeared into the bushes—or, rather, the *Leopardo* disappeared above it. I heard birds screaming; they were mobbing the airship to the sound of the Gatlings. The searchlight swirled wildly, then swept away from me as the *Leopardo* swirled, fighting to stabilize itself despite the attack of the birds.

I breathed hard; I was in so much pain, and feeling my stomach churn. It was familiar. Had I dislocated something? Jesus, it could be anything. *Pick a joint…*

The searchlight started moving again, started describing a meticulous, circular path, trying to find me. The Gatling hummed on its mount, tracking.

My rifle was empty after my encounter with Tatiana; I hadn't paused to reload it.

☠

I fished a mag out of my vest. I moved nice and slow. I knew any motion could tip off the sausage. This time, the Gatling tracked identically to the searchlight; they would not fuck around this time. The next time they found me, they'd open up when I was pinned there, like a bug to a board.

I pressed the magazine release on the rifle. I pulled the mag free and dropped it in the bushes.

The searchlight passed very close to me. I froze. It didn't slow or stop; it moved beyond me.

I got the new mag inserted. I chambered a round. I braced my back against the ground; from the way my shoulder felt, this was going to hurt like hell.

I peered down the iron sights of the rifle and waited for the searchlight to sweep past. If I shot when they were at their closest point, or directly overhead, or even right over me, I knew they'd open up with their Gatlings.

So I waited until the beam of the light was pointed away from me.

Then I took the shot.

But someone was waiting, up there in the *Leopardo*—looking somewhere other than the circle illuminated by the searchlight.

Someone was up there, with goggles just like mine.

By discharging my rifle, I gave away my position; that's when the shooting began.

☠

All that belly-aching ignores the fact that I took a hell of a shot. I caught the searchlight with an armor-piercing 5.7mm round.

It winked out in a shower of sparks.

But whoever was on the opposite side of the *Leopardo*'s gondola had low-light goggles and an assault rifle. Probably an AK—or something very like it. They opened up wide, on full auto, raking the bushes around my position.

☠

I leapt into darkness.

That's when I found that I had dislocated something.

My hip.

I tumbled ass-over-teakettle, exploding in pain.

The Gats opened up and the mountain exploded.

☠

Dirt rained down on me everywhere; half of the mountain came down. Those Gatlings were *big*.

Through the flash of ripe agony I saw a great disturbance above me; fog swirled everywhere. The props started making noise—as much noise as they ever make. Strained to the limit, they whined; Even with the echo of the Gats still bleating through the canyon and my ears all but slaughtered, I heard the props fighting valiantly to stabilize the *Leopardo*.

They didn't do all that good of a job. She waggled back and forth, fighting for purchase. She spun in a circle and almost hit the mountain.

So those pricks couldn't do the impossible.

Birds swirled everywhere, chirping and bleating, mobbing the sausage.

The sausage careened crazily up and away, swirled as I froze in the shadows, my hip spasming.

The vessel huffed away on the wind, its whiny eco-motors on full, almost dominating the ringing in my ears from my shot and the Gatlings.

I held tight, breathing hard through the pain.

I smelled smoke—not gunsmoke; the Gats had ignited the mountain.

A big wet sloppy wad of Twin Peaks oozed past me, glowing like lava, smoldering in the fog.

Then I saw the vessel again: nose at me, Gatlings at the ready.

I left the rifle.

I started crawling.

One more blast from the Gats, forward-on this time, with a stable platform. That's all it took to get me moving—really moving.

Unfortunately, it got Twin Peaks moving too. Big parts of it came down wet, fog-soaked, waterlogged. Mud slid underneath me. Shrubs went up—those Gatling rounds were *hot*. Even the foggy-wet couldn't stop the blaze; it started burning up the mountain.

I wrenched myself up onto my hands and knees; I couldn't stop screaming in pain for a few seconds. My hip popped back into place and I swear to you, nothing I felt on the table of Virgil Amaro or Dr. Ava Sorzano or all the field hospitals where I got stitched up even came close to what I felt in that instant.

I hauled my ass up and started running.

I saw a big dark thing ahead.

I saw an opening.

I saw a tunnel.

I made for it.

The airship, swirling high in the grey shooting down into green, into black, left big plumes of mud behind me as I slid and I hurt and I ran and I—

—made it.

A service opening in the side of the mountain—leading into its bowels, into its tunnels.

Waves of gunsmoke poured all over me, mingled with the fog; The *Leopardo*, destabilized again, whirred and trembled.

I heard the chirping of birds; they were mobbing it.

I crept into the shadows of the service tunnel, fumbled in the darkness for the latch.

I hauled the gate open.

The Gatlings whirred softly overhead on their mounts, searching for me.

I crept inside and slammed the gate.

☠

It was dark and wet and totally black inside the tunnel. I had lost my light-sensitive goggles in the fall, so I couldn't see shit. The tunnel smelled like mold. My ears rang from the Gatlings.

I pulled my pistol and hit the tac light. It was dead. I holstered it and tried to reach for the gun on my left thigh; my left shoulder screamed. Waves of nausea cooked me alive. I grabbed my left upper arm hard —*hard*—with my right hand, feeling the fingers of my right hand tight from being peeled back as I scrambled on the ground; the knuckles were raw.

I heard the sobbing—high-pitched, juvenile, close in tight the smoky, sodden shadows. Too close. All tangled up with the night, just inches from my side, at elbow-level.

With a hot scream of agony blasting through my torso, I shoved my arm back into place. I fumbled; I scrambled; I tried to get back away from it in the dark and I had to reach down desperate to fumble out my gun, right hand to left thigh, safety-snap slippery from the fog, not wanting to give; I got it out and groped for the tac light with my teeth.

The sobs turned to laughing.

How many hours of training? How many hours doing this shit while being strafed from Russian-made copters by assholes who couldn't hit the side of a barn? How many times had I got my tac light on in a second; with, tonight, did it take me two?

I saw her face blaze to life in my tac light, halogen glare setting sharp teeth on fire. I opened up a fragment of a second too late; pieces of her throat blew out behind her in a radiant spray, lit up by the flash and the halogen as I tried to ward her off with my dislocated arm; it didn't go that well. Her teeth sank into my left hand and I went down, kicking furiously, shoving her off of me. She tore a strip off; I hit the mud hard and started firing.

Hot brass five-seven cartridges rained everywhere till the slide locked open; smoke poured out. Hurting *bad*, I played the tac light around, and that's when adrenaline lost its sweet taste.

I said, "*Son of a bitch!*"

A piece was out of me; she'd taken a good bite. Blood poured from my left hand, slippery.

Sitting on the hard filthy concrete, I did a circuit with the tac light and saw no more laughers anywhere. The big black yawned into nowhere, the tunnel plowed into the mountain. I could hear running water.

I aimed the light at the thing I had killed.

She might have been twelve; she had purple streaks in what had been her hair. She wore a nightgown. Great big chunks were ripped out of her; I had fired wildly. Whether any of that damage was someone else's, or something's, I didn't know. Her knees were bloody, flesh worn off, smooth kneecaps sticking out visible. She'd probably worn her kneecaps open rocking back and forth on the concrete, sobbing.

Above the red hairy smear that had been her head, someone had stenciled:

DPW ACCESS TUNNEL. GARDENSIDE DRIVE.

The first time, I read it "Gardenslide." I woulda thought that was pretty fucking funny if I hadn't been in so much pain.

I propped the pistol in my lap; I grabbed my arm and shoved it back in place. My vision swarmed with fireflies. Tears cooled my cheeks.

I fished a field dressing out of my vest. I wrapped the wound on my hand. I clamped that shit between my knees and held it tight while I felt for a mag in my vest. The snaps of the vest had come free; I'd lost a mag somewhere. I felt around.

I was dizzy with pain and adrenaline; I wasn't perhaps functioning quite at my optimum. The tac light pointed toward my feet; I couldn't hear shit after the sound of gunfire in that closed space. I'd be lucky if I could ever hear again.

So when they came up close behind me, back around from the hidden shadows of the tunnel's sewer-side tributaries, I didn't hear them till the double-barrel rested on my shoulder and a white-hot flashlight blazed a few inches away.

Someone said, "I've got to put you down, son."

I wasn't in the mood.

I turned and glared into the blinding light.

I growled, "I'm immune to them, dirtbag. Lower your weapon."

"I don't think so," he said. "No one's immune."

I said, "I am. In fact, my doctor tells me I'm Jesus. Put the gun down."

"I can't do that."

"Then put me down, prick! I'm sick of this shit. Pull the trigger or let me tape my fucking hand up; it hurts like a motherfucker and you, 'son,' are working my very last nerve."

I was up before I knew what I was doing, the pain in my hand and my hip and my shoulder barely slowing me. My empty pistol spilled to the ground. Had I been fresh and uninjured, I honestly think I would have probably taken the coach gun out of Bubba's hand and beaten his weak ass to death with it.

But sometimes grievous bodily injury is a good thing, at least for my soul. When I reached for the twin-barreled piece, every muscle, every bone in my body just *hurt*.

So I stood there and glared.

He was just a big hairy mass, wiry beard and moppy grey hair illumed by the flashlight, sticking everywhere: a giant hedgehog haloed in the darkness. Someone said, "Do it, Screech! Do it! Pull the trigger! Pull both triggers! Blow 'im away! He's gonna turn!"

I stood with my feet planted and said, "I'm not gonna turn."

Someone said, "He's gonna turn! Do it, Screech! Don't be a wimp. Fine, I'll do it!"

There was movement just out of my peripheral vision. I heard a slide being racked: handgun. In the glare from the flashlight I saw a glint of dirty silver. My hand hung loose near my thigh. Should I pull my right five-sev?

Sure seemed like an awful lot of effort.

"William, chill out. I'll do it, I'll do it. Just give me a minute."

William, the guy with the .380, said, "I'll do it!" He held the gun on me, and trembled.

Behind them, I heard someone say, "*I don't think so.* Put down the shotgun, Screech."

It was a girl, or more properly a young woman. She was seventeen or eighteen, maybe, dark of flesh and pink of hair. She wore tattered skull stockings and harness boots, a short cotton skirt with syringes, a black Danger Bitch hoodie and a carved-up hot-pink T-shirt that said SKOL. Café-au-lait skin shimmered milky in the darkness. She held my rifle aimed at Screech, while William aimed his .380 at her. She didn't even flinch when I got my five-sev out and aimed at the side of William's head.

I told them, "See, if this was a movie, now is when I'd get all up in your face and start biting, and the audience would scream and we'd all learn a valuable lesson about killing dumb pricks who get bit. But this isn't a movie, this is real; I'm not a laugher, and you're all douchebags."

Screech said: "Huh?"

I snarled: "Put down your fuckin' weapons *now*! I'm fuckin' bleeding, and I'm really not that fuckin' into it."

"You got a foul mouth, son."

"I take after my grandpa; he was a gorilla. Now put your fuckin' gun down."

Pink said, "You heard the man, Screech, he says this isn't a movie. I thought it was some kinda weak Tarantino-ass shit—Mexican Standoff, right?"

I growled, "Hey, that's what I was thinking."

She said, "But Dante Bogart should know. He says it isn't a movie, then this shit ain't a movie."

I growled, "Has my reputation preceded me?"

Pink howled with pleasure.

"It *is* you! Say, 'They sent me to Mars!'"

I said, "Maybe later."

Screech said, "Who?"

She said, "Dante Bogart. The world's most famous star of viral science fiction videos!"

"Oh, man," said Screech. "You have got to be fuckin' kidding me. That is fuckin' crazy."

I growled, "That's what I keep saying, but no one will listen to me."

"Don't you old-timers know anything?"

William knew me. He waved his pistol and said, "Iggy, don't be an idiot. That's not Frosty Bogart, it's just some asshole. He's been bit! He's gonna turn!"

The pink-haired black chick said, "He's Dante Bogart! You wanna shoot a viral movie star? He's famous."

Three-eighty said, "Famous? He's not even internet-famous!"

I said, "But am I Facebook famous?"

"Maybe you're MySpace famous, asswipe!"

Screech said, puzzled, "Who is this person again?"

Iggy said, "He's a viral movie star!"

William said, "I say he's an asshole!"

I growled, "That part's hard to argue with, but I still haven't turned. So this is all just, like, hypothetical, and you're all still douchebags. Can we please put our guns down?"

We did. The flashlights, too; suddenly I could see. Three-eighty glared at me.

I holstered one pistol, reloaded and holstered the other.

Iggy said brightly, "Here's your rifle back, man."

I tried to take it; pain jabbed through my shoulders.

I said, "You keep it."

Tank Girl liked that.

☠

Ig, Screech and William had lived in the Big Beneath since well before this happened—Iggy on an itinerant basis, Screech and William more permanently. They camped deep beneath the City in the spiderweb network of transit tunnels that stretched in varying degrees across six to eight counties—and, depending who you asked, for eight, ten, twelve, fifteen, maybe twenty stories. Maybe even further. No one knew.

"There's maps and shit, but no one can find them. They're probably in basements somewhere, but nobody even really knows where. They don't let people like us in the planning office. Someone told me the schematics are all on the internet, oh, yeah, thanks, that's a big help. Zzzzzaaappp! Apocalypse! Arreviderci, internet!"

I asked her, "Why don't the laughers come down?"

"They do, sometimes. You can hear them. It echoes everywhere. But mostly they don't, 'cause there are gates and stuff, and trenches; they can't navigate the maze. That's what we call it. They can't work doors and gates. And have you noticed that sixth sense they have?"

"Yeah, what about it?"

"It'll work through walls. But get more than a couple feet of dirt between you and them—they don't even know you're here."

I told her, "Interesting shit, Iggy. But, listen. I need to get back to the surface so I can get to the Armory—"

Screech and Ig started laughing hysterically. William just glared.

I growled, "Is this where I blow your guys' brains out?"

William snapped bitterly, "Are you stupid?"

Screech said, "If you want to get into the Armory, the *last thing* you should do is go to the surface. You can't get ten blocks from that place. The laughers all know the survivors are there."

"He's right. Dante, there's no way you'll get anywhere near that place. The laughers are packed in by the thousands," said Iggy.

I said, "I'll jack a car."

They laughed.

"An SUV."

They laughed.

"A bus or something."

Screech said, "I knew someone who jacked a cop car on Army Street and tried to drive it up Mission to the Armory. Wanna guess how far he got?"

I said mildly, "Sausalito?"

Screech said, "Nah, he got all the way. He's still in the car, laughing his ass off."

William tried to top him: "I knew this guy who tried to hand-over-hand it on the power lines and drop down on the roof? Assholes in the Armory figured out how to turn on the juice and—"

What pissed me off is that of course I knew this shit. I had been planning to improvise, as per usual. Problem was, it was time to improvise, now, and I had *diddley*. That can make a man a little sensitive.

So I growled, "You know, I think any day now would be a pretty good time to start with the productive input."

William sneered, "Why should we help you?"

Iggy punched him: "This guy is Frosty Bogart. He doesn't get sick when they bite him. He's a *rockstar*."

I said, "I'm a rockstar."

Iggy grinned, "If you can't go above, go below. That's where we come in."

Screech made a horror-movie face and said: "We're the Lurkers Beneath. We're the bogeymen zombies tell their kids about."

Iggy howled, "We're the nightmares guys in leopard-print sausages wake up from, screaming! I'm doing *you* again, Frosty."

William finally liked that; his grapefruit face sloughed off its sourpuss; he showed me jazz hands and flipped me a double-bird.

He wailed, "We're the Moles, motherfucker."

I glared at his birds and said, "Moles don't have fingers."

"This one does."

"Not for long," I growled.

He put 'em away.

☠

Iggy and I left William and Screech under Twin Peaks. Iggy led me through the tunnels of the city—down deeper with every passing minute.

While she did, I asked questions.

Without explaining shit, Pink said "Come on!" and led me down the access tunnel. I was in so much pain and moving so fast that I didn't ask questions for a minute, as she led me into the bowels of Twin Peaks.

She found a rusting spiral staircase and started us going around and around and around in the dark. If she was leading me to, like, a cult of cannibals, I was either on the menu or about to start kicking cannibal ass.

The way I felt, I was pretty OK with either.

Then she started talking a mile a minute again.

"Dante, your videos—y'know, they were kinda… prophetic. I know they were supposed to be about your real life as a mercenary—"

"Please," I said. "Contractor."

"—but there were some, you know, monster things that… well, they seemed like science fiction. Looks like they ain't."

I growled, "Yeah, here and there I laced them with elements of, you know, *truth*."

"Is it true what you said in that first video? The one the bad guys jacked?"

"Oh, you heard about that, huh?"

She said, "That some rich-people outfit sent you around trying to get them, like, viruses and shit so they could live forever?"

I said, "Something like that."

She said, "'Cause when this started happening, I figured it was those DePop weirdos."

I growled, "Funny you should mention them."

☠

Iggy and I found a nice cozy switching room, switches long dead. She held the flashlight so I could stitch up my hand with the med kit. I might not come down with the Panama Laugh, but the bite was wide open and oozing.

"Doesn't that hurt?" she asked me, getting all up in my shit and thrilling to the sight of the open wound.

"The Novocain helps," I said, gritting my teeth as I forced the needle through. I'd given myself an injection. "But I'm not gonna be able to shoot for shit with my left hand. Are you sure you can get me into the Armory?"

"Fuck yeah. Before this all happened, I used to sneak in there and steal dildos and sell them on Haight Street. You know you can get like fifty dollars for *one dildo*? I can get in there any time I want, I'm just not stupid enough to go. They're crazy in there."

"Who the fuck is 'They?' And do they know there's tunnel access?"

"I know some of the hostages do, because this little Latina poet dominatrix friend of mine told me about the tunnel in the first place. She wanted me to be able to sneak into their parties before I turned eighteen. Don't give me that Dad look, Frosty, I lived on the street, you think I'm gonna be shocked by a little lesbian fist-fucking? Anyway, I'm pretty sure the assholes don't know about it."

"Okay, so I think you skipped the part about assholes. Who the hell is in charge there?"

"Frosty, you decidedly fail to be the first person to ask that person about the Inferno, or even the ten thousandth. It's a little bit complicated."

I drew surgical thread through my flesh and growled, "So complicate me, Iggy. Ow."

"Okay, so like I was saying, I used to do poetry slams with this chick who worked at the Inferno, and her shit is, like, totally autobiographical. So here's what I know. This guy Ellis Osborne made a bunch of money in dot-com shit and so he started Purgatorio. Okay, so he's the guy with the airship. And he's totally in love with this girl, right?"

"What girl?"

"The *poet*! My dominatrix friend who writes autobiographical poetry. Aren't you listening?"

I said, "Is her name Lupe?"

"No fuckin' way, you know her?"

"I think we might have met once at an asshattery festival."

"Isn't she awesome?"

I deadpanned, "Totally. Love her. *Love* her."

"Her poetry is, like—so, then, you must have already heard this story?"

"Let's pretend I haven't."

"So he's in love with her, but she's like, 'Marriage is a tool of the patriarchy,' so he makes her like this total famous dominatrix strap-on celebrity star, and follows her around like a puppy dog, I swear, there's this one story about how this one guy posted some shit about her online, and Ellis actually got in that fucking airship of his and followed the motherfucker on his motorcycle and the FAA's all, *say what?* Over a city, dude? You serious?"

"Let's back up," I said. "Is Ellis one of these DePop Art people?"

"Fuck no! None of them are—well, not most of them. Mostly they're like, artists and hackers and stuff. Wikileaks people. But it's totally democratic so no one's sure who's in charge. After what happened in Japan, Ellis works out this disaster preparedness plan, right? So he stocks the place with food and stuff, biodiesel, solar panels, satellite dishes—he's big into solar panels. And he has this blimp, right?"

"Zeppelin."

"Whatever. Other people try to talk him into guns and stuff, but he won't have it. He's, like, fine with crossbows and stuff, but he has a strict no gun rule in the Armory, right?"

I growled suspiciously, "Right."

She said, "But other people there do this weird *Anarchist Cookbook* stuff. Their theory is to post the plans to, like, genetically-engineered viruses and shit, chemical weapons, how to hack into nuclear bombs—to, like, post that shit because then it makes the world a safer place. How does *that* work? And that's the most fucked-up thing. It turns out there's this splinter group, inside the Inferno. Just like five guys, but they're these completely fucked-up weirdos. They're into this global depopulation movement, and Ellis is like, free speech, right? Nobody knew they were serious."

"Why is he trying to kill me, if he's not on their side?"

"'Cause they've got Lupe, see?"

I said, "*Claro*. Did they do this?"

"The plague? Are you crazy? The news said they did, but that was just disinformation. You gonna find out who did it and crack skulls, Dante?"

I growled, "Hopefully among other bony tissue."

She cackled and said, "That's the spirit, Colombo."

"How do you even *know* about Colombo?"

"Dude, don't you even watch your own videos? Anyway, if they didn't do it, they're still pretty excited about it. And they knew it was going to happen."

"How?"

"Well… dude, they're *hackers*."

"Right," I said. "Hackers know everything. *Claro*."

"That's what they'll tell you. Anyway, they took over the Armory like four days before this all happened. The cops were about to bust in when everything went to shit. Under all those laughers you'd probably find lots of cop cars."

"And these DePop people took the others hostage?"

"That's what I hear. You wanna get moving?"

"Now seems as good a time as any."

As we climbed and crawled, Iggy filled me in on life in the tunnels. There had been hundreds of them living down there before the laughers came. There might have been thousands—nobody knew how deep some of the tunnel people lived. Most had gotten caught above ground—or been naïve enough to think, now that the cities were emptied of the living, that it was safe for them to come up and scavenge carelessly.

Iggy said she'd lost a lot of friends. Now many feet below the surface and passing through an open segment of tunnel, we passed a little alcove at the edge the Muni station.

In it was a rotted-out homeless encampment that had obviously been abandoned quickly. A sleeping bag and someone's personal effects crawled with rats. The site had police tape across it:

CAUTION—POLICE LINE—DO NOT CROSS

Glancing at it, Iggy said; "I've been down here in the tunnels since I was fifteen. It fuckin' sucks what happened. It's just another round of patriarchal government bullshit. It's rough up there. But if you lived down here it was pretty fuckin' rough before."

I said, "*Claro.*"

☠

As she steered me through a cracked-open sewer-stink canyon, I looked at her hair and asked her, "Iggy, where do you get hair dye?"

She said, "Same place I always do. Hot Topic at Westfield."

She shrugged.

"It's a lot easier to shoplift lately."

We went down, down, down, down, down, down the hill from Twin Peaks to the Mission, through the Muni tunnels, the pylon supports, the long-disused basements with their cracked-open walls, the abandoned sub-basements with their dirt floors, through the sub-sub basements with their through lines. She knew service tunnels, old gas mains, drainage channels, electric access points, switching stations. She threaded me through blackness lit up by my tac lights and her half-assed scavenged flashlights. I saw old homeless encampments—years old. Maybe *decades.* I saw bodies—not fresh ones. Not laughers. Not victims of the laughers. Not even victims of the chaos after the laughing. We're talking old bodies—the bones of the forgotten. We're talking *moles.*

We made the river.

It stank like mold. Storm drains emptied into it, the river that flowed beneath the City to the sea. Fog poured: fog become condensation become drainage become drip become river become sea. Five miles that-a-way, maybe six or seven, give or take, with the winding, was the beach where I'd pulled an Anzio.

What the fuck was I thinking?

☠

Mission Street used to be a narrow little waterway called Mission Creek. The Armory had been built around the creek like a tree grows around a street sign. The water still ran through the basement. Iggy explained: that meant that Mission Creek overran its banks every time it rained, and sometimes when it didn't. A huge array of drainage channels had been drilled through the rock of the Armory's basement, feeding the excess water into the storm channels that kept the whole City from flooding.

That meant that even if you couldn't get to the place from above, or from street level, its belly was unprotected. The Armory was like a battleship just begging for a torpedo—with only the ground between us and it.

We went down.

Iggy took me through basements, through tunnels, through root-over-grown, tangled, sewer-choked drainage routes and through an abandoned transit station. She took me down, straight down, to the vertical limit. Any deeper, you'd be dying. The monsters would eat you.

I loaded subsonic rounds into a five-sev and screwed on the silencer.

Iggy's pink hair glowed in the tac light.

She pointed up.

She said, "This must be the place. Straight up, Frosty B."

I said, "*Gracias.*"

She held out my rifle.

"Keep it," I told her. "You need it more than I do."

"I doubt that, Frosty. You're sure I can't come?"

"I just met you. Let's save that for our second date."

"You're too old for me, dude. Besides, dating movie star's not for me. All those paparazzi…"

I said, "If I'm still alive in an hour—"

She said, "You can Facebook me."

I grinned and said, "*Claro.*"

☠

I left her in the depths with her nightmares—far less troubling to her than mine to me. But nonetheless, I mused as I ascended, probably shit I couldn't handle. Because I didn't have to. That's how it worked.

I spiraled up like a nightmare myself, surfacing from the depths.

Every cell in my body screamed with pain. I thought, *All right, people. Let's depopulate.*

I came up dark and deep and pissed and steamed and hurting.

I came up through the drainage channels.

I came up past the Creek.

I came up through the tangle of rubber-tubing pumps and scored shattered Gold Rush foundations that writhed with rats.

I came up through the metal ladders that wound into the guts of Earth where the Bogeyman lives.

I said, *I'm viral, fuckers. Open up and say Aaaah.*

☠

Without the goggles, I couldn't see shit. I didn't use tac lights or flashlights or penlights or anything. I just climbed. I heard the chittering of rats and mice in the darkness; I grinned at them; they shied away.

I ascended Jacob's Ladder to Paradise.

I came out in the dungeon.

☠

The Inferno had generators, but fuel was in short supply. It always has been.

Without power, there were very few lights on the dungeon level—not even safety lights.

So I had no choice but to use a tac light. I refrained from using the one on the five-sev, so I could filter it through my fingers. The technique gave everything a pink, rosy glow.

The room in which I'd emerged from the deep turned out to be on the dungeon level—which had originally been the stables. Now it was a storeroom, with giant crates and barrels just behind me. A complex series of hoses and foam-rubber-wrapped PVC pipes were tangled and twisted all over, to the point where I had to thread my way through them just to move. They must have been designed to pump out the groundwater, which would have been no problem if they hadn't been wrapped up with electrical cables that looked like they were begging for a short—assuming they were still live.

Behind that, there were six crates marked:

MEDICAL CENTRIFUGE EQUIPMENT
RADCLIFFE MEDICAL SUPPLY
Chautauqua County, NY
"FOR THE LIFE OF THE FLESH IS IN THE BLOOD"
(Lev. 17:11)

From somewhere, I heard the soothing strains of "Video Killed the Radio Star."

It took me two full rounds of that shit to realize where it was coming from: My breast pocket. Christ, you spend all that time loading subsonic rounds into your five-sev, and you forget to silence your cell phone.

Augie Amaro's cell phone.

I remembered, vaguely, someone in this very basement saying to me, *If there's a nuclear war? We're gonna be the ones still updating Live Journal.*

I pulled out Augie's phone.

When I saw who it was, I got woozy. I got goosebumps. I got all, like, hyperventillatish and shit.

It was a text message from "Uncle John."

John Amaro.

It was timestamped a week ago.

It said:

hey neph i just heard about teh mercy
glad ur ok... where pick u up 4 trip 2 frisco?

I didn't know what part of that bugged me more—that John Amaro was alive, that he thought Augie was alive, that he was on his way here, or that he called it Frisco.

I silenced Augie's cell phone and made double-sure it was silenced this time.

Then I killed my tac light.

I put my ear to the crack in the storeroom door. I couldn't hear much beyond. I eased the door open and stuck my head out.

It looked clear. Beyond the door was the firing range—a giant open area, two or three hundred feet across. I crept out, racking my brains to remember the layout from my one trip here, years ago.

Mission Creek was where the extra ground water came from. The unfinished dirt floors were crisscrossed by the remnants of badly-poured asphalt eighty years old. Cardboard and wooden crates were stacked everywhere, providing me sufficient cover to make it across the big open area. They were marked things like *Peaches, Tomatoes, Corned Beef, SPAM*. It all stank like mold and dirt. The place smelled ancient, like simmering rot, like earth, like soil, like decaying vegetable matter, like the crotch of the devil. There was gunpowder on the air, too—someone had been shooting recently.

A concrete trench had been cut to guide the river past the range, and chunks of old stone had been tossed in the river. I crept along through the half-darkness, till I reached the place where someone had set up hay bales to serve as makeshift "cover" for target practice. Beyond that, against the crumbling stone wall, were what looked like five crash dummies with chunks blown out of them.

Beyond that there was a narrow corridor leading to the main dungeon level, which was mostly a huge hallway, and stables beyond. I saw the glow of halogen work lamps. I crept toward the light, keeping down low and threading through the piles of crates.

The place was freezing.

I got to the main drag—the giant, open hallway, twenty feet across.

Metal bars had been installed on both sides of the hallway, to create two huge cells that looked more like an Old West county jail than any real jail ever had—even in the Old West.

It had been built that way for entertainment purposes, but the locks and the bars weren't for show.

And neither were the prisoners.

On the left side of the huge hallway huddled about twelve shivering prisoners in a bizarre assortment of filthy half-destroyed fetishwear in PVC and leather, hospital gowns. Some were wrapped in tattered blankets, and ruined robes emblazoned with the Inferno logo.

On the right side were laughers—maybe twenty of them. They had been locked up with shackles and rope at the wrists and ankles, and gagged with ball gags, belts, strips of cloth.

You could still hear them laugh. The sound gurgled out from under gags wet with drool. If anything, it sounded *worse* for them being gagged.

The living people on the left looked worse for wear.

Two guys pacing up and down between the cells cradled AKs with bayonets. At the moment, one was facing me—but he was in the glare of the halogen work lights, so his eyes weren't adjusted. He hadn't spotted me yet, lurking in the darkness.

The other one—the one facing away from me—howled:

"We're clearly not making an impression on you. I guess one of you wants to be next? You saw what happened to Lupe—she's over here now—"

He gestured at the laugher cell, where dozens of naked laughers twisted and writhed. I felt a stab of recognition—like I gave a shit? Apparently I did.

I think I must have issues.

Someone howled, "That was Karen! Fuck, you don't even know our names after all these years?" I recognized her voice—it had berated me for being a baby-killer.

☠

I was faced with a dilemma. I had no way to know if these asshats had a clue about what had happened. I needed information. Furthermore, I had no meaningful intel about the situation. None at all. I had a visual on thirty prisoners, their safety being immediately threatened. But if I started spitting lead, I could be placing other prisoners in—

The guy facing me had just turned away.

The red dot showed on the back of his head.

The five-sev chirped.

The subsonic round took the top of his head off.

☠

Even a professionally silenced round is not *silent*. And a subsonic round, sound-suppressed, is not as accurate as a typical round. I thought I could get two accurate headshots off in the time it took Mommie Dearest to react—but I didn't. The second round went wide by a fraction of an inch.

The guy heard the action of the five-sev cycling. He dropped to his belly and got his AK up and started firing at me in moments; stone, dirt and sparks kicked up all around me.

That was his first mistake; in dropping to his belly, he'd failed to accurately gauge the distance between himself and his prisoners.

They weren't armed; they didn't have anything that could be turned into a makeshift weapon.

But the guy I'd just shot had fallen haphazardly across the hallway, his head in pieces.

Someone with long arms grabbed his AK; as the guy fired at me, they shoved people out of the way. The shooter thought the commotion was just garden-variety panic, until it dawned on him.

Whoever grabbed that rifle had thought fast; it would have taken a moment to chamber a round, find the safety and get it off. So she didn't bother.

She put the bayonet through the shooter's eye.

I got up and started running.

☠

As I crossed the hallway, a female voice rang out: "Hey, fucko! On your six!"

The voice was Lupe's, but I didn't clock that until after I'd tried to turn and been blinded; I felt the blow as a string of hits cut across my side. They knocked the wind out of me; I hit the cement. I skidded.

The fucker had a tac light on his AK, which was what blinded me. I couldn't see shit. I raised the five-sev and opened up with underpowered rounds that chirped—underpowered rounds that didn't penetrate the asshole's body armor.

Lupe's did.

Leaning through the bars of the cell, she opened up wide with her captured AK—on full auto.

The whole world exploded. Only the first ten or so rounds hit the shooter; the rest put holes in the ceiling. Chunks of rock hit alongside light fixtures, as the shooter went down wet.

☠

The prisoners were starved and covered with bruises. The looked weak; their flesh was papery.

Lupe's voice was hoarse; she looked thin and wasted.

On the far side, the laughers chattered and yowled behind their gags. They twisted and jerked in their bonds. I heard bones cracking as they thrashed, maybe agitated by the activity.

I double-tapped the one Lupe had shot and the one she'd bayoneted.

I said: "That's three. Any more on this level?"

Lupe said, "Not that I know of."

"How many total?"

"Three more," she said. "Choke, Ghandi and Bill."

I said, "A terrorist named *Bill?*"

Lupe shrugged. "I think *Ghandi's* weirder."

"Where?"

She said, "Out. Flying with Ellis."

"In the sausage?"

"No, fucker—Hawaii air. What do you think?"

"Any idea how long they'll be gone?"

"Not a clue. They're after some government special forces guy—whoa, is that Dante Bogart? This is like being rescued by George Clooney!"

I said, "Save it. Keys?"

Lupe pointed at the guy with the missing forehead.

"He's got 'em."

I got the keys and got the cell door open.

I said, "Get somewhere safe."

One haggard blonde in shredded PVC nurse's uniform said, "I'll get where I want, fucker. Like to the gun locker and the pantry, not necessarily in that order."

A brunette in a ruined pink pinafore said, "Yeah, dick, thanks for rescuing us last week."

A tall shirtless guy in mangled leather pants and a leather harness said, "Corporate stooge," as he passed me.

"Yeah," said a short, hairy guy in a backless hospital gown. "We'll arm ourselves and form a democratic militia. Then you can have a vote like everyone else."

I growled, "Okay, that's cool, too."

Lupe said, "What's your next move, Brainiac?"

"How do they moor that sausage?"

"To the back turret. There's a mooring tower."

No shit. That had been what I thought was a radio tower on the fourth turret—the one without the flag.

"How do they get down?"

"Rope ladder."

I said, "Doesn't sound very secure."

She said, "Why would it be? Everyone's dead."

I said, "Take me there. I want to be waiting for them."

"Don't let them see you."

I said, "No shit. Take me there."

We mounted the stairs.

☠

I was sweating. I felt dizzy.

Lupe looked at me. "Dante, you don't look so good."

"I don't feel so good."

"You didn't get bit, did you?"

I said, "Actually, yeah. But I can't get sick, I don't think."

"You don't *think*? You've been, like, vaccinated?"

"That's a long story, but let's just say yes, for now. If I start laughing, shoot me."

"I thought you'd never ask," said Lupe. "But those enema nurses took all the guns."

I unscrewed the suppressor from my five-sev as I got all up in her shit. "Did you assholes do this?"

"Do what?"

I jerked my thumb downstairs, toward the laughers.

"Fuck you very much for asking, shitbag!"

"There's centrifuge equipment in the storeroom," I growled.

"Yeah? There's centrifuge equipment at Genentech, are they on your shit list too?"

"Somebody did it."

"Yeah," said Lupe. "Your fuckin' employers."

"You're sure it wasn't these DePop asshats?"

"They couldn't cause a global plague if their lives depended on it. Bad choice of words, maybe. Dante, you sure you're okay? Your shoulder's like in seven different places at once."

I was getting woozy.

As we mounted the big marble stairs that led to the second floor, I gave her the five-sev.

I said, "Don't shoot me unless I start laughing. I'm pretty sure I can't get sick."

She said, "*Pretty* sure?"

"I don't know who's on what side, but your boyfriend's been trying to kill me. He's probably out there right now looking for me or dropping bombs on my ride."

Her jaw dropped. "No fuckin' way! Some bad-ass battleship, right?"

I said, "That's going a little far, but yeah."

"Ellis has been having a shit fit. They told him it's a pirate invasion."

"It is."

"Hey, Dante, don't blame Ellis. They threatened to feed me to the gigglers if he doesn't do everything they say. And they thought it was some corporate fascist asshole's ship, like, your old employers or something."

"Imagine that."

"You're not working for those fuckers again, are you? With all that happened? I figured you'd switched sides."

I said, "Yeah, I did—in fact, lately I do it so often I can't keep track of my cell phone bill. No, I'm not working for Virgil."

"You mean Bellona? I thought that Virgil guy died."

"Oh yeah," I said. "Slip of the tongue."

"Seriously, don't blame him."

"Who?"

"Ellis. He's been the only thing keeping us alive down there. They need him, because with that airship he can get stuff. They keep threatening to feed us to the laughers. They actually did feed Karen—" her drained face got haunted. She shook all over. "Oh, fuck, man. Sorry. It's been a long few weeks."

I said, "No shit."

"Anyway, Ellis has just been doing what he thought he had to do. They lock him in at night, and they never let him go up without two of them going along—usually three. They practically keep a gun to his head. I mean, I'm not saying I'll forgive him, and shit, but don't kill him. He's one of the good guys."

"Yeah," I growled. "Like Marshal Petain."

Lupe said, "After he pulled that bomb attack they gave him a ten-minute 'conjugal visit' with me as his reward."

I said, "Ten minutes? What the fuck?"

She said, "Ha ha! You don't know Ellis, it's like, three woulda done it. But I told him, 'Conjugate this, fucker! Get me out of here!' Finally I just kicked his ass for like, eight minutes, but he was into that."

I said, "Same old Lupe."

"Same old baby-killer?"

"Fuck yeah," I said. "But I still don't let them play with napalm. How many fuckin' floors in this place?"

Lupe panted, "Just one more."

One floor up, there was a scream.

We ran.

☠

As we climbed, I drew my pistol. Lupe was still holding the one I'd given her.

We arrived on the top floor just in time to see a guy in black fatigues dragging a blonde up the narrow stairs to the roof. She was the blonde that had mouthed off to me that she was headed for the pantry—and he had a short-barreled revolver to her head.

He screamed "Back! Stay back! This door opens, I'll fuckin' kill her!"

The door slammed behind them.

Two other women and one other man stood on the marble floors looking shocked.

I said, "What happened?"

All three glared at me.

Lupe said, "What happened?"

It burst out of the guy's mouth in a rush: "It's Ghandi. Tish was going for the gun locker. He grabbed her."

"Fuck's sake," said Lupe. "I thought he was flying."

One of the chicks said crisply: "Not this time, I guess. She looked me up and down, pissed. Way to rescue us, *Die Hard*."

I said, "You're welcome."

While we were in the basement, the sun had started coming up; light spilled down from the skylights.

Then it stopped, as something very big passed very close overhead.

I said, "Sausage. Fuck!"

Lupe nodded. "That's the ship. If Ghandi gets on it, we're fucked. They'll either kill Ellis—"

(—which, after the good time he'd shown me, sounded pretty fuckin' good to me—)

"—or they'll keep him flying that thing, and—oh, man. This is some bad shit."

I said, "Is there another way onto the roof?"

Lupe said, "Just the fire ladder. But… Dante, you don't look so good. You shouldn't—"

I holstered my five-sev.

"Show me."

☠

The fire ladder was rusted. It groaned under my weight and felt about ready to collapse. It led up the turret beneath the mooring tower. The stern of the airship was directly ahead.

Below, there was about fifty feet of empty space—and then the laughers, crawling like maggots on the rail containers blocking the roll-up doors.

My shoulders hurt like hell. About halfway up, I realized just what a great idea this wasn't.

The laughers chattered and howled. They giggled. They guffawed. Impaled on jagged metal thrusting up from the shipping containers, they reached for me with their bony hands.

The ladder strained under my weight.

It threatened to give.

Above, the *Leopardo* hovered, mottled in the dawn light. I saw a mooring hook hanging free—they hadn't moored yet. The electric screws started up and the thing rose about five feet. The mooring rope drew back inside the gondola.

I heard a speaker crackling: "I don't think so, Ghandi!"

Over the edge, on the roof, I heard Ghandi screaming:

"It's not my fault! It's some special forces asshole! Let me come up! She's our hostage!"

I heard someone else talking through a megaphone:

"If you come up, buddy, we're screwed."

Just beneath the corner, I drew my five-sev and hit the laser sight.

Then I made the turret.

The red dot was on Ghandi's head; I was about to take the shot when someone right above me shouted: "Freeze!"

I didn't have to look up to know it was the asshole who'd emptied an AK from the *Leopardo* on Twin Peaks, because he somehow felt raking the area with Gatlings just didn't make my life interesting enough.

Well, it was pretty interesting now.

I did not look up; in fact, I did not take my eyes off Ghandi.

The guy's eyes widened; he gaped. He had his revolver to the blonde's head and his hand gripping her hair. She looked pissed.

Without looking up, I shouted, "You better put me down with your first shot. It'll be an eye for an eye. Or, if you'd rather, we can work this out. There's not enough people left for us to keep blowing each other away."

This was, of course, bullshit. I was not in the mood to get along with my fellow humans. There were two DePop fuckers and one garden-variety asshat in that vessel, plus Ghandi on the roof. If they were dumb enough to let me get a crack at them, the most they could hope for was that when I relapsed into my old inconsiderate ways and pulled about six weeks of Gitmo with them, I'd feel bad about it afterwards. However, with the night I'd had, I suspect I wouldn't, so they woulda had to have been idiots to turn themselves over to my tender mercies.

Ghandi's eyes were wild. He looked from me to the ship and back again. He never let his revolver leave the side of the blonde's head.

For what it's worth, I probably would have shot him if the guy with the AK hadn't been directly above me—maybe even then. I couldn't imagine that without being moored, the *Leopardo* would provide a stable shooting platform—even at this range. If he fired on full auto, that dipshit upstairs would probably scream like a girl and drop his AK. If he fired single-shot, he'd just flat out miss me.

And I knew I wouldn't miss. The red dot of my five-sev's laser sight rested squarely between Ghandi's eyes. Ghandi knew it, too—in the moist morning air, he could see the faint stream of the laser.

A few bad moments passed for all of us—but they were probably worst for Ghandi, as it dawned on him just how much his friends valued him.

Plus, I was watching his breathing so I could gauge the exact moment to blow his brains out, and minimize the chance he'd give the blonde the same treatment.

Then the guy with the AK shouted: "Fuck that! He's yours! Take her up, Osborne—that's an order!"

The speaker crackled; the other guy said, *"Hasta la vista!"* The *Leopardo* started rising.

Ghandi howled, "No, no, no, no!"

I heard an electric whine.

The blonde whirled and bit.

The guy with the AK opened up.

☠

I had been basically right; he didn't drop the rifle, sure, but his shots went wide. Unfortunately, there wasn't much left of that ladder.

Rust peeled away in strips, and I started going down. I had already pulled the trigger three times, but I was not on my game, and the AK had startled me. I missed Ghandi.

I didn't miss AK, though—that was just a lucky shot. As the ladder peeled away from the turret, I opened up with the pistol and got another three shots off. I saw a red spray on the window of the *Leopardo*, and the guy disappeared back into the gondola.

Then the whole world exploded, as the Gatling opened up—just short hot buzz of lead, coughed out before anyone knew what had happened—including me.

Then there were pistol shots from inside, and more blood appeared on the windows of the gondola.

As the ladder collapsed, I dropped the five-sev and jumped for it. I caught the edge of the turret as the pistol spun down into the writhing mass of laughers.

There was the scream of electric motors.

The Gatling mount circled wildly, out of control. The motor spun, the barrels rotating but empty. If it had been loaded, I would have been dead—along with anyone on the top floor of the Armory.

The hold I had on the turret was not a good one. My fingers hurt like fuck, and my shoulder was killing me. The other shoulder was not doing much better. My grip was weak. I started slipping.

The airship's screws made a howling sound.

Below me, the laughers seethed. They could see me or sense me coming, and they started going crazy. The laugher stew churned. Directly beneath me, things writhed and chortled, impaled on spikes on the shipping containers.

Above me, the shadow was gone. The airship had drifted up and away, tipping at a crazy angle. The shadow spun across me as the wind caught the airship and it pirouetted up and away. Birds mobbed it.

The airship disappeared into the fog.

Dangling, I looked down. Laughers howled and squirmed under me. One made it off the shipping containers and getting enough purchase up the wall to gain on me. I was helped by the fact that it only had arms to work with—the climbing thing had bisected itself on the jagged piece of rebar jutting out of the container.

I kicked at the half-laugher. It tried to bite my foot, guffawing. My steel-toed Bates caught it right in the forehead.

Someone grabbed my wrist.

"Hey, fucko! You wanna be rescued, or what?"

Lupe was above me. The blonde joined her with a length of stylish black rope. The blonde poured blood from a flesh wound on the side of her face. It dripped on my face.

Lupe climbed to the edge of the turret and clipped the rope to my load-bearing vest.

It bore its best load yet. They hauled me up onto the turret, the shirtless Daddy type with leather pants doing the heavy lifting.

I sprawled on the tarpaper, hurting.

☠

Ghandi was gone. One round from the Gatling had turned his face into... well, let's just say he won't be yukking it up. Also, the top floor had a new skylight. But Osborne had managed to avoid hitting the blonde. Good thing the asshole waited until his last moments to become Annie Oakley.

The *Leopardo* was nowhere to be seen. It had vanished in the fog and didn't come back.

Maybe it's floating up there—a ghost ship sailing over the laughers.

The radio was worse than ever—Tibetan bells. We got through to the single one-way FM frequency—the pirate radio station that had been broadcasting MP3s of the Panama Laugh, recorded live at the Armory in the weeks before—as some of the hostages turned—and the DePop fuckers fed others to the laughers.

There had been fifty hostages; now there were twelve.

None of them seemed to be stoked with my performance as a commando. "Thanks for rescuing us last week" seemed to be the refrain for the first few hours.

Then I had other fish to fry—like sorting out the centrifuge equipment on the dungeon level. And the level below that—the one Lupe didn't know about. The one with the tunnels into adjacent locked-down basements in other buildings. The one where the DePop fuckers had *operational* centrifuges—at least, operational until the power went. You can't run a centrifuge on solar power, so they sat, unattended, amid big vats gooey with cultures—overgrown, and seething.

The place was a biohazard site. One way or another, Ava Sorzano has a lot to work on.

So do I… but since I ran out of bubblegum in the Kuna Yala morning, I've been working on it. I've got a lifetime's blood to wash off my hands— but I've got a lifetime, unfrozen, to wash it with.

But then, we watch the skies, waiting for John Amaro to show with his Pale Bird fuckers. No sign of him yet, but if there's one thing I've learned it's that the asshole you don't want to show up to your party is always the one who shows. So maybe someday soon I'll have more blood to wash off my hands.

Tatiana still roams, hunting laughers. She did me a solid; I figure I owe her. Any prick wants to write a Siberian lullaby in this burg? I'll hand 'em a slingshot. She and I will be waiting for you, washing our paws on 19th Street.

See? This is the new Frosty Bogart; at one with nature, in love with the Earth and friend of the little guy. Big into cats. Digs midnight walks on the beach and French kissing. Lots and lots of kissing.

Speaking of which, remember how Virgil told me that men like him and me, without women, are monsters? Well, he still agrees with me. But you ask the women in question, we're both monsters anyway. If you want to imagine how interesting my life got once Trixie got a chance to shoot the shit with Lupe and Iggy, you're a braver man than I. Trix and Ig got along famously. It's kind of creepy. William still scowls at me. Screech sometimes makes me plug my ears.

Virgil Amaro, what's left of him, slumbers ugly in the Old West cell where we euthanized the laughers the day I arrived. They moved out; Virgil moved in. Given his mental state, it seems cruel and unusual to put him in a jail cell. But what do you do? You can't just let a guy like that walk, ha ha ha. Incarceration seems the only option. And for all I know, the Old West cell at the Armory is the very last operational prison in the world.

And since Ava Sorzano won't even look at him, Virgil is my problem.

What's left of his mind seems to have crumbled under the strain of knowing what he did. When I think about that, I ask myself... *Yeah, and?* Some of the worst of us have sins that simply can't be forgiven. My heart goes out to those of us unable to undo even a small part of our most grievous errors, but... in Virgil's case, compassion only goes so far.

In some sense it's creditable to crumble under such burdens, but it's hard to see. The pain in his eyes bugs the shit out of me. It hurts to watch a man suffer inside like that.

But I spend time with him, because letting him do what he did is one of *my* most grievous errors.

Sometimes, when I'm there, Virgil calls out my name, sadly, and asks if it's okay what he's done.

I never really know how to answer that shit. Do I hand the fuckhead a comforting lie? That seems crueler than telling him the truth.

So I say, "Not really, asshole."

Sometimes, all he asks is:

"Dante, is it Easter yet?"

And then I tell him:

"Yeah, it's Easter, shithead. Why don't you rise from the dead?"

☠

ACKNOWLEDGEMENTS

Jeremy Lassen at Night Shade Books was the one who suggested that the Armory would be the place for survivors in San Francisco to hole up in time of zombie apocalypse. He asked me to write this book. Many thanks to you, Jeremy.

Violet Blue and Alan Beatts were incredibly helpful in composing this manuscript. They both gave me extensive, valuable feedback. Alan was particularly helpful with the weapons and details about the world of military contracting. Any errors here are mine, not theirs.

Zille DeFeu and Ross Lockhart also reviewed the manuscript and gave me very helpful feedback—thank you.

Additional facts were provided by Chris O'Sullivan, graduate of the California Maritime Academy, by Christophe Pettis, Kent Garner, and Kenton Hoover. Errors are mine, not theirs. Thank you.

Much of this novel was written at Temple Coffee at 28th and S Streets in Sacramento. Their charming and gracious staff pull great espresso and also roast their own amazing gourmet coffees. Thank you.

Thanks to my immediately family—my mother, my father, my sisters—plus my sisters' husbands and kids, and my wonderful uncles, aunts and cousins. You've been incredibly supportive—thanks.

Last but far from least, my partner Bridgitte Rivers was patient and encouraging throughout the composition of this work. Thanks and love.

For purposes of the narrative, I have taken liberties with the topography and geography of Panama. As her topography is famously unforgiving, I must leave it to her inspired and inspiring citizens to give me a pass on this one, and trust that this reorganization was done with great affection for their nation. Viva Panama!

In case you don't know, the Armory is a real building in San Francisco—a nearly 200,000 square foot Moorish castle built in 1914. Extreme gratitude must go to its current tenants, Kink.com. They provided me with the opportunity to study this incredible building from the inside in 2008–2009. Kink.com and its owner, Peter Acworth, have launched an effort to preserve and share this magnificent structure, which is a living piece of history like no other place in the world. Acworth and crew are doing much to restore the beauty of this unique building.

While I have attempted to reflect the real structure and personality of the building, and borrowed Kink's general category of business (adult entertainment) to be the business of Purgatorio, the only character traits that the Armory occupants in *The Panama Laugh* share with Kink.com's employees are an iconoclastic passion for celebratory self-expression, a fondness for Burning Man and some amazing tattoos.

No element of any character or institution in the novel is intended to represent anything about any individual, any group of individuals, or any of the Armory's tenants or visitors, past, present or future. The novel is fiction. Also, zombies aren't real.

Night Shade Books is an Independent Publisher of Quality Science-Fiction, Horror and Fantasy

ISBN: 978-1-59780-285-7 • $14.99 • Look for e-Book and Audio

Recent World War II veteran Bull Ingram is working as muscle when a Memphis DJ hires him to find Ramblin' John Hastur. The mysterious blues man's dark, driving music--broadcast at ever-shifting frequencies by a phantom radio station--is said to make living men insane and dead men rise.

Disturbed and enraged by the bootleg recording the DJ plays for him, Ingram follows Hastur's trail into the strange, uncivilized backwoods of Arkansas, where he hears rumors the musician has sold his soul to the Devil.

But as Ingram closes in on Hastur and those who have crossed his path, he'll learn there are forces much more malevolent than the Devil and reckonings more painful than Hell . . .

In a masterful debut of Lovecraftian horror and Southern gothic menace, John Hornor Jacobs reveals the fragility of free will, the dangerous power of sacrifice, and the insidious strength of blood.

Night Shade Books is an Independent Publisher of Quality Science-Fiction, Horror and Fantasy

ISBN: 978-1-59780-282-6 • $14.99 • Look for it in e-Book

Night Shade books is proud to present the debut novel from Jonathan Wood, NO HERO.

"What would Kurt Russell do?"

Oxford police detective Arthur Wallace asks himself that question a lot. Because Arthur is no hero. He's a good cop, but prefers that action and heroics remain on the screen, safely performed by professionals.
   But then, secretive government agency MI37 comes calling, hoping to recruit Arthur in their struggle against the tentacled horrors from another dimension known as the Progeny. But Arthur is NO HERO.

Can an everyman stand against sanity-ripping cosmic horrors?

Night Shade Books is an Independent Publisher of Quality Science-Fiction, Horror and Fantasy

edited by
ROSS E. LOCKHART

the **BOOK** of
CTHULHU

Tales inspired by H. P. Lovecraft from:

**KAGE BAKER   LAIRD BARRON   ELIZABETH BEAR
RAMSEY CAMPBELL   DAVID DRAKE   CAITLÍN R. KIERNAN
THOMAS LIGOTTI   TIM PRATT   CHERIE PRIEST
W. H. PUGMIRE   CHARLES STROSS   GENE WOLFE**
and many others...

Ia! Ia! Cthulhu Fhtagn!

First described by visionary author H. P. Lovecraft, the Cthulhu mythos encompass a pantheon of truly existential cosmic horror: Eldritch, uncaring, alien god-things, beyond mankind's deepest imaginings, drawing ever nearer, insatiably hungry, until one day, when the stars are right....

As that dread day, hinted at within the moldering pages of the fabled Necronomicon, draws nigh, tales of the Great Old Ones: Cthulhu, Yog-Sothoth, Hastur, Azathoth, Nyarlathotep, and the weird cults that worship them have cross-pollinated, drawing authors and other dreamers to imagine the strange dark aeons ahead, when the dead-but-dreaming gods return.

Do you dare open The Book of Cthulhu? Do you dare heed the call?